Pr

The Mad

"A refreshing change from the usual madman-turned-murderer storyline… a complex, engaging thriller."
– *Kirkus Reviews*

"Flawless writing, great characterization, and a twisting plot that will keep you surprised until the end."
– *Akros Books*

"Not for the squeamish… an exciting character-driven page turner."
– *Phoenix 2000 Reviews*

"Fantastic characterizations and a well-developed plot. It's a mystery with multiple twists, most of which readers won't see coming. Highly recommended."
– *Paul Dale Anderson*

"Great story… you're constantly turning the pages."
– *Hampton Reviews*

"Riveting in its unpredictability."
– *Weldon Reviews*

THE MADMAN'S DAUGHTER

M. C. SOUTTER

C&T&L Books

Also by M. C. Soutter

Undetectable

Coming Soon by M. C. Soutter

Pod Ten

For Lynne

THE MADMAN'S DAUGHTER

We are in strange waters here, where all the usual considerations may be reversed – where illness may be wellness, and normality illness, where excitement may be either bondage or release, and where reality may lie in ebriety, not sobriety.

- Oliver Sacks
The Man Who Mistook His Wife for a Hat

One Kind of Genius: Melissa

1

From *Growing Up Fast*, by Melissa Hartman. Reprinted with permission.

I never had a chance with my father. When I was older – much older – people who knew him well told me stories about what a "man's man" he was. About how he would shout at women he didn't think were dressed properly. About the way he would get after a night at the bar. That was when he would go looking for women he called the tramps. "Let's go teach the tramps a thing or two," he would say, tossing his empty beer bottle into an alley.

On the quiet nights, when he couldn't find anyone suitable, he would conveniently decide that my mother was one of those tramps. She often needed to be taught a thing or two, it seemed. That she was his wife seemed to make no difference.

These people who knew my father, they told me that when they found out Martin Hartman had had a baby girl, they thought it was the best thing they had ever heard. Maybe, these people said, Martin would be changing his mind about a few things.

I told these people that maybe they didn't know my father so well after all.

2

With his first baby on the way, Martin Hartman was in a good mood. He had not been to a bar in weeks, and on some days his wife, Janet, could see the man she had married three years ago. His short black hair seemed neat, rather than severe. The faded tattoos on his thick arms suggested protection, rather than abuse. He was home most evenings, spending his free time in the spare bedroom. "Setting up the little guy's home plate," was how he described it. He put up posters of Joe Montana and Wayne Gretzky. He lined the shelves with books about baseball and soccer. He went out and bought a set of *NASCAR* bed sheets.

"Oh, Martin," Janet said. "The baby won't be sleeping in a bed for months."

"We want the whole room to be ready, don't we?" He beamed at her. "Every detail should be right for him."

She smiled in spite of herself. "Martin," she said softly, "what if it's a girl? Are you going to go out and buy a few pink things, a dollhouse just in case? Not that girls don't like sports," she added quickly. "But still."

For Janet Hartman, asking such questions constituted a rare show of bravery.

Martin looked up sharply at his wife, and he scowled. It was an expression Janet knew too well, and for a second she thought he was going to come at her. He would start shouting, and before she knew it, she would be pinned in a corner. She would cover her face with one arm, her breasts with the other…

But then Martin's eyes cleared. "Don't worry about that," he said. He walked over and gave his wife's belly a little pat. "I know a boy when I feel one."

Janet looked uncertainly at him, trying to share his confidence. Martin had refused to let the doctor tell them the sex of the child during the ultrasound procedure, claiming that such information was unnecessary. "Wouldn't make a difference what they told me anyway,"

Martin said. "Going to be a boy, and that's all."

He turned and left his wife standing in the living room. He wanted to get the new racing sheets set up on the bed before dinner. She was a good wife, Martin thought. Stupid, and with no sense of duty, but that was a woman for you. At least she was attractive. Most of the time. Not half as nice-looking as his secretary, Pauline, but what did that matter? There was fucking at home and fucking at work. No sense in comparing the rickety chair at your dinner table to the plush, ergonomic one in your office.

Both served their purpose.

He pulled the printed sheet over his future son's mattress, and the bed was transformed into a tapestry of speeding, decal-covered stock cars. Martin stepped back for a moment to admire the effect. As he unwrapped the bright red Mobil Gas pillowcases, he began to whistle.

The midwife was impressed with the first sounds Melissa Hartman made as her life began. She was a good crier, and there is nothing more comforting in a delivery room than the outraged sound of a newborn stretching its lungs.

"Congratulations!" said the doctor. "You have a beautiful, healthy baby girl."

Martin spun toward him, pulling his own mask down as if it were suffocating him. He glared at the man. "What did you say?"

"Mr. Hartman, please put your mask back on. Your wife will still need surgical attention before – "

"That's a mistake!" Martin shouted, his neck cords standing out like tent ropes.

The doctor was taken aback, and he paused before responding. "Don't worry, Mr. Hartman, her color will be normal in no time. This bluish tinge is only because of – "

"You shut up!" Martin yelled. "I'm the father here, and I'm telling you that you have made a very big fucking *mistake!*" He turned and stormed out of the room, peeling off his surgical gown and gloves as he went. "A MISTAKE," he shouted again, his voice echoing from the hallway.

There would have been a stunned silence in the delivery room, except that little Melissa Hartman was not concerned with her father's behavior. She continued crying with enthusiasm.

The midwife, for her part, continued to be impressed.

Dr. Ryan clipped the umbilical cord and performed a quick suctioning of the baby's mouth and esophageal passage, and then he wrapped the little girl up and handed her to her mother.

Janet looked fearfully at her new child.

"It's all right," said the doctor reassuringly. "New fathers go through all sorts of strange emotions. I'm sure he'll be fine in a few hours."

Janet stared back at Dr. Ryan. If she had not been so drained from the delivery, she might have laughed in the man's face. Instead, she began to cry.

Melissa Hartman lay on her mother's trembling chest and found that she liked the sensation just fine. While Janet sobbed from exhaustion and fear, Melissa stopped crying and began to breathe regularly. The smell of her mother's sweat and tears was strong, and these smells found their way into Melissa's tiny nose and settled there, heavily.

Janet Hartman stood over her baby's crib and cried. She had read about postpartum depression in one of the pregnancy books, and she wondered if this was what she was feeling now.

Melissa was five months old, and already she was a happy child. Martin had retreated to the office and to the bars, where the indignity of having a daughter seemed less real. He was far from happy, but no one would have looked at former tailback Martin Hartman and called him sad.

Furious, maybe. Or dangerous.

Alone in her misery, Janet looked down at her gurgling, grinning baby and asked what she should do. "Am I crazy?" she whispered.

Melissa looked up at her mother and made a cooing noise. Janet interpreted this response to mean "maybe."

"Will I feel better soon?" Janet asked. "I don't know how long I can do this."

Some shift in Janet's tone, or gas, or one of the dozen other things that may irritate a baby, suddenly caused Melissa's expression to change. Her face froze momentarily in that nothingness between smiling and crying, and then her mouth curled slowly open as she began to wail.

Quickly, Janet reached down into the crib and put a finger gently under her daughter's nose. Melissa stopped crying immediately. She clutched at the offering with her tiny baby hands. She did not put the finger in her mouth, but held it there, her pudgy legs bicycling slowly through space.

Janet threw her head back, closed her eyes, and sighed deeply. She would have liked it if her own mother had been there to comfort her. Though perhaps not with the scent of maternal skin, which seemed to be Melissa's favorite thing.

A bowl of soup would have been nice. Or even just a willing, patient ear. Someone to listen.

Martin came home at five-thirty one evening. Which was not like him. Janet was in the kitchen, warming up a pot of water. "Martin?" she called. "Is that you?"

Because at such an early hour, who could tell?

Suddenly he was behind her, his hands on her waist. She hadn't heard his footsteps on the linoleum. "It's me," he said. His breath reeked of gin. "Come out of here."

"Let me put this bottle of formula into the pot," Janet said, speaking over her shoulder. "Just a minute."

"No." Martin pulled her roughly away from the counter, and she didn't have time to set the bottle down. He walked her ahead of him, into the living room, leading her with pressure on her hips and shoulders.

"Martin, I need to put this somewhere. If you would – "

"Quiet."

They came to the big easy chair, the one he sat in on winter weekends when there was a game on and nowhere to go. Janet moved to step around it, but Martin pushed her forward. She almost fell.

"Martin!"

Janet's legs were pinned up against the side of the lounger, and now Martin's hands were on her back, pushing her over. She raised her arm to avoid tipping the bottle. Martin reached under her house dress, began clawing at her underwear.

"No, Martin! What – "

"I said *quiet.*"

She heard the thud of his belt buckle as his pants dropped to the floor, and then he was pushing her forward again, from inside.

"We're starting this… whole thing again," he said, breathing in gasps. "The… right way."

Then it was over. He stepped back, releasing her. Janet looked at the bottle of formula, still clutched in one hand. She had kept it steady; no spills. With her other hand, she adjusted her underwear and smoothed out her dress. Martin's pants were already back on, his belt refastened. "I'll be back tonight," he said, turning to go.

Janet didn't move. She stood next to the easy chair and concentrated on taking slow breaths. She wouldn't cry. Not while he was still here.

The door closed behind him, and Janet gave herself permission to let go. She waited for the tears, but nothing came. A sound from the kitchen made her blink, and she remembered the bottle. And her baby.

She hurried back to finish fixing Melissa her supper.

That night, after three hours of trying, Janet finally fell asleep. She had come close to drifting off earlier, but then the baby had needed to be changed and fed.

Martin's return later on did not wake her, because she was accustomed to sleeping through his 2AM arrivals. He stood in the doorway to their bedroom, looking at Janet's sleeping form beneath the covers. If he squinted his eyes just right, he could imagine that Pauline, his secretary, was lying there. Pauline in one of her checked, gingham skirts and cotton, high-necked tops. Those high necklines were Pauline's attempt at hiding her tramp tendencies, but Martin knew better. The so-called "conservative" tops were even sluttier than the rest, he thought. Because there was no cleavage to distract you. There were only the breasts themselves, sheathed in fabric, thrusting up and forward with the aid of some unseen underwire fakery.

Pauline had let Martin touch them once. And then, that same night, she had let him do everything he wanted with her. He had been trying for weeks, inviting her to dinner after work and complimenting her hair. Then, suddenly, she had given in.

Because she was a tramp. He had known it when he met her.

But a few nights later, just as suddenly, Pauline had decided that Martin didn't have permission any more. He had been disappointed, but not terribly so. He assumed that this was just Pauline's way of keeping him interested. And that was okay with him. To a point.

After two more months, however, Pauline hadn't given him anything else. Not a feel. Not a kiss. Nothing at all.

Martin was livid. He confronted her in the office.

"How long is this going to go on?" he said.

She looked at him evenly. "What?"

"Enough. When are we going to dinner again?"

"Dinner?" She didn't smile, but her eyes were laughing. "I don't remember you inviting me to dinner," she said.

He clenched his teeth. "Would you like to go to dinner?"

"I'm sorry, Mr. Hartman. I don't think that's a good idea."

Martin cringed. *Mr. Hartman.* She never called him that.

"Let's stick with business," Pauline said. She nodded solemnly and shook his hand, as if they were finalizing a negotiation.

"Fine." He turned away, smoke rising from his head.

That afternoon, Martin had gone home early. There, at least, he could find one woman who would do whatever he said. And whenever he said it.

It had been quick in the living room with Janet, but Martin was surprised to find that it had also been good. Very good, he thought, especially tipping her over the barcalounger like that. She did what he wanted, and that was right.

He felt pleasantly omnipotent afterward.

Anyway, it had been high time for him to get working on a baby boy. The little girl was getting old – eight months last week, if he was counting correctly – and having a son would set things straight.

Speaking of making new babies, he was pretty sure he had something left in him. It was late now, but thinking about Pauline's smooth cotton sweaters had gotten him ready in a hurry. Her sweaters always had that effect on him. Her stuck-up attitude, too. She acted as if he were nothing to her. As if she didn't have to do what he said.

She was his *secretary*, he thought, seething. She was *supposed* to do what he said.

He set his jaw, and advanced toward his wife's sleeping form.

Janet awoke to the sound of Melissa crying. She tried to sit up, but there was something holding her down. Some*one*.

"Martin?"

He was on top of her, his breathing ragged. Melissa cried out again, louder this time.

"She needs me," Janet whispered. She tried to push him off.

"*Stop* that," he hissed, "or I'll strap you to the bed and do this all night." He arched his back so that he could glare at her. "Do you believe me?"

She nodded silently.

Martin shook his head and returned to work, as if he had been interrupted in the middle of repairing a broken light fixture.

Goddamned women, he thought. *No sense of duty.*

Janet turned her head away and stared at the egg-white wall of their bedroom. She tried not to listen to her daughter's cries, which were becoming louder. Martin gripped the end of the bed and focused on a mental image of Pauline. In the fantasy, his secretary was bent over the office copy machine, asking for help. "Can you take a look at this?" she was saying. Martin noticed that the bottom of her already-short gingham skirt had ridden up a few extra inches. As he walked toward her, he began giving instructions. *I can take a look*, he said, *but you'll have to do exactly as I say*, *exactly when I say it.*

Melissa finally became impatient in her crib, and she began screaming in earnest. The midwife, had she been there, would have been pleased at the child's pluck. Even for an 8-month old, she sounded very lively.

Very strong.

There were no scenes in the delivery room this time. Martin Hartman was at his wife's side throughout her labor, offering supportive words of encouragement. He held her hand. Five months earlier, during the ultrasound, the OB-GYN had looked hesitantly at Martin, but Martin had nodded and told her to get on with it. "So?" he said impatiently. "Are we good or not?"

The doctor turned to Janet. "You're going to have a boy," she said.

Janet almost cried out with relief.

Martin began bringing home special vitamins for Janet. He took her out to dinner six nights a week, and refused to let her carry the clothes hamper down the stairs. Now, five months later, he was there, helping, coaxing, cheering her on. Bring our boy into the world. Our Jimmy. Let me see my little Jimmy.

It was the second pregnancy, and so it should have been easier. But after three hours of pushing in the delivery room, Janet's cries suddenly became louder, more urgent. Martin saw the midwife glance up at the doctor, saw the doctor frown. Martin was hustled out of the room like an intrusive teenager, and then he could only wait.

Dr. Ryan came to him soon after, and Martin studied his face. It was difficult to read. "Your wife is fine," the doctor said. "She'll be groggy from the anesthesia for a while, but the C-section went well." The doctor waited for the customary outburst of relief, but none came. Martin Hartman stared at him, breathless. "Your son is alive," Dr. Ryan went on, "but we've placed him in the NICU. His lungs are not fully developed."

Martin seemed not to hear the last part. "I have a son!" he announced to the scattering of expectant fathers in the waiting room. Heads looked up. There were congratulatory nods and smiles.

The doctor took Martin by the shoulders and spoke to him with an exaggerated clarity, as if trying to communicate with someone suffering from dementia. "This is still an uncertain time," Dr. Ryan said slowly. "Your son is not yet strong enough to survive on his own."

Martin finally seemed to hear. "But Janet took all the vitamins. What happened?"

Dr. Ryan shrugged. "Nothing 'happened.' Every child is different.

Some need extra help at the beginning."

Martin considered this. Then he grinned at the doctor. "Yes," he said. "Of course. At the beginning." He nodded to himself, as if this were exactly what he had been hoping for. "It will make him even stronger in the end."

Dr. Ryan kept silent.

Martin did not lose hope easily. His small, silent son was making progress, after all. Jimmy was able to leave the NICU after two months, and that was a triumph. Three months later, he began taking milk from Janet's breast with something like real appetite, especially in the evenings. After nine months and endless encouragement, Jimmy finally succeeded in rolling himself over onto his stomach. Exhausted from his efforts, he lay in this face-down position for several seconds before Janet realized that he was smothering, and she plucked him hurriedly from the mattress. Jimmy took a relieved but unenthusiastic breath.

When Jimmy was eleven months old, Martin came home one evening to find his wife standing over Jimmy's crib. Her eyes were red from crying, but this in itself was nothing new. Janet was always crying.

"How's our little guy?" Martin said. He peered into the crib and smiled. "Huh? How is he?"

Jimmy did not smile or kick his legs. He made no sound. Nothing in his eyes gave any indication that he recognized his father.

"He's so small," Janet whispered, almost to herself. "He's so… weak."

"Don't ever say that," Martin snapped. He stood up from the crib and looked at her. "Why would you say that?"

Janet's nerves were frayed by anxiety over her son's health, and she had not been sleeping well. She was not herself. "Don't you remember Melissa at this age?" she said. "She was laughing, crying, standing up in her crib. I could barely buy her enough formula. She was twice this size. She was so much more *alive*."

"I don't give a shit what that girl was doing at this age," Martin said. His voice was soft.

His wife barely heard. She was on a roll. "Melissa would look you in the eyes," Janet went on, "and you could tell that she was really seeing you, connecting. I don't think Jimmy sees *anything*. By the time Melissa was Jimmy's age, she already understood words like 'mommy' and 'bottle' and 'sleepy.' She's incredibly smart, Martin. She's good at drawing. She likes – "

Martin slapped her.

Janet stopped in mid-sentence, her mouth frozen open in shock.

It wasn't the first time. He had hit her harder before, and with worse things than his hand. But in the past she had always been able to see it coming. When he was drunk, for example. Or if she had said something disrespectful. This time, though, she had simply been talking about their child.

She had been praising their own daughter.

Martin spoke through clenched teeth. "I said, I don't give a shit what she likes. We're talking about our son here. And he looks just fine. He looks *better* than fine." He glanced down at Jimmy, whose head was turned to the side, his eyes at half-mast. He might have been drifting off to sleep. It was hard to tell.

Martin walked quickly out of the bedroom. He grabbed his coat from the hall closet and strode past Melissa, who was curled up on the floor of the living room, concentrating on coloring with crayons. She didn't notice her father as he stormed by.

He paused at the front door. "Don't get any of that crap on the rug," he growled.

Two-year-old Melissa sat back from her work and smiled. The look on her face could have charmed a marble statue. "Daddy?"

Martin was unaffected. "Jesus," he muttered, and walked out. He slammed the door behind him.

Melissa's lips pouted forward. Daddy was having one of his "grumpy times," as her mother would say. Daddy was a strange and unpredictable character. Seldom available for quiet time. Often distracted.

She returned to her coloring.

Martin came home late that night. It took him a while to locate his own bedroom, and it confused him to find his wife not there.

"Janet?"

"In here."

He stumbled into the children's bedroom, where he found both his wife and daughter standing at Jimmy's crib. Janet held Melissa's hand in her own.

Melissa looked up at her Daddy with an expression of infinite sorrow.

Martin blew air through his lips like a man who has just discovered a parking ticket on his Jeep. "Fuck," he said. He reached into the crib and gave Jimmy a little shake. When Jimmy did not respond, Martin began poking him roughly, as one might poke a raccoon carcass on the highway.

"Martin, please," said Janet.

"Oh, shut up."

All four of them were silent.

"I'm going out," Martin said finally.

"Martin, what about Jimmy – ?"

"Shut *up*." He turned to go. Conveniently, he had not yet removed his coat.

When he was gone, Janet and Melissa walked into the living room and sat down on the couch. Melissa's bare feet did not reach the edge of the cushions. She held onto her mother's hand and waited.

Eventually, Janet began to cry. The tears came down in thick, steady streams, and her body shook. It was a behavior Melissa was used to, and she was not distressed. She gripped her mother's hand as tightly as she could manage with her toddler's forearm muscles, and she breathed in the familiar scent of sweat and tears.

"It's okay, Mommy," she said quietly. "It's okay."

Another Kind: Nathan Kline

1

They took hold of him, and they didn't let him up. There were too many hands for him to break free, and he was weak from the treatments.

"There won't be any more of that," said a voice somewhere behind him. The voice was stern. "Put him under." A pause. "Don't look him in the eye, you idiot. And check your nose plug – it's slipping."

"Sorry." Another voice, more hesitant. "But do you think he meant to – "

"I said *put him under*." Real anger now. "Or would you like to be in charge?"

Silence.

There was a tug at his catheter line, and a few seconds later he felt his eyes grow heavy. He might have struggled, but he couldn't think of a reason why he should bother. As his eyes closed, he hoped they had given him enough to kill him.

All things considered, it probably would have been for the best.

2

The selections below are taken from *Getting to Know Patient Nathan*, by Dr. John Levoir. They are reprinted here, and in later chapters, with permission from the author.

Dr. Levoir published his essays fully two years after the incidents at Dartmouth had already occurred, but these writings are still the only confirmed, first-hand accounts of Dr. Nathan Kline and his strange condition. Reliable testimony from other sources has proven difficult to obtain. Dozens of enthusiastic "witnesses," all of whom claim to have encountered Kline in the weeks before his death, have given descriptions that are both logically inconsistent and medically implausible.

The few players best suited to accurately describe Dr. Kline's behavior are either unavailable or unwilling to comment.

Most of them, of course, are dead.

From *Getting to Know Patient Nathan*:

Everything about Nathan Kline's stay at our facility was irregular, even his arrival. A psychiatrist from the state ward in Concord, New Hampshire, brought his notes to our clinic personally. This surprised me. We are a small, privately run facility just outside of Boston, and we receive most of our transfer data by fax or mail. Sometimes we get nothing but the patient and a set of dirty linens. But the state psychiatrist was intent on making his delivery by hand. He caught me in the main hallway, where I was returning from my early morning rounds. He was very direct.

"Are you Dr. Levoir?"

I nodded.

"These are for you." He thrust a stack of folders at me. "From the N.H.S. facility."

"Thank you. And you are – ?"

"What?" He stepped back, as if trying to put space between himself and that pile of notes. "Oh. Bjorn Larsen." He looked up at me then, but only for a moment. His blue eyes were unsteady.

"I think I saw your name in the papers," I said, trying to make conversation. "From the trial, right? That must have been something."

"Why?" he said quickly. "What do you mean?"

I shrugged. "Testifying in a murder case. I've never been called up for one."

"Waste of time," he said.

"How so?"

Larsen sighed. "What does a jury know about psychiatry? Or neurology, for that matter? They don't want to hear a real diagnosis. I start talking about behavioral disorders, treatment options, and they start falling asleep. No one can handle any big words. No actual terminology. It has to be either, 'He's perfectly normal,' or 'He's completely crazy.' "

I nodded and gave him my supportive face. I am the senior attending neurologist at Clancy Hall, and this face is one of my specialties. Yes, I understand, the supportive face says. And I want to hear more.

It was a look I usually reserved for my patients.

"You know what else kills me?" Larsen was saying. "Half of the jurors were probably taking one kind of drug or another – anxiety meds, some SSRIs – but none of them cared about Kline's 'scripts. He was the defendant, for Christ's sake. They should've wanted to know what he was taking. But everyone looked at me as if I was making excuses for him. *He's* the one who killed a lab tech, not me."

I kept quiet for a minute. Larsen was agitated and defensive, as if someone had accused him of a crime. He struck me as jumpy, especially for someone in the business of treating psych patients. To change the subject, I said, "Speaking of medications, could you tell me what you've been prescribing for him?"

Larsen nodded. "We started him with a standard antipsychotic. Risperidone. But it caused side effects I've never seen. Delusions, increased paranoia. Claimed we were poisoning him. So I tried haloperidol. But that was even worse. Strange reactions."

I stared at him. Larsen wasn't making any sense. Risperidone didn't create schizophrenic symptoms; it treated them. "So it didn't work?"

The psychiatrist smiled sourly. "Oh, it worked. For an hour after each dose, he was the model patient."

"And then what?"

"Everything changed. Look." Larsen put his hands up as though he were showing me how to hang a picture frame on the wall. "Let's say he's hearing voices in his head. So we start him with the risperidone. It kicks in fine, just like you'd expect. But an hour later, he's fully manic. He's chatting up the nurses like he's looking for a date."

"Manic? So he's bipolar?"

Larsen pointed at me eagerly. "Right, that's what I thought, too. Bipolar. So we hit him with divalproex, which was great. Worked like a charm, and he settled down. He left the nurses alone. But another hour goes by, and he's totally incoherent, claiming his left leg doesn't belong to him."

I blinked. "He said it didn't *belong*?"

"Yup. He called it a disgusting, dead piece of flesh. Accused me of attaching it to his body while he was sleeping."

"But what could be causing so many different – ?"

"It didn't stop there," Larsen interrupted. "After a while, he came full circle. He was hearing voices again."

"He started over?"

"Exactly. He was a regular schizophrenic again."

"What about the risperidone?"

"It wore off."

I shook my head, wondering if I had misheard. A dose of

risperidone doesn't just wear off, like some over-the-counter cold medicine. It takes hours. "What are you talking about?"

Larsen shrugged. "It was as if he never took it. We tried upping the dosage a quarter milligram, which worked beautifully until his next round, when he was just as bad again."

"And the cycling from one symptom to another? Is that why…?"

Larsen nodded, anticipating me. "That's why he's been on so many different kinds of medication. I can't get him pinned down. He's ten different psych patients wrapped into one."

I studied Larsen for a second. "He'd make an interesting case-study," I said. "Don't you want to keep him for yourself?"

The doctor shifted his weight, suddenly nervous again. "Ordinarily, yes. All my interns want me to stick with him."

"It's what I would do."

"I know – he's a career-maker. I could be the first to describe the pathology. It's just…" He hesitated.

"Just what?"

"Kline gives me the creeps."

I almost laughed out loud. The creeps? Larsen couldn't be serious. State employees overseeing psychiatric prison wards didn't get the creeps. You were cured of that sort of thing during your first semester at med school, in Gross Anatomy.

I clamped my mouth shut and tried to show him the supportive face again. "Perfectly understandable," I said mildly, when I had brought myself under control. "I have a number of patients who rub me the wrong way."

"That's not it," he said, shaking his head with dismay. "He catches me off-guard. His pathology is too unpredictable."

"Not surprising. Patients with severe schizophrenia can display dramatic – "

"Please, Dr. Levoir." Larsen looked insulted. "Don't give me a psych lecture. I know the pathology of a schizophrenic."

"Of course," I said gently. "Of course you do."

"And Kline is not that simple."

"Apparently not."

Larsen ran a hand through his thinning blond hair and sighed. His face relaxed. "Anyway, now you have all my notes. Maybe someday you can write that case-study. Oh, and be sure to ask him about Charcot's Postulate. He claims to have found a way to prove it, you know."

That got my attention. I knew a little about Kline from the stories in the paper, and he had been a respectable neurologist before his meltdown. Before the murder. But respectable was one thing, and proving Charcot's so-called Genius Postulate was something else altogether. "No one's made that claim in almost fifty years," I said. "The last time I even heard Charcot's name was in med school."

Larsen nodded. "I know, but you should hear him talk. He really believes in the thing."

I grinned. Maybe I had been too conservative before. Kline was starting to sound like the ultimate case study. The man would keep me busy for months, if not years. Imagine, someone who actually thought the Postulate was real.

Larsen said, "Any other questions?" and began inching backward as if I might grab him and have him locked in a room with one of my patients. "You can always reach me through the state institution if you think of anything later," he said.

"One more," I said quickly. "After all that switching around, what's he taking right now?"

"Ah." Larsen stopped and looked at the floor. He hitched up his belt and put his hands on his hips. I have been in the business of reading emotions for nearly half my life, and some are easier to spot than others. Larsen looked like a seven-year-old who had been caught in the act of taking money from his father's wallet.

"Actually," he said, still fiddling with his belt, "he's been on a course of thorazine and Xanax for the last several months."

I relaxed. "That sounds reasonable. If it's effective, then by all means – "

"At two thousand mill and ten mill per day," Larsen added quietly.

I was too shocked to control my reaction. "A day? The Xanax is high, but the thorazine… two thousand every twenty-four hours… you could be inducing seizures with that dose. What were you thinking?"

"Me?" Larsen was suddenly indignant. "Try taking him off it. You'll see soon enough." He looked up at me then, and there was something new in his eyes. Something that looked like desperation. "He's not normal."

I was furious on behalf of my new patient, but I took a minute to slow my breathing. "I thought you testified that Kline wasn't crazy."

"I did. But it's always more complicated." Larsen looked away. "Eventually you'll agree with me."

"The doses you've prescribed are ludicrous. I'm surprised he's still alive."

Larsen shook his head. He faced me again, and his expression was now strangely calm. Those blue eyes were finally steady, and the defensiveness I had seen before was gone. "Not this one," he said. "You don't understand the whole picture."

"Paint it for me."

His face went dark. "I don't think so."

And that was it. Suddenly the conversation was over. He turned to go, this time with conviction. "I've given you everything I have," he said over his shoulder. "If you want to change the medication I prescribed, go ahead. You're his physician now."

I watched him hurry through the sign-out, property-return, and security search procedures at the exit. His step was already lighter. He moved like a high school senior leaving for summer vacation. The guard at the watch station unlocked the gate for him, and Larsen didn't look back.

3

Kline's former partner, Professor Frederick Carlisle, was having breakfast at Lou's Bakery in Hanover when he saw the story in the Globe. It was on page two of the City/Region section. The bold print said that an orderly in the state ward down in Concord had been severely injured.

The professor wiped the crumbs from his yellow cardigan, put his glazed doughnut to one side, and read the story line by line. Most of the article focused on the orderly's injuries and expected recovery. There was an interview with the man's mother, who related an endless anecdote about her son's brave boyhood encounter with a rabid dog. Few details were included about the incident itself or the person who had caused it; the reporter mentioned only that the orderly "had been attacked by one of the patients in the ward, who was being transferred to another facility immediately."

What about the name, Carlisle thought angrily. *Can't you give me the name of the patient?*

No name. And there were no descriptions of the circumstances surrounding the incident, either. It was impossible to tell whether the orderly had simply made a mistake, or if the patient had been improperly medicated, or anything at all.

Some patients, Carlisle thought, *have reasons for wanting to hurt people. Or for wanting to escape.*

Carlisle put the paper down. The story had not been written very well, he decided. After staring out the restaurant window for a moment, he sighed and returned to his breakfast. Main Street in Hanover, New Hampshire, was so peaceful, so comfortingly ordinary with its white clapboard storefronts and Dartmouth students everywhere, that it was easy to feel safe.

It doesn't mean anything, he told himself. *It's probably not Kline.*

He would keep an eye on the papers, both here in New Hampshire and in Boston. But he wouldn't let himself become overly distracted. There was no sense in getting worried.

Kline's Problems

1

From *Getting to Know Patient Nathan*, by Dr. John Levoir:

When I saw the patient for the first time, he was strapped to a gurney. He seemed even taller than his listed height of 6'4", probably because he was remarkably thin. "Gangly" is the word Nurse Bailer always liked to use. Considering the quantity of thorazine and Xanax Dr. Bjorn had prescribed, I expected to find a man lost in a deep, sedative swamp. Physically, this was true.

"Nathan?"

He turned his head toward me with an agonizing slowness. I was surprised that he was able to move at all.

"Nathan, I'm Dr. Levoir. I'll be your doctor from now on."

His eyes found mine, and they locked into place with an unsettling intensity. It was as though I were a spot of firm ground, and he was using me to steady himself.

"Nathan, I understand you have been placed on a high dose of tranquilizers. The first thing we are going to do here at Clancy Hall is take you off of them. Start fresh, okay?" I put one hand on his arm. I'm not sure he felt it. "Going off the Xanax will create some significant withdrawal issues. But we'll help you though the process."

He blinked once. It may have been my imagination, but I think he was thanking me.

Detox was a struggle, as it always is. The details are not relevant, though I will say that Nathan endured his period of deprivation with more than the usual stoicism. Toward the end, I visited his room to discuss treatment options.

"Good morning, Nathan."

He turned his head and nodded silently, his face set in concentration. Beads of sweat stood out on his forehead.

"You've been doing very well, and it's almost over."

"Thank you," he whispered.

"I have an idea about how we are going to proceed from here. I wanted to ask you about it first."

He waited.

"I'd like to give you a few days – perhaps a week – with no medication whatsoever. I know this has not been tried with you, but at this facility, we have the luxury of – "

"Yes," he said. "Yes, please."

"Keep in mind that this will probably be only temporary. We need to get a better understanding of your symptoms."

He nodded, keeping his eyes fixed on me. "I understand," he said. "I won't let you down."

I smiled. "There's nothing to accomplish here, Nathan. It's not a test. No matter how you behave, we will find a way to help."

"I won't let you down," he said again. His face was gray.

"All right, Nathan. That's good. I believe in you."

He continued looking at me for a beat, then turned away, apparently satisfied that he had made his point. His breathing returned to its slow, regular rhythm, and his eyes went blank.

The next few days were some of the worst for him. The nurses and I repeatedly offered to turn on the television; most patients suffering from chemical dependency withdrawal enjoy the distraction that T.V. provides. But Nathan was never interested. He preferred to use the window in his room as a point of focus. The view was nothing spectacular – just a small yard with a tree and a few patches of grass – but he looked out at that little green yard for days at a time.

Later he told me that he was usually thinking about his daughter, Alexandra, during these difficult days. "Her face," he explained. "Just remembering her face always made me feel better."

I now know that Nathan was only using Alexandra as a cover-up. He may well have been thinking about his daughter, but she was not *all* he was thinking about. I had forgotten, you see, about what Bjorn had told me: that Nathan believed he had found a proof to the Genius Postulate.

But Nathan had not forgotten. The Postulate was always on his mind. In retrospect, I suppose those were the days when he started to make his plans.

2

We have visitors occasionally here at Clancy Hall, most of them family members. Dr. Kline's file listed a wife and daughter living in Hanover, New Hampshire, but neither one had contacted me or anyone at the clinic about coming to see him. I had read in the news that they were moving to another state. I didn't blame them. Even his beloved daughter, Alexandra, whom he always talked about with such affection, never sent a letter or called even once.

I don't think he ever saw her again.

Still, Nathan never wanted for company. He always had plenty of attention from other visitors, even though none of them were relatives. When people saw him, they naturally wanted to know more. They found him fascinating. I can remember one woman in particular coming up to me – she wasn't even on the right floor, I don't think – to ask about him.

"Why is he walking like that?" she said.

I had been contemplating Nathan on my own for several minutes, and I was caught by surprise. I stood back and faced the woman, who was the sort of earnest, weary-looking aunty type who could often be found visiting our ward. Her hair was a gigantic, badly-dyed snarl of unkempt curls and rogue barrettes.

"Miss?"

She pointed to Nathan, who was in the process of navigating one of our long, banister-lined hallways. He was trying to move without touching the railing, and having a hard time of it.

"He looks like a human bowl of Jell-O," the woman said quietly. I was grateful to her for keeping her voice down. "What's wrong with him?" she said.

I took a moment before answering. There were so *many* things wrong with Nathan, it was difficult to know where to start. "At the moment, he's going through what I've been calling his scarecrow phase."

The aunty lady gave me a disapproving glance. "That's a charming term, I'm sure," she said. "But I was actually wondering about the pathology."

Ah, I thought. *An aspiring clinician.*

"Well," I said, "he's lost his proprioception. The condition is transient, but until his parietal lobes resume normal function he'll have to rely entirely on external visual cues for skeletal orientation."

The woman's eyes clouded over. Apparently the term *proprioception* didn't show up in any of the standard waiting-room pamphlets. I started over. "You know what it's like to be dizzy, right?"

She nodded.

"Okay. Proprioception is one of the things that helps you keep your balance."

"No," she said, shaking her head. "I thought balance was controlled from the inner ear. The vestibule-something."

"The vestibular system, exactly," I said with a grin. The lady was in over her head, but she was still game for the conversation. I liked her spirit. "You're on the right track. The inner ear does account for most of your sense of equilibrium. But proprioception is essential, too. It's an internal sense, a sort of 'joint-to-joint' monitor that helps your brain keep track of *where* your limbs are. For example, proprioception is what lets you touch your nose even when your eyes are closed. Or catch a ball without actually watching it hit your hand."

She looked toward Nathan, who had fallen to the floor again. "He doesn't know where his hands are?"

"Hands, arms, legs, feet – he can't tell where any of his body parts are going. Not unless he actually looks at them. And in his case it's a system-wide deficit. There have been plenty of documented cases of proprioceptive impairment over the years, but that's not what we're dealing with here. His proprioception is *gone*."

She nodded slowly, sympathetically. "So how do you help him?"

I shrugged. "Actually, I don't. I wait, and it goes away after an hour or so."

"Goes away?" Her eyes grew wide, and she opened her hands in a gesture of confusion. "Then what's he doing stumbling around? Wouldn't it be easier for him to sit it out? Wait until he's normal again?"

"Yes," I said. "It would. Controlled movement without the benefit of proprioception is incredibly difficult, and *walking* without it is almost impossible." I let out a long breath. "I don't know what he's trying to accomplish, but if I understood what made him tick, he wouldn't be in here."

The woman shook her head and turned to go. "Guy looks like he's on a mission," she said.

That's true, I thought, watching the aunty lady waddle away. *But in an asylum? Nathan can barely stand up on his own. What kind of mission could he possibly have in mind?*

Unfortunately, not all of Nathan's problems were so benign as the scarecrow phase, which was, after all, not much more than an advanced case of the wobbles. There was the "half-blind" phase, for instance, which was actually first identified – quite by accident – by Nurse Bailer. She had me paged one evening near the end of Nathan's second week. It was dinner time, and I had been hoping to have a minute to myself and my cold ham sandwich. But then I heard my name announced over the PA system, and I knew the meal would have to wait. When I arrived in Nathan's room, Nurse Bailer was standing at the foot of his bed with her arms crossed. "He's making trouble again," she said, her mouth drawn tight over her teeth.

Nathan didn't seem to notice me, though he had looked up briefly at the sound of my footsteps at the door.

"What's the matter, Nathan?"

"Doctor?" His head moved as if he were searching the room, but there was something strange about the way his eyes darted about. He never actually looked in my direction.

I glanced at his dinner tray, which was still half-full. "No appetite this evening, Nathan?"

"Dr. Levoir, I'm not trying to be difficult – "

"He's a liar," Nurse Bailer cut in coldly. "He's trying to get me to bring him a new tray."

"I'd like to hear his side," I said, doing my best to sound impartial. Bailer huffed loudly to emphasize her contempt for the patient, but I knew she wouldn't interrupt again. "Nathan?" I prompted him.

"I… I don't understand," he said haltingly. He sounded apologetic.

"What, Nathan? What don't you understand? It's okay."

"It just seemed like… like there wasn't very *much* tonight," he said finally.

"But you only ate half your dinner."

Nathan's brow furrowed, and he stared down at his supper tray as though it contained a complicated mathematical formula. "That's what *she* said," he said under his breath. "And I know you're only trying to help, but…"

I watched him carefully, letting him work it out. Meanwhile, I was doing some serious thinking of my own. I saw him reach out and grasp at the empty half of his plate, and something occurred to me.

"The rest of the meal is on your left," I said slowly. "Your *left*, Nathan. Do you understand me?"

He froze. "Left… I know the word, yes. But it's nothing to me now. It has no color."

I nodded and came toward the bed. I had never witnessed this particular form of hemi-inattentive deficit before – and certainly not with a presentation so extreme as this – but by now I was beginning to expect remarkable things from Nathan. Moving very slowly, I reached out and gave his plate a careful, 180-degree turn. The untouched portion of food now lay in his right field of vision.

His eyes lit up immediately. "*There* it is," he said, and he breathed out a huge sigh of relief.

"Oh, give me a break," Nurse Bailer growled, and she went stomping out of the room. I didn't call after her, or even try to explain. She wouldn't have understood anyway. The condition Nathan was suffering, as I had suspected, was due to a severe, recurring deficit in his right temporal lobe. It was one of his most difficult phases. I referred to it, as I mentioned before, as his "half-blind" phase, but the word "blind" is misleading here. Blind people can be told what they are missing, and can understand the scenes described to them; Nathan's experience was nothing like this. During these episodes, any object not in his right field of vision would simply cease to exist in his mind. Not only that, but he could never remember that turning his head to the left would help his situation. Nathan was blind not only to objects on his left, but to the very *idea* of a left side. There was a hole there; a nothingness. It was a void in his mind.

So yes, it would be accurate to say that Dr. Nathan Kline was fascinating, both to me and to others. The visitors never stopped asking questions about him. About why he moved in that strange way. About why he refused to speak in anything but a whisper. "What is he doing sticking his head out the window?" they would ask, as Nathan tried to escape the stench of the asylum during one of his dog phases. "What's *wrong* with him, Dr. Levoir?" Then, invariably, they would ask me about his prognosis, and at this I could only smile and shake my head. The word "prognosis" is a statistical term, referring to a probability for survival. A patient's prognosis is based on data that have been collected from similar cases over the years. The problem, of course, was that no one had ever seen anyone – or anything – like Dr. Nathan Kline. Looking at his chart was like looking at the map of an undiscovered country.

There never *was* any prognosis. Not in the traditional sense. Because the only person at Clancy Hall with a clear vision of Nathan's future was Nathan himself. Not that this slowed him down; his vision was clear, even if mine wasn't.

A vision of revenge is, by all accounts, a vision of finely focused clarity.

3

Eventually I convinced Nathan to sit through a formal interview with me. He was becoming more trusting every day, and I considered it significant that he was willing to submit to such a thing. I told him so.

"My pleasure," he whispered, easing himself down into the chair across from me.

"How are you feeling right now?"

"Terrible."

"Why?"

"This table, this chair, this whole room."

"What about them?"

"They all smell very, very bad." He grinned. "But not nearly as bad as you do."

I smiled back at him. This condition, which we had been calling Nathan's "dog" phase, was one of the easy ones for him. Having a hyperactive sense of smell was obviously unpleasant, but it didn't require medication.

"And what's coming?"

"Fear," he said.

"Of what?"

"You. Anyone. Everything."

"How soon?"

"Soon. Maybe ten minutes."

"And it will last an hour, like the others?"

"About that."

"Can I get you something?"

He glanced up at the window behind me, where we both knew security personnel would be watching. "I'd like to try it clean, if you don't mind. Alexandra's not going to want a father who's always hopped up on anti-psychotics."

I nodded. "Good point. You can do it. I believe in you."

These interviews became a ritual for us. Sometimes we would just talk. Nathan would describe what he was feeling, always in that tight whisper of his. On other days he would pass the session by struggling through one delusional state after another: the room would spin on its head, or my face would become inhuman and ghoulish. His memory would desert him. He would lose the ability to speak.

The right-brain deficits were the most difficult, as they are for all who suffer them. The right hemisphere of the brain carries out the most basic cognitive functions; there is no "thought" in the sense that most people would recognize. Patients with tumors or seizures in the right hemisphere go through experiences that are unfathomable to the rest of us. Can you imagine, for example, what it would be like if you couldn't recognize your own face in a mirror? Or remember the word "hello"?

When Nathan had returned from one of these netherworlds of neurology, we would try to discuss what he had been feeling. Our progress was slow, but it helped that he had been a neurologist himself, a researcher in the neuro-lab at Dartmouth's medical center. He had the training to approach each of his deficits with an objective attitude, and the vocabulary to communicate precisely what was happening to him. He was a very engaged patient, always trying to aid in his own treatment.

Sometimes the delusions became too powerful, and he would have to be sedated. His bouts of Transient Global Amnesia, for instance, were terrifying for him. "Who are you people?" he would shout at me. "Why am I being held here? What *is* all this?"

I always did my best to explain, but the true TGA sufferer (and Nathan was clearly one of these) cannot be calmed by logic. It is an experience of almost pure panic. Without memory, all context is lost. The patient forgets not only what he or she had for breakfast that day, but everything else about the years leading up to that moment. The life, the whole internal history that lets us place ourselves – that lets us *know* ourselves – is wiped away.

Afterward, when his hippocampus had resumed its normal behavior, Nathan would become deeply frustrated with himself. "My own mind betrays me," he would whisper. "I am someone else."

Always I would try to be encouraging. "You're improving every day, Nathan. I believe in you."

Sometimes, when he was in a better mood, he liked to chat about his life before the murder. "Do you know what I was working on?" he asked me one day.

I did have an idea, but I wanted to hear him explain it. So I kept quiet and waited.

"Charcot's Last," he said, and a rare look of excitement came into his eyes.

"The Postulate, you mean?"

He smiled. "Do you know the precise definition of that word, Doctor?"

"Postulate?" I shrugged. "An underlying assumption. An axiom, like in geometry: two points determine a line."

But Nathan shook his head. "Strictly speaking, a postulate is one step further up the logic chain – it's an idea that seems as though it *should* be true, but one that isn't sufficiently self-evident to be considered axiomatic."

"Like Jean-Martin Charcot's alleged claim about intelligence?"

"Exactly," Nathan said, grinning. "Because his idea made sense, right? Your brain, my brain, the brain of some accountant on Wall Street – they're all put together in essentially the same way. So if Isaac Newton can be a genius, why can't we all? If a hit of methamphetamine can make me more creative, then why shouldn't some *other* treatment make me – "

"Because that's just wishful thinking," I said, trying not to sound patronizing. "Let's remember a few things. First, no one has ever been able to conclusively link Charcot to that idea."

"Oh, but you've got to admit – "

"Second," I said, not letting him interrupt, "you know as well as I do that people's minds are set up in subtly different ways, and that those differences are what count in the end. We *can't* all be geniuses. Experience tells us that we all have our limits."

Nathan was suddenly animated. He brought his fist down hard on the table. "That's a lie!" he shouted. "I've seen what's possible. I *am* what's possible. And it's not just intelligence. There are other kinds of mental capacity. You don't understand the concept behind – "

"Nathan?" I looked at him steadily. "I need you to calm down."

His expression changed immediately, and all at once he was contrite. Deferential. "I'm sorry," he whispered. "I'm such a damn *mess*."

It is distressing to look back now at those times with him, and to have to wonder how often I was being deceived. The progress he made was real enough, I suppose. But the frustration was an act. So few of the patients at Clancy Hall are even aware of the outside world, and it never occurred to me that Nathan might be thinking about leaving. It was something *I* had considered, but only in the sense of rehabilitation. If I could help someone like Nathan reinsert himself into everyday life, it would be, I thought, a real victory for Clancy Hall.

And, yes, a victory for me.

But Dr. Nathan Kline was always two steps ahead. He had been making plans from the beginning.

Plans, and a list.

Melissa

1

When Melissa Hartman was in kindergarten, she brought home a permission slip for a class field trip. The kindergarten class was going to visit the children's museum in downtown Boston, and Melissa was excited. She gave the slip to her mother. Janet could see the eagerness in her daughter, and she filled out the form as best she could. "There won't be much *real* art there, honey."

Melissa shrugged and smiled. Any art was better than none at all. It was fun to make, and fun to look at. Art never argued. Or cried.

She was the first student to hand her slip in the next day. Ms. McCartney, the kindergarten teacher, glanced at the slip, then stopped. "Melissa, Dear."

Melissa looked up.

"Permission slips are serious. You must have one of your *parents* fill this out." She frowned and picked out a fresh sheet from her drawer, and gave it to the little blond girl.

Melissa stared at her with wide, uncomprehending eyes.

"I'm glad that you can write your own name, Dear. But did you really think you could fool me with this?" Ms. McCartney patted her on the head, then shooed her away, back to where the rest of the class was playing with blocks. Melissa sat by herself, silently, for a long time, studying the blank permission slip for answers.

Now, a flash of understanding on her face.

Melissa sighed. It was a long, adult sigh. She put the permission slip in her pocket. Later, when Ms. McCartney was not looking, she took a pencil from her backpack and wrote out the necessary information herself. Ms. McCartney's class had not yet covered writing, so there was no need for her to disguise her penmanship.

She handed the slip in the next day.

"That's more like it," Ms. McCartney said with a satisfied smile. "Have you ever been to a museum, dear?"

Melissa nodded happily. Her mother liked museums. They calmed her. Janet Hartman had been taking her daughter on regular weekend visits since before Melissa could walk. "I've been to every one in the area," said Melissa. "But never the children's museum."

Ms. McCartney pursed her lips and looked sideways at the child. She did not approve of telling stories.

At eight years old, some of the blond was starting to leave Melissa Hartman's hair. It lay in great, unruly tangles across her face while she worked on her drawings. There was no one to tell her to cut it. Her mother now spent most of her time in the den, where the television delivered its soothing, mindless balm without end.

Martin Hartman made only rare appearances on the premises. The Hartmans were not divorced. Why bother?

On those few occasions when Melissa's father did make his way through the house, he would usually stop just long enough to exclaim over Melissa's drawings.

"What *is* all this crap?"

Melissa would pause in her work, and look up, and smile as though her father were a breeze on a late July day. "Hi, Daddy. You like my drawings?"

"Is that what all this crap is?"

Then 8-year old Melissa would take a slow, deep breath through her nose, and tell her father something about himself.

"You smell like smoke, Daddy. Were you at a fire?"

"Did you bring the car to a garage this morning, Daddy? Something smells like oil."

"You smell *pretty* today, Daddy. Like a lady."

Martin Hartman would stare at his daughter for a moment, and then he would grab the bottle of Jack, or the handle of Stoli, or whatever it was he had been looking for in the kitchen, and he would go stomping out the door. Sometimes he would kick loose drawings out of his way as he left.

"Okay, bye," Melissa would call. Her head would go back down, and she would return to her work.

The little charter school in Fitchburg did not have much money for courses outside of the standard, Math-English-History ilk, but the administration did what it could. When students reached the fourth grade, they were given the option of taking a general art elective.

Melissa did not expect much. Still, art was art, so she signed herself up for the elective and prepared for the worst. They would have large, flat tables she could use, at least. Her living room was getting crowded with papers and canvases everywhere.

The art teacher, Ms. Cooper, was a wide, strong woman with a round head and sparkling eyes. She wore her white smock fitted snugly about her apple-shaped body. Melissa saw her and breathed her in. She smelled of scrubbed surfaces, and the turpentine for washing paint off brushes. Like a kitchen that had been cleaned by a professional.

"Someone tell me the rules of drawing, please," Ms. Cooper demanded of the class on the first day.

Melissa raised her hand. "There aren't any I am aware of," she said.

"Now we're talking," said Ms. Cooper.

Melissa could barely contain her smile.

"You need a haircut," added Ms. Cooper.

"Yes, ma'am."

Martin came home one day to find his house more orderly than he remembered it. All that crap seemed to have disappeared somewhere. It looked as though someone had even vacuumed. He poked his head into the den, but no, his slack-jawed wife was still wrapped in a blanket in front of the television. When did that fool woman get her meals?

He made his way slowly into the living room, as though expecting an ambush. There he found a girl he barely recognized. A girl with long but neatly trimmed hair that still had a few streaks of blond left in it. The girl looked up, and Martin was surprised to find that she was his daughter.

"Hey," he said. "How old are you these days?"

Melissa smiled. "Hi, Daddy. I'm eleven."

"Uh-huh. Is there something cooking in the kitchen?"

"Sure is. You staying for dinner?"

Martin considered. "Dinner" was no longer part of his regular vocabulary, but he remembered the concept. "I guess."

Melissa nodded. "You better go wash," she said, sniffing the air like a beagle. "You smell like the man on the corner by the bus station."

Her father's eyebrows shot up, but he did not argue. He went to the downstairs bathroom and splashed water on his face.

When Martin arrived at the kitchen table, there was a plate of scrambled eggs, spaghetti, and chopped carrots waiting for him. He sat back in his chair and glanced around the room, as if searching for a waiter to bark at. "You call this dinner?" he yelled.

Melissa came walking in from the den, having delivered a plate of food to Janet. "You didn't wash very well," she said, her nose wrinkling.

"Who eats eggs and spaghetti together?"

"I do. Mom does."

"Did Mom teach you to cook?"

Eleven-year old Melissa Hartman paused and looked at her father.

Martin shook his head, momentarily embarrassed at having asked such an absurd question. He pulled his chair forward and began eating the food that had been given to him. When he was finished, he pushed away his empty plate and burped. "We got anything to drink?"

From the living room, Melissa's voice: "Good drinks or bad drinks?"

Martin thought about this. "Bad drinks."

"No."

"Then I'm leaving." He rose from his chair. "God-damned loony bin around here. Freaking me out."

He paused at the front door. "Get that idiot mother of yours out of the den," he shouted, loud enough for the neighbors to hear. He slammed the door behind him. "Can't figure out why I don't just sell this place," he grumbled from outside.

Because you don't own it, Melissa thought, as she prepared herself for bed. *Good thing, too.*

There was a noise from the den, and Melissa headed downstairs to see what her mother might need. A drink of water, perhaps. Or some help making her way to the bathroom.

2

On the first day of Melissa's eighth-grade year at Fitchburg Charter School, Ms. Cooper greeted her with a hug and a strange expression. The art teacher stood back and looked at her star pupil as though examining a fresh canvas for defects.

"You've grown," Ms. Cooper declared.

Melissa smiled uncertainly.

Ms. Cooper began nodding to herself, as if suddenly realizing something important. "Lord, *look* at you," she said.

Melissa's eyes widened, and her hands went to her face. "What?" she said. "What's wrong?"

"Nothing, nothing. Never mind."

"You sure?"

"Yes. Now let's talk about your project for this semester."

Melissa clapped her hands with excitement. Art projects were wonderful things. They took her mind off everything else.

When she was painting, she never thought of home.

Melissa Hartman's growth spurt ended at age fifteen. Walking through the crowd outside the high school each morning, she was now a shade taller than most girls.

"Hey, Melissa!"

This was Charlie, who had been in Melissa's art class every year. Not necessarily because he liked art.

She changed direction to meet him. Melissa enjoyed Charlie. He never yelled. And even to Melissa's exquisitely sensitive nose, Charlie smelled clean enough.

She talked to Ms. Cooper about him that afternoon.

"I think Charlie Lane might ask me out pretty soon."

Ms. Cooper nodded seriously and said nothing. The middle-school student she had met six years ago was gone. The girl in front of her was a different creature. This girl's hair had no more blond left in it. She had the smooth, curving face of a mother who had once been beautiful, and the hard, bright eyes of an angry father no one saw anymore. The combination was striking, and Ms. Cooper had seen people noticing. She was tall, this girl. Tall and shapely and strong. She ate well, and she played on the field-hockey team. Other students' mothers gave her rides to the games in their minivans. They enjoyed her company.

So, Charlie Lane. Ms. Cooper supposed that Charlie might not be the only boy at the high school thinking about a date with Melissa Hartman.

Maybe the only one brave enough, though.

Most of the other boys seemed intimidated by her. Or at least by the way she made them feel.

"Will you say yes?" Ms. Cooper asked.

Melissa shrugged. "Maybe. I could fix Mom some dinner ahead of time, I guess."

Ms. Cooper waited, and Melissa was silent for a while.

Then she turned to her teacher. "When's the deadline for that art competition?"

Ms. Cooper paused to think. Melissa had switched subjects abruptly, probably in an effort to avoid dwelling on her mother for too long. "Entries are due October first," Ms. Cooper said.

"I'm going to make it into the finals, right?"

Ms. Cooper laughed. Her round, solid body shook from the shoulders, and the string-ties of her white smock strained at the waist. "Not if you don't get busy," she said.

"To work, then."

"Yes. To work."

Melissa labored on her entry for the autumn art festival. Ms. Cooper pressed her to take risks with her work, and in the end they were both proud of what she created. It was an oil on canvas, the scene of a girl running through a city that might have been Boston. Melissa had used two distinct color palates for the buildings and the running figure, and the effect was one of clear separation. The girl in the painting seemed only coincidentally associated with the city through which she ran. Light struck her from an unseen sun. She floated above the sidewalk.

"It's a mature work," Ms. Cooper told her when it was done. "I'm proud of you. Let's wrap it up and send it in."

In a month the reply letter came, and they opened it together.

Melissa put her hand to her mouth.

"You should go home and tell your mother," Ms. Cooper said.

Janet Hartman was awake and alert when Melissa got back that afternoon. The television volume was turned low, which told Melissa that her mother was available for discussion. She ran to the den and threw herself onto the couch. "Mom! My painting got into the finals!"

Janet turned and looked at her daughter. She shook her head slowly, as though coming out of a dream. "You? What?"

Melissa was unfazed. Her mother often needed a few tries to get going. "My painting! The one Ms. Cooper's been helping me with. It's going to be in the autumn festival!"

A significant interval, in which Janet Hartman appeared to weigh the information she had been given. Her eyes moved over her daughter's face. She clutched at the blanket wrapped around her shoulders. "Oh, don't worry, honey." Janet said finally. She took a breath, and the tears began flowing down her cheeks. "It's okay. Everything's going to be okay. I promise."

Melissa took her mother's hand and nodded. "I know, Mom." They sat together while Janet sobbed. Melissa reassured her that everything *would* be okay. Eventually her mother tired herself out from crying, and Melissa wrapped her up tightly in the blanket and left her there, sleeping on the couch.

The judges at the autumn festival tried to appear thoughtful and professional. They took extra time to wait and stare critically at every entry in the high school division. Some tilted their heads at different angles, scribbling illegible notes in their little books. They stood like statues in front of one work or another, frowning with concentration. These pieces are *all* so good, one murmured. Yes, said another. This is very difficult.

None of them seemed to study Melissa's painting very carefully. The judges, and everyone else, had plenty of time to admire it after they had awarded it the unanimous first-place prize that afternoon. Melissa let out a little yelp when she saw them pin the ribbon on her stand.

Ms. Cooper could not be there that weekend. She was at home, nursing a fever. No matter. Melissa would tell her all about it on Monday. She took her blue ribbon and ran home, because even someone as chronically depressed as Janet Hartman would surely understand that a blue ribbon was a good thing.

She would see that this was a *happy* thing.

And indeed she might have. But when Melissa burst through the door she detected a new smell. A very bad smell that reminded her of the time she had fallen hard off her bike and hit her head, and the blood had run down the side of her face in a dark, sickening stream.

She dialed 911 and gave the information quickly and clearly, and they came fast, as a small-town ambulance team will.

The E.R. doctor came out to the waiting room, and Melissa, gorgeous in her exhaustion and her strong, smart eyes, stood to meet him. The doctor hesitated. He considered asking her if her father was around.

"Doctor," Melissa said, to prod him along.

He was a professional, and he regained his composure. "Yes. She's going to be fine."

Melissa nodded. She had seen what her mother had done to herself. Janet's work with the knife had been sincere, but sloppy, and lacking in the necessary skill. "Can we call someone for you?" the doctor asked.

A father? An older brother? Someone?

Melissa shook her head.

Not knowing, Charlie Lane chose the next afternoon to ask Melissa to the movies. She smiled without reservation, and told him that she would have gone with him, that she so definitely *would* have.

She left him standing in the school parking lot.

He stayed there for a while afterward, feeling happy that she had smiled so brightly at him, and that she had said what seemed to be a very nice thing. He was sad, too, at the knowledge that somehow, for reasons beyond his understanding, he would probably never get to kiss Melissa Hartman. It was something he had been looking forward to.

Kline's Plans

I can make it, he thought.

As soon as the Xanax withdrawal symptoms had passed, Dr. Kline began setting goals for himself. He liked goals – they helped him stay focused. The first one had to do with getting out of this place; he had decided that he should try to have himself released before a full year had passed. A deadline was really the best sort of goal, Kline believed. It created a sense of urgency.

I'm going to New Hampshire next year, he wrote in his journal. *To find Alexandra. And to visit some old friends.*

He admitted to himself that this was not precisely true, but it wouldn't have been wise to write down *everything* in his journal, despite Dr. Levoir's assurances.

"It's a place for your own, private thoughts," Levoir had said.

Well, maybe, Kline thought. *But some thoughts are more private than others.*

Sitting now in the quiet solitude of his little white room, Kline opened the journal. He selected one of the black crayons from the box Dr. Levoir had provided – patients at Clancy hall were not allowed pens – and he waited.

He listened.

After a few seconds, he heard it – the sound of someone whispering to him – telling him things. Awful things. That Dr. Levoir wanted to keep him here forever. That nurse Bailer was slipping arsenic into his food each day. That the government of the United States was behind all of it.

As calmly as he could, Dr. Kline wrote down each piece of information. The truth of what he wrote was so clear, so undeniable, that it was all he could to do keep himself from leaping out of his chair and screaming for help. This went on for almost an hour, and he filled several pages with those horrible words. At the corner of the desk was a little plastic container with a pill. He knew the pill would make him feel better, but he tried not to look at it.

He listened for as long as possible, and eventually the whispering began to fade. When he could no longer make out the words clearly, he took a shaky breath and sat back in his chair. The pill was still there, sitting at the corner of the desk. No Haldol tonight. Four nights in a row and counting.

"These are all lies," he whispered, looking down at his journal. "Lies. None of it is true." He could hear the voice in the background, even as it faded away, shouting that he was being tricked. That it was *all* true.

"No, it's not. Not a single word."

Feeling pleased with himself, he turned to a fresh page and waited for his hands to stop shaking. With the paranoia now at a low point, he knew that a better time was coming. A happy, creative time.

The manic phase.

For the next hour, Dr. Nathan Kline wrote poetry. He wrote stories. He wrote with his head moving in a slow, back-and-forth rhythm above the table, as if he were composing music on the page. Occasionally he would pause to look at what he had just written, and he would smile to himself.

He was always sad to leave this phase behind.

Afterward there was the Voice phase, during which there was no writing. The Voice made him persuasive. Even alone in this room, with no one to hear, he could feel the authority it gave him. He would practice sometimes, going barely above his usual whisper:

"Put that down. Bring that over here. Give it to me."

He could hear it. There was something powerful there. Something sexual, too – he experienced a strange and unprovoked tingling of lust every time the Voice arrived – and there was a smell. He couldn't identify this smell, but he knew that it was *good.*

The rest of the night was filled with one phase after the other. After the Voice came the problems with his left side: what Dr. Levoir called his half-blind phase. The journal entries from these times were hard to read. Then the balance problems: the spinning-room phase and the scarecrow phase. And, of course, the memory holes: the awful, alone-in-the-dark feeling of the amnesia phase. Always he kept writing, recording as much as he could, though sometimes he was barely coordinated enough to hold the crayon. During the scarecrow phase, for example, he could barely keep himself from falling out of his chair.

There were many more. Twelve distinct conditions, at last count. Dr. Levoir had seen perhaps seven of these. Quirks and feelings and abilities. Like finding a box of mysterious new tools in your basement. Some of these tools were rusty and dangerous-looking. Others gleamed with possibility. You didn't know exactly what each one did, or how they worked, but you knew you could build… something.

So much potential, Kline thought. And still plenty of time to get ready. Eleven and a half months to go.

The deadline, he reminded himself.

Always the deadline.

Melissa

1

Melissa turned seventeen. She came home from school one day to find Martin, whom she had not seen in three years, sitting in the den talking to Janet.

"Hey, Dad."

Martin did not look away from his wife. "Melissa, your mother and I are having a discussion. Give us a minute, please." He waved his hand behind him impatiently. Scat.

Melissa glanced at her mother, whose eyes still had the soft, fog-filled blankness of something the word *depression* could not describe. "No, that's okay," Melissa said. "I'll sit with you guys."

Martin turned to face her with sharp, angry words rising in his throat. "Didn't you hear what I – "

The end of his sentence trickled away as he took in the sight of his daughter walking toward him. She was so beautiful, he almost smiled in spite of himself.

"I heard you," she said, sitting down next to her mother and adjusting the blanket around her shoulders. Janet stirred on the couch, and her body settled automatically into her daughter's arms. Her glassy-eyed expression did not change. "How are you, Dad?" Melissa said. "I haven't seen you in a long time." Her delicate nose twitched. "You smell a little bit like the man on the street corner again."

Martin waited before answering. He was having difficulty

organizing his thoughts. "Your mother and I have *adult* things..." he began, then stopped as the look in Melissa's eyes unbalanced him. She stared at him as if he were a beetle. A small, fascinating beetle. Martin Hartman was not accustomed to being stared at in this way.

"Cut it out," he said, standing up from the couch.

Melissa cocked her head. "I thought we had things to discuss," she said. "What do you want?"

"You are my *daughter*," Martin said, backing away. "I'm not about to talk about these serious, *adult* things with my baby daughter."

Melissa laughed, and there was movement behind Janet Hartman's eyes. A hint of life. She had always loved the sound of her little girl's laugh.

"No?" Melissa said. "Then I suppose your business here, whatever it may be, is done." She felt a shudder in the body pressed against her, as if Janet were falling asleep. But the opposite was true.

"My *will*," Janet whispered. Her eyes still stared straight ahead. "The house."

Melissa stroked her mother's head and began to rock her. "Okay, Mom," she said. "Okay." She looked up at Martin, who was now standing in the entryway to the den. "Visiting hours are over, Dad. But come back again, all right? And maybe bring a lawyer if you're thinking about messing around with things that don't belong to you."

She turned away from him and began wrapping her mother more snugly in the blanket. Janet sighed with pleasure.

"This isn't over," said Martin. With a more comfortable distance now between himself and Melissa, he had regained some of his confidence. "I have just as much right to this place as you do. You can't make me leave."

Melissa shrugged. He was partly right.

"I'll be back in a few days," he said. "We'll talk more about this."

"Let me know if you'll be staying for dinner next time," Melissa said.

Martin glared at her. Glared at them both.

Janet Hartman's eyes cleared briefly. She looked as if she might begin to laugh. Melissa did it for her. She laughed and held her mother as she did, and the sensation was shared between the two of them. Janet closed her eyes.

Martin slammed the door behind him as he left.

"Bye Dad," Melissa called after him.

Janet made a small sound. "That's right," Melissa said to her. "He's gone."

Senior year, and Melissa turned eighteen. Ms. Cooper was talking to her about colleges. "You should apply to Dartmouth," she said.

Melissa shook her head. "I can't leave my mother."

"It's only three hours from here."

"That's three hours too many."

"I can write you a recommendation – "

"No." Melissa turned away from her. Ms. Cooper looked at the floor.

That night, Melissa talked to her mother about it. She talked about everything with Janet, who was an infinitely patient listener. The subject matter wasn't important. The sound of her daughter's voice seemed to please her, and listening to Melissa talk was how she got to sleep every evening after dinner.

"Ms. Cooper says I should apply to Dartmouth," Melissa whispered. "She says college is the way to get out of this place. But I don't want to leave. I want to stay right here."

Janet Harman may have heard, but she made no reply. Melissa

didn't expect one. She assumed Janet was already asleep.

"I'll never leave you," Melissa whispered.

It was an unusually cold October day in Fitchburg, and Janet Hartman wrapped the quilted blanket around herself as snugly as she could. She stood at the front doorstep of her little white house and looked out at the New England fall. It had been months – no, years – since she had gone outside, and she did not remember everything being so bright as this. The clouds were too white.

She made her way out into the quarter-acre yard. The grass was brown and dying in patches, and there were places with no grass at all. She eased herself down onto a still-green, still-soft spot, and sighed as she was relieved of the uncommon effort of standing. The quilted blanket billowed and fell around her in the shape of a small tent. She looked like an Indian squaw now, squatting there in her tent-blanket. Her face was turned toward the wind, and she squinted.

A bottle appeared from beneath the folds of the blanket. The top was gone, and the contents were emptied carefully. Evenly. She waited patiently for her unwashed clothes to be properly soaked.

Janet Hartman smiled and thought of her daughter. Beautiful, strong Melissa. Where had such a child come from? From somewhere inside her, maybe. Or so she hoped. It didn't seem possible now, so many years later.

And now her child needed to leave. But would not. Could not. She was stuck tending to her sick mother, and periodically fending off a drunk, belligerent man named Martin. A man who had called Melissa a *mistake* in the delivery room.

Janet wondered how long Martin would keep coming back to this place.

Will he ever stop?

No, she decided. He wouldn't. Not ever. And the three of them would go on like this, in a limping, gruesome imitation of family life, until Martin figured out a way to snatch the house out from under them. Or, failing that, he might try his hand at something more aggressive. He was capable of it, she knew. She had seen it in him.

Janet opened the box of matches she had taken from the kitchen. She felt good for the first time in years. Purposeful. The match lit on the first try, and the EasyLight lighter-fluid that had soaked through her blanket and clothes caught immediately. The wind pushed the flames up and around her. In seconds, Janet Hartman became a tent-shaped, human bonfire.

She didn't make a sound.

2

The deed papers and the early acceptance letter and the bill for the funeral services – they all came at once, on the same day. The postman, handing Melissa a stack of easily recognizable envelopes, did not trust himself to utter condolences, or congratulations, or wishes of God Speed and good luck, or anything. So he touched the tip of his hat and turned on his heels.

Melissa sat in her house, alone in the den, while Ms. Cooper stayed in the kitchen and handled the phone. The calls were all from people at the school – mostly boys – and Ms. Cooper chatted and thanked and disposed of them with the efficiency of a corporate secretary. She also opened the follow-up letter from Dartmouth, the one that came a week later.

"You have a full ride," Ms. Cooper announced. She stood in the entrance to the den and waved the letter at Melissa. Like a lure. "Academic scholarship. Sponsored by the art department. Want to read it?"

Melissa shook her head. She barely seemed to hear. The smell of her mother in this room was overpowering, and she wondered absently if all the rugs and upholstery would have to be replaced.

Ms. Cooper shrugged. "Lunch time in a few minutes," she said.

"Don't bother."

A grunt of endurance from the kitchen. "Oh, I'll bother," Ms. Cooper said, raising her voice. "I'll bother and bother and bother until you get *up*."

Two weeks, and Melissa was up. She opened the windows to the frigid November air and cleaned for three days, working in a sweater and hat. Her cheeks were red. On the last day, Charlie Lane came over to help. He talked to fill the empty rooms. Melissa's eyes shone with the work, and sometimes she did not seem to be listening to him.

When they were done they sat on the floor in the living room, pleased with themselves. Charlie brought two glasses of water from the sink. When he leaned over to kiss her, she let him.

"That was nice," she said.

Charlie Lane, who would never leave Fitchburg and who would never, ever meet another girl like Melissa Hartman, leaned back and smiled. He nodded in agreement, and he did *not* try for more. It was then, and continued to be for years afterward, one of his finest moments.

Martin did not show up for the funeral, but he appeared several months later, at the end of the following summer. Melissa came home from saying her final goodbyes to Ms. Cooper, and she found him sitting on the couch watching television.

"Where's my big chair?" he said when she came in.

"Hey, Dad. Nice to see you."

"I said, where's my chair?"

"Mom hated that chair. I threw it out years ago. You're just noticing now?"

Martin snorted as if he had expected as much. "This place smells weird."

"It's clean."

"Where's all the *stuff*?"

"Sold most of it."

He shrugged. "Any beer in the fridge? Mine's almost done."

"No." Melissa continued upstairs. She had a call to make. Martin flipped the channels, settling eventually on a program about fixing cars. After a few minutes, Melissa came back down. She was carrying a large suitcase.

Martin glanced at her without interest, then turned back to his program.

"You'll have to leave now," Melissa said.

Martin laughed and turned up the volume. "Yeah, right."

"Dad, you can't come here anymore. You can keep the Cadillac – that's my goodbye gift to you – but this is your last day in this house."

That woke Martin up. "What? I can keep…?" He silenced the television and turned to face his daughter. She looked ready to go somewhere, he realized. "It's *my* damn Cadillac," he said, his eyes flashing with anger. "Of course I can *keep* it. And the house is just as much mine as it is yours. Nobody's throwing me out of my own house. Least of all my own *daughter*."

Melissa looked evenly at him. "I'm eighteen, Dad. Mom left me the house. You never owned it in the first place, and I'm selling it."

"You can't *sell* – "

"You have to leave. Right now."

Martin Hartman stood up from the couch and squared his shoulders. His expression said that he had endured about enough of this bullshit, thank you very much. He was still the man around this place, and that still counted for something. No *bitch* was going to throw him out of his own home, daughter or not. "I'm going nowhere, understand that? Absolutely fucking *nowhere*." His thick arms, still hard with muscle after all these years, flexed beneath his shirt. He took a step toward her.

Melissa didn't move. "I called the police three minutes ago, Dad. When I was upstairs. They're on their way now, but if you're gone when they arrive, I don't think they'll bother arresting you."

Martin's eyes goggled. "Arrest me? *Arrest* me?" He shook his head quickly, as if he had the shivers from eating something spoiled. "I'm your father, Melissa. Your *FATHER*, get it?"

Melissa smiled. "You remembered my name, Dad. That's good." She looked out the front window, as if watching for someone. "Don't come back, okay? They're going to change the locks, and the real estate agent will have you thrown in jail if he finds you here." She picked up her suitcase. "Good luck."

Martin didn't move. He was frozen to the spot. His face trembled with rage. "And just where the fuck do you think you're going?"

She turned her back on him. "College, Dad. Dartmouth College."

"Oh, that's perfect," Martin said. The door closed, and he was left standing alone in the room. He could hear the sound of an approaching siren. "That's just jack-piss *perfect!*" He hurled his almost-empty beer bottle at the door, and it shattered into a hundred caramel-colored pieces. "You're a mistake!" he shouted. He walked to the door and threw it open. "You're nothing but a big, shit-covered MISTAKE!"

A cab was waiting at the curb. Melissa put her suitcase in the trunk, then paused briefly before getting into the backseat. She spared one last look for the house and her father.

"Okay, Dad," she said. She gave him a little wave. "Bye, Dad."

The cab pulled away.

Students

1

Lea Redford had known she was going to Dartmouth since the age of nine.

Both of Lea's parents were ecstatic when she was born. They had been told they might not be able to have children in the first place, so Lea had always been their little miracle. No one *ever* called her a mistake. Growing up, Lea's responsibilities at home were limited to making her own bed each morning and taking out the trash on Tuesday nights. Lea's father didn't drink, except for maybe half a beer on New Year's. Her mother was seldom sick, and she didn't usually cry unless something sad or painful happened.

If Melissa Hartman had known Lea before college, she would not have recognized such a life as anything close to normal.

Charmed was more like it.

Lea adjusted her glasses and checked her hair. She told her parents to wait in the minivan. Tom and Mary Redford exchanged a look and a smile, but they didn't protest.

"We'll be right here," her father said, hands on the wheel.

"Don't be afraid to introduce yourself in line," her mother added.

Lea rolled her eyes and hopped out. Parkhurst Hall was about fifty yards away, just across the main quad. Other students were cutting across the green as well, all of them converging on the same building. Most of them, Lea saw, had left cars and parents waiting in the street, exactly as she had. Some had probably made their parents park two or even three streets away, so that it would appear as though they were already on their own.

Time for a new life, Lea thought, quickening her pace.

The wait inside was long, but no one seemed to mind. Lea was in heaven. She felt surrounded by smart, motivated people, and every one of them seemed open to meeting… everyone. She could see it on their faces, the way they were all nodding and smiling at one another. That tall boy there: his body posture was open and relaxed. And that small, energetic-looking girl just ahead: her expression was unabashedly friendly. There was not a clique to be found.

Good.

Forty-five minutes later, Lea walked back across the green toward her parents and the family Windstar. She was giddy from the sheer potential of the place. An Ivy League college. Freshman year.

There was a girl walking toward Lea on the path. Another freshman, she supposed, since upperclassman registration was not until tomorrow. But this girl didn't look like a freshman. She looked older. As though she had experienced things. Life things. There was real confidence in her walk.

Physically, the girl reminded Lea of some of the popular girls at her old high school, at least in the superficial, boy-obvious ways: tall, gorgeous, built like a swimsuit model… all of it. Then again, this girl was *nothing* like that, somehow. Her eyes had more behind them. Much more. And there was none of the jittery excitement that had been so clear in the other freshmen's faces. In fact, she looked almost sad.

Unlike the other students streaming toward Parkhurst Hall, this girl was carrying a suitcase. *One* suitcase. As if she had arrived for her first day of college on a bus. But no, that was impossible. Her parents had to be around here somewhere.

The girl slowed slightly as she neared Lea, and her eyes brightened a little. But Lea put her head down and quickened her pace.

As soon as she was past, Lea regretted it. The girl *wasn't* from her old high school, after all. And she had been giving Lea an obvious "hey-what's-up" look. Lea could have read that expression almost with her eyes closed. Still, she hadn't been able to pick her head up and say hello. She had been frozen, somehow. Or maybe she had been misreading the situation. Because the girl wasn't a freshman at all, but some world-weary senior who would never bother chatting with a wet-eyed first-year.

That's not true. I was just scared, that's all.

Lea wondered what she must have looked like to such a girl. Inconsequential, probably. Thin, geeky, and irrelevant.

She kept walking, and focused on getting to her parents' Windstar. It didn't matter, she told herself. That girl wouldn't have any trouble meeting people. The whole campus would want to get to know her. No one looking like *that* would care whether or not Lea Redford paid her any mind.

Even from a distance, Lea found Melissa Hartman intimidating.

She reached the minivan. Before opening the door, Lea turned and looked back along the path. The gorgeous girl with the suitcase had climbed the short flight of stairs at Parkhurst Hall, and was heading inside. She really *was* a freshman, then.

Lea wondered what the other students in the registration line would make of her.

"All set?" asked her father, as she stepped into the Windstar.

"Yes."

"Meet some cute boys?" asked her mother.

Lea rolled her eyes.

Melissa saw that there would be a long wait in Parkhurst Hall, and she put down her heavy suitcase with a sigh of relief.

She noticed, as Lea Redford had before her, that the atmosphere in the building was festive. As if this were a dorm party rather than a registration line. She could smell freshly applied makeup, deodorant, perfume, and even some cologne. Underneath those, there were more subtle scents: the warmth of hot breath from small-talk, the cool sweat of excited eighteen-year-olds meeting each other for the first time.

Melissa Hartman saw the world with her remarkable nose.

The line continued growing behind her, and new conversations filled the space like water from a hydrant. The two girls ahead of her had already begun talking like old friends – it sounded as though they happened to be from the same town in Connecticut – so she turned around, in search of new acquaintances.

The boy behind Melissa was already occupied. He had seen her walking a few steps ahead of him as he entered the building, and he had felt his chest tighten up. He had *hoped* he would run into girls like this at college, but he hadn't expected to be standing right next to one in line. Not on the first day. He didn't have a social routine ready for someone like this. She probably wasn't even a freshman. Couldn't be. She was too beautiful.

So before Melissa could turn around, the boy panicked. A little. There was a short, plump girl behind him who looked friendly. He turned to her quickly and asked what dorm she was in. The girl looked surprised.

"Me?"

"Absolutely, you. My room's in Ripley, across from the gym. I'm Nick. What's your name?"

"Jennifer."

"So what's up, Jennifer?"

Jennifer looked puzzled by the question, or maybe by Nick's unsolicited enthusiasm, but she responded gamely. "Um. This is a long line."

"Damn right it is!" Nick was relieved. He was having an animated conversation within sight of the hot girl. He would, therefore, be able to talk to her later without fear of being judged a loser on sight. You couldn't just *approach* a girl who looked like that. She would eat you for lunch. And then you'd be finished. Your request would be officially denied, and you'd never be able to talk to her again. Not until you had won some sort of statewide sporting event. Or been nominated for a cabinet position. Or something.

Melissa Hartman looked hopefully past the couples immediately behind and ahead of her, searching for someone to talk to. But no. Everyone seemed to have found a friend instantly, and there was no room for interlopers. She adjusted her heavy Samsonite bag, which was wide and tall enough to make a passable chair, and she sat down. She glanced at her watch.

Every few minutes, the line shifted forward. Melissa moved her suitcase when this happened, and then she sat down again. She kept her eyes and ears open, in case there might be a pause in the chatter around her.

In the thirty-five minutes it took for the line to work its way up the stairs and through the hall to the registration table, no one dared speak to the gorgeous girl with the strong eyes and the big suitcase.

Surrounded by her future classmates, Melissa Harman waited alone.

2

Jason Bell, former starting left wing on the Dartmouth Hockey squad, opened the calculus book without much hope. The book's cover had a large picture of an airplane on it. There were streams of red and yellow-tinted gas flowing around the wings, as if the plane were flying through a rainbow. Jason had failed calculus last year, and he couldn't remember seeing any problem sets about planes and rainbows. Not that he had actually attempted the homework. He had been too busy training. And skating. And getting ready for the NHL.

But all those things were finished now. One blind-side hit on the ice, one perfectly placed knock to the head – and he was through.

He did remember being capable in math once. Long ago. When he was in fifth grade. There had been some tricks with fractions that he had learned to do well. And the teacher, Mrs. Hawes, had told him he was the only student who remembered all the formulas she put on the board.

Well, of course he *remembered* the formulas. He remembered almost everything. But that was before his hockey career started to pick up. In sixth grade his mother had entered him into the club leagues. Because the school athletic program wasn't giving him enough chances to shine, she said.

And so math was pushed aside. Along with all his other subjects. He had passed his high school courses, but that was high school. He was able to memorize everything the night before the tests and squeeze by. College was different. Calculus was different. There were things in calculus that had to be studied. Understood.

Learned.

While he was in the hospital, recovering from the concussion in his head and the hairline fracture in his neck, his mother told the doctor that he *couldn't* learn anything new. Not now. "You've got to *fix* him," she hissed.

"He's had too many concussions, Mrs. Bell. It wouldn't be a good idea – "

"It's *Ms*. Bell, and I'm not interested in your opinion. Your job is healing, not career advice."

"Perhaps we should have this conversation in another room…"

"Oh, he can't hear us," she said dismissively. Nevertheless, she began whispering: "He's been out for hours."

But that wasn't true. Jason could hear everything his mother was saying.

"He's *useless* without hockey," she whispered, her frustration giving way to worry. "What will he do?"

Now, in his dorm room, Jason frowned and bent his head over the book. The position made the pain in his still-healing neck bones flair up, but he didn't care.

It was the first official day of classes. Jason sat in the second row and wrote down everything Professor Braden said. Everything that he put up on the board. Jason had questions – so many questions – but the professor did not pause during the hour-long class. Jason looked behind him once, at the endless rows of seats in the lecture hall, and saw only scribbling hands and shining eyeglasses. No confused faces. No expressions of dismay. Apparently he was the only one having difficulty.

"Assignments are on the syllabus I gave you," Professor Braden said, wrapping up. "Homework number one is due Tuesday. We have a T.A. – Lea, could you stand up? – who will be available for tutoring tonight from seven to eight."

The girl at the end of Jason's row stood and faced the class. She looked so young, Jason thought.

How can she be the teacher's assistant?

"Could I have a show of hands?" the girl called out. Her voice was surprisingly strong. "I know it's only the first night. Is anyone planning on coming for extra help?"

Jason held his hand up high.

The girl scanned the hall. Jason cleared his throat, and she turned and saw him. She looked annoyed. Jason smiled sheepishly, but the girl continued frowning. Behind her glasses, her eyes were cold.

She looks like the smartest girl on the planet, Jason thought. *And she looks mean.*

"You're late."

Jason hurried into the now-empty lecture hall and unzipped his backpack. "Sorry. I was doing some reading for History, but I forgot that I was supposed to – "

"What's confusing you?"

Jason hesitated. "What?"

Lea Redford took off her glasses slowly. She was pretty, Jason saw with some surprise. Thin, yes. And young. And clearly not nice. But very pretty. "What's confusing you about *math*?" she said. "That's why you're here, right?"

"Right. Yes. Um." Jason opened his notes from the day's lecture and flipped through the pages. "Oh, here." He pointed to his notebook. "Limits."

"Fine. One problem in particular, or the whole concept?"

"Uh, both. I think."

The girl sighed and stood up. She took a piece of chalk and went to the board. "What's your name?"

"Jason."

"Okay, Jason. I'm Lea. Let's talk about limits." She began to write.

He sat down in the first row and watched her.

An hour had passed, and Lea Redford's expression had not thawed. She put the chalk down on the desk and stared at the big kid sitting in front of her. He was bent over his notebook, writing.

Lea had wanted to go out tonight. She had been thinking about investigating frat row. But instead she was stuck here, teaching first year calc to some underachieving junior.

At least he's trying, she thought.

Yes, he was. Trying *hard.* If she hadn't been so annoyed about the wasted time, Lea might have thought he was cute. Clearly nothing but a jock, but still cute. It was endearing, somehow, the way he kept insisting that he couldn't learn this stuff. Actually, he was doing fine. And he had been scribbling in that notebook without a break for over an hour.

"Okay, wait a minute," Lea said. "Stop. Come over here."

Jason held up his hand while he finished writing something. Then he got out of his chair and walked to the board. "It's still weird…" he began.

"Be quiet and listen."

Jason stopped and looked at her. She didn't seem angry anymore.

He's a big one, Lea thought. *Strong.*

"Do you understand this?" she said, pointing to a spot on the board.

Jason nodded. "Sure."

"And this?"

"Definitely."

"Good. And this over here?"

Jason considered. "Um. Yes. That's okay, too."

Lea threw up her hands. "Then we're done. You understand limits."

Jason shook his head. "No, I don't pick up new ideas well, and – "

Lea Redford snorted. It was a sudden, involuntary reaction, and it startled both of them. Jason looked uncertainly at her. Lea smiled for the first time. "Jason, that's not true. Limits are the basis of calculus, and you obviously understand the concept." She grabbed her backpack and threw it around her shoulders. She looked at him seriously, like a coach giving a pep talk. It was a look Jason had seen before, but never from a girl. "You're smart," she said. Her voice was stern. "And you learn quickly. Come to class. Do the homework. You'll be fine."

Jason felt like laughing. This pretty girl with the amazing brain had told him that he would be fine. That he was smart. And that he learned things quickly.

She turned and left him there, standing by the blackboard. He watched her go, and he didn't return to his seat until she was out of sight.

3

Garrett Lemke's first day as a Dartmouth senior did not go the way he had planned it. He did avoid running into his ex-girlfriend, but that small piece of luck was the one bright spot in an otherwise abysmal afternoon. Everything was awful. *He* was awful. It wasn't just the headaches; there was something unbalanced, something *wrong* with him. His rhythm was off.

Way off.

A friend on the football team had given him a half-full bottle of Tylenol codeine caplets for his head. He gulped down a few that morning, and in half an hour the pain at the base of his skull had retreated slightly, to a level that was just bearable.

The pills made him feel strange. Murky, as if the air around him were thicker than usual. But he decided it was worth it. For the first time in weeks, his appetite had come back. He was genuinely hungry, and he couldn't believe how good it felt to want food.

He made for the dining hall.

On his way, he ran into Allyson Morrone. And Naomi Reed. And – hey, now – it looked like the entire Dartmouth women's swim team. They were all headed to lunch in a group. Garrett would have rubbed his hands together at the sight of the girls, but he didn't want to seem too obvious. He slowed his walk to a casual saunter, and waited for the right moment. He needed eye-contact before he could start.

There it was. Allyson. She had noticed him, and Garrett saw his chance.

That was when things started to go wrong. Something about his head suddenly felt peculiar. The pain was still there, but there was something else, too. Something different. It was as if he had been drinking. He had a quick flashback of an especially late night the year before, when he had let a friend give him one too many cups of cheap beer. He had said some very stupid things that night.

Garrett tried to ignore the feeling. There was work to be done here.

"Hey, Allyson!" he called out. "How are you – "

And then, without warning, his own mouth betrayed him.

"Hello – " He stopped short. "Hi… it's Garrett." He paused for another second, and his expression turned from bravado to concern. "See you!" he managed to blurt out.

Whoa.

He stopped walking and opened his eyes very wide. His voice just now – it had sounded horrible. Strained, and far too loud. And *nasal.* Nothing like the laid-back, smoking-jacket style he had cultivated over the last few years.

And what the hell did I just say? It's Garrett… see you?

What does that even mean?

Allyson Morrone's brow furrowed briefly, but she shook it off. Probably she had misheard. "Hey, Lemke." She waved at him and smiled. "What's up?"

Garrett couldn't help himself. His habits were too strongly ingrained, and he responded without waiting to think. "Hey, Allyson, not much… but I'm… I'm looking forward to bringing you back to my place tonight… so bring your bathing suit because it'll be on the floor before long… can't wait!"

Fucking hell.

Garrett lowered his head slowly, like a man who had just lost his house on a single hand of poker. Allyson looked at him and frowned. So did Naomi and the rest of the swim team. If he was trying to be funny, their faces said, it wasn't working.

He waved a hand at them without looking up. Go away, never mind, forget you saw me here. This is all just a dream. A horrible dream.

And please, don't say anything else to me.

But Allyson tried one last time. Her tenacity was maddening. "You going to lunch?" she said.

Garrett's head didn't come up, but his voice came out just the same, as if he were speaking to the ground: "Wanted to go to lunch on *you* but

– ”

He clamped a hand over his mouth and ran. A car honked at him as he sprinted through a red-light intersection. Allyson Morrone and her swim team companions watched him go, confusion in their eyes.

He didn't look back.

The swim team shrugged collectively and headed up the stairs to the dining hall.

Garrett ran all the way back to Zimmerman house. When he got there, he locked himself in his room and pulled the shades. He lay down and waited for his breathing and heart rate to slow.

After a few minutes, he sat up and swung his legs over the edge of the bed.

"Hello," he said slowly, to the air in the room.

Shit.

It was still there. His voice was pinched. He sounded like a thirteen-year-old going through puberty.

He tried another one: "Hey, Allyson."

Garrett waited, but nothing else came out. No sexual comments about bathing suits. No bursts of uncensored innuendo.

Must be the pills.

That was it. He had taken too many Tylenol codeine tablets, and he was having some sort of psycho reaction. No problem; he would just stop taking them. A replacement would be necessary, of course – he couldn't endure these headaches without some kind of drug – but he had to fix this… thing. Immediately. Whatever was happening to him, it needed to stop. Right now.

After a few hours without the benefit of codeine in his system, Garrett's headaches returned, and with authority. As the pressure above his neck grew steadily worse, he found himself reconsidering his convictions. Maybe it didn't matter if the pills made him talk in a strange voice.

Getting laid isn't worth this much pain, he thought. *Nothing is.*

It was too quiet in his room, too easy to think about the pounding in his head, so he stumbled out into the common area, turned the television to ESPN, and collapsed onto the couch in a heap. His breathing was faster than normal, and sweat dripped down his nose. He clenched his teeth as an extra-heavy wave of pain hit him. His head lolled back on the cushions of the couch, and the whites of his eyes began to show. After another minute, the mercy of unconsciousness came at last. Garrett's body went limp, and he slept.

That was the way Melissa Hartman found him three hours later: on the couch, passed out, looking like something barely alive. She came walking through the Zimmerman commons, and Garrett was still unconscious. She had gone to the library after her first day of classes. Not because she wanted quiet – everyone still seemed to be avoiding her for some reason – but because academics at Dartmouth were surprisingly difficult. She had known it would be hard, but not like this. Classes at Fitchburg High had never challenged her. She showed up consistently and paid attention, and that had been enough. She was smart, after all. But *everyone* at Dartmouth seemed smart. And the stack of homework she had accumulated after just one day was unreasonable. She couldn't understand where she would find the time.

I can't work on art projects if I'm buried under history essays and chemistry labs, she thought.

So she went to the library, where there were few freshmen doing any work – only a scattering of graduate students surrounded by thick reference volumes.

When she finally got back to Zimmerman House at eleven that night, at first she didn't see Garrett's sleeping form. She did see the blaring television, though, and she stopped on her way through the common room to silence it. There was a groan behind her. Melissa turned around, and what she saw made her mouth drop open.

It wasn't that the boy on the couch actually resembled Melissa's mother. Not really. Janet Hartman had been a slight, limp-haired woman, and this was a 20-year-old college student. He had stubble on his face. His long frame sank into the cushions in a way her mother's bony body never could have. He took up *space.*

But Garrett Lemke had also broken out into a full, cold sweat, and his face was pale. He was not sleeping peacefully; he had taken his arms out of the sleeves of his oxford shirt and created a little cotton cocoon. His dark hair fell on his forehead in damp threads. He shivered.

And so Melissa shifted into caregiver mode. It was not a conscious decision. She sat him up slowly on the couch, being careful with his head. As she would have with a newborn. "Okay," she said softly. "Okay, now." Garrett's eyes fluttered open, and Melissa saw the pain there as easily as she smelled the ammonia musk of his sickness-sweat.

"Hi," Garrett said weakly. "You look like Teresa my ex-girlfriend but stronger and that's okay but where is she now she was so *beautiful…*" He trailed off as his strength failed him.

"Where's your room?" Melissa said gently. Her voice was perfectly clear, and very kind.

Garrett thought about the question. "8-C but don't go there it's dark and lonely and Allyson will never meet me there not after today." He looked at Melissa with sad, bloodshot eyes. "Oh my head hurts," he added.

She nodded and took hold of him under the armpits. With a strength that would have surprised even Ms. Cooper, Melissa leaned back and hauled the sick boy up, off the couch, onto his feet. She lifted him slowly, so that he would not fall.

Garrett suddenly found himself standing, and he looked at Melissa with surprise. "You're very nice and pretty like Teresa but I don't think we'd be good together but I don't know why okay?"

"Okay." She smiled and tried to ignore the smell of sickness. It was very strong on him. "Let's walk slowly. You said 8-C, right?"

Garrett looked at her suspiciously, as though wondering how she had come by this information. Then he nodded.

"Okay," Melissa said. "Here we go." She guided him into his room, and then down onto the bed. She took a blanket off the floor and wrapped it around him snugly. She put out the lights and turned to go.

"Wait wait wait no wait."

Melissa looked back. Garrett was pointing at something on the desk.

She picked up the bottle of pills and studied them. The date on the prescription was two months old. "Are you supposed to have these?"

Garrett nodded frantically at her. "Yes please yes *please* my head hurts so much."

Melissa considered. "I'll give you one."

"Three."

"*One*. That's it. And I'm taking these to my room. I'll come and give you another in a few hours. If you're awake."

Garrett looked disappointed, but he held out his hand. Melissa gave him a Tylenol, which he popped into his mouth like an M&M.

She walked to the door, then paused and looked behind her before stepping out of the room. Garrett's eyes were already closed. He gathered the blanket tighter around his shivering body.

Melissa did set her alarm for a few hours later, and she did check room 8-C at around four that morning. Getting up in the middle of the night for such things was a familiar task for her. It was almost automatic. She poked her head inside Garrett's door, and the smell of sweat inside the room nearly made her choke.

Always the sweat, she thought. *I need an off-switch for my nose.*

She listened carefully. There was the steady breathing of sleep, but no tremor anymore. He had stopped shivering, which was probably good. Melissa crept to the far wall and opened the window a crack, being careful not to make any noise.

Her patient slept on.

She checked on him once more that night, and found him still asleep. She nodded to herself, then closed the door and went back to bed. Fifteen years after first holding the hand of her sobbing mother, Melissa Hartman was still wrapping people in blankets, comforting them, putting them to sleep. It was a habit she had hoped to leave behind.

Kline's First Kill

1

From *Getting to Know Patient Nathan*:

The standard neurological workup on Patient Nathan yielded nothing useful. His EEG showed the sharp fluctuations of an epileptic, but with periods of electrical quiet – almost as if portions of his brain were dying rather than becoming excited. The Functional MRI and SPECT tests confirmed it: Kline's cerebral functions were shutting down and powering back up like a computer system performing self-diagnostics.

Unfortunately, the data didn't fit my own observations. Nathan was experiencing some depressed states – the balance problems, the memory deficits – but most of his symptoms involved excited behaviors. The paranoia, for instance. The euphoria, and the hyperphasia. None of it made any sense.

At least, it didn't make sense to me at the time.

In any case, I had decided that the only sensible way to treat Nathan was with an empirical approach; that is, to focus my efforts on precisely what I could see and hear, rather than what my diagnostic instruments were telling me. I would watch *him*, rather than his test results. We continued the interviews, and I kept prescribing low doses of various antipsychotics.

On several occasions I tried to broach the subject of the accident itself. And the murder. But I never made any real progress. Nathan's memory blackout of this short, violent period of his life was total. He had killed his own lab assistant, a young man who had worked with him for several years, but he could not seem to remember anything about the event. At first I was skeptical that such a trauma could be cleanly erased. Memories of the lab assistant himself, for instance, did not seem to have been affected at all. Nathan did not pretend any affection for the young man. "Ah, Stefan," he said with a frown. "They testified in court that I killed him. I suppose, then, that I must have."

"Does this bother you?" I asked. "That you killed someone?"

He shrugged. "From an intellectual point of view, perhaps. I don't think of myself as a murderer. But I don't remember it. I would feel no different if you told me he had been killed by an unknown assassin."

"But you knew him. You're not upset that you killed your own friend?"

Dr. Kline's face was unreadable. "He was not my friend. He was an employee."

"Your own employee, then."

"He had turned lazy. His work was substandard."

"And for that he should die?"

"No, for that he should be fired. But apparently I killed him before I had the chance to hand him a pink slip."

"All right, Nathan." I decided to let the subject drop. "I believe you. And I believe *in* you."

Over time, I became convinced that Nathan had truly lost all memory of the murder. His episodes of amnesia during our own interview sessions were certainly authentic – they always left him badly frightened – so I took him at his word. And even now, I don't think he was ever lying about the memory problems. It would be more accurate to say that he was dodging the issue.

I now believe that Nathan did remember *why* he killed Stefan, if not exactly where or how. The memory holes served as a sort of mental shield for him. A way to escape the act itself, as well as the sense of responsibility.

I wish I could ask him about these things now.

It was a terrible oversight. But I never made the connection, even after the incident with Nurse Bailer. The idea that Dr. Kline might kill someone on purpose never occurred to me.

I should have been more cautious.

2

After almost six months of making journal entries in black crayon, Dr. Kline decided that he was making significant progress. He could control himself during the paranoid phases, and he didn't panic during the amnesia phases. The little plastic container of Haldol on the corner of his desk had not been touched in weeks.

I think I'm ready, he wrote in his journal.

He knew it was true. He would make a good candidate for the out-patient program. Nevertheless, he didn't want to rush things. After all, he still had over six months until his self-imposed deadline. And there was no reason to hurry into the review procedure.

Better to practice first, he thought. *With a more forgiving audience.*

But there lay the real problem: practicing. Kline was worried, at first, that he would never find anyone to practice with him. All he needed was someone to talk to, but insane asylums were filled with… insane people. His talking partner couldn't be some psycho. It had to be someone normal.

He was lying in his bed one night, wondering how long Alexandra's dark brown hair might be by now, or how tall she might be. His daughter was surely growing more beautiful by the day. He had almost drifted off to sleep when a sound in the corridor made him open his eyes and sit up. One of the night watchmen had walked past the door. Just as they did every night.

Dr. Kline smiled.

Those guards on the midnight shift had nothing to keep them busy. Kline knew most of them were probably bored, and he reasoned that at least one of them would be glad to talk for a while each evening. Just to pass the time.

The security staff worked in shifts: Mr. Simmons covered Monday through Wednesday, and Mr. Door had Thursday through Sunday. Of the two, Kline had his sights set on Simmons, whom he could often hear talking to himself. The man was desperate for conversation.

"Hey, there," Kline called out the next night, when he heard Simmons' footsteps moving past his room. "I hear the weather's starting to get nice again."

The footsteps paused. Turned and came back. "Yup, sun's coming up earlier these days."

And that was it. Mr. Simmons and Dr. Kline struck up a friendship of sorts. When they spoke, they did so through the slots in the thick metal door to Kline's cell. Kline didn't care what they discussed; he let Simmons dictate the conversations. Often they talked about other patients, one of the few subjects they had in common.

The fearsome Timmy, for example.

The patient who lived two rooms down from Dr. Kline, a giant named Timmy Hollingshead, was a constant source of morbid entertainment. Kline and Simmons talked about Timmy the way teenaged boys would talk about an axe-murderer on the loose. What would happen if that man ever got his hands on you, they wondered. How would you get away? Timmy was a huge, near-mute simpleton. He was also what Dr. Levoir called a 'pure' psychopath. Unlike Dr. Kline, Timmy was never allowed out of his room without multiple restraints, and multiple guards. Timmy was not sneaky. Or clever. There were no misunderstandings with Timmy. If you were stupid enough to get near him, he would simply grab you and begin breaking things. Timmy loved breaking things. It made him laugh. His massive hands could snap bones like popsicle sticks.

"How much you give me to go in there?" Simmons asked once.

"I don't have any money, Ben. I'm locked in a little white room."

"I know, I know," Simmons said, waving his hand as though he were swatting away invisible flies. "But I mean, how much *would* you give me? If you *did* have the money."

Kline considered. "Two million?" It had been a while since he had played this kind of game.

"No way. Ten."

"*Ten*?" Kline tried to put some hurt in his voice, as if he were being duped on a mattress sale. "I'll give you four, tops."

"Seven."

"Five."

"Five and a half."

Kline relented. For venturing into a cell with giggling Timmy Hollingshead, he thought 5.5 million dollars was probably a fair asking price.

When they became tired of discussing death-defying dares, the conversation moved to whatever Simmons had seen on television earlier that evening. If it was something the guard didn't understand, Dr. Kline would try to explain.

Explanations required sustained speaking. These were the real tests, because Mr. Simmons was not an especially polite man, and he was not careful with his words. If Dr. Kline said something strange, or said it in a strange way, Simmons reacted immediately. "You sound funny," he would blurt out suddenly. In Simmons-speak, this could mean almost anything. "Should I call someone? You need a pill or something?"

"No, Ben. Hold on." And here Dr. Kline would check himself, examining what he had done wrong. "I'm all right now."

"Yeah, okay," said Simmons, the worry lingering in his voice. And then it was forgotten. "Anyway, you were saying about the fire on T.V.?"

"Yes. The fire from the explosion was so hot that it began melting the steel in the building."

"Melting the steel?"

"Melting it, yes."

And so Dr. Kline would continue, until the next time his friend noticed something awry.

"Have you seen the new Porsche they're making?" Simmons asked one night.

Dr. Kline was in the middle of a deep, deep memory hole – an amnesia phase – and he was struggling to avoid the panic that accompanied such times. "I'm not sure," he said slowly.

The response didn't activate Simmons's weird-sensor, and he plowed ahead. "It's an awesome car. I wish I could have one. You ever have a car like that? A sports car, I mean?"

Dr. Kline concentrated. He recognized neither his surroundings nor the voice of the man talking to him, and the feeling of panic was closing in like a dark, asphyxiating cloud. He supposed that he might have owned a sports car once. Why not? He didn't remember his own name; anything was possible. "Yes," he said, trying to sound confident.

"No kidding." Simmons was ecstatic. "What kind? What color?"

These questions were too difficult, and Dr. Kline felt himself beginning to lose his grip on reality. He summoned his last bit of strength. "I think I need to go to sleep, friend."

Simmons reacted with his usual equanimity. "Okay, Nathan. Talk to you tomorrow. Sleep well."

The next night, Kline asked Simmons to remind him what they had discussed the day before. It was difficult to make his voice sound casual. He wondered if he had blacked out, or had suffered a particularly severe paranoid episode, or what.

"Oh, this and that," Simmons replied. "Then you got tired all of a sudden and went off to bed, remember?"

"Ah, yes."

Kline did *not* remember, but he knew that his bouts of Transient Global Amnesia were frequently followed by fatigue. Dr. Levoir had told him that. So maybe he had just been having one of his forgetful spells. And if he had managed to get through an amnesia phase without Simmons noticing anything amiss, then that was cause for celebration. "What were we talking about before I went to bed?"

"The Porsche. Don't you remember?"

No, he certainly didn't. But Simmons didn't seem worried. Good.

After two months of practice, Dr. Kline believed he was ready for the next stage. Ready, that is, to try his luck with people who were more critical than a night watchman.

Surely I can handle the idiots on a review board, he thought.

It was a little bit ahead of schedule – he had budgeted another four months before his targeted release – but the possibility of getting out was too exciting to ignore. There were so many old friends he wanted to visit.

So many… discussions… that needed to be had.

Just days before Kline was going to broach the subject of the review board, Dr. Levoir arrived at their morning interview session looking concerned. Looking almost upset. And Dr. Levoir never looked upset. "What happened last night, Nathan?"

Kline froze. He thought quickly, but could not resurrect any memory of the night before.

"Benjamin Simmons came to me this morning," Dr. Levoir said slowly. "He seemed shaken up. I wasn't able to get anything specific out of him, but he did say that you two had been talking."

Silence, as the patient searched his leaky brain. If it was another amnesia phase, that was one thing. But there were other possibilities. A more acute form of the paranoia phase, for example. Or maybe it was something else.

Maybe it was something I couldn't control.

"What did you talk about, Nathan?"

"I swear I don't remember."

Dr. Levoir nodded, but his dour expression did not change. "All right, Nathan. Mr. Simmons will be taking some vacation, starting today. Nurse Bailer has agreed to stand in for him."

Kline had difficulty hiding his disappointment. With Simmons gone, he knew he would never find out exactly what had happened the night before. And he would have to revert to self-assessment from now on.

Also, Nurse Bailer was not his favorite employee.

She came to him without warning that night, just minutes after the call for lights out.

"Kline." Her flat voice at the door.

He was nearing the end of a dog phase, and he could smell the detergent on the nurse's freshly laundered white uniform. The soap overwhelmed most of her natural odors, but nothing could block out the oil on her skin, the grease in her hair. Dr. Kline had decided that Nurse Bailer did not bathe often enough. He brought his plastic chair to the front of the room, just as he always had with Mr. Simmons. "Nurse Bailer?" he whispered. "How nice to hear – "

"Drop it, mush-brain. I don't get paid enough to listen to nut-fucks like you."

Kline's mouth snapped shut. He could not have been more surprised if she had come striding into the room and hit him over the head with a wrench. Nurse Bailer was usually unpleasant, but this was a new level of spite.

"I don't know what you've been feeding Simmons," she said, "but I'm not hungry, got it?"

Kline did not respond.

You don't interrupt an angry dog, he thought. *You keep still, and hope that the barking, drooling thing will continue on its way.*

"And don't confuse me with Dr. Levoir, either."

No danger there.

"I don't know why that man is so taken with you, but there it is." She sounded disgusted. "I'd have you strapped to a bed around the clock, if I ran this place."

Then I guess I'm glad you're not a doctor.

"I don't want to hear one more fucking *word* out of you tonight, understand?"

Absolutely.

"I can hardly wait until you come up for review. I'm going to have so *much* to say."

Kline's breath stopped in his chest. Insults were one thing, but he didn't like to hear her talking about the review board.

He didn't like it at all.

"You may have made Dr. Levoir your little pal," the nurse went on, "but I can see what you're doing. You're like one of those 'reformed' child molesters who can pick up a little girl, smile for the cameras, and put her down again. But you're nothing but rotten underneath. I can see the crazy in you like a bull-turd in a glass jar."

Dr. Kline took a deep breath. It was too early for this, but he knew what he had to do. Nurse Bailer had crossed the line. "I'm so sorry you feel that way, " he said.

"Don't you say one more goddamned… what?"

Kline had felt the Voice phase approaching, and he had been planning to keep his mouth shut. But then the nurse had started threatening him with this review board nonsense. And that was unacceptable.

His plan was risky. The Voice had not been field-tested, not even with Simmons. If it didn't work the way he hoped, Bailer would rat him out. Then Dr. Levoir would start asking questions, which would be a disaster. If the doctor got wind of his special abilities, he would never get out of this place.

So Kline closed his eyes and tried to speak in a tone that was both firm and clear. "It's just that I thought we were getting along so well," he said.

"We were *not* getting along," the nurse said. "What are you talking about?"

Kline hadn't won her over yet, but her tone had softened a few notches. She didn't sound so sure of herself anymore. He pushed on.

"You're right," he said. "Of course you're right. We weren't really. Not at first. Maybe we started off on the wrong foot."

"Wrong foot…?" She was hesitating now. Her breath was unsteady.

"Exactly. The wrong foot. The thing is, I didn't realize how important you were around here. How much responsibility you had." The words were slow, delicious.

It sounds right, he thought. And the smell was there too, just as it had been when he was practicing on his own. It made him think about sex. His dog phase was over, so he couldn't smell the nurse anymore, but he hoped she was being affected through the slots in the door. He knew she had a master key, and he considered inviting her into his little room for some play-time. God knew it had been a while.

But he had a better idea.

The nurse sighed. "It's true," she said. "I have a lot on my plate."

"That's right. I can see that now. You're the real engine of this place. You keep the wheels spinning."

"I do oversee most of the staff."

"Levoir would be lost without you."

She let out a little laugh. "He doesn't know the first thing about running a ward." Now her tone had changed completely. She was speaking easily, as though to a good friend. Or to a very attractive man at a bar. "I take care of everything," she said.

"Naturally. And you make every patient's comfort your business."

"Yes… that's right."

"But do you know what I like best about you, Nurse Bailer?"

"What? Best?" Her voice was light. Almost giddy.

"I like how you're always talking to the patients. I love these visits of yours."

"It's my job," she said, the sound of pride welling up in her chest.

"And you do that job so well. Could you do me a favor, Nurse Bailer?"

"Anything. And call me Charlotte."

"Charlotte, yes. Could you give Timmy Hollingshead a visit?"

Charlotte Bailer turned to look in the direction of Timmy's room, two doors down. Even in her dreamy state, she seemed cautious at the sound of that name. "Timmy?" she said, and paused. "Oh, I'm not sure I should."

Kline kept talking. "Charlotte, come on. I don't want to monopolize your time. Couldn't you just go into his room and say hi? It would mean *so* much to me. And to Timmy. He and I are good friends, you know, and he told me that he's been feeling neglected lately."

"Has he? Well…"

"Please?"

"I suppose it's part of my job."

"Exactly right," Kline purred.

He heard her move away from the door, heard her sneaker footsteps padding down the concrete hallway. There was the ringing of a set of keys being pulled from a pocket. He held his breath and waited.

How long do the effects of this little parlor trick last? Kline wondered. *Is she actually going to let herself into Timmy Hollingshead's room? Does the Voice really work that well? Does it really?*

He heard the groan of hinges as a heavy door opened and closed, and then the click of a latch snapping shut.

Yes, it really does.

There was the sound of Nurse Bailer talking quietly, waking Timmy up. Dr. Kline walked over to his bed and eased himself slowly down onto the thin mattress. He could feel a vertigo phase coming on, and he didn't want to fall and knock his head against anything.

Seconds later, Charlotte Bailer screamed. There was a clarity to the sound, as though the first broken bone had made the nurse suddenly understand her mistake. She screamed, desperate and pleading, for Timmy to stop. The next bone snapped, and her voice went up an entire octave, into a register that woke the few patients who had not already been jolted from their beds by the first yell. Nurse Bailer took great, gulping mouthfuls of air and *screamed*, screamed as one who could see her own death suddenly so near, and was not, not, *not* ready. The sounds she made filled the Clancy Hall ward and pressed up against the concrete walls. The metal doors trembled.

Beneath Nurse Bailer's terrified wailing there came another sound, much softer, this one like the bells in a child's toy. It was the sound of Timmy Hollingshead's laughter, delighted and musical. Like a girl's.

Lying in the dark, the room spinning around him as his vestibular sense began to fail, Dr. Kline closed his eyes and smiled.

He was ready.

3

From *Getting to Know Patient Nathan*:

I have said publicly that I felt pity for Dr. Kline, both during his stay at Clancy Hall and afterward. It is easy to understand why this sentiment is not a popular one. Kline's name has come to symbolize many things, but pity is not one of them.

The whole story of Patient Nathan, though, is one that I do think deserves pity. He lost his family. He lost his job, his coworkers, and many of his closest friends.

He lost his mind.

"But Dr. Levoir," I can hear someone say, "Kline himself was responsible for the losses you describe."

To this observation, I can only respond, "Good point."

And still I find it sad.

4

Nurse Bailer had been dead a week, and Kline was delighted to find that no one suspected anyone other than Timmy Hollingshead.

Delighted, but not really surprised.

When Kline was told what had happened, he managed to look appropriately shocked. It wasn't hard for him. He had been putting on an act of one kind or another for months now.

As far as Dr. Levoir was concerned, Kline was still the model patient.

Kline's Escape

1

The review board was not what he had expected. Kline had been picturing a long table of men and women dressed in suits. They would face him with stern, thoughtful expressions. He would sit in a single wooden chair, and if he had owned a cap, he would be holding it in his hands. A large fan would turn slowly overhead while the men and women asked him probing questions. He would nod thoughtfully, and then he would describe all the progress that he and Dr. Levoir had been making. All the neurological demons that had been found, catalogued, and quarantined.

Afterward they would smile wisely at him, write a few notes with expensive pens on official stationary, and then he would be on his way.

But that wasn't the way it happened.

Exactly forty-five weeks after Nathan Kline's arrival at Clancy Hall, Dr. Levoir brought another doctor into the daily interview session with him. "Nathan, have you met Dr. Bender?"

Kline spoke without hesitation. "From the third floor? University of Pennsylvania, I believe. Then Stanford."

Dr. Bender's eyes opened wide. He reached out to shake the patient's hand. "Dr. Levoir prepared you?"

"The nurses discuss everyone," Dr. Kline said smoothly. He winked. "I think you're one of their favorites. I hear about you all the time."

But of course this wasn't true. Kline was in the middle of a mnemonic phase, one of several that he had not discussed with Dr. Levoir. For the next hour, his memory would be perfect. Every stray sentence that had ever been uttered within his earshot; anything he had seen, touched, tasted, or smelled; it was all right there in front of him. He could have named Levoir's necktie choices for the past 288 days. He could have recited the recipe for meatloaf his mother had taught him 20 years ago. But he stuck to pleasantries. He knew it was what the doctor expected. "Are you here to meet the fearsome *Patient Nathan*?" Kline said, trying to sound amused. "I worry that I may disappoint."

Dr. Bender sat back, a man at leisure. "Not at all. We often observe one another's interviews. Helps for collaboration. Nothing to do with you."

"Of course."

Liar.

The next day, Dr. Bender did not return. Kline was pleased; he took this to mean that the doctor had been satisfied with his visit. In Bender's place, Levoir brought Dr. Haven. Dr. Haven arrived in the middle of one of Kline's dog phases, when he could smell absolutely everything.

Dr. Haven put out his hand to greet Kline, who struggled to return the favor. The man reeked so strongly of semen that it was difficult to concentrate.

"Pleased to meet you, Nathan." said Dr. Haven. "How are you feeling?"

I was feeling all right, Kline thought. *That is, until I noticed the fresh sperm on your breath. Your companion seems also to have dripped sweat on you in the process. Tom Harwell, is it? I can smell that man from two hundred yards away – he's a greasy one. Is this part of Tom's treatment, doctor? Or do all the patients in your wing get that kind of special attention?*

"I'm feeling very well, thank you," Dr. Kline said. "Although my stomach is a little uneasy this morning."

"Probably the breakfast meat," Haven said, smiling.

Dr. Kline tried to breathe through his mouth for the rest of the interview.

There were more. Each morning, a new doctor joined them for an hour or so. No special reason, they said. Just stopping by. Kline could tell by Levoir's reactions that the process was going well. The first goal – getting released – was *close*. Which meant that phase two – the list – was approaching. It all made his heart race, and he began to have difficulty sleeping.

When he did manage to sleep, he had vivid dreams. His daughter was the subject most of the time. Alexandra was tall and beautiful, as always. She asked him why he had to stay at the lab so late. "Come home, Dad," she said. "Come home and talk to me."

His wife, Joanne, was often there as well, but she never spoke. She blamed him for what had happened. Only his daughter was willing to forgive. Alexandra called out to him and opened her arms. He was cured of his mental problems, acquitted of the murder. Those terrible things were only illusions. *This* was the reality.

They were wonderful dreams, and waking up was a disappointment. He would close his eyes and try to return, but it never worked.

The doctors kept coming to observe him. Usually the visits were easy. All he had to do was act normally. Interact without seeming unstable. He had done it for weeks with Mr. Simmons, and the simple-minded security guard had probably been his most critical audience.

There was one small scare, however: the interview with Dr. Sonya. She had pretty eyes, and she seemed kinder than the others. Kline was in the middle of a phase change when she arrived in the interview room, but he tried to give her his attention as Levoir made the introduction.

Suddenly, Dr. Levoir's speech began to sound foreign, and Dr. Kline felt his chest constrict.

No, please.

If he went aphasic now, he would never be able to make the kind of humdrum conversation that was expected of him. Dr. Sonya would surely be fascinated by his inability to understand language, but she would not be likely to recommend his release. He had seen a tape of him trying to speak during one of these phases, and it was embarrassing. Instead of speech, he could produce only a series of strained bleating noises. It made him sound like a wounded sea lion.

Kline painted a permanent half-smile on his face and waited for the senseless jabbering to stop coming out of Dr. Levoir's mouth. The aphasia was in full effect now, and he could no longer see how such sounds had *ever* held any meaning.

When Dr. Sonya reached out, he automatically did the same. They shook hands.

She was a real talker, which was a blessing. Kline watched her with a burning concentration. When her eyes seemed to brighten, he smiled in agreement. If she leaned forward in an earnest pose, he nodded and bit his lip. He did everything possible to keep her talking.

Dr. Sonya turned briefly to look at Dr. Levoir, as if to get his opinion on something. Levoir paused, then shrugged and looked at Kline. There was a question in his eyes. Dr. Sonya turned to face him as well. She waited.

Dear Jesus, Kline thought. *They're trying to ask me something.*

He didn't panic. He put on a thoughtful expression and looked at the two doctors, studying them. The wrong response now could cost him everything. If he shook his head when they were expecting a yes, his coherence might become suspect, and incoherent patients did not get released into the outside world; they got remanded for six months of additional high-security observation.

If the question required more than a yes or no, he was finished.

Kline looked again at Dr. Levoir, whose familiarity made him easier to scrutinize. The doctor's face seemed open, neutral. Kline could find no real curiosity there.

The question was something simple, he decided.

He checked Dr. Sonya. Ah, there it was: her cheeks were waiting to fan out into another smile. All she wanted was a yes.

Dr. Kline nodded slowly, and the two doctors smiled back at him. Levoir rose immediately from his chair and went to the television that was mounted high up in the corner of the room. He turned it on and spoke to the mirror at the back wall, where unseen security personnel were watching every move.

The television screen switched from static to a clear picture, and Dr. Kline almost laughed out loud. He realized that they were going to watch a tape. A tape of one of his first interviews with Levoir, who always recorded everything for his research. Both doctors would want Kline to comment on it afterward, but by then everything would be fine. It was a long interview, and he would be able to speak English again before it finished playing. He also might turn into a paranoid schizophrenic by then, or discover that he couldn't remember his own name, but never mind. One problem at a time. He had developed techniques for getting himself through those phases.

Dr. Sonya left an hour later. By then Kline was able to tell her, in glowing tones, that he was sorry to see her go so soon.

After two weeks of these team-style examinations, Dr. Levoir finally arrived one morning without any extra doctors in tow. He sat down and looked at his patient, a little smile playing at his lips.

Kline held his breath.

"I'm not promising anything," Dr. Levoir began.

Kline would have clapped his hands like a child at a birthday party, had it not been for the profound deficit affecting his right temporal lobe at that moment. His left arm and leg would both be useless for at least another half-hour, so he knocked his right fist enthusiastically against the top of the table.

"We'll see," said Dr. Levoir. "But I think we'll get it. I believe in you, Nathan."

Dr. Kline had vivid dreams again that night, but his wife and daughter were nowhere to be found. Instead, Frederick Carlisle appeared, wearing the same thin, yellow cardigan that had covered his sloping shoulders all the years they had worked together. He was standing right there, so close. Kline found himself wanting just to kill him and be done with it. But his arms didn't seem to be working.

"Want to try it again?" his partner was saying.

Kline tried to shake his head no, but nothing happened. He was paralyzed. That didn't seem fair, since total paralysis wasn't one of his twelve symptoms. Carlisle seemed to take Kline's silence as a yes.

"Let's get you hooked up, then," he said cheerily. "Stefan, if you would?"

Back from the dead, Stefan LeCoeur scurried around Kline like a monkey, double-checking the wires and straps that sprouted from the device resting on Kline's head.

I changed my mind! Kline tried to yell at them, but nothing happened. *The machine doesn't work right! The prototype wasn't constructed to specs! The field is compromised!*

Nothing. His voice was useless. He could only bleat at them wordlessly.

"And you've taken the pill, I assume?" said Professor Carlisle.

I shouldn't have done that! It was impure! Laced with something! Stop this, please!

"Good, then," Carlisle said. "Let's get moving." He began speaking like a boxing announcer: "Dr. Nathan Kline! You are about to become the first man on the planet to experience the effects of a globally administered TMS treatment! With a few key modifications, of course!" He let out a small giggle, making him sound strangely like Timmy Hollingshead.

No! Dr. Kline shouted. But the sound was still only in his head. He searched in vain for Stefan, who was supposed to be in charge of safety. *Stefan, where are you? Why don't you stop this?*

There was a humming noise. He felt no pain. The room went white, as though they had all been engulfed in the flash of a nuclear detonation.

Dr. Kline woke up, and he sprang from his bed as if someone had doused him with a bucket of ice water. A moment later, his limbs collapsed beneath him, and he fell awkwardly to the ground. After a moment, he saw where he was. His face tightened into an expression of forbearance, and he did not try to get up.

When the morning nursing staff arrived twenty minutes later, they were surprised to find Dr. Kline there, still crumpled on the floor. They had never known Patient Nathan to let himself be seen in such a vulnerable, compromised position. He even allowed them to pull him to his feet, which was a first. His eyes were wide open and unblinking, much as they had been when he was suffering from Xanax withdrawal eleven months ago.

The focused look, Dr. Levoir had called it.

Kline recovered himself before it was time for his daily interview. When Levoir asked if he had slept well, he replied, "Yes, wonderfully. Thank you." He was not about to let a bad dream get in the way of his long-term plans. That would have been pointless. Instead, he used the dream as inspiration. As a way to clarify, and to re-commit.

To remind himself of the mother-fuckers who needed scolding.

2

From *Getting to Know Patient Nathan*:

On his last day at Clancy Hall, Nathan seemed distracted. I had been expecting him to be excited about his release. Or proud of himself, for his long months of steady progress. Nervousness would have been normal, too, I suppose. He was returning to the world after a long, long absence.

But Nathan was not excited, at least not in the happy sense. And I wouldn't have described him as nervous. Keyed-up was more like it. He acted like a college quarterback on the night before a big game.

"You're going to be fine," I told him.

"I know." His face was so serious.

"Remember that you can always call me if you need anything."

He nodded.

"And you have the number for the rental agent I told you about?"

"In my pocket."

"Good. Now, if you have trouble with sleeping during the first week, you should try to – "

"Dr. Levoir?"

I stopped, and Nathan looked at me across the table. I couldn't tell which phase he was in, but he suddenly seemed tired. As though the pressure of whatever big game he had tomorrow was finally starting to wear him down. "You helped me," he said.

It was a nice thing for him to say, and I relaxed.

"Thank you for always being honest," he said.

I grinned. "Maybe this was all for my benefit. You're my prize case-study, remember?"

"That's fine. You deserve it."

"*You* deserve it, Nathan. You learned trust, which is a concept that's almost as difficult for normal people as it is for paranoid schizophrenics.

People are dishonest, and there is no real way to tell the liars from the truth-tellers. Trust is the only social currency. And you found yours again."

Nathan turned his head half a degree, as if he had heard a strange noise in the distance. "That's interesting," he said.

"What?"

"You think it's impossible to tell truth from lies."

"Well. No *sure* way exists. You can't tell. Not consistently. Not really."

He looked at me then with sorrow in his eyes. Like a parent staring at a particularly well-meaning, particularly stupid child.

"Of course you can," he said. "You just have to watch."

He stood and shook my hand before I could ask what he meant. Then he turned to go. He left our facility the same way he had come in. Not on a stretcher, though. Not this time. He walked, and with purpose. His tall, gaunt frame looked stronger than I remembered it.

He walked like a man with places to go.

"I believe in you, Nathan," I said to his back.

He put one hand in the air, acknowledging me for the last time.

3

Dr. Kline's first significant encounter occurred one week after his release from Clancy Hall. It happened in the bus station at the corner of Atlantic avenue in downtown Boston, where he spoke with a ticket lady named Hanna Dee Corley. The date and time, September 14, at 6:20 PM, took on no special significance for Hanna Dee afterward. Her name was nowhere on Dr. Kline's list, and she survived the encounter.

There was a long line that night at gate seven, the New York route. Hanna Dee was thinking that it was funny with buses, that you could never tell when there was going to be an overflow. The computers were fine at printing out tickets and credit slips, but they didn't work so well at anticipating customer demand.

A round man in a bulky, ill-fitting black sweater stepped up to her window. He had thick lips and a weak chin. He looked annoyed before he even started talking. "One roundtrip to Manhattan," he said. "Lewinston. I have a reservation." He nodded his head in the direction of Hanna's terminal. "I have a reservation," he said again.

Hanna Dee sighed as she typed the man's name into her computer. Whether his name came up on the list or not, she knew it wouldn't make any difference. This wasn't the Delta Shuttle. "Sir, you're probably going to have difficulty getting on." She glanced in the direction of gate seven. "That's the line for the New York bus over there."

"No," Lewinston said curtly. "No difficulty. I made this reservation two weeks ago."

"Yes, sir, but seating on USA Coach service is on a first come, first serve – "

"That's *not* what they said on the phone. They said it would be *fine*."

"Certainly. But that particular bus will be filled to capacity. If you'd like, I can give you a ticket for another coach to New York. That one would leave at – "

"No, dammit! They said it wouldn't be a problem!" He was

shouting now, and people were turning to look. "I have a reservation on the 6:45 to Manhattan, and my name is Jake Lewinston, and I want a seat on that bus!"

The line of travelers waiting at gate seven became very quiet. Most of them could not hear exactly what the pudgy man in the black sweater was saying, but they had the general idea. Everyone knew that traveling on buses was a crap-shoot. Everyone except this guy, apparently.

"I want to speak to your manager!" Lewinston yelled. The skin around his fleshy lips was jumping. "Right now!"

"Sir, this is just a ticket booth. Anyway, Mr. Morse leaves at five. He's – "

"Bullshit! I want to talk to him right now! Are you deaf?"

Movement behind Mr. Lewinston caught Hanna Dee's eye. She could see someone coming up to the booth. Someone very tall. She cocked her head to the side to get a better view. Lewinston did not appreciate the distraction. "Look at me, you moron! If you think I'm going to let you just brush me off like some – "

A large, gaunt hand came down gently on the shoulder of Jake Lewinston's sweater. The hand rested there for a moment, as if its owner were pausing for strength. Lewinston turned around to stare at the towering, hollow-faced man who had come up so quietly behind him, and his eyes narrowed into slits. "And just who the fuck are *you*?"

The tall man said nothing. He bent slowly at the waist. Hanna had the impression that the movement required some concentration. When his mouth was at the same level as Mr. Lewinston's ear, the man began to speak.

His voice was just barely above a whisper.

Hanna could not make out the words, but she saw Lewinston's face change. First there was surprise. Then confusion. Then, miraculously, calm. And then Jake Lewinston simply turned and walked away.

Hanna Dee was delighted. "Next!" she sang.

The tall figure stepped up to the window, and Hanna Dee looked up, preparing to give the friendliest two minutes of ticket service ever witnessed. When she saw the man's face, however, her voice caught in her throat.

She saw something… unstable.

It's like he's holding his face together, Hanna thought. *Through sheer will. And if he loses his concentration, even for a second, the whole thing will go flying apart like a big flesh grenade.*

Hanna shuddered and tried to collect herself. She had encountered stranger-looking people than this during her three months behind the counter, and she had sold all of them bus tickets without a hitch. She couldn't understand what had come over her. "Where to, sir?"

The tall man looked at her carefully. He seemed to be studying her mouth. If Hanna hadn't just seen him talking to Mr. Lewinston, she would have guessed that he didn't speak any English. Then she saw his upper lip begin to tremble, and she let out a startled little yelp. She put a hand self-consciously over her mouth.

The man closed his eyes and took a deep breath. When he opened his eyes, the lip tremor had stopped. Hanna returned her hand to her computer's keyboard, waiting.

"I beg your pardon," the tall man said. Hanna found his voice surprisingly deep. And rich. "Could you repeat that, please?" he said.

"Of course," said Hanna. All at once she felt much better. Warmer, and more relaxed. And something smelled very nice. "I asked where you would be traveling this evening."

"Ah, yes," rumbled the man. "Concord, New Hampshire."

Hanna smiled. New Hampshire. Such a beautiful name. For a beautiful state. And now she realized that this man's face didn't look ugly at all. It looked handsome. And strong. "One way or round trip?"

"One way."

Yes, one way. Nothing could be better. God, what *was* that smell? It was so beautiful. "Phone number?"

The tall man smiled gently, and Hanna almost melted. Someone else might have pointed out that the man's teeth were dull and uneven, and that his lips seemed to slide open with a mind of their own. But Hanna saw only brilliance. "Do you really need my phone number?" the man asked softly. "What about if I just pay for the ticket instead?"

Hanna giggled. "It was worth a shot," she said shyly.

"Yes," said the tall man. "I understand."

Of course he understood. He understood everything. "I knew you would," Hanna said with a sigh. "Here's your ticket. Gate eleven."

"And where is gate eleven, please?"

"Over there, to your left," Hanna said, and pointed.

The tall man hesitated. He stared at the mousy, love-smitten ticket lady before him, and his eyes were uncertain. Hanna Dee Corley felt a great wash of sadness and confusion come over her. She was afraid she would start crying soon if this feeling continued for too long.

"Where?" asked the man again.

"There. On your left." Hanna was pleading now. If this man didn't find gate 11, she thought, it would be a tragedy. A profound loss for her and for everyone at the bus terminal. She had to make him see. "Just turn to your left," she said. "It's over there."

The tall man stared at Hanna, and something behind his eyes changed. "Left," he murmured to himself. "It's there. On the… on the *other* side." He paused and looked to his right. Then he began turning. He turned in place, to his right, all the way around past 180 degrees to 270 – a three quarter turn – so that when he stopped, he was facing gate 11. "And there it is," he said. His eyes lit up. "Right where it should be."

Hanna leapt from her chair. "Yes!" she shouted, and she had never been so happy. "Right there!" She felt like kissing someone. Anyone. She ran over to Franklin's booth and planted him one, right on the lips.

Franklin froze in the middle of counting out a customer's change. "Well, I don't…" Franklin began, then stopped. He looked at Hanna Dee and grinned. "I guess I'll be starting *this* over, then," he said, throwing the money down into a pile.

Hanna Dee Corley laughed and went skipping back to her own booth.

Dr. Nathan Kline proceeded quickly to gate 11, where the bus to New Hampshire was waiting for him. He knew that he would need to find a seat within the next two minutes, before his left side deserted him altogether. He had never experienced this sort of multi-phase problem before, with so many symptoms occurring at once, but for a first try at interacting with the real world, he thought it had gone very well. The important thing was to avoid making a scene, and in this he believed he had more or less succeeded. He was on his way, after all. On his way to Concord, New Hampshire. And then, after that, to Dartmouth. At last.

He didn't notice the man sitting in the opposite corner of the terminal, the man with the eyeglasses and the tweed coat, watching him carefully.

Kline's List

1

From *Getting to Know Patient Nathan*:

I have read so much, in the papers and the magazines, about how senseless Dr. Kline's murders were. About what a madman he was. "A ruthless, mindless psychopath," they called him. But there was nothing senseless about what Nathan did after he left Clancy Hall. Not one thing.

I understand that my opinion in these matters is looked upon with skepticism. Because I am conflicted, the papers would say. After all, I am the one who set this "psychopath" loose on the world in the first place. And yes, he killed other human beings. With malice aforethought. Even with brutality, as some have said. And I agree that there is no excuse for these things. Kline deserves every bit of the anger directed at him. He was a cold-blooded murderer, in the end.

But – and you may accuse me of dealing in semantics here – it was never senseless. Never mindless. At least, not in the way that I use those words.

Have you read the police reports yourself? Have you seen the names Kline had on his list?

Have you thought about why?

I have.

And it all makes perfect sense.

2

Dr. Kline enjoyed his bus ride up to New Hampshire, and he was sorry when the USA Coach pulled into the little terminal on Stickney Avenue in Concord. It had been nice to just sit. To watch the New England scenery go by. As if he were a teenager on his way to camp. Or college.

There were errands to run now. First to the Bank of America on North Main, where he made the maximum allowable single-day cash withdrawal. He grinned when the money came riffing out of the machine. Dr. Levoir had assured him that his account would be unfrozen – he was being released, after all – but it was still a relief to see the stack of twenties come shuffling into his hands.

As he stepped back from the ATM, the world began to turn around him unnaturally. Dr. Kline compensated almost without thinking. He kept his eyes fixed on large, distant objects, just as a ballet dancer would spot the back of a recital hall between pirouettes. He walked the six blocks to the Centennial Inn on Pleasant street without anyone giving him a strange look.

Months of practice at Clancy Asylum.

Thank you again, Dr. Levoir.

The man behind the desk at the Centennial might have noticed something unstable about the tall, gangly figure who walked through the door that afternoon, but he didn't see any reason to comment. Not when the man put down two nights in advance. In cash.

Kline went to his room as quickly as he could without risking a fall. He made it to the bed with perhaps thirty seconds to spare. Soon after he lay down, the ceiling above him began to spin with authority. To spin *fast*. As though his bed were attached to a huge, turbo-charged Lazy Susan. He closed his eyes and waited.

The phase cleared an hour later, and Dr. Kline sat up on the bed. He went through a series of practiced movements designed to detect the onset of any obvious motor-related deficit: proprioceptive, hemi-inattentive, vestibular. Everything seemed normal. He could touch his nose with both hands. He could follow his own finger as it moved past his face. And he could probably… yes. He could stand up.

He looked around the room, continuing his diagnostics. His own name came to mind easily, as well as what he was planning to do. There was no sense of dread in his chest. And he could both recall and understand the phrase 'I am not aphasic.' Then it occurred to him that he had taken 820 steps from the bus stop to the Inn, and that if he were to repeat that number 12 more times –

Ah.

Analytical phase. Good. This would be a perfect time to go shopping. He was confident that he could get what he needed and be back within the hour.

Probably closer to 54 minutes, actually.

The desk clerk almost missed the tall man go sweeping through the lobby. He looked up from his portable television just in time to see someone – it might have been the old, bony guy from an hour ago – walking briskly out the door. The clerk would tell the police later that he had thought it was strange. Because the guy who came in earlier had looked like he was about to fall down. The man on the way out, though – he was *moving.*

"He looked… focused," the clerk would say.

And the cop would look up with doubt in his eyes. "You got that from watching his back?"

"That's what I said, right?"

Dr. Kline returned to where the bus had dropped him off. The terminal was next to a string of cheap restaurants, a huge department store with no name on the front, and a hardware store that had been modeled to resemble a Home Depot. He headed into the nameless place first. The only salesman he could find was a slouchy teenager in Birkenstocks, looking as though he didn't want to be bothered. Kline flagged him down.

"I need a backpack, please. It should be light – not more than five-point-six pounds. And I need a capacity of at least three thousand cubic inches. Single compartment."

The teenager looked at him for a beat. Then he pointed. "Larger packs are on the far wall, right-hand side." Kline nodded and went to make his selection. He did not linger.

Hardware was next. The Home Depot clone was clean and well-stocked, and Kline double-checked his mental list as he scanned the isles. He also kept count of the number of steps he took per breath, updating the average ratio continuously. He did this because it was fun to keep track of such things. That, and because he was curious to know whether the mean and median ratio values would begin to converge, despite fluctuations in his heart rate and oxygen consumption. He suspected that they *would* converge. Asymptotically, of course.

The salespeople in this store were helpful. And quick, which Dr. Kline appreciated in his hyper-literal state. They showed him where to find the copper wire, the toilet plungers, the DC power inverters, and the wall-mounting sets for hanging oversized mirrors. Oh, and the portable nailers. With the .22 caliber cartridge included. No outlet required.

The Hilti nailer, a specialized piece of equipment, was the most expensive item by far, though not the heaviest. The DC power inverter held that honor. The toilet plunger, on the other hand, would take up the most space per unit weight. Kline would have liked to create a comparison chart with these characteristics, but there wasn't time. This phase would pass soon, and the numbers would lose their charm.

He paid with a credit card – it worked just as well as his ATM card had – and then zipped everything up inside his new North Face Explorer backpack. He still had a few hundred cubic inches left in the pack. There was plenty of room for a car battery.

The man at the Meineke Car Care center was friendly. He wanted to chat.

"Died on you, huh?"

"Died?" Dr. Kline smiled. "No, not quite yet. Soon, though."

The man nodded. "Just buying a backup, then?"

"Backup….yes. Is this the most powerful battery you sell?"

"Oh, sure. Get her up in the middle of February, that one. Turn over an old diesel block like flipping a burger. Start a '79 pickup just on *guts*, you know? You could – "

"Good. I'll take it."

"All right, then."

"And I need a lockout kit. With an air wedge and a reach tool."

The attendant's demeanor cooled a few degrees. "Um. Thing is – those are only for sale to tow-truck companies, law enforcement, or registered locksmiths with documentation of – "

"Yes," Kline said, taking the roll of cash from his back pocket and peeling out five twenty-dollar bills. "Of course. But I don't have time for that. I just need to get into my car." He put down a sixth twenty. "You understand."

"Well, sure. I guess I do."

He made it back to the motel in just under 53 minutes. The desk clerk was taking a bathroom break, and he didn't see the tall man come in. Dr. Kline went up to his room and spread his purchases out on the bed, like a child gloating over his Christmas bounty. He had only minutes before the next phase, and that wouldn't be enough time for any real prep work. So he went to the phone and dialed a number he had looked up before leaving Massachusetts.

A young voice picked up at the other end.

"Is this the Baxter residence?" Kline asked.

"Uh-huh. You want Donny?"

"No, don't bother Donny right now. I'll call back."

Indifference on the other end. "Okay."

He hung up and returned to the bed, where his supplies waited. The DC inverter would need some modifications – the fuse, if it had one, would need to be bypassed, along with any other safety mechanisms – but everything else was going to be easy.

Now, if he could just get lucky on a phase.

As he stood there, the items on his bed seemed to take on a new quality. He could sense a texture, somehow. The roll of copper wire, so clean and cold when he had picked it up at the store, seemed more alive than before. As if he could taste it, even from a distance. And the stainless-steel picture-hanging set had changed, too. The metal had turned harsh. Bitter.

Dog phase, Kline thought.

Every item in the room now had a distinct odor, a flavor of its own. The new backpack reeked of leather and plastic, and he could smell the fresh rubber bell of the toilet plunger as if it were wrapped around his head.

And Lord, the bed mattress.

That mattress had cradled a thousand tired, unwashed bodies. It almost knocked him over with its stench. The dog phase often made Kline's stomach turn, but he could work through it. His natural technical aptitude, while not up to the standards of his analytical phase, would be good enough for the modifications he needed. He moved the power inverter from the bed to the small desk by the window, and he opened the window as wide as it would go. Concrete and exhaust fumes rushed in like poisonous gas, but both were better than the smell of the mattress. He sat down in the little wooden chair, and set to work.

The inverter was easier to modify than he expected.

It was not until the next afternoon that Dr. Kline was ready to go out again. He suffered through one particularly long and terrifying memory hole that night, and the fear was made worse by surroundings that really *were* unfamiliar. Several hours passed before he could remember himself. As always, the dread lingered, even after the amnesia itself was gone. He remembered, after a while, why he was lying alone in a tiny, ugly motel room. But the knowledge did not comfort him. He could not relax until the sun came up. Then he fell asleep. Finally.

He dreamed again of his wife and daughter. Both were more beautiful than before. Alexandra, especially. The image of her was clear and bright, like a picture taken under the noon sun. She called to him, welcomed him. Her skin seemed to glow.

He awoke suddenly, feeling as if he had slept through an important meeting. The sun came through the window and shone on his face. Through force of habit, he resisted the temptation to sit up, and instead he lay there and took stock of his mental state.

Someone was talking to him. Apparently the clerk downstairs had ratted him out. The police would be coming soon. There was an exotic nerve gas being pumped into his room through the vents. Spies were watching him through the television set. The government was trying to take over his brain with the help of the people who lived on Sirius-B.

Voices told him these things. Smart, honest voices. Kline almost smiled. The paranoia phase was such an easy one. Compared to some of the others, anyway. "That's all in my head," he said out loud. The voices protested, but Kline didn't listen.

Ironically, none of the voices mentioned anything about a man with glasses and a tweed coat, sitting in a car outside Kline's motel. Sitting so patiently, watching.

Kline got up from the bed and went to the little chair, where his backpack was waiting, loaded up and ready. It was time to pay Donny Baxter a visit.

He didn't bother trying to be stealthy. An undernourished, 6'4" man cannot easily blend into the New Hampshire countryside, and Dr. Kline had never been any good at blending. Even before the accident. So when he reached Donny Baxter's place, he walked up to the front entrance of the two-bedroom, vinyl-sided ranch house as if he were coming to visit old friends. He knocked, and the unlatched door swung open with the tired rasp of cheap metal hinges. Kline stood at the threshold and peeked inside carefully, like a neighbor stopping by to borrow a cup of sugar.

There was a boy sitting on the thin carpet, perhaps six years old, playing with a toy fuel-truck. He pushed the truck around him in an endless circle, making rumbling, truck-engine noises with his cheeks.

Dr. Kline smiled. "Hello, there." He was in the middle of a Voice phase, and the words came out in full, stereophonic resonance. A beautiful sound, he thought.

The boy looked up and paused in his trucking maneuvers. He didn't respond, which Kline found surprising. He tried again. "Is your brother at home?"

The boy frowned. "Why are you talking like that?"

"I'm a friend of Donny's. Could you tell me – "

"You sound weird." The boy shrank back from the door.

"I'm sorry, I only want to… "

"Stop!" The boy clapped his hands to the side of his head.

Dr. Kline stopped. He looked at the frightened child on the rug. The boy was wincing and covering his ears against the strange noise.

Kline held his breath.

What's happening?

The Voice sounded the same as it always did. Nurse Bailer would have been on her knees by now, awaiting instructions. So why was this child – ?

Dr. Kline closed his eyes. Of course. The Voice worked with sexual attraction somehow. He didn't understand the specifics, but specifics didn't matter.

It would never work with someone this young.

He squatted down on the floor and began to whisper. The boy took his hands off his ears.

"I'm looking for Donny," Kline whispered. "Could you tell me where he is?"

The boy pointed.

"Donny's asleep?"

"No. Working."

"In the other room?"

The boy shook his head and pointed again, with more energy this time. As if he were throwing a ball. "No, *working*. At school."

"Okay," Kline whispered. "Donny works at the high school?"

The boy shrugged. "I guess." He returned his attention to his toy truck.

Dr. Kline had an idea of the sort of "work" Donny Baxter might be doing at the public high school, and it wasn't teaching. He had seen the press clippings from the Hanover paper: Donny had been fired from Dartmouth Hitchcock for stealing supplies from the pharmacy storeroom.

Not the first time he'd done it, either, Kline thought. *Just the first time he'd been caught.*

It was a ten-minute walk to the high school, and Kline used much of this time to picture his daughter's smile. Alexandra could look both serious and happy when she smiled, because her eyes always stayed so focused. So steady. She would forgive him, he thought. Surely she would. When all of this was finally done.

There were only a few cars left in the school parking lot this late in the afternoon, and he spotted Donny's immediately. The same beat-up Honda, the same sagging muffler. It was the car Donny had been driving when he worked up in Hanover.

There were several ways to do this. He would check the vehicle first, and if it was locked, he could still –

But the door wasn't locked.

It was an old car, and there were no valuables inside. Donny was probably half-hoping someone would steal it so that the insurance would take over. Dr. Kline opened the door and climbed in. He waited.

Twenty minutes after his old boss had snuck into the back seat of his Honda Accord, Donny Baxter closed up shop for the day. It had been a good afternoon for him. There were plenty of customers, and no trouble from teachers. No cops, either. It was dusk, and the light was low. With its tinted windows and charcoal seats, the inside of Donny's Honda was murky. Still, the man sitting in the back seat was tall, and there was nowhere to hide. Donny could have seen him. If he had checked.

He didn't check.

For Donny Baxter, the next few seconds were surreal.

He opened the door and began lowering himself into the car, and Kline began sitting forward, hands at the ready. Donny settled back into the seat and reached for the door; at the same time, Kline brought his hands above Donny's head, as if preparing to spring a *guess who?* surprise. The two men moved in tandem, like a pair that had practiced together for countless hours. Each movement was fluid. Donny Baxter neither heard nor saw anything amiss until the stainless steel wire was already around his neck, snug like a collar. The entire process took less than three seconds, start to finish.

Kline spoke before Donny had a chance to react. "If you move or say a single word, you'll be dead inside of a minute."

Donny Baxter, in a remarkable show of sangfroid, did *not* move.

Did not say a single word. His breathing quickened, but Dr. Kline did not hold this against him. Donny assumed that he was being held up for the drug money he had made that afternoon. So after a few moments of stillness, he began moving his hand – ever so slowly – toward his right front shirt pocket.

"Put your hand down, Don."

Donny did as he was told. Kline made some adjustments in the back seat, and the steel wire drew briefly tighter. Donny Baxter uttered a short, surprised gurgling noise, but nothing more.

"Whoops," said Dr. Kline. "My fault." The Voice was gone, and he was speaking in his normal register. He was also feeling wonderful. Energetic. And happy.

The creative phase.

"Here's the situation, Don. That's a length of 200-pound-test, picture-hanging steel wire wrapped around your neck. So don't strain against it. You'll lose. The wire is looped, at both ends, around the wooden dowel of a good, old-fashioned toilet plunger. Strong, thick shaft. Bought it yesterday. I've removed any slack in the wire, so if I twist the plunger rod in either direction – "

Donny made another choked, half-gasping sound.

" – the wire draws tighter. Neat, right? As you can imagine, the length of the plunger gives me significant leverage. I'm not positive, but I think I could take your head off with this thing." He sat forward between the seats and looked Donny in the face for the first time. "I think I could do it with just two fingers. It's physics, you know."

Donny's eyes went wide with recognition. His broad cheeks, tanned brown from hours outside in the sun, flushed red. "Oh my God. When did you gehhh – "

The smallest turn on the wooden dowel of the plunger, and Donny Baxter stopped in mid-sentence. Kline sat back, releasing the pressure slowly, and Donny's breathing resumed. "No talking, Don. Not unless I ask you a question." Kline began rummaging through his backpack. "Do you understand that rule? You can answer."

Donny remembered to avoid nodding, and thus saved himself some pain. "I understand," he said.

"Good. You're going to do fine. I just need to ask some questions."

Donny tried to relax. Questions were okay, he told himself. He could handle questions. He would invent answers, if it came to that.

"Put your hands back here," Kline said. "Behind the seat."

Donny did as he was told, and he felt his thick wrists being wrapped tightly together with more wire.

"Great!" Kline was almost laughing. This manic, creative phase was his favorite, and his voice was light. "This is going to be terrific! Just give me a minute to get some other stuff arranged back here, okay?"

Unsure as to whether a response was called for, Donny Baxter made a quiet, affirmative humming sound. He kept his large head as still as possible, and waited while Dr. Kline tinkered in the backseat. Donny's eyes scanned the now empty parking lot, searching – praying – for one of the local cops to show up. They were always making sweeps of the high school. Harassing him, scaring off his customers.

Where the fuck are you now, Officer Shaw?

"Okay!" Kline said. "First things first. Special earphones for you, Don."

Donny twitched briefly at the sensation of cold copper on his skin. Dr. Kline made several careful loops, wrapping both of Donny's ears with nine inches of copper. "Good. Now, first question."

"I'll tell you anything you need to know," Donny blurted out suddenly. "Anything. Just ask me – "

"DONNY!" Dr. Kline gave the plunger a quick twist, and Donny's eyes bulged. "You *need* to be quiet."

The pressure eased off, and Donny breathed again.

"Donny, you're going to be quiet, right?"

"Right," Donny gasped.

"Okay. Back to business. Here's quiz question number one." Kline paused, then began speaking in a sing-song, game-show tone of voice.

"Let us suppose, Don, that we have a brand-new, DieHard truck battery rated at two thousand cold-cranking amps. What would happen if the leads of such a battery were connected, by means of copper wire, to someone's ears?"

"Oh, Jesus, I don't know but listen I've got money you can have and – "

"Donny?"

"What?"

"Trick question. You're already connected." Kline held up the huge battery so that Donny could see it in the rearview mirror. The copper wires were securely connected to the positive and negative terminals. Donny shuddered.

"Oh."

"The answer, as you can see, is that *nothing* happens. And do you know why?"

Donny would have shaken his head, but he restrained himself to avoid being cut by the steel wire around his neck. "No," he said, feeling not quite relieved. "Why?"

"Because human skin has a remarkably high natural resistance to current, Don. Especially *your* skin, which is so dry after being outside all day long. I'd say you're rated at somewhere around three or even four thousand ohm. Cuts the amps down to nothing. Very fortunate for you."

"Uh… yes."

"Yes indeed, Don." Dr. Kline removed the copper coils from Donny's ears. "But what if… bear with me for a second, okay?"

Donny heard more tinkering in the back. He checked the rearview mirror, but Dr. Kline was making his preparations too low to be seen.

"Remember to keep still. Okay, Don?"

"Okay, but what – ?"

The sound of the Hilti nail gun firing was very loud inside the car. That, and the sensation of a two-inch roofing nail driving through the right side of his skull, convinced Donny Baxter that he had been shot. He did not lose consciousness, however – he was clearly not dead yet – and so he began bellowing with pain and outrage.

Using the wooden plunger dowel like a volume knob, Dr. Kline twisted gently until Donny's yells were reduced to gargled sputterings. "Quiet, Don. Quiet. You're fine."

Donny did not feel fine, but he did seem to be alive. And he couldn't see any brains splattered on the windshield, so apparently he had not been shot. Not by a bullet, anyway. When the wire loosened enough for him to breathe again, he forced himself to stay silent. His face trembled with the effort.

The next blast from the Hilti was not as shocking as the first, but the pain of another roofing nail embedding itself in Donny's skull – through the back this time, just to the left of the seat's headrest – was no less intense. He managed to keep his mouth shut, but he could not stop the muted groaning that welled up from his chest. It made his whole body shake.

"So you see, that's how we get around that little difficulty," Kline said cheerfully. "We wrap the copper wire around a couple of nails, and then we put the nails *under* your skin. Way under, in this particular example."

Donny Baxter felt his concentration beginning to fail him, but he was past caring. "Listen," he said through gritted teeth. "There's over seven hundred dollars in my pocket. Just take it and go. Take it and do whatever you – "

Dr. Kline closed the circuit at the DieHard's positive terminal, and he watched Donny's body go rigid as electricity coursed through him. He waited a few seconds, and then removed the copper wire from the battery post. The current stopped flowing, and Donny's muscles relaxed.

Kline continued as if Donny had not spoken. "With the contact points *under* the skin," he said, "your ohm rating is lower. Considerably lower. And it hurts." Kline sighed. "I damaged your brain with that last one, Don. Not very much, but still."

"Why – " Donny took a slow, shaky breath. "What are you trying to – ?"

"Shhh. Pay attention. Last few questions, coming up. We've talked about electricity, but what about drugs?" Dr. Kline sat forward. His mouth was right next to Donny's ear, and there was a thin line of blood tricking down from the nail embedded there. "What if someone wanted to run an experiment, Don? A very delicate experiment involving electricity and the brain. And what if, in addition to electricity, that experiment also involved a small dose of stimulants?"

There was a flash of understanding on Donny Baxter's face. Understanding, and a fresh jolt of fear. "No, I – "

"What if someone happened to be selfish?" Kline went on, ignoring him. His voice was rising now. "What if someone didn't care about the consequences of his actions?"

Donny could hear the tension building in Kline's voice, and he tried to interrupt. To make eye contact. To do anything. But Kline was on a roll. "What if someone turned out to be a fucking *drug dealer*?" He was shouting now, and the noise was deafening inside the car. "What if *someone* borrowed a bunch of equipment from the lab, and then *used it to cook up a fucking batch of methamphetamine?*"

"I swear I didn't…" Donny began.

"*YES YOU DID!*" Kline shouted, and connected the battery again. Donny's body jumped, and Kline let him feel it for a slow count of five. When the current stopped flowing, Donny began speaking immediately.

"STOP OKAY yes, I did." He was breathless from the electricity, and sobbing in between his words. "I know, I'm sorry. But I needed the money, and that equipment was perfect. Meth is like gold now. Like *gold.* I couldn't… I didn't know the equipment was so important. Anyway, I only borrowed it. What's the big deal?"

Kline sat back and nodded slowly, like a disappointed father. After a moment, he turned his attention to the setup in the back, reorganizing the wires to include the DC power inverter in the circuit. One battery terminal was left unconnected. "Of course you didn't know," Kline said as he worked. "But it would have been better if you had just stolen the equipment, Don. You brought it back, and there's the real problem. That crap from your crystal-kitchen got mixed in with what I was supposed to take. You see, Don? The impurities created a neurotoxin effect. What should have been a delicate stimulant turned into a fire-cracker in my head. And then there was the substandard device construction, which induced a relapsing behavior…" Kline shook his head. "But never mind. *That* part wasn't your fault. The point is this: the equipment you borrowed was important." Kline nodded, as if agreeing with himself. "And you fucked it up."

Donny tried again: "But I swear to God I didn't know – "

"Quiet, Don. We've been through all that, and we're moving on. All right?"

"Um. Okay."

Donny tried to tell himself that Kline was calming down. At least he wasn't shouting anymore.

Maybe my punishment is over. Maybe we're coming to end of this.

He was mostly right.

"Okay, next question," Kline said, sounding cheery again. "The human body can withstand 10 times as much direct current – the kind that comes straight from a battery – as alternating current. The DC hurts, but the AC is much more dangerous. Do you know why?"

Donny didn't want to respond, but he feared the penalty for non-cooperation. "No," he said hesitantly. "Why?"

"This is why."

Dr. Kline closed the circuit. The power inverter took the direct, 12-volt power in the DieHard battery and converted it to an alternating-current flow oscillating at 60 Hertz, suitable for household electric appliances. What had simply been painful to Donny a minute ago suddenly became lethal. The AC interfered with the electrical signal paths in both his pulmonary and cardiovascular systems, and his lungs and heart locked solid.

They would never work again.

Dr. Kline sat forward. He spoke quietly while Donny asphyxiated. "This is a little bit what it felt like," Kline whispered, "when I was using my TMS device with that crystal shit of yours in my system. Like having my brain put in a fucking deep-fat fryer." He nodded, and waited a beat. "I set this up very carefully, Don. So that you could share the experience. I hope you appreciate it."

Kline sat back.

Donny didn't respond. He couldn't. Deprived of both oxygen and blood circulation, he was dead in less than a minute.

Donny Baxter's body was found the next morning by the school secretary, Ms. Shen, who was usually the first person to pull into the parking lot each day. She had arrived early, as always, hoping to get some work done before the rush of students could destroy her concentration. Ms. Shen was not a nervous woman, and she did not cry out when she saw the body. She touched nothing, walked straight into the school building, and called 911.

When the police got there, they found an elaborate set of electrical equipment connected to the dead man, whom they recognized immediately. Donny Baxter was a well-known meth dealer in the neighborhood. A repeat offender.

The forensics team was called in, and they were delighted by what they found. There were dozens of fingerprints in the car, most of them clean and complete. Easy to lift, too. An amateur could have handled the job. There were prints on the door. On the plastic casing of the DieHard battery. On the back of the seat.

Everywhere.

"It's like this guy *wants* us to catch him," one of them said.

After electrocuting Donny Baxter, Dr. Kline stowed the Hilti nail-gun in his North Face backpack and left everything else in the Honda. He didn't need the battery arrangement any more. Or the power inverter. He wasn't planning on doing any more brain-frying, and those things were difficult to carry.

He felt tired. The euphoria of the creative phase had left him, along with the adrenaline rush that had come from confronting and disposing of Donny. He was afraid he might lose control of himself if a bad phase hit him now, and he needed a place to sleep. But not at the inn. By the time he got back there, he might be mid-scarecrow phase. Or mid-memory-hole, God forbid.

Still, he wasn't worried. He had planned ahead.

The little town streets at the outskirts of Concord's downtown had almost no traffic at this late hour. Kline walked slowly, studying the cars parked at random intervals along the curb. The New Hampshire trees had started reacting to the cooler September weather, and some of the more delicate leaves had already begun to change and fall. Each parked car had a leaf or two on the hood, or on the roof.

Here was what he was looking for: a Buick station wagon with many more leaves on it. Looking neglected. As though it had been sitting in this one spot for several days. Or several weeks.

Kline stopped and fished for the lockout kit stored in his backpack. He slid the plastic corner of the air wedge into the seam between the Buick's door and its frame, and gave the hand bladder several quick pumps. The wedge inflated quickly, and the car door bent outward just enough for Kline to slip the steel super-jimmy inside, hook the lock, and open the door. He stowed the kit and threw his backpack into the passenger seat. Then he sat down inside, closed the door behind him, and adjusted the driver's seat to go as far back as possible.

It felt good to stretch out again. He was asleep in minutes.

His dreams were horrible. Worse than anything he had experienced since the accident. There had been plenty of bad dreams before, especially when they first locked him up, and of course when he was in detox, coming off Xanax. But nothing like this.

This dream seemed real.

He was back at Clancy hall, having one of his interview sessions with Dr. Levoir. Except that this session was different somehow. He was dazed, and a little too happy. As if he were a young child being plied with sweet treats. Dr. Levoir was asking him questions, and he was answering. In detail.

"Tell me how all of this started," Levoir was saying.

"We were studying autistics," Kline said, a goofy half-grin stuck on his face. "Carlisle had always found them fascinating."

Levoir nodded. "Go on. Tell me."

And Kline did. Even in the dream, he was vaguely aware that he should be fighting it, shutting up and keeping this stuff to himself. But his mouth seemed to have a mind of its own. "We were looking for treatments," he said. "As you know, there are over two hundred thousand people living with autism in the U.S. right now, and that number is going up every year. The current rate is something like one in every five hundred births. A new treatment would have been an instant success."

"Did you have any luck?"

"Not even close. We were trying to come up with an atypical antipsychotic, something to compete with Clozaril or Seraquel, but we couldn't get a handle on the side-effects."

Levoir put on a supportive face. "That must have been frustrating."

"Definitely. But it didn't stop us. We went off in a whole new direction. That's the beauty of university-funded research – you can change course right in the middle of things, and it doesn't matter as long as you can publish something interesting at the end."

"And so? Where did you turn your attention?"

"We got into savantism."

Levoir smiled knowingly. "Rain Man strikes again."

Kline found his doctor's cynicism understandable. The movie *Rain Man* had convinced millions of Americans that autism was not just a developmental disorder, but some sort of undiscovered superpower. Anyone with autism was suddenly expected to be a savant. Autistic people were closet geniuses, the movie seemed to say, able to stroll into a casino, count and memorize the cards being dealt out of a six-deck poker shoe, and walk away millionaires.

The reality, of course, was that most autistics had no such abilities. And those who did display savant characteristics were severely handicapped in other ways. They might be able to do startling mathematical tricks, but most of them couldn't navigate their way around a city block without getting lost.

"The sheer variety was what intrigued us at first," Kline said. "We wondered why savants came in so many different flavors. It wasn't just the human calculators. You had the mnemonic savants with their perfect memories. And the creative ones, with their wild inventions. And of course the language prodigies; not that they could communicate *with* anyone on any normal level, but if you happened to be searching for a word in Spanish – or Hindi, for that matter – there was nothing they couldn't tell you."

"Yes, interesting," Levoir said, sounding not at all interested. "Still, it takes on a bit of a side-show flavor after a while. I'm surprised the Dartmouth administrators let you pursue that sort of research."

Kline shrugged. "We wrote the abstract with broad language: '*Where do these abilities come from? What can they teach us about our own mental function?*' Stuff like that. It was enough to keep our grant going."

"Okay, but then what?"

Kline smiled. "Then we hit the jackpot."

"A new drug?"

"Not at all. We were doing the background research, and one

subheading in the case reports caught our attention: injuries. We had assumed going in that autism and savantism were inseparable, that there was something unique about an autistic's cerebral development that created these special abilities. But in the cases we were reading, perfectly normal adults would develop savant-like behavior as a result of head trauma. A guy would get into a car accident, and he'd wake up spouting Latin."

"You're talking about some very rare cases," Levoir said. "Cracking open someone's skull doesn't turn them into a polyglot."

"Of course not. But don't you see the larger point? Savantism doesn't have to be a part of you from birth. It can be *induced*."

Levoir sat back and considered this. He stayed silent, waiting for Kline to continue.

"Have you ever heard of TMS?"

Levoir grunted. "Transcranial magnetic stimulation? Of course. Some clinics use it to help schizophrenics, or for controlling depression. I'm not a believer, personally."

"You will be. Do you know what it was originally designed for?"

"Brain operations, right?"

"Exactly. Induced stimulation in real-time, to help surgeons keep track of how the patient's mind was holding up. But it did more than just assist with the surgery. Some patients experienced savant episodes in recovery."

Levoir raised his eyebrows. "You've been working with TMS?"

"At first, yes. We did some low-level trials with Dartmouth students, just to get an understanding of the concept. We got promising results, so we decided to design a brand-new device. A more powerful, more focused device, unlike anything that's commercially available. By the time it was ready, we knew it would work. From our research. Because when you get right down to it, the brain is infinitely malleable. It can change."

"But it couldn't have been that simple," Levoir said. "Let's face it, Nathan. You apparently tested that new device on yourself, and your brain *wasn't* malleable. It got damaged, in fact."

Kline waved a hand dismissively. "We made mistakes, that's all. There was a neurotoxin issue, and the device construction wasn't up to par. Not to mention that we had things all flipped around."

"Flipped around how?" Levoir leaned forward, suddenly very attentive. "This is important, Nathan. What exactly do you mean?"

"I mean that hyperactivity isn't the answer," Kline said. "We were trying to create savantism through TMS stimulation, but that's backward. Look at an infant's ability to learn language; do they learn quickly because they're geniuses? Of course not. Infants absorb information and new skills like sponges, but it's precisely because they *aren't* geniuses that they succeed so well. Their minds are simple and unsullied. A young child isn't yet distracted by the thousands of neuro-synaptic connections that every adult has to wade through during every second of every day of his life." Kline put his hands over his ears to illustrate, as if trying to drown out the noise from the distractions all around him. "We're victims of over-stimulation," he continued. "Savants aren't smarter than you are – they're just more focused. And their abilities are inside every one of us. Literally buried inside our crowded minds." He tapped his head and grinned. "I didn't see it at the time, but it seems obvious in retrospect. And the basic concept is still viable, even if I didn't figure it out until recently. We can *all* be savants."

Levoir took a long slow breath, and he put down the pen and pad he had been using to take careful notes. "That's a good story, Nathan. And an interesting idea."

Kline awoke with a start. He didn't bother with diagnostics, because he could smell the fake-leather steering wheel of the old Buick as if it had been rammed up his nose.

Dog phase, simple as that.

His relief at waking – and at realizing that it *had* been a dream, since he would never have willingly given up such information to Levoir – was immense. He grabbed his backpack and stepped out of the car, into the brisk New Hampshire morning. Besides scaring him, the dream had served as another reminder.

I should give Carlisle a call, he thought.

He would go back into town for a minute, and use his credit card at a payphone. Then he would be on his way to the Patton brothers. He was looking forward to having a talk with those two. They were next on his list.

The man with the glasses and the tweed coat waited until Kline had walked a short distance away from the parked Buick before keying the ignition on his little Ford *Escort*. Then he put the car in gear and pulled out slowly, following.

Melissa's Professor

1

"What do you think, Frederick?"

Professor Carlisle paused with his fork halfway to his mouth. He glanced at the people sitting around him at the dinner table and tried to let his mind catch up. Perhaps the topic of conversation would occur to him. These department dinners were always filled with the same blather every time anyway.

It was a technique his old partner, Dr. Nathan Kline, would have recognized immediately. "I'm sorry," Carlisle said, tugging at the sleeves of his yellow sweater. "What do I think about *what*?"

Jeff Gooding piped up, as Carlisle had known he would. "Dr. Lerner brought up the topic of modifying intelligence," he said slowly, as though Carlisle might have trouble understanding the words.

And you couldn't call him 'Sydney,' Carlisle thought. *It had to be 'Dr. Lerner.' You think that's going to get your tenure track moving a little faster, Jeffy-Jeff?*

"The brain's just a machine," Carlisle said. He took another bite of the steak, which was quite good for a change. Sheila loved hosting these dinners – probably because she liked showing off the work she put into her house every year – but she seldom did anything impressive with the menu.

The department head sniffed. "Our atheist declares that brains are machines," Lerner said. "And so the mystery of the mind has ended."

"It's a *complicated* machine, Sydney." He glanced at Gooding. *See, Jeff? I called him Sydney. Not so hard. And my head didn't split open.* "When something is sufficiently complicated, it's difficult to modify," Carlisle added.

Jeff Gooding thrust his mouth forward eagerly, like a fish gulping at a line. "I'm sure Dr. Kline would agree with you there."

Carlisle closed his eyes.

The other professors at the table froze. Bringing up Kline was taboo in the department. Especially with Carlisle around. "Yes, thank you for that observation, Jeff," he said quietly.

Gooding bristled at Carlisle's patronizing tone. "It's true, isn't it? You both thought it would work. That you could just throw a switch and treat Dr. Kline's mind like a piece of stereo equipment."

"You're *vastly* oversimplifying…"

"Am I? The goal of the project was to 'amplify' certain mental capabilities, yes? I've read your paper, you know."

"Congratulations on being able to read – "

"But I don't remember this department approving any *human* trials. So tell me, Dr. Carlisle, whose idea was it to subject Kline to that special device of yours? Carlisle glanced around the table. He could feel the rest of them waiting breathlessly for an answer. "We covered all of this in the departmental hearing," he said slowly.

"That's nothing but smokescreen," Gooding said. "Especially since you never included any of the details on *how* your custom machine was put together. So don't you think – "

"No, Jeff. I don't." Carlisle wiped his mouth and pushed back from the table. "I'm too tired for thinking tonight. And thinking *about* thinking? No." He put on a smile. "Sheila, this was delicious. As always." *Part truth, part lie. Close enough.* "I look forward to seeing you all at the department meeting tomorrow morning." *Pure lie.* He would have preferred to stay in the lab all year long, but there were classes to teach.

So many bothersome college students.

He walked quickly across the campus, heading for the lab. His heart rate was way up, but just thinking about his little white office was already helping to calm him. When he arrived, he walked straight to the wall-safe in the corner. He spun the combination wheel quickly, expertly, and opened the heavy metal door on the first try.

And there it was, just where it was supposed to be.

The TMS device, safe and sound. It was polished and beautiful, an elegant configuration of capacitors and spun copper, and it made him smile to see it.

In a way, he wished Kline could be here with him.

The accident last year had been a huge setback. And so much time had been wasted in the hearings afterward that he worried he would never get back on track. Even several months later, when he had been officially cleared of wrongdoing by both the College and the State, he was still too shaken to do any real work. But then, standing in the shower one morning three weeks ago, something had come to him.

Something wonderfully simple.

Now he reached into the safe and picked up the newly redesigned machine. "TMS device" was the name he still used in his head – the name both he and Kline had always used – though of course this machine took the concept of TMS to brand new heights. Transcranial magnetic stimulation was a technique commonly used to treat patients in psychiatric wards all over the world, but he and Kline had made several fundamental changes in their design. There were three figure-eight loops of copper on this unit, instead of the more common single-mobius; also, it had an array of independently wired capacitors, for precise discharge control; finally, there was a small iron disc in the center of each copper loop. The iron was key: it helped the unit create a magnetic field that was twice the strength of regular TMS devices.

But even with all that, it was still a very simple machine. You could tell just by looking at it; nothing but a handle, a small housing for the capacitors, and the copper loops with their iron centers. The device looked like a strange, old-style television antenna.

Simple changes, yes. But with significant results.

And now he had made another change. A *vital* change.

I'm a visionary, he thought. *An absolute wunderkind. And I'm going to be the richest man alive.*

That tenure-track fool, Jeff Gooding, had actually been fairly close to the mark at dinner. The original plan *had* been to treat the brain like a stereo amplifier. But what Gooding didn't understand – and what he and Kline had understood only too late – was that turning up the volume on a mind could only take you so far.

The real trick was turning the volume *down.*

He reached farther back into the wall-safe and brought out a small stack of papers. They contained the latest data from his diagnostic tests. He had hooked up pigs, dogs, and even a small monkey – the department had access to several primate facilities through a grant from the Parker Foundation – and all of the experiments had confirmed his intuition.

If you could shut down sections of an animal's brain – not subdue them, but actually *shut them down* – then the other sections of that brain would compensate with new behavior.

Extraordinary behavior.

That's the key. That's what we missed.

In a Rhesus monkey, "extraordinary" meant only that the animal could recognize patterns and signals too complex for an average member of the species. But in a human, of course, it could mean far more.

He sat looking at the data, still nodding his head. All of it was good, but the next step was a problem. He jotted down a note in the margin: *More complex test subjects?*

Leaning back in the office chair, his eyes drifted up to the ceiling.

He closed his eyes and enjoyed the feeling of his chest rising and falling with the rhythm of several deep breaths.

And then he knew.

It wasn't a problem. Not really. He had all the test subjects he needed, right here at the Hanover psych clinic. There were so many of them, all ready and willing.

They're willing in the legal sense, anyway, he thought.

Trying to experiment with human subjects was always tricky. You needed something called "informed consent," and that meant convincing people to sign lots of scary-looking forms. But the term "informed" wasn't relevant in this case. A paranoid schizophrenic wasn't capable of giving informed consent for *anything.* Neither was a convicted sociopath. Because who was to say what those people did or didn't understand? He admitted to himself that such a claim wouldn't necessarily hold up in court, but he didn't care. It would never come to that. No one would believe the word of an asylum inmate against that of a Dartmouth professor.

Too bad Kline won't be here to share in the glory, he thought.

2

It was easy to round up a few patients from the ward under the pretense of administering extra treatments. No one questioned him about it.

Two days later, Professor Carlisle walked slowly around the large, restraint-equipped chairs in Examination Room B, taking his time. Three of the four chairs were occupied, and the professor's clipboard was out. His pen moved rapidly across the page. Carlisle liked writing notes, especially when an experiment was going well. The room smelled strongly of vomit, but he barely noticed. He watched the man in the first chair carefully, waiting for more.

No?

Carlisle stood at a safe distance, took a deep breath, and then exhaled strongly in the direction of the man in chair number one.

The man's eyes bulged. His body lurched against the chair's thick canvas straps. From his mouth came a desperate, choking rasp. Then, finally, a thin stream of yellow-brown fluid.

"That's it?" Carlisle said.

The patient stared at him with large, vacant eyes. The eyes of an animal that has endured unspeakable things.

Hour 59, Carlisle wrote on his clipboard. *Sensitivity remains high.*

He turned to the second chair. "How are you feeling?" he asked sweetly.

A thin, trembling man looked up at him. He seemed surprised to hear Carlisle's voice. "Please," he said. "Take me out of here. We can go together."

Carlisle appeared to consider this. "Where would we go?"

"It doesn't matter." The man became excited. "Away. Not here. Outside."

"But what do you mean?"

The man hesitated.

"Outside?" Carlisle said, as if trying to understand. "What is outside?"

The thin man's lips moved silently. He seemed as though he were trying to say something, but no words came. He looked at the door of the examination room, then looked away. "I… I just want to…"

"But *what* is outside? What are you talking about?"

The man suddenly broke into tears. "I don't know," he said miserably. "I don't remember. It's gone."

Carlisle smiled and nodded. *Preliminary adaptation*, he wrote. *But hippocampus deficit is unaffected.*

The man in the third chair spoke up suddenly: "I'm going to cut your tongue out."

Carlisle turned to him. The man was small, with a pointy nose. "Are you?" said Carlisle pleasantly.

"And then those hands of yours. I'm going to slice them off and chop them into little pieces."

"And then?"

"I'll grind everything together, tongue and hands and fingers, into a special Carlisle paste."

"It sounds wonderful," Carlisle said. "Who's this for?"

"For?"

"Yes, the Carlisle paste. I assume someone will be eating it?"

The man in the third chair looked briefly amused. His pointy nose crinkled. "It's a sealant, you idiot," he said. "There are some cracks in my wall that need fixing."

Carlisle grinned. "Of course." He returned his attention to his clipboard.

Aggressive. Sociopathic. Coherent and precise.

He pressed a button by the wall. "Eddie. Come in here and clean this mess up. And get these men back to their rooms. I'm done with them."

"I'm done with *you*, ass-face," said the pointy-nosed man in the third chair. "You're nothing but wall-grout to me."

"Yes, yes. That's fine, Peter."

Before leaving the building, Carlisle took a minute to prepare four fresh doses of oxytocin. He used an eyedropper to mix exactly two milligrams with five milliliters of water, and then he poured each solution into one of the little bottles he had bought at CVS. The bottles had originally contained antihistamine solutions for treating clogged sinuses.

Oxytocin was one of his favorite tools. He used it in any experiment involving human subjects. A hormone associated with childbirth and parental attachment, it evoked a feeling of confidence and trust in patients who inhaled it. Test subjects described the smell of oxytocin as "delicious," or "friendly," or even "sexy." Whenever Carlisle needed unquestioned cooperation from someone, he simply gave them a small dose. "It will keep your sinuses clear," he would explain to them.

With enough oxytocin in their bloodstream, patients would do virtually anything they were told. They would submit to unspecified injections, or go without food and water for as long as necessary. Carlisle suspected he could have asked for his patients' life savings if he had wanted to. More important, he could convince them to take a turn with the new TMS device.

Carlisle loved oxytocin. He couldn't imagine what he would have done without it. And now he had four fresh bottles of the stuff, all ready to go. Four little bottles that looked like nothing but nasal spray.

Now he was walking briskly on the path leading back to the main campus. The experiments were going better than planned, and he was ahead of schedule.

The next step was *normal* test subjects, and the oxytocin would become even more important. Mental ward patients could be manipulated, but regular people often resisted being told what to do. Especially if they were scared. A trust chemical, then, was exactly what he needed. And it was exactly what he had.

He looked at his watch. Fifteen minutes until the first class. A new year, a new semester, and a brand new group of students.

So many minds, Carlisle thought. *All fresh and ready for the asking.*

Surely a few of them would show up late. He hoped so. It would be easier that way.

The first time around, he only needed four.

3

Melissa Hartman got out of bed slowly that morning. The alarm had gone off far too early. It had to be a mistake, she thought. A malfunctioning circuit. But when she rolled over and looked, the clock said 7:00.

Stayed too late at the library, she thought.

Right, but there was something else. Something that had reminded her of home.

The sick guy. The one who smelled of pain. Like her mother.

She hoped he had made it through the rest of the night okay.

Her schedule was pasted on the wall next to her bed. She glanced at it and saw that there was time for a shower and breakfast before her first class. Psych 10A. It was the only class she hadn't seen yet. She hoped the homework would be light for once. The professor was someone named Carlisle. Frederick Carlisle. Melissa grinned at the name. She thought he sounded scholarly, like all of the Dartmouth professors. He'd probably have a beard, too.

In the dining hall, Melissa loaded her tray with eggs and cereal and sat down at an empty table. When no one joined her after a few minutes, she realized her mistake.

Should have taken a seat next to a mob of freshmen.

At that table over in the corner, for instance. She remembered the registration line from a few days ago, and she shook her head. Dartmouth students were obviously smart. But they all seemed socially stunted.

She was suddenly aware of a group of boys at the table next to her. Aware of them being aware of *her*. But they didn't come over. They didn't introduce themselves. Melissa put her fork down. She had had enough. She put her hands flat on the table and stood up. If no one was going to come over to her, than she would just march over and –

"Hi. Can I join you?"

Melissa stopped. A skinny girl with glasses had come up. She stood there with a tray in her hands, beaming.

"Absolutely," Melissa said. "Have a seat."

"I'm Lea."

"I'm Melissa."

"You want some breakfast company?"

"*Hell* yes."

The skinny girl's eyes went wide behind her glasses, and Melissa worried that she had just offended her only friend. Her only *almost* friend. But then Lea Redford smiled, and Melissa relaxed.

"How's the food?" Lea asked.

"Pretty good, actually."

"Glad to hear it. Can I ask you a strange question?"

Melissa looked up from her eggs and grinned. "You're the only one talking to me, Lea. You can ask me anything."

Lea nodded. "Yeah. That's my question."

"What?"

"*Why* am I the only one?"

"Um…." Melissa pressed her lips together. She scanned the dining hall. The boys at the next table suddenly became very busy, looking anywhere except in her direction. Several boys – and girls – at other tables put their heads down quickly, as if their breakfast plates had just become incredibly interesting.

"I don't know," Melissa said. "Because you're not weird?"

Lea smiled. "I don't think so, but I'll take the compliment anyway." Lea sat forward and lowered her voice. "I think everyone else is just afraid."

"Of…?"

"Of *you*."

Melissa stared at her for a minute, saying nothing.

The boys at the next table looked over quickly, startled. The gorgeous girl with the strong, angry eyes was laughing. Her head was thrown back for a moment, her dark hair hanging over the back of the chair like a curtain. It made them want to *be* that chair. The skinny, pretty girl sitting opposite her was smiling. The boys thought it was a beautiful sight, and they wanted to go over and join them. Each privately cursed his own hesitation from earlier. They *would* join them, they decided. Not now, though. Later, when the girls were not in the middle of something. They would get their chance. In a few minutes.

But Melissa and Lea did not give them a chance. They talked and laughed and forgot about the food in front of them, and there was never a good moment to interrupt. The time came for first-period classes, and the two girls were still talking, nodding, exclaiming to one another. The boys cleared their trays grudgingly, hating the requirement of attending class. Hating the whole concept of studying in college. Especially when there were things – much more important things – that needed their attention.

Eventually Melissa calmed. She took a long, happy breath and looked at her new friend.

"You really cheered me up, Lea."

"My pleasure."

"It's not true, of course. But it was a nice thing to say."

Lea shrugged. "You can keep telling yourself that. But you should start getting used to the idea that you're attractive."

Melissa put her hands up. "My luck with boys is nothing to brag about."

"Uh-huh." Lea's voice was skeptical. "You get turned down a lot?"

"Well." Melissa thought about it. "Actually, I've never – "

"Yeah," Lea said, sounding dismissive. "You've been sort of busy until recently, haven't you?"

Melissa looked at her carefully. She took a long time before answering. "Yes," she said, speaking slowly. "I suppose I have. But how do *you* know that?"

"It's a specialty of mine."

"What, reading minds?"

"No, faces."

They were silent for a while. Melissa seemed to be studying her. Then she nodded. "Fine, then. You know, we should – " She stopped suddenly and looked around her, at the now quiet and empty dining hall. Then she looked at her watch. "Aren't we supposed to be in class?"

Lea didn't wait to answer. She jumped up from the table, sweeping up her tray as she moved. "I've got psych," she said over her shoulder.

"Me, too." Melissa followed her, and they threw their trays on the conveyer belt.

"We're going to get in trouble," Lea said.

"Why? Isn't intro-psych a huge class? Who's going to notice?"

Lea threw her backpack around her shoulders and started to run. Melissa stayed close behind her. "It's Professor *Carlisle's* class," Lea said.

"So?"

"So I've heard he's a pain."

"Oh." Melissa smiled in spite of herself. It was good to have a friend. Friends could tell you which profs they had heard were pains. "So let's run faster."

They did.

4

Jason was almost finished with the last question on his math homework, and he didn't hear the phone ringing. He felt he was close to getting this stuff – really *getting* it – and that meant he could pass calculus. With regular tutoring, of course. He was already looking forward to more help from that Lea girl. She was sharp. And pretty. And she had told him he could do it. It made him smile just remembering the way she–

"Jason, will you pick up the PHONE!"

His mother's voice, amplified by the answering machine, almost knocked him out of his chair. He fumbled for the receiver. "Hello? Sorry, Mom. I was distracted."

"Jason, honey. How's your head?"

"Fine, mom. No different. But it's – "

"And your neck?"

"Still a little sore."

"I have news."

Jason closed his eyes.

"I've talked to a doctor here in Connecticut," she said. "He can – "

"Mom, we've discussed this."

"Jason. Honey, please. Trust me, will you? This doctor is very, very good, and he said that he'd be happy to take a look at you."

"That was nice of him."

"He'll give us a second opinion. I've scheduled an appointment for you tomorrow afternoon."

Jason was silent.

"Honey?"

"Mom, I have *class*."

There was a pause on the line. "Jason, *please*." She was starting to sound angry. "What's more important than your career, honey?" The shrillness began creeping into her tone, and visions of grade-school hockey games flashed through Jason's head. Games in which his mother had berated not only the opposing team's coach, but his own coach as well. "This is your *chance*," she said. "Your shot at being someone. You're not going to the National Hockey League by writing history papers, you know. Academics are not your strong point."

Thanks for reminding me. "I'm not going to the NHL, Mom."

Another stunned silence. "Don't say that, Jason." Her voice was shaking. As if he had insulted her. "Don't *ever* say that. Without hockey, what would you do?"

"I don't know, Mom. There are plenty of possibilities."

"*What* possibilities?" Frantic now. "What? Tell me. What would you do?"

"I said I don't know. You may have noticed that I'm still in college."

"Well. That's a terrific plan. Why don't you just throw away everything we've ever – "

Jason held the phone away from his ear. He looked down at his calculus homework, so close to being finished, and he wondered about what his mother had said. *Academics aren't your strong point.* Maybe she was right.

He put the phone back to his ear. His mother was still talking.

"…and to think that I sacrificed hours, days, *years* of my life to bring you to those games…"

"I have to get going, Mom. Thanks for calling."

"Jason, don't you *dare* – "

He put the phone down gently, then removed it from the cradle and lay it on its side.

When the last calculus problem was done, he went back and checked his answers. It was satisfying to see all those numbers lined up. So orderly. And he had done it himself. The whole thing. He smiled. He thought

Lea would be proud of him.

The alarm rang faithfully the next morning at 7:30, just as it had been programmed to do. But Jason Bell, former Dartmouth hockey star, was still growing accustomed to the scholar's life. He briefly forgot that he was no longer a member of the hockey team, and he punched the snooze button.

When the alarm rang again, Jason was closer to lucidity. He suddenly remembered that he was expected to attend classes from now on. He glanced hurriedly at his schedule. What was today? Tuesday? So that meant his first period was… Psych. 10A. With Carlisle.

Total gut class, he thought with relief. *Nothing but freshmen. Easy pass.*

But wait a minute. He had heard that Carlisle was a bastard who liked to mess with people. Especially people who came late. That was the rumor, anyway.

Crap.

He sprinted out of the dorm, shirt-tails flying. And Lea Redford would have been proud to see *that*.

5

What – ?

Garrett Lemke, veteran of the Dartmouth College fraternity scene, was accustomed to waking up in strange places. And with strange people. He knew from experience that the best thing was simply to lie there. To let your alcohol-addled brain provide as much information as it could before you got out of bed.

But this was different. He recognized this room. And this bed. Because they were his own.

Garrett didn't have many rules about partying, but this one was clear: If you got drunk enough to black out, you didn't go back to your own bed. And you never, ever went to bed alone. So he couldn't understand how he had ended up here. It had never happened before.

He waited for his leaky memory to fill in some of the blanks.

After a few more seconds, Garrett had a terrible idea: maybe he had finally gone too far. He was an accomplished drinker, and he prided himself on an ability to hold his act together. Even when he was blacking out. He believed that this special ability was one of the things that made him a Dartmouth Man. A Dartmouth Man who got *action.*

But perhaps he had lost control last night. Had one too many. It wasn't out of the question.

Did someone have to help me to bed last night? Like I was some drunken invalid?

Unthinkable. Anyway, none of his friends would ever bother to –

There was a sudden twinge in his head, and Garrett realized he was forgetting something much more important than any frat party.

The headaches.

He turned slowly to one side, as if he were afraid of dislodging something. The pain was a little better, he realized. Not all the way gone, but definitely an improvement over the last few weeks. Maybe he was over the hump.

Now he was remembering more. An encounter with Allyson and the women's swim team yesterday afternoon. An awful encounter. He had behaved like an idiot, somehow. The details weren't available, but the sensation of embarrassment was clear. After that, he remembered only pain. And more pain. So maybe he hadn't even gone to a party. Or gotten drunk. And that meant he might have made it to bed all on his own.

He hoped – *prayed* – for this to be true.

Garrett looked at his watch and saw that he had woken up in time for first period. He'd probably be a little bit late, but that didn't bother him. He had organized his senior-year schedule to provide maximum free time, which meant that he had signed up for as many intro-courses as possible. In those big freshman classes, it was easy to show up late. No one noticed. Or cared.

He double-checked the schedule. Psych 10A with Carlisle.

No problem.

He'd make his way over there in a few minutes, after a stop at the dining hall for some breakfast.

6

Melissa and Lea were breathless when they arrived at Silman Hall. Room 10A was the largest lecture auditorium in the building, but they still had trouble finding it. The two of them went around back, hoping to sneak in undetected. They were six minutes late.

Professor Carlisle was already lecturing as they crept through the door.

"…will be covering only the most basic, introductory concepts of psychology," he was saying to the packed auditorium. He paused and looked to his right, where an eager-looking young man was standing. "This is Jeff Gooding," Carlisle said. "He is the second teacher for the course. After today, half of you will be going with him." Carlisle stopped, and a little smile crept over his face. "Still bucking for that tenure position, Jeff?"

Gooding took a breath. "Yes, Professor Carlisle."

"Been a few years now, hasn't it?"

"Only two, actually."

"But you're still just teaching the intro course?"

With an effort, Gooding maintained his composure. His eyes flashed. "Is this something you want to discuss here, Professor? Now?"

Carlisle turned to the class. "You see?" he said loudly. "Anger. Shame. Embarrassment and barely-controlled aggression. These are just some of the emotions we experience every day, and look how easy they are to draw out. Bare millimeters below the surface, all of them. Just waiting to emerge." He turned to Gooding again. "Okay, Jeff. Thanks. Great demonstration." Carlisle winked at him. He used the eye closer to the students, so that they could see.

Jeff Gooding looked at the floor, and his mouth twitched. The words he was muttering were impossible to make out.

Melissa and Lea found an empty row of seats near the back, and they sat down silently, hoping Carlisle hadn't seen them.

"There will be two midterms and one final exam," Carlisle went on. "Homework assignments will be based on lectures…"

Melissa saw someone slide into their row. Someone big. He sat down next to Lea and gave her a friendly nudge, then started whispering to her. He sounded excited. Lea made a shushing noise and turned away from him. She craned her neck forward, as though trying to hear the professor better.

Melissa thought she could see Lea trying to hide a smile.

The big boy leaned forward and tried to get Lea's attention again. He was whispering louder now, and Melissa could hear what he was saying.

"I got all the Calculus done," he whispered. "Every problem. And I think I'll be able – "

"HELLO THERE," Professor Carlisle shouted out suddenly. He was looking toward the three of them. The boy stopped whispering and froze. "YES, YOU," Carlisle yelled. "Could you stand up please?"

Jason Bell rose slowly from his seat, and a hundred young faces turned toward him.

"Mr. Bell!" Carlisle said. He sounded delighted. "I'm surprised to see you here. Shouldn't you be at the rink? Or perhaps you're just arriving from practice. Is that it?"

Jason didn't say anything. He shook his head.

"Was that a no? Then I'll assume you were very tired this morning. Tired from a hard workout yesterday, perhaps. And that's why you were late, yes?"

"No, sir."

"No again?" Carlisle put a hand to his chin, feigning confusion. "Are you no longer playing on the Dartmouth hockey team, Mr. Bell? I've heard so much about your abilities over the years."

Jason said something very quietly. Even Melissa could barely hear him, and she was sitting two seats away.

"What was that, Mr. Bell? You were speaking so clearly before, to your friend. But now I can barely hear you."

"I got HURT," Jason said. He dropped his head, as if he had just admitted to stealing a ten-year-old's lunch money.

Carlisle nodded. "Oh, yes. I do remember seeing an item about that in the college paper." He smiled as if this were a wonderful piece of news. Then his expression turned serious. "But where does that leave us, Mr. Bell? Are you telling me that you were simply late? For no good reason?"

Jason shrugged. His eyes were closed.

"And what about your girlfriend there?"

Jason's head came up, and Lea stiffened. Melissa glanced at them. Even in the darkened lecture hall, she could see that Lea's face had gone red.

"Yeah?" Jason said finally. "What about her?"

"Would you stand up as well, Miss?"

Lea got up slowly. So did Melissa.

Carlisle's eyebrows jumped. "I don't remember asking *you* to stand, Dear."

Melissa didn't reply.

"Excuse me," said Carlisle. "Can you hear me speaking?"

Melissa smiled. "Of course, Professor. You're practically shouting."

"Then why didn't you answer me?"

"Because you didn't ask a question."

Lea glanced quickly at her. "What are you doing?" she whispered. "He'll kill us."

Melissa sighed gently, and she turned to look at her new friend. "Not likely," she whispered back. "There are scarier men in this world. Trust me."

"Enough of this," Carlisle shouted. He sounded genuinely angry now. "You're all wasting valuable class time. The three of you have just volunteered for the first student experiment of the semester. I'm going to need a fourth participant, so let's see if I can find anyone napping…"

At that moment, Garrett Lemke entered the lecture hall. He didn't come through the back, however. He used the main entrance, right up where Carlisle was standing. Melissa recognized him. *The sick guy*, she thought. *At least he's walking on his own now.*

"Good morning," Carlisle said. "What's your name?"

Garrett didn't seem to hear. He walked right past the professor and headed up the stairs of the lecture hall. He was looking for an empty place to sit.

"Excuse me," Carlisle said. "Hello?"

Garrett found a seat and plopped down. He carried no backpack, and no pencil. After adjusting himself into a comfortable position, he finally looked up. Carlisle was staring right at him.

Garrett jumped.

"Yes, HELLO," Carlisle said. There was a scattering of laughter in the hall. Nervous laughter, Melissa thought, from those who were glad they were not the object of this professor's attention.

"Who are you?" Carlisle asked.

Garrett squinted, as if the professor's voice were a bright light that hurt his eyes. "Garrett Lemke," he said quietly.

Carlisle studied him for a moment. "Sophomore?"

"*Senior*," Garrett said, sounding offended.

Carlisle threw his hands up. "What are all these upperclassmen doing in my course? We've got Mr. Hockey-Boy-Bell up there, and now you?" He scanned the room, looking peeved. "Hear this," he said, addressing the whole auditorium again. "If you are taking this class, and you are *not* a freshman, I consider you to be lazy. Lazy, and distinctly uninspired."

This proclamation was followed by silence. There was no more nervous laughter. "But back to you, Mr. Lemke," Carlisle said. "You are my fourth volunteer."

Garrett made a face. "Volunteer?" he said. "For what?"

7

Professor Carlisle was walking quickly along the path leading from Silman. The four students were trailing a few yards behind. "Come on," he said, sounding annoyed. "Keep up, all of you. I don't have all day."

The four of them glanced uneasily at each other. The professor still hadn't told them where they were going. They had arrived at the classroom at 3PM that afternoon, on the dot, just as he had asked. But at first he hadn't been there. They had waited for ten minutes, in a tense silence.

Jason spoke up. "How long should we stay here?"

Lea shook her head. "As long as it takes."

"What?" Garrett put a hand to his temple. "I'm not sitting here for – "

"Relax," Melissa said. "I'm sure he's coming."

"Yeah, but what if – "

Then Carlisle had appeared at the door, and the conversation ended. He waved to them impatiently. "Over here," he said. "Let's go." He turned and walked away.

Lea jumped up and followed him. After a beat, so did the others. They walked for a while without saying anything. Carlisle was moving quickly, and he didn't seem to like them falling behind. "Come *on*," he kept saying.

Melissa thought he sounded like a spoiled, excited child. As if he were leading them to an amusement park.

Jason was the first one to ask the question. "Professor, where – ?"

"Hitchcock," Carlisle said without turning around.

"The medical center?"

"Is there another Hitchcock around here?"

"But I thought we were – "

"Participating in a student experiment, yes." The professor glanced behind him, making sure they were all still there. "Everything is set up at the med lab, which is where I do most of my work. And I'm giving you a brief tour of the ward first."

They all looked at him.

"The ward?" Lea said slowly. As if she had misheard.

Carlisle nodded. "You're all going to need some background before we do this thing. It's part of the assignment."

Garrett rubbed his head and frowned. He looked as though he had just joined the conversation. "Do what thing?" he asked.

Carlisle ignored him. He stopped in front of a small white van waiting in the street. "Hop in," he said. "We could walk, but I'm not willing to wait that long."

When they arrived, Carlisle ushered them quickly through Hitchcock's main entrance, through two sets of double-doors, and into the main atrium. "This is the non-violent ward," he explained. He stood with them at the edge of the common room, which was huge and spotless. There were pictures on the walls, plush chairs and couches, large tables for playing cards, and enough televisions to prevent arguments.

"This is nicer than the commons in Zimmerman," Melissa said.

Lea turned around with a grin. "Hey, I'm in Zimmerman."

"So am I," said Jason.

Melissa pointed to Garrett. "*He's* in our dorm too."

Garrett frowned at her. "How – ?"

"I helped you get to bed last night."

Garrett swore under his breath. "I knew it. I fucking *knew* it…"

"You were sick," Melissa said with a shrug. "It's okay."

Garrett shook his head. He seemed to think it was decidedly *not* okay.

"HELLO," Carlisle said, stepping into the group. "Were any of you listening?"

Jason made an attempt: "Absolutely, sir. You were saying about the aphasics?"

Carlisle stared at him for a second, then returned to the lecture. "Yes, aphasics. The term is derived from Greek words meaning 'speechless'." He pointed to a small group of patients on one of the couches. "They have difficulty with language, but they still enjoy watching television. They pick up a lot just through tone of voice and body posture."

The professor paused and turned to face the four of them. There was a look of mischief in his eyes. "It is very, very difficult to lie to an aphasic. Even if they don't know quite what you're saying, they can spot the contradictions in your face and attitude."

He waited, still staring at them with that amused look.

"What?" said Jason finally.

"Don't you think," Carlisle said slowly, "that it would be interesting to have such an ability?"

"*What* ability?" Garrett said, still sounding confused.

Carlisle sighed. He turned away from them and pointed to another section of the common room. "Over here we have the autistics. They don't usually stray from their area, which suits the staff just fine. Their space has to be kept very neat and orderly so that they don't get upset. No changes, ever." Carlisle was quiet for a beat. A little smile began played around his lips, as if he were remembering something pleasant. "Autistics have always fascinated me," he said quietly. "The savants were how we got our start."

Melissa nodded to a quiet corner of the room, where a woman with a frightened expression sat talking to a nurse. "And her?"

"Amnesiac, right-brain deficit," Carlisle said, coming out of his reverie. "We only have a few of them. She stays far away from the television, as do the others with similar conditions. It confuses her to see images of modern life; she's stuck in the world as it was twenty-six years ago."

The professor got that amused look in his eye again. "Of course," he said, "what's really interesting is the opposite of amnesia. Imagine how much more productive all of us would be if we never forgot *anything* – "

"What's wrong with that guy?" Garrett interrupted, pointing to a man walking toward the window. His head was cocked to the side, as though he were listening to something no one else could hear. And his gait was uneven, like a drunkard's.

Carlisle shrugged. "Several things. He has a large, inoperable brain tumor in his temporal lobe, and it's causing all sorts of problems. Auditory hallucinations, severe vestibular deficits, and a low-grade dementia, to name a few. Gets worse every day. He'll be dead in a month. Maybe less. He shit his pants for the first time yesterday."

The students looked away. Lea glanced at the Professor. She was surprised at his tone.

He doesn't talk the way a doctor is supposed to talk, she thought. *There's no empathy in his voice.*

"On we go," Carlisle said, as if leading a museum tour. "To the secure rooms."

"This man," Carlisle began, "sustained damage to his frontal lobe in a car accident. He has no impulse control, and he is categorically homicidal." Carlisle clucked his tongue thoughtfully. "He can also be quite charming."

"My kind of man," said Melissa.

Carlisle looked at her for a beat, debating whether or not to take her seriously. Then he shrugged. "Over here," he said, walking to the next door and stopping at the window, "we have an extreme case of paranoid schizophrenia. This man's psychosis is purely chemical, and we do our best to medicate him."

The students looked through the window, but none of them could see anything.

"Unfortunately, he doesn't respond well to traditional treatments. His delusions are not improving, and he is very unpleasant."

Carlisle motioned to Jason. "Here, Mr. Bell. Have a closer look."

Jason stepped forward hesitantly. He peered into the window.

"Hey, Carlisle!"

Jason flinched. Someone inside the room was speaking. *Shouting*, actually, but the tightly sealed door reduced the voice to a dim, faraway sound. Jason still couldn't see anyone through the little glass view-hole.

"I can *hear* you out there, ass-face," the voice shouted. "I still need some grout for these walls. Some Carlisle-paste, remember?"

Carlisle grinned. "As you can tell, this patient is not charming in the least. He is often delusional – "

"If you put me in that chair one more time, I'll make paste from your DICK, you worm-eating bitch."

A little man with a pointy nose stepped suddenly into view. His face was inches from the window. Jason stepped back quickly.

The pointy-nosed man looked at each one of them. "What is this, a field trip?" He shook his head. "Oh, Carlisle," he said. "You are *such* an ass-face. Setting up the next round, are we?" He took an extra second studying Melissa. "Don't let him touch your tits, honey. You may be the prize in this group, but to him you're just a body and a brain."

"Moving on," Carlisle said smoothly. "Don't let his ranting scare you. Half the time he doesn't even know where he is. Lots of paranoid schizophrenics behave that way." Carlisle urged them forward, onto the next door. "Here we have an *apparent* catatonic, but this is deceptive, because as you can see…"

Lea hung back for a moment, staring at the little window. The pointy-nosed man was still standing right there. He didn't *seem* delusional, despite what Carlisle had said. He had been unpleasant, certainly. And he had obviously hated Carlisle. Lea had no medical training, but anyone could see that the pointy-nosed man was angry. Outraged was probably a better word. Like someone who had been taken advantage of.

Abused.

Up ahead, Carlisle lectured on. Lea hurried to rejoin the group.

The little man with the pointy nose watched her go.

8

Professor Carlisle peered through the little window at the next door. He was so fascinated that he seemed almost to have forgotten the students standing next to him. "This patient has developed a hyper-sensitive olfactory condition," he said quietly. "His sense of smell is somewhere on the order of ten *thousand* times better than normal…"

Garrett whispered something to Melissa. She looked at him and shook her head. "What?"

"I said my name's Garrett."

Melissa shrugged. "I know. And I'm Melissa."

"Right," he said, smiling even wider. "So, Melissa, I was wondering – "

"I don't think so."

Garrett stopped. "What? You don't even know what I – "

"Yes," she said. She fixed him with a look of disapproval. "I do."

Garrett found himself at a loss for words. He had never been rejected quite that fast. And yet he felt good, somehow. He liked the way she was looking at him, even if she had said no.

Weird.

Garrett nodded slowly, making a show of being embarrassed. "Okay, then," he said. This was only the first stage, after all. "So tell me your objections."

Melissa scanned the ceiling, as if extra time would be necessary to catalogue such a towering heap of issues. "For starters, you're a senior and I'm a freshman."

"My dad's older than my mom," Garrett shot back. "It doesn't seem to bother them, and – "

Professor Carlisle spun around suddenly, and he glared at the four students as if they might have been making faces while his back was turned. "Any questions?"

They shook their heads silently.

"Fine. To the examination room, then."

He headed back the way they had come, toward the entrance of the building. "Mr. Lemke," Carlisle said, pointing at Garrett as they walked. "Can you tell me the point of this little tour?"

Garrett's focus on Melissa was momentarily broken. "To... prepare us?"

Carlisle grunted. "A vague and slippery response, Mr. Lemke. But essentially correct. Could you expand on that, Miss...?" He nodded at Lea.

"Lea Redford," she said helpfully. "Probably you wanted us to appreciate all the strange things that can happen when someone's brain isn't working quite right."

Carlisle's eyes widened. "Well, Miss Redford. Aren't we sharp this morning?"

Jason nodded, and Carlisle spotted it. "You agree, Mr. Bell?"

"Um, yes." Jason was caught off-guard. "She is. Definitely. Extremely smart. It's amazing, she – "

"No, Mr. Bell. I meant, do you agree with Ms. Redford's *statement*?"

Jason's face turned bright red. Almost as red as Lea's, but not quite. Melissa smiled to herself.

"No response?" Carlisle said. "It doesn't matter. Miss Redford is exactly right. I wanted you all to see that the brain is a machine. More specifically, you should understand that it's a machine with problems." He smiled. "The brain malfunctions. In fact, it malfunctions *often*. The general public likes to think of psychiatric patients as fundamentally different creatures – as if they all come from another country, or perhaps another planet – but we're all just one step away from being exactly like the people you saw today. When the structure or chemical make-up of your brain changes, there's very little you can do. There is seldom an operation or pill that will help you, despite what the antidepressant commercials would have you believe. It doesn't matter if you're in good physical shape, or have been eating healthy foods, or have studied Latin and Calculus. None of those things mean anything where neuropathy is concerned."

He stopped walking and pointed to his forehead. "Because you *are* your brain. If it changes, you change."

They nodded at him. Lea and Jason seemed to be making an extra effort to pay attention to what the professor was saying, perhaps so that they wouldn't have to look at one another.

"Makes sense," Garrett said. He glanced at Melissa. "People change their minds about things all the time."

She shook her head and sighed.

"True enough," Carlisle said. "But hardly the point I was making, Mr. Lemke." He led them to a door just inside the entrance to the building, and he fiddled for his keys. "Have a seat in my office, all of you," he said, opening the door. "I'll explain how this experiment is going to work."

They stepped inside.

9

Carlisle stood behind a little desk, and he directed the four of them to sit down on a pair of couches by the far wall. They all noticed how neat the office was. Not a single stray paper, no piles of books or overflowing file cabinets. They did notice one strange thing on the desk, however: a small, gleaming object, oddly shaped. It reminded Jason of an old television antenna, the kind with all sorts of strange loops and wires.

"This experiment is about smell perception," Carlisle said. "The procedure is very simple. I'll be giving each of you a small nasal spray bottle. All I want you to do is take a good sniff, and then write down what you smell. Be as clear as you can. The descriptions should be your own, and each of you will be getting a different scent." He looked at them expectantly, as if he had just finished telling a gripping story. "Questions?"

"This is a joke," said Garrett. "We sniff a little white bottle and write down what it smells like? What kind of experiment is *that*?

Carlisle's eyes brightened. "Some of the simplest experiments are the best, Mr. Lemke."

"You're the professor," Garrett said with a shrug.

"Other questions?"

Carlisle waited, but no one else spoke up. "Fine, then." He opened a drawer in his desk and pulled out four small white bottles. Each bottle had a smooth, round end at the top.

"Those look like the things for unclogging your nose."

"Yes, Mr. Lemke. Except that these are filled with specific scent chemicals, rather than antihistamines." He pushed them across the desk. From another drawer came a stack of papers and four pens. "Take one each, and then fill out these forms. Be sure to record which bottle you are using."

They each stood up and took a little white bottle, a form, and a pen.

Carlisle was being cautious, and he didn't smile. This was the moment of truth. *Go ahead,* he thought. *Have a nice big snort of oxytocin. Then we can all get down to business.*

Melissa sat down and glanced at the others. They were already pushing the tips of the bottles up their noses and spraying.

She hesitated. The idea of introducing a chemical directly up her nose didn't seem like a good idea. She saw Lea and Jason put their bottles down and begin to write. Garrett looked as though he wanted to take another spray before filling out his paper form. All three of them seemed okay. No one acted revolted.

She didn't notice how carefully Carlisle was watching her.

Melissa put the bottle gently inside one nostril, then gave the tube a little squeeze. A cold mist went squirting up her nose.

She felt herself relax immediately.

That's not a bad smell at all.

She had been expecting something harsh and artificial, like the oily stink of a fast food restaurant. But the mist in the bottle didn't remind her of burgers or fries. And it wasn't like any perfume she had ever encountered. In fact, she thought it smelled sort of nice. A memory of Ms. Cooper suddenly filled her head, and a little smile came to her face.

Maybe it smells like art supplies, she thought.

No, that wasn't it exactly. Could it have been something in Ms. Cooper's hair? Shampoo? No, that wasn't it either. She couldn't put her finger on it. Either way, she decided that it was a good smell.

A *happy* smell.

"I think all of us are ready now," Carlisle said, coming out from behind the desk. He spoke with a sense of anticipation, like a grandfather getting ready to dole out birthday presents. "How is everyone feeling?"

The students looked up at him and nodded. All four wore identical expressions of calm satisfaction.

Carlisle smiled. Even if someone had come into the room at that moment, they would not have suspected anything unusual. The students would experience no motor-skill impairment or disorientation from the small dose they had received. The only way to detect a change in behavior would be to ask them to do something requiring an unusually high level of trust.

Which was exactly what Dr. Carlisle was planning.

"You can all stop writing," he said. "Just listen for a minute." They put down their pens and sat back in their chairs. "I've been doing some very interesting experiments over the last few weeks," he said. "I'm not going to go into all the details, but there is one important thing I think you'll enjoy hearing about." He stopped and stared at them, widening his eyes. "You'd like to know what I've learned, wouldn't you?"

They nodded like a row of trained seals.

Carlisle spread his arms in a gesture of inclusion. "I've discovered that when it comes to neuroscience," he said, "everyone is abnormal."

Lea put up her hand, and Carlisle grinned. He was glad to see that her sense of curiosity had not been subdued by the drug. "Yes, Ms. Redford?"

"What do you mean?" she said, sounding quite girlish. "*I* don't feel abnormal."

"Not abnormal in a bad way." Carlisle said, and he smiled reassuringly. "In a *special* way."

Lea looked ready to accept virtually anything the professor told her – they all did – but she still seemed confused. "Special how?"

"Let's start with you," Carlisle said, walking over to her. "What's your favorite subject?"

"Math."

"So you probably have an *abnormally* well-developed frontal lobe," he said triumphantly. "That's where most mathematic processes take place in the human brain. It's a good thing, Lea. You should be proud of yourself."

She nodded dutifully. "Okay, then. I'm proud."

"But we can find more," Carlisle said. "Because the first thing is not usually the only thing. Think hard, Lea." He squinted his eyes at her, as though helping her to think. "Is there something else? Something you've always had a flair for? Never mind school work for a minute. This could be anything – your ears, your eyes, how you speak… what is there about *you*, Lea, that's just a little bit better, a little bit stronger than everyone else?"

Lea's face changed, and Carlisle knew she had found it. He'd seen this look before, on psych patients who had gone through a similar interview process. It always took longer with the crazies, of course, since it was difficult to convince criminally insane patients that there was anything special about them. But Lea was no criminal. "What is it?" Carlisle said eagerly. "You can tell me, Lea. Don't worry, it can be our secret."

She didn't hesitate; no one in the grip of oxytocin ever did. "I can read people really well," she said happily. "What they're feeling, I mean. It's something I've been able to do forever. Since I was little. Since before I could even talk."

"Perfect," he said to her. "And listen, Lea." His voice became quiet, conspiring. "What if I could make you even better at reading people?"

Lea brightened. "That'd be fine."

"Of course it would."

Jason spoke up suddenly. "I have a really good memory," he said, sounding hopeful.

Carlisle turned to him with an approving smile. "Yes, Jason. Good. Thank you for sharing." That was the other wonderful thing about the oxytocin – it made everyone so much more willing to offer up personal information.

Melissa put up her hand. "I think my nose is more sensitive than most," she said.

Carlisle nodded at her. This was going to turn out even better than he had planned. "Terrific, Melissa. That's just the sort of thing I'm looking for. Smell is one of the most ancient and fundamental brain functions – it's controlled in the temporal lobe, by the way – and it's an area of enormous potential. You'll have the nose of a bloodhound by the time you leave this office." He pointed back to Jason. "And Mr. Bell, your memory will be flawless after today."

Melissa and Jason looked at him, then at each other, and they nodded simultaneously. They looked very happy. Neither one seemed interested in how the professor was going to accomplish all these things.

Carlisle glanced at Garrett, who hadn't spoken yet. "What about you, Mr. Lemke? What makes *you* special?"

Garrett didn't reply immediately, which Carlisle found surprising. "I'm not sure," Garrett said finally. "I get migraines more than other people, I guess." He rubbed one of his temples absently. "And I'd say my headaches *hurt* a lot more than the regular ones." He shrugged sadly, as if he knew that this wasn't the sort of specialty the professor was looking for.

Carlisle walked over to him. He almost looked concerned. "How long have you had these headaches, Garrett?"

"Not sure. A few months, maybe."

"Do you have one right now?"

Garrett let out a painful little laugh. "Bet your fucking PhD."

Carlisle knelt down so that he could get a better view of Garrett's eyes. He frowned deeply. "Okay, Mr. Lemke." His voice was soft now. "We'll see if we can do something about that." He stood up, shaking his head. "At least for the time being, anyway."

Garrett nodded slowly. Then something seemed to occur to him. "I'm good with the ladies," he said, a hint of excitement in his voice.

"Are you, now?"

"*Really* good. At least, I was before this whole headache business started messing up my game, you know?"

Carlisle seemed to reconsider. "You're not just boasting?"

Garrett shook his head vigorously, wincing from the pain the motion caused him. "No, seriously. It was like some kind of gift, you know?"

Carlisle nodded. He seemed hopeful again. "That could be something," he said thoughtfully. "Probably being obscured by a cerebral pathology of one type or another, but maybe the ability is still buried in there somewhere." He put a hand to his chin and dropped his voice, as if conferring with a colleague. "Go for the hypothalamus?" he whispered. "Sure. And temporarily subdue the paraneoplastic symptoms…" His voice trailed off. Then he turned back to Garrett. "We'll make you a sexual *machine*, Mr. Lemke. How does that sound? And maybe we'll even get those headaches to ease off for a day or two, okay?"

Garrett grinned like a wolf, and he looked hungrily at Melissa. "Just tell me what to do," he said.

Carlisle laughed. "Oh, I will, my young friend. I will."

Carlisle took Garrett into the examination room first. After half an hour had passed, he came back for Jason.

The door swung shut behind them, and Lea and Melissa were sitting alone in the office together. They were both still smiling.

"Hey, Melissa?"

"Hmmm?"

"What do you think about Jason?"

"I think he likes you."

Lea did not blush this time. She closed her eyes and let her head drop back, as if she were remembering her first time tasting ice cream. Then a new thought occurred to her, and her expression changed. "But what if he likes *you*?"

Melissa hooted. "Lea, he hasn't even looked at me."

"Everyone looks at you."

"You don't know that. You just met me."

"Right," Lea said. "But so far, everywhere we go, people are looking at you."

"Jason's not."

"Promise?"

"Yup."

Lea nodded slowly. "I believe you, Melissa."

"I know. And I believe *you*, Lea."

"About what?"

Melissa paused. "I don't know. About anything."

"Yeah," Lea said. "Me, too."

"Hey. You know what?"

"Hmmm?"

"That little white bottle smelled really good."

"Shhh, we're not supposed to discuss it, remember?" Lea sat quietly for a minute, her eyes focusing on nothing in particular.

Then: "You're right, though. It smelled great."

Sometime later, Carlisle came to collect them. He led Lea in first, then Melissa. Neither one resisted. Or even asked what was being done to them. When he brought them into the examination room, they found Garrett and Jason strapped into a pair of large chairs with canvas restraints. Neither girl asked why. Carlisle explained to them that it was okay, that both boys were simply recovering from their treatments. He suggested to the girls that they might like to make themselves comfortable in the other two chairs.

The girls thought that sounded fine.

They waited patiently as Carlisle secured their arms and legs, and they didn't mind when he came toward them with the thing that looked like an old television antenna.

There was no sound from the examination room. A careful listener might have been able to detect a very faint, very low-frequency humming, but nothing more. It sounded like a high-powered halogen lamp, or a noise that might have been coming from some sort of lab equipment. Nothing that would arouse concern.

Inside the examination room, Professor Carlisle walked back and forth among his four test subjects, grinning broadly.

He took pages and pages of notes.

Modifications

1

From *Getting to Know Patient Nathan*:

What made Kline so special? Not the symptoms themselves, surely. Nathan did present with more varieties of neuropathy than anyone I have ever observed, but sheer symptom volume is not, in any systematic analysis, worthy of special consideration. An accumulation of compromised cerebral function is more often simply an indication that death may be approaching.

And yet Nathan *was* unique. Not because he had a greater number of maladies, or because each problem was so severe. Rather, he distinguished himself with awareness.

Self-awareness.

Now someone asks: Why should this be so remarkable? Are the sick not capable of self-diagnosis? When someone has a fever, for instance, are the effects not most easily detected by the patient himself? "I'm hot," he says. "I need a glass of ice water. Someone get me a cool towel."

And indeed, this is normal behavior.

However, we must remember that cerebral deficits of the right hemisphere are usually difficult – if not impossible – for patients to view objectively. This is because the viewing apparatus itself has been altered. We must imagine, then, a patient with a fever *and* a lack of ability to sense his own internal heat. "Perhaps you would like a glass of ice water," we say to him. But the patient, with sweat pouring down his flushed-red forehead, turns to us with a glassy-eyed smile. "No thank you," he says. "Why would I want such a thing? I'm not thirsty. I think I'll go for a jog."

Dr. Kline had *several* right-hemisphere conditions. Taken together, these should have reduced him to a state of total self-oblivion. And yet they did not. He could discuss his issues intelligently, and this is something I still struggle to understand. Dr. Kline could "see" the problems while he experienced them, as if he were diagnosing another patient from afar.

Granted, his vision in these situations was never perfect. But he did know, for example, when to discount paranoid delusions, even when he was in the grip of the fear they generated. At such times, he was like the brave child in the middle of a thunderstorm, hiding under the covers of his bed. He was deathly afraid. And yet he knew, somehow, that his terror was not realistic.

Such presence of mind is unheard of in schizophrenics.

For Nathan, this ability to see was both therapeutic and damaging. On the one hand, he was better able to treat himself than any similarly affected patient. He could give himself counsel and support. This was a blessing, since it allowed him to avoid the medication he so despised. On the other hand, his awareness made him far more self-critical than any "normal" schizophrenic. He could comprehend, as so few patients can, that his own mind was not working correctly.

He could see that he had been damaged, and it made him very angry.

2

Dr. Carlisle was dreaming of money. Not in any specific, story-oriented sense, though. It was more of a *feeling*. He dreamt of the concept of money. Of wealth.

Vast wealth.

He pictured stately, high-ceilinged rooms in sprawling summer houses. European cars pulling out of too-wide, gravel-lined driveways. Sparkling water. Sparkling women.

The phone rang, waking him, but he almost welcomed the interruption. For once, being awake was nearly as exciting as having the dream. Because he would be living the dream soon. The experiment with the students was going well. Before long, the fame would come. And then the money, and then –

The phone rang again, breaking his trance. He glanced at his bedside clock as he twisted and reached.

6 AM.

Who the – ?

"This better not be one of my students," Carlisle said groggily.

"No, this is just a courtesy death notice."

Professor Carlisle sat up quickly. He recognized that voice. It was different now – strained and whispery, as if there were a bad connection – but it was the same underneath.

"Kline?"

"Do you have any idea what it's like?"

Carlisle took a long, shaky breath. It *was* Kline. "What?"

"You heard me."

That's true, I did. "No," he said.

Kline huffed. "You *will* know. Starting today."

"Where are you?"

Kline kept talking as though Carlisle hadn't spoken. "It's interesting," he said. "When I'm in the paranoid phase, I can never shake the fear. No matter how well I control myself, I still suspect everyone. Every*thing*. Even the moon and stars are out to get me."

"I never forced you – "

"It's hard to describe with words. But I've been trying to give people a little taste of what it's actually like. You know, to be *insane*?"

"You made your own decisions," Carlisle said, a little too loudly. He was trying to sound calm, and not quite succeeding.

"Yes, Frederick. Of course. My own decisions. And now I'm making another one." He sounded tired. "I'm calling to let you know I'm on my way."

"Here?"

"Fool. Yes, there. To kill you. Sometime in the next few days. Does that make you nervous?"

"Go to hell, Nathan." A slight tremor in Carlisle's voice now. He couldn't control it. "Where *are* you?"

Kline coughed. "Maybe close, maybe not. Hard to know for sure. Anyway, who says you should be watching out for *me*? I've made some new friends lately. One of them might come in my place."

Carlisle gripped the phone. "What's that supposed to mean?"

"It means look out behind you, partner. Look behind, look around, look down in the ground. Just be *afraid*, Frederick."

"You're bluffing."

"Am I? You've been distracted lately, I suppose."

"Why?"

"You should check the Concord Star. Or the Boston Globe – I think they'll pick it up."

"Pick *what* up?"

Kline ignored him. "You're the last one, Frederick." He paused. "Well, that's not true. Not yet. But you *will* be last. There's the Patton brothers first, but I don't think they'll take more than a moment of my time."

"What have you done?"

"Afraid yet?"

"No, you lunatic, I'm – "

"Yes, you are." There was satisfaction in Kline's voice. "I can hear it. I know the sound." He laughed. "See you soon, Partner. Watch out for me. Or for anyone."

"It wasn't my FAULT – !" Carlisle yelled into the phone.

"*There* it is," Kline said sharply, sounding pleased. "*That's* what it's like to be paranoid. Keep it up, Frederick."

The line went dead.

3

Melissa woke up, leapt from her bed, and ran to the bathroom. She was quick, and she almost made it. A roommate, if she had had one, might have remarked that this was nothing more than the classic college freshman scene: the attractive girl leaning over the sink, spewing up a foul, green-brown sludge. Her shoulders trembled.

When she was finished, Melissa stood up slowly. A string of saliva hung from her bottom lip. She looked back toward her bed, where a trail of vomit marked her path. Thank goodness this dorm room came with its own little sink.

It was that smell.

Where is it coming from?

Slowly, she approached the window. Maybe a pack of dogs had been hit by a car outside. Whatever it was, it had to be coming from something dead. The smell was *rotten*. And huge. When she found it, she knew it would be covered with flies.

Thousands of flies.

She opened the window, and immediately regretted it. There were no dead dogs outside, but there was something else. A combination of mulch and grass and cement and *exhaust* – oh my God so much car exhaust – and it all seemed to be pumping straight into the window and up her nose and right into her brain.

She slammed the window down and concentrated on not throwing up again.

I don't know what's going on outside, Melissa thought. *But I've got to find this dead thing first. Because it's apparently* inside *my room.*

Which was ridiculous, she knew. Because the smell was strong enough to be coming from a whole *bunch* of dead bodies, and there was no space in her little single-occupancy room to hide a stack of corpses.

Melissa began drawing small sips of air through her nose. She was careful not to breathe all the way in, for fear of setting off another appointment with the sink. The smell was so strong, it seemed to come from everywhere at once. Then, very gradually at first, she began noticing small differences. She turned first one way, then another. Tasting the air. She tilted her head back a few degrees. She began to walk. Slowly, one step at a time. She was still taking those little sips of air, and making delicate adjustments to the direction her nose was pointing.

Here, she thought. *Right here.*

Melissa looked down. She had walked to the corner of the room, just behind her bed. The shadows from the bed frame made it difficult to see. There was a cheap lamp on the desk, one she had bought at the beginning of the week when she arrived, and she turned it on and picked it up, shining the light down into the corner.

There it was.

A baby mouse.

She stood there for almost a minute, peering down at the lifeless thing. There was an expression of disbelief on her face.

That can't be it.

To create the stench Melissa was smelling, there would have had to be a hundred, a thousand, *ten* thousand dead mice.

Maybe they're in the walls. Piled up in heaps. Families of them, And they're all dead because the exterminator came.

Right. And when had the exterminator come, exactly? Last night, while she slept?

No. She knew there wasn't any exterminator. Just as she knew there weren't any other dead mice.

This is the only one. I can tell.

Her nose told her so.

Melissa didn't touch the mouse. She pulled on a pair of jeans, grabbed her keys, and bolted out the door. The most important thing was just to get *away* from that smell for a few minutes. Or a few days.

Walking into the Zimmerman common room was like walking into a wall. The stench of garbage hit her so hard that she actually stumbled. She closed her eyes and put her hands on her knees, willing the nausea to pass. She didn't have to look, or even turn her head, to know where the smell was coming from. There was a huge bin next to the television, where students dumped old pizza boxes, soda cans, banana peels, and anything else they didn't want stinking up their rooms.

Melissa tried not to picture each festering item in the bin. Her stomach turned over again, and she bit down hard. Someone entered the common room from outside, walking fast.

Girl, hung-over on peppermint schnapps, returning from the room of a boy who eats too much red meat and drinks too much Coke.

The information came so quickly that Melissa didn't have time to wonder how she knew it.

She's perspiring from the walk. She had sex last night… twice.

The girl continued on to her room, leaving a floating trail of decaying odors in her wake. Melissa waited until her nausea had receded to a manageable level, and then she stood. She looked around the room, and a sudden memory occurred to her. It was so vague that she wondered if it might be something from a dream.

She and Lea had walked back here together.

But that wasn't everything. All four of them had walked back here. After… something. With a professor, maybe? Lea would remember. She would go talk to her. And Lea's room was… right over there. Even if this really *was* from a dream, Melissa was sure Lea lived in 12B.

Maybe Lea had told her that earlier.

She went and knocked on the door. Almost at once, Lea's voice came floating out. "Yeah?"

Before stepping inside, Melissa reminded herself not to breathe through her nose. That precaution had only been partly successful so far – the smells seemed to find a way in regardless – but it was better than nothing.

Lea was sitting on the edge of her bed. She had a strange expression on her face. She looked up as Melissa came in, and her expression changed. She looked horrified.

"What?" Melissa said. Suddenly she was afraid, though she wasn't sure why. "Lea, what is it?"

"You're so – " Lea turned away, as if the sight of Melissa hurt her. "You hate me."

Melissa was shocked. "No, Lea. What are you saying?"

Lea didn't look at her. "You think I'm disgusting," she said. "I make you sick."

"That's ridiculous," Melissa began, and she stopped. She had been so distracted by the distress in Lea's eyes that she had forgotten to control her breathing, and a full dose of air had gone sweeping up her nose before she could think to do anything about it. A flood of information came with this breath, and it unbalanced her briefly.

Lea hasn't showered since last night. The shirt she's wearing has sweat stains in the armpits. She's getting a cold.

To be honest, it *did* make her a little bit sick. Not like the garbage bin in the commons, but still. "That's ridiculous," Melissa said again, with more authority this time.

Lea finally turned to face her. "Please don't lie." She sounded miserable. "Your face twists like a wrinkled towel. It's painful to watch."

"I'm sorry."

Lea relaxed slightly. "Okay," she said. "Better. But why do you think I'm so gross? I feel weird – my ears are ringing a little, as if I drank too much – but I don't *feel* disgusting."

"You're not – " Melissa saw her friend wince. "All right, all right. Yes. Just wait a second, okay?"

Lea breathed a little sigh of relief.

"Something's wrong with my nose," Melissa said slowly. She tried to choose her words carefully. "Everything smells strange."

Lea squinted at her. "Now you're just covering. Can you please *talk* to me?"

Melissa thought for a moment, wondering how to proceed. Finally, with a little shrug, she gave up. "I smell you," she said. "I smell every piece of you. The oil in your hair, the bits of food caught under your nails and between your teeth. You have a slick of bile at the back of your throat because you just woke up. Your feet are dirty." She paused and waited for Lea to yell at her, or throw something, or start crying. But Lea didn't. Instead, she nodded as if Melissa had just described the choices on a breakfast menu.

"Okay, good," Lea said. "Now, what's your question?"

Jesus, that was weird. How did she –

"It's all there," Lea said. "Like you're carrying a big, flashing neon sign. The question expression, and now the confusion expression. You can smell me? Well, I can *see* you."

Melissa stared at her for a beat. "I'm wondering about last night," she said at last. "What were you doing? Was I with you?"

"Oh, I – " Lea stopped. Her face clouded over. "I don't remember."

"Nothing? What about your boyfriend? Was he with you?"

Lea tried to frown, but her face lit up. "Jason's not my boyfriend."

"No?" Melissa smiled. "Maybe not yet. But you're hoping he *will* be."

"Maybe."

"Who's covering up now?"

They heard a crash from the common room, as if someone had thrown open a door too fast. Then heavy, running footsteps. Another door opened, followed by muffled shouts. More running. A second later, there were several hard knocks on Lea's door.

"Lea!" A boy's voice outside. A strong voice. A former hockey player's voice, if there could be such a thing.

Melissa winked. "I wonder who that is."

Lea leapt up from her bed.

"You going to put on some pants?"

"Right. Thanks."

"Come in."

Jason flung open the door and burst into the room. The doorknob slammed into the wall, making Melissa glad that she had taken a step back ahead of time. There was a quick billow of air from the common room, and she cringed. The smell of *boy* wafted into the room, strong and sharp. It was an animal scent, nothing like Lea's smells. Melissa felt her eyes begin to water, as if she had just walked into an unventilated holding pen for breeding horses. She would have liked to suggest that Jason march off to the men's room and take a shower, but he obviously had something pressing on his mind.

Jason looked at Lea for a beat, who stood there saying nothing, studying his face. She studied his posture, his hands, the tilt of his head. She must have liked what she saw, because she bit down on her lower lip to keep from smiling. Melissa wondered what secrets Jason had just unwittingly given up.

He smiled back at her. "I am *so* glad to see both of you. Could one of you talk to me, please? Say anything, put on some music, I don't care, just make this stuff *stop*."

Lea's expression of girlish delight turned to concern. At the same time, Melissa realized that she had almost missed an important piece of Jason's scent profile. So many things were obscured by his "maleness," it was difficult to catch anything else.

He smells exhausted, she thought. *And a little bit afraid.*

"What's wrong?"

"Everything. I don't think we should have done that yesterday, but it's more than that. Because you don't even know what *everything* means, right? I mean, no one does. Or no one *did*, until now. You know?"

Both girls shook their heads. "No," Lea said. "What are you talking about? And what happened yesterday?"

"You don't remember?" He stared at them with disbelief on his face. "Wow. I guess that's good. And you're not going through anything weird this morning?"

The girls glanced at each other.

"I wouldn't put it that way," Melissa said slowly.

"There's maybe a couple of odd things here and there," Lea added.

"You have a nice voice," Jason said, taking a step toward Lea. "It makes the crap in my head get less loud."

Lea looked as if she might start giggling. They stared at each other.

Jesus, Melissa thought. *We're never going to get anywhere like this.* "Listen," she said briskly, "what happened to us?"

Jason shook himself out of his Lea-trance. "You really don't know?"

Melissa sighed. "Jason, if you can remember what happened yesterday, please spill it. Spill it now."

"*If* I can remember?" He laughed. A little too hard, Melissa thought. As if he hadn't slept enough. "I remember everything," he said. "And not just about yesterday. I remember what Lea told me when she tutored me. I remember what she was wearing in class the first day." Lea smiled at this, but Jason didn't even notice. "I remember what all the people around her were wearing," he went on. "And my mother…" He put his hands to his ears, as if blocking out the screech of a fire-alarm. "She will not shut *up*. Everything she's ever yelled at me. It's all there. Like a really bad record. Over and over."

Melissa turned to Lea. "What's the last thing you remember from yesterday?"

"Going to Carlisle's office."

Melissa nodded. "That's it for me, too. Although I could barely remember his name until you said it just now." She looked at Jason. "Can you give us the details after that?"

Jason's face tightened up suddenly. "What?" He tapped his head as if he were trying to clear water out of his ear. "Sorry, couldn't hear you. End of game five in the high school division playoffs. Mom went *ballistic* that day. Say it again?"

"Just tell us what happened. Start from the office in the afternoon."

"Should we get Garrett in here first?" Lea asked.

Jason shook his head. "I checked his room. Empty."

Melissa shrugged. They could always fill Garrett in later, assuming he had forgotten too. She turned to Jason. "Come on. Let's have it."

"Okay," Jason said. "For starters, that was no T.V. antenna."

"What? Start at the *beginning*, please."

Jason sighed. "You guys are like a couple of Alzheimer's patients. First we went to this psycho ward, okay?"

Lea nodded. "Right. I remember that."

"And do you remember the pointy-nose guy?"

"I do," Melissa said. "Now that you say it, I do. That guy was pissed."

"Yes, he was. Pissed off at Carlisle. And I think I know why."

Jason laid it all out for them.

For the first time in almost two months, life was smiling on Garrett Lemke. His memory of yesterday – of the last few days actually – was spotty, but he attributed that to the headaches.

Ah, the headaches. He loved thinking about them now. Because they were gone. Not gone as in "tolerable." Not gone for a little while. Just gone. All the way. Whatever the problem had been, he was apparently cured. And it was better than that. He was more focused; everything seemed easy. His mind was flying.

He had woken up far earlier than usual, and instantly his head had been filled with thoughts of the women's swim team. He had to go find them. Right that minute. He got out of bed, showered, shaved, and was ready in less than fifteen minutes. By the time Melissa Hartman was waking up to the stench of a dead mouse, Garrett was already out the door and on his way. There would be no problems with Alyson Morrone this time. He would say the right things. And in the right voice. He would be irresistible.

I can feel it, Garrett thought. He almost started running.

He headed for the breakfast hall. With any luck – and surely this morning he couldn't help but have good luck – the swimmers would all be there when he arrived. It was still early, and there were not many students on the paths around campus. As Garrett walked, he saw few people he knew by name.

But here came Amy Till.

That was too bad. Amy had never liked him, and she was a close friend of his ex-girlfriend. He hadn't run into Teresa yet in this first week, but he didn't expect a warm reception from any of her friends. Amy least of all.

Garrett thought quickly. Feeling as he did this morning, he decided to risk going on the offensive. It was a narrow path – he'd have to say *something* to her – and it would probably be best to speak first.

"Amy!" He held out his arms as she came toward him. Her head was down, and she only looked up and saw him at the last minute. She would have had to veer sharply off-course to avoid the embrace, which might have been awkward. She submitted to the hug, though stiffly. Then she stepped back and looked at him. Her expression was not quite as hostile as Garrett had been anticipating; she seemed cold, but not frozen.

"Amy, good to see you," Garrett said. "How was your summer?" He noticed, somewhere in the back of his mind, that his voice sounded *perfect* now. Deep, and rich.

Like a man's voice should sound, he thought.

Amy took a long, slow breath through her nose, as if trying to calm herself. It seemed to work. Her face smoothed out a bit. "Summer was fine," she said. "Where are you living this year?"

Garrett ignored the question. "You look *fantastic*. Were you on the beach a lot in August?"

Amy's expression warmed another half degree. "Um, sure. I mean, yes. A little." She looked down. It was almost a shy gesture.

Garrett didn't let her up for air. His offensive strategy seemed to be working. "Just a little? How come you're *glowing*, then? You look like you just stepped out of a calendar shoot!" He touched her affectionately on the shoulder.

Was that going too far?

No, it wasn't. Incredibly, she didn't shrink away. In fact, Garrett thought she might have even edged closer. He gave her his warmest smile. "We should get some breakfast or something." He congratulated himself on the delicate diplomacy of such an offer. Not dinner. Not even lunch. Breakfast. Anyone could have breakfast together. It meant nothing. *Nothing.*

She surprised him again by smiling back. "Sure," she said. "What are you doing right now?"

Garrett lost his momentum briefly. This was not the response he had been expecting. His goal had been a smooth getaway, nothing more. He was good, but not *this* good.

Amy didn't seem to mind the silence. She stood and looked at him. Then, inexplicably, she actually took a step toward him. Garrett was so surprised that he thought for a second she might have been hit by a gust of wind. But she didn't try to step back. They were standing only inches from each other now. He studied her face, searching for a trap. Or maybe a joke.

No joke.

Garrett felt like laughing. Instead, he looked seriously at Amy and took her by the shoulders. "What about this?" he said quietly. "Why don't you and I get to know each other a little better?" He managed to do and say these things without cracking even the smallest smile, and Amy let herself relax against him.

They kissed there on the path. Garrett wondered what would happen if Teresa were to happen along right then, and see her best friend sticking her tongue into her ex-boyfriend's mouth. *That* would be interesting. But Teresa didn't happen along.

After a while Garrett told Amy that he had to go, but that he would call her up later that afternoon. She looked up at him, and he sensed that he could have taken her behind a patch of bushes if he had suggested it. Just a couple feet away from the path.

I could take care of this in three minutes, tops.

"But I do need to go grab breakfast," he said quickly.

And Allyson Morrone, he thought. *She's the one I really need to take care of, that's the thing. And I'm not going to have any difficulty this time.*

He walked away, heading for Taylor dining hall. Amy Till watched him go. She looked mildly disappointed. Mostly, though, she just looked smitten.

Life was smiling on Garrett Lemke.

Jason was finishing his story of the previous day's events. Normally the task would have made him stumble over his words, especially considering the audience – two good-looking women, one of whom he was definitely starting to like – sitting right in front of him. But his new memory didn't seem to be affected by nerves.

"After he gave Garrett and me the treatment," Jason said, "Carlisle brought you two into the room. Then he hooked you both up, and that was it. Once we were all out of the chairs and back on our feet, he told us we should come back to see him tomorrow for a second interview and the start-up."

Melissa frowned. "Start-up? What's that supposed to mean?"

"Who cares?" Lea said, suddenly sounding unhinged. "I'm done talking to that man. He should be in *jail*."

Melissa shrugged. "I agree, but we still need to see him." She tapped her nose delicately. "This thing is awfully sensitive. I don't know about you two, but I'd like to get back to the way I was before. We should go see him right now."

"Not an option," Jason said. "He won't be on campus today. Some conference or something. He said we shouldn't even bother trying to find him before tomorrow." He sighed and glanced at his watch. "Anyway, all of us have classes now."

Lea looked stricken. "Class*?* I don't know if I can."

But Melissa was already nodding. "Yes, you can," she said sternly. Her voice was clipped and cold. "This is your freshman year at Dartmouth College. Fall semester. Third day of classes. Don't let some manipulative, bonehead professor throw you off-course."

Jason and Lea were silent. They stared at Melissa, and her face reddened. "Sorry," she said quietly. "That was for me, not you. It wasn't easy for me to… to *get* here, you know? To get to Dartmouth, I mean."

Lea nodded supportively. Her emotional hyper-sensitivity was getting stronger all the time, and Melissa's distress was having a profound effect on her. "We'll all go to classes," Lea said. "One day is nothing. And then tomorrow Carlisle will fix us up. Things will go right back to normal."

Melissa looked encouraged. "That's right."

"Back to normal," Jason said, as if repeating the phrase would make it more likely.

"Can we meet back here this afternoon?" Melissa suggested.

Lea and Jason didn't say anything. They had made eye-contact, and were now gazing at each other as if hypnotized.

Melissa threw her hands up. She walked over and punched Jason in the shoulder. Hard. He barely seemed to feel it, but it did wake him up.

"Um," he said.

"We'll meet here after classes," Melissa repeated.

"Okay," said Jason dreamily.

"Got it," said Lea, barely controlling the goofy grin on her face. "Right here, this afternoon."

"For crying out loud," Melissa said. She took Jason firmly by the wrist and lead him out of the room, trying to hold her breath. At this range, the smell of boy – *horny* boy – was so strong that it almost obscured the reek of the garbage bin in the commons. She could feel herself starting to respond involuntarily, and she decided that it would not be safe for her to maintain this closeness. She let go of Jason's wrist and pointed him toward his room. He thanked her and shuffled happily away, thoughts of Lea dancing in his head.

4

Professor Carlisle sat in his office at the medical center, biding his time. He was wondering about his four subjects' progress so far. Despite what he had told them, he had not left campus for any conference. He wanted them to grapple with their new experiences for at least a day on their own – twenty-four hours was the minimum for a meaningful test run – so he had fed the hockey player a little lie about taking a day trip.

They would probably be upset at him by now.

Then again, they might not remember who was to blame, at least at first. If that turned out to be the case, the hockey player would be able to help them piece it together. And most of their hippocampus function would return after a few hours anyway. Not like Jason's, of course, but enough to fill in the bigger gaps.

Carlisle could hardly wait to interview them tomorrow. He was so excited that he had almost stopped thinking about Kline's unpleasant phone call that morning.

Almost.

He was still taking extra precautions. He locked doors behind him whenever possible, and he was very aware of anyone approaching him. Especially from behind.

Someone might come in my place, Kline had whispered.

5

On her way to art class, Melissa tried to prepare herself. She thought back to all the smells from Ms. Cooper's room at Fitchburg High. The oils and the acrylics. The cotton canvases, the wooden easels, and the caustic, alkaline cleaning solutions.

The horsehair paint brushes.

She tried to imagine it all multiplied by a thousand, filling up her head like a dense, black smoke. If she thought about it enough, maybe she could avoid making a scene when she entered the classroom. It was difficult to concentrate as she walked, because the smell of car exhaust kept pushing every lucid thought from her brain. Almost as bad was the dog feces everywhere. The Dartmouth campus was always filled with happy dogs – faculty dogs, frat dogs, dorm dogs – but now it seemed to Melissa as though every one of them did nothing all day except poop and pee.

She hoped that her stomach would be strong enough to withstand the art department. It had been a stressful morning, and she needed to do some painting. Ms. Cooper would have understood.

The class started out well. Melissa arrived early enough to get a spot by the window, where the breeze could help dilute scents in the room. She would still have to deal with the stench of car engines and dog shit from outside, but she was becoming slowly accustomed to those things.

The real problem was the *inside* of the room.

The odor of art supplies was stronger than she had anticipated. The cloth canvases had a living, almost personal smell to them, as if each were a separate character. She had been prepared for the oil paints to be pungent, and they were. But the metal tubes they came in were *more* pungent, sharp and bitter in her nose, almost as if they were burning her. And the brushes – the supposedly horsehair brushes – were not horsehair at all, but donkey-hair.

She didn't know exactly how she was able identify the smell of donkey, but there it was.

She smelled the first student coming before he had even arrived. Melissa tried to keep her nose pointed out the window, but this didn't help much.

Male. Hasn't showered since Sunday – Sunday! – *and he didn't brush his teeth when he woke up.*

The boy took a seat at the other side of the room, and Melissa took a little breath of relief. She could handle him at that distance, even though he –

Two females. Shared the same eye shadow this morning. Ditto with the deodorant, although it's not really working. And they just smoked up. They're practically made of pot.

The hashish ladies sat down in the middle of the room, a little closer to her than the unwashed boy, and –

Girl. Bulimic, threw up a few minutes ago.

Two Boys. Obviously gay and dating, since their smells are all mixed around.

Girl. Boy. Two more girls. All of them filled with nothing but coffee and booze. It's in their sweat. Profoundly hung-over.

Melissa bent down and tried to slow her breathing.

One more girl. Advanced case of athlete's foot.

That was it. Melissa rose from her seat and went staggering out of the room, one hand over her mouth. The four students who smelled like hangovers watched her sympathetically, imagining that they knew how she felt.

Melissa lunged for the public bathroom in the main hallway, but this turned out to be a mistake. The bathroom had recently been used, and not kindly. Even as she dry-heaved into the sink, Melissa felt her body gearing up for a much stronger, deeper response. The industrial bleach used by the janitor wasn't helping; it seemed to amplify the fecal rot.

Her stomach contracted powerfully, and bits of food she thought had been digested days ago found their way up her throat and into the sink. The veins at the side of her neck bulged. Her head throbbed. Tears of pressure poured from her eyes.

I wonder if this is what it's like to be in labor.

She didn't wait for the spasms to subside. Instead, she forced herself out of the bathroom, through the double doors at the stairwell, and straight outside, all while her stomach was still twisting itself like a towel on a ringer.

Several students running late for class saw a very tall, very beautiful, very sick-looking girl come stumbling out of the Farley Art Center. If they had not been so late already, they might have stopped to ask if she was okay.

It was good that they didn't stop. In her weakened state, Melissa couldn't have withstood the morning breath.

Lea's English 5 class was in a large, dimly lit lecture hall. The space resembled Professor Carlisle's Psych 10A auditorium, though it could not hold quite as many people. The smaller size was supposed to allow more questions and answers from the students. Lea chose a seat at the back. She hoped the shadows would hide her face. Like Melissa, she didn't want to make a scene.

When the professor, Jane Wilkes, resumed the discussion of *Othello* from the day before, Lea felt herself tense up. Yesterday Professor Wilkes had seemed clear-spoken, energetic, and open-minded. But now, with Lea's improved face-reading abilities, it was unpleasant to watch her. The cynicism in her demeanor was like a dark brown stain. "As we have seen," Professor Wilkes said, "Shakespeare's examination of love and its dark companion, jealousy, is a moving and painful work. It is, in every sense of the word, a tragedy."

With this, at least, Lea could agree. She had read *Othello* twice already in high school, and it was still awful to watch the main character's downfall. Even when you knew Othello was going to screw everything up, you still found yourself hoping that maybe, *this* time, he wouldn't murder his own wife. And if Professor Wilkes had said the same thing yesterday, Lea would have nodded along. Maybe she would even have jotted a quick line on her notepad: "tragedy."

But today things were different. Today it was obvious that Professor Wilkes was nothing but a con artist. Lea squinted and leaned forward, watching the professor closely. Was she seeing this right?

Absolutely. Look there, at the lines around her mouth. And the tightness in her neck. The teacher was practically laughing. She was a picture of badly-concealed cynicism. Professor Wilkes, Lea realized, thought *Othello* was nothing but a hack-job. A piece of middle-millennium pulp. She half expected the teacher to stop in the middle of her lecture, hock back, and spit a glob of phlegm into the first row of seats.

Very slowly, Lea reached into her backpack and brought out a pair of earphones. After putting them gently over her head, she felt around in the bag for the *play* button on her iPod.

She sat there for a minute, and then reached in again. She turned the volume way up, to drown out the professor's voice, and she closed her eyes.

Better.

Jason was having a wonderful time in Calculus. In fact, he thought it was the best class he had ever attended. Right up to the minute when the teacher threw him out of the lecture hall.

Professor Braden started the lesson by going through a quick review of the concepts from the previous class. Most of it was limits stuff, and Jason now felt supremely confident with limits. Lea had explained the material clearly to him, and he could remember every word she had said or written on the board. He could also remember everything Braden had written – it was no different than reviewing a video tape in his head – but he preferred to remember Lea's explanations whenever possible.

The mental tapes with Lea in them were more fun to review. They were *prettier*.

Professor Braden paused for questions. Just for the hell of it, Jason put up his hand. Braden looked surprised. "Yes?"

"The second example, there, for finding limits by factoring?"

"Go on."

Jason smiled. "Wouldn't it be more helpful to give an example in which the answer could *not* be found using simple division?" Oh, that was good, Jason thought. It came out sounding just the way Lea had said it. Maybe even better.

"What did you have in mind, Mr. – ?"

"Bell," Jason said quickly. "I don't know, maybe something that would lead to a zero in the denominator without factoring." He tried to sound as if he were coming up with the information on the fly. "For example, you could try the limit as X approaches three of X minus three over X squared minus nine."

Professor Braden gave him a strange look. Then he turned to the board and began writing. "That sounds fine, Mr. Bell. I'll put your example up as well. Thank you."

Jason sat back and tried not to look too smug. "No problem."

After a few minutes of review, Braden moved on to a discussion of the projects that they would be working on. "You may work in groups if you want," he said. "But each member of the group will need to turn in his or her own report. The written product from each student must be no less than six pages, double-spaced, with a full explanation of the concept being explored."

The class groaned.

Jason couldn't resist. "Professor, I think you said five pages yesterday." *And I don't think. I know.*

Braden turned to him. “Excuse me?” He sounded annoyed, but Jason didn’t back off. He felt his heart rate going up, and he liked the sensation. It reminded him of being back on the ice in Ledyard arena. “Yesterday it was five,” Jason said again. “Ask the other students if you don’t believe me. You changed the page count.” He could already see people nodding around him.

Braden’s eyes narrowed. “Did I? Well *today* it’s six pages. Tomorrow it might be seven. Comments?”

Jason shrugged.

Not if you’re going to get all uppity, he thought.

“STOP BEING SO RUDE!”

His mother. Her voice almost knocked Jason out of his seat. He turned around to look, even though he knew he wouldn’t see her. Still, you could never tell. Cynthia Bell might have decided to drop in on her son’s math class. Just to make sure he was getting enough playing time. Or board time. Or whatever kind of time you were supposed to get in a calculus lecture. Coach Dixon, Professor Braden; they were all the same. None of them gave her son the credit he deserved.

But of course she wasn’t there. Jason shrank down in his seat and closed his eyes. The mental tape had switched over for some reason. Instead of Lea’s supportive voice, now his mother’s shriek was stuck in his head. “MY SON IS A HOCKEY PLAYER!” she yelled. It was the scene from the hospital room. She was barking at the doctor. “HE CAN’T LEARN NEW THINGS! NOT ANYMORE!”

“Quiet,” Jason whispered. He put his hands over his ears.

“WHAT ABOUT YOUR NHL CAREER?” Now she was on the phone with him, trying to convince him to see the doctor in Connecticut.

“Shhh.”

The girl sitting next to Jason turned to look at him. He waved her off and tried to smile.

No, no. Not you.

The girl shifted her weight to the side, inching away from him.

"GET IN THERE AND HIT SOMEONE!" Fourth grade now. Division playoffs. Jason began shaking his head back and forth. He needed to get back to the memory of Lea's tutorial. Lea had told him he was smart. That he could do it. He loved that memory.

"ACADEMICS AREN'T YOUR STRONG SUIT." Back on the phone. No, anything but this. "WHAT ARE YOU GOING TO DO WITHOUT HOCKEY? HOW–?"

"Oh, will you please shut *UP*!" Jason shouted.

Professor Braden stopped in the middle of writing and turned around. He didn't look mad anymore. Now he just looked disappointed. "Okay," he said, pointing at the door. "That's enough. Out."

"Right, right." Jason got up and grabbed his backpack with one hand. He kept the other hand over his ear. "I'm a little distracted, that's all. See you tomorrow."

"*Out*," said the professor, pointing again.

Jason kept talking as he left. It helped to drown out his mother. "I'll get the homework off the website, okay? And, uh… six pages on the report. Got it. But that's for the end of the semester. Great. Okay…"

As soon as he stepped out of the building, his mother's yelling stopped. Jason lifted his head and sighed with relief. A lone German Shepherd, trotting across the green on its way to a frat or a lunch hall, glanced at him without slowing down.

"This has *got* to stop," Jason said, to no one.

Garrett was not concerned with classes. After his encounter with Amy Till on the way to breakfast, he decided to make it a skip day. He couldn't afford to be wasting his time listening to lectures. Not when he was feeling like this. There were serious matters that needed his attention.

Serious matters like Allyson Morrone.

He quickened his pace to the dining hall. When he arrived, Allyson was already there. So was Naomi. And, yes, so was the rest of the swim team.

Athletic schedules are so beautifully predictable, Garrett thought.

They looked at him cautiously when he brought his breakfast tray over to their table. Many of them remembered the strange things he had said a few days ago. And the strange way he had acted.

He was acting like a dork, they thought collectively.

But as Garrett sat down he made a vague reference to some bad meth a friend had given him, and that covered it. He was just a fun-loving guy who had been partying a little too hard, that's all. They had caught him on the tail end of a long trip on crystal.

Oh, of course.

They laughed about it with him.

He pretended to look at them critically, then told them they all looked strong. That they were going to be fast in the water this year. "You're like a pack of lady *sharks*, right?"

They smiled and looked back at him shyly. As a group. Told him that *he* looked strong. That he must have been working out over the summer.

He smiled confidently and shrugged. It was probably just the shirt he was wearing, he said. And managed to imply with his tone of voice that it was *not* the shirt. That he *had* been working out. Allyson Morrone still hadn't said anything so far. But Garrett saw her watching. The conversation began to accelerate, moving from summers to weekend plans to upcoming swim meets. Then the wisecracks about senior year, the blasé references to jobs, and the inevitable panic over the idea of post-college life. He sympathized with their anxieties. They laughed at his jokes. Then, slowly, the pack began to thin out. One by one, they began to clear their trays. They thought they were deciding to go, but it wasn't up to them. Not really. Garrett could feel himself *letting* them go. Choosing the ones who would stay. Every few minutes, he would narrow his focus a little more.

Now eight left. Now five. Now three.

He held on to Allyson until the end. And then it was only the two of them sitting there, she and Garrett, as if they had planned to meet up in the cafeteria. Yes, well. *He* had planned it, anyway.

The thing about sex: it was always a good thing, and Garrett had never struggled with convincing women to go to bed with him. They usually broke down in the end, with enough cajoling and flattery. Not just any women, either. Teresa had been beautiful. And April, before her. And Wendy, before *her*. They were beautiful, and they made him glad to be a man. Plus, they always seemed to enjoy themselves. Teresa had maybe started to go overboard with the whole relationship thing, but that was another story. Whether his girlfriends liked him as a person or not, they all clearly appreciated his performance.

But it had never been like this.

They had left the dining hall together, and now he was walking back to Zimmerman with Allyson at his side. She was sticking close to him. *Close*. Several times she almost tripped over his legs as she leaned her head into his shoulder. He was reminded of a cat asking to be fed.

Garrett took her by the waist as soon as they were inside the common room, but she was already ahead of him. Her hands moved to his belt, to his chest, then back again. As if she couldn't decide where to touch him.

They barely made it to his room. She pawed at his clothes, tearing off his shirt and pants with a carnal urgency. Garrett worked to get her naked as well, but she was so fixated on rubbing her body up against him that he almost couldn't manage it. She began kissing him, *tasting* him, and Garrett was struck again by how much she seemed like a hungry animal. As though he were food to her. Or a drug.

He finally succeeded in taking her clothes off, and the reward was worth the effort. Allyson's body was soft in all the right places, firm everywhere else. She was smooth, and warm. He smiled, lay back, and enjoyed the view. He let her do most of the work, which seemed to be what she wanted anyway. He had a great time.

But Jesus, not as great a time as *she* seemed to have.

When they were done – and he had to physically push her away, because he *was* done, even if she still seemed eager for more – he lay there and thought about it. This in itself was odd. He usually went to sleep afterward.

He didn't feel sleepy. He felt like taking a run. Or playing some lacrosse. He felt competitive. Aggressive, and relentless. Like a machine.

A machine. Someone had told him…

He would be a sexual machine.

The memory was faint, but it was worming its way back into his head. Something about yesterday. The psych professor. Professor… Carlisle.

Yes, Carlisle. He had brought them to his office. And then he had asked them questions. *Personal* questions. Garrett's eyebrows drew together as he waited for the details of their conversation to become clearer. But they didn't. The memory was stuck in a permanent fog.

He did remember the room, however. Carlisle had taken him into a little white room with special chairs. And then he had put that antenna thing behind Garrett's head. All of this had seemed fine at the time. Thinking about it now, he wondered *why* it had seemed fine.

The memory ended there. He woke up in his bed the next morning – *this* morning – feeling better than he had in months. Headache gone, energy to burn, and sexual prowess fully restored. More than fully restored, in fact. And something told him it was all thanks to Carlisle. He loved that man. And he would thank him, just as soon as he –

A hand moved across Garrett's stomach. A soft, pleading voice: "Baby?"

Garrett glanced at the sophomore girl next to him. The look in her eyes was unsettling. If he didn't give her some more attention, that look said, she might start howling like a dog.

He was about to roll away – there simply hadn't been enough time yet – but he paused to be sure. She was gloriously naked next to him, and he found himself staring at the rise of her hip where it joined the downward-sloping curve of her waist. That naked hip and waist were rocking gently, moving with anticipation. Anticipation of *him.*

So he rolled toward her.

And still she was hungry. As if she were in estrus, and he, Garrett, simply one of the herd necessary to satisfy her. He was tireless today. He began thinking about trying for number three, but then something got in the way. Something horrible. Way, way deep inside his head, he felt the beginnings…

It was just a tingle at first. No one else would have noticed it. Garrett, however, had become an expert. The start of another headache. Carlisle's trick with the television antenna hadn't cured him after all. Not all the way. He guessed that he would be needing another treatment.

And *soon.*

Complications

1

The body of Professor Frederick Carlisle was found the next morning at approximately 7:15 AM in his office. The student who made the discovery, a freshman girl enrolled in Carlisle's Intro Psychology course, arrived at his office seeking extra help on a homework assignment. She knocked twice before trying the door. It opened a few feet before she felt it hitch up against something heavy and soft, and she poked her head in to see what was causing the obstruction.

The next thing the freshman saw was difficult for her to identify, though the dental examiner did later make a positive ID based on a four-point match with Carlisle's wisdom teeth, which had never been removed.

The sight of the professor's fresh corpse was so disturbing that the student fainted briefly. When she revived a moment later, she found herself on the floor, staring at what looked like the remains of a face. She tried frantically to get up, but was unable to move, either because of the shock at being so close to a dead body, or because of the residual effects of having fainted.

Lacking any other recourse, she screamed. The mangled thing in front of her seemed to scream right back, and this made her scream louder. Her ability to move her arms and legs returned, but she was by this time too panicked to raise herself back up to a standing position.

Instead, she began thrashing around on the floor like a drowning fish. Remarkably, she did not injure her head on the edges of the door or doorframe.

At the sustained sound of screaming, orderlies and nurses came scampering from the adjacent ward. The girl was duly rescued from her prone position, though not before a certain amount of cajoling from the staff members. "Please, dear," they said. "We need you to be calm. Please try to lie still."

Ultimately, they were forced to give her a sedative. There were several hypodermic needles handy.

"It was a *monster's* face," the shaken freshman told her mother over the phone that night. She said the phrase again and again: "A *monster's* face."

Her mother whispered kind, supportive words, but nothing seemed to calm the girl. She withdrew from the college a month later. In her exit interview with the school psychiatrist, she cited an inability to sleep through the night.

"Do you have dreams?" asked the psychiatrist.

The girl nodded. "Of monsters," she said, sounding like a very young child.

The psychiatrist made a note, and said nothing. He had access to the pictures from the crime scene, after all. He didn't blame her.

The first person on the scene of Frederick Carlisle's murder – the first *official* person, anyway – was Officer Jim Watts. One of the orderlies at the ward put in a call right after they had finished sedating that screaming freshman girl, and Watts was there in minutes. He didn't have to break the speed limit, either. His electric-powered cart happened to be near the Hitchcock Medical Center already.

When he saw the body on the floor of the office, Watts put in a call of his own. Because before too long, someone would say it: "Shouldn't there be some *real* police here?"

And even though Jim Watts was licensed to carry a gun; even though he had a crisp green uniform and a sparkling badge issued by the college; even though he was in better shape than any of those Hanover cops…

He was still only campus security. Yes, some people called him "Officer." But no, he wasn't one. Not really.

That semantic detail had never stopped him from taking a look around, however. He had made his call, and the Hanover Dispatch would do the rest. So now he had five minutes before the boys in blue would crowd in here and push him out. He hoped it would be enough time to get what he needed.

ID was first, and that was easy. You checked the name on the door. Then you asked a nearby nurse if the body on the floor was Carlisle.

"His face is *gone*," the nurse said with a nervous shrug. "How should I know?" Her voice shook.

Watts nodded. "Right. But are those the clothes he usually wore?"

"Oh." The nurse looked again. "I suppose."

ID, done. And no fingerprint lab necessary. Next came the time-of-death stuff, which was harder.

"You see him yesterday?"

"Yes."

"Morning, afternoon, night?"

"Once in the afternoon. Around four."

Watts raised his voice so that others could hear. "Anyone here see Professor Carlisle after 4 PM yesterday?"

An orderly in the back looked up. "He came in after we had finished serving dinner."

"He was visiting a patient?" Watts was speaking quickly. No one had asked about the "real police" thing yet. He could keep peppering these people with questions as long as he didn't let them think too hard. "Was that a regular routine?"

The orderly shook his head. "Wasn't usual, but yeah, he was visiting patients."

"Know which ones?"

"No."

"See him leave?"

"About nine. Just before lights out."

Watts turned to the freshman girl. She was sitting in a chair, quiet now, calmed by the tranquilizers they had given her.

"Young lady?"

Something flickered in her eyes, but she didn't look up at him.

"What time did you come to the professor's office?"

She answered immediately, in a flat, expressionless tone. It surprised him. "Seven o'clock," she said. "For extra help on the homework."

"Good, thank you."

"It was a *monster*," she added.

Watts nodded. "I know."

So: time of death sometime between nine last night and seven this morning. Not a very small window, but better than nothing. So far, so good. The cops would be there any minute. Watts turned back to the nurse. He needed one more thing. "Anybody have a problem with this guy?" he asked her. "Anyone bearing a grudge? Have it in for him?"

The nurse glanced at him quickly. She looked puzzled by the question.

"Not that anyone would *dislike* him," Watts said, back-peddling. "All I mean is, was there anyone who – "

"I know what you mean," the nurse said. "Give me a second, okay?"

Watts put up his hands. Of course. No rush.

The nurse took a breath and steadied herself. Then she smiled. Her teeth were surprisingly white. "*Everyone* had a problem with Dr. Carlisle, Officer."

That was nice. She called him Officer.

"Check around," the nurse said. "Ask any of the staff here. Ask his coworkers. His students."

Watts nodded. He would, if he got the chance. Or if the Hanover Police didn't beat him to it.

"People *hated* that man," the nurse said. "He was a slime."

Security Officer Jim Watts ran a hand through his hair. "I guess that doesn't narrow the field much, does it?"

"You know, he used to have a partner," the nurse added.

Watts perked up. "Used to?"

"Dr. Kline was his name," she said, and smiled again.

Such a pretty smile, Watts thought happily. *And good information, to boot.*

So now he just needed to get some information on this Dr. Kline.

2

On his way out of Concord, Dr. Kline made one final stop at the hardware store, where a man in a bright red smock directed him to the gardening aisle. The lady at the register offered to give him a bag for the extra-large pruning shears he purchased, but Kline preferred to carry them in the open.

Ready for use.

He had never actually visited the prototyping facility on route 89. Not in person. He knew the address from memory, and he had seen pictures. The cab driver raised an eyebrow when Kline told him where he wanted to go, but then three twenties came fluttering over the front seat. That settled the matter. For sixty bucks, the driver would have been willing to go twice as far.

Kline would have been willing to pay twice as much.

The *Kinetech* building lay in a sparsely settled area just north of Concord, NH, with great stretches of untended land on all sides. Kline had the cabbie drop him off at exit seven, a half-mile away, and he began making his way through the rough, un-mowed crab grass. A minute later he found himself in the middle of a huge, featureless expanse of meadow, with no idea where he was or how he had arrived there. One building – a small, squat, cinderblock structure – was visible in the distance, but he could see no other evidence of human settlement. He stopped walking and listened carefully. There were sounds of a highway somewhere behind him.

Kline sat down in the grass and tried to think. The sun was out, which calmed him somewhat. But why on earth – ?

And *who* on earth – ?

The amnesia phase settled over him like a huge, heavy blanket. He decided to stay sitting. He would wait.

A little more than an hour later, it occurred to him that his name was Nathan Kline, and that the cinderblock building in the distance reminded him of the pictures he had seen of the *Kinetech* prototype center. That got him thinking about the Patton brothers, Jerald and Brian, who had obviously fucked up something when they built the first version of his TMS Isolator device.

Those Patton brothers, Kline thought. *They're next on the list.*

And look at this: he was holding a pair of extra large pruning sheers. Exactly what he would need for this type of errand.

How nice.

With the last wisps of his amnesia phase evaporating like a fog in the morning sun, Kline allowed himself a small smile. He rose to his feet, and headed for the cinderblock building.

The brothers were easy to catch unaware. He saw Jerald first, bent over something at a large work table. Kline approached him with the Hilti at the ready, and by the time the engineer looked up, there was a single-cartridge, .22 caliber nail gun pressed to the side of his head.

"Don't move," Kline said. "Get your other half over here."

Jerald did as he was told. "Brian!"

They were meek academic types, and it took Kline fewer than five minutes to convince them to take the sedatives he was offering. He didn't want to kill them, he said. He only wanted to prove a point. He would leave as soon as they cooperated. The old "do as I say, and nobody gets hurt" routine. It was a tired strategy. Tired, and predictable. But it was also effective. "Your prototype malfunctioned," Kline explained. He tried to sound reasonable. As if he were discussing a misunderstanding at the post office. "There has to be some retribution. Take one pill each, and this will all be over. I'm letting you off easy."

The smaller brother, Brian, looked at the pill suspiciously. "It won't hurt us?"

"You won't *like* it," Kline said. "But you owe me. And this is fair payment."

"What if we refuse?"

Kline inclined his head at Jerald, who was still trembling. Jerald's eyes moved restlessly, searching for a better view of the nail-gun pressed to the side of his head. "I'll shoot your brother here with a two-inch roofing nail," said Kline.

Jerald winced at the thought, and he gave Brian a plaintive look.

Kline waited patiently. He could see the mental calculus at work, and he knew that he had already won. Brian would go with the choice that seemed the safest.

Even though it was the *wrong* choice.

They took the pills.

When they were both unconscious from the thorazine, Kline got to work. First he went looking for restraints. The building was well-stocked, and there were more than enough stainless steel lock-fasteners available. He tied the brothers to a couple of large office chairs, which he then secured to two of the steel support poles that ran from the floor to the ceiling. They would not be able to move. At all.

He waited until they were awake. Then, with the two of them positioned so that they were facing each other, Kline took his place at Jerald's side. There was a brief delay while Brian oriented himself. His eyes took a moment to focus, to understand. When Kline was sure he had the man's full attention, he began firing nails into Jerald's ears.

Jerald responded more vigorously than Kline had expected. His screams were startlingly loud, welling from deep inside his diaphragm. For such a frail-looking man, he had terrific power in his lungs.

Kline did not rush. He pulled the Hilti's trigger with a studied regularity, being sure that each nail drove home before following it with the next blast. Throughout the process, he kept his eyes locked on Brian.

To see the reaction.

Jerald's screams were music to Dr. Kline, but Brian's horrified expression was the real reward. Besides, the screams began to dwindle after nail number eight or nine, whereas Brian's face only grew more twisted with horror over time.

Afterward, Kline untied Jerald and let him stumble around for a while, like a boat on a rolling sea. The man was still alive – barely – but his vestibular system had been obliterated by the fifteen nails now embedded in each ear. He looked like a child learning to walk for the first time.

That's what it's like to have no balance, Jerald.

Kline pushed him to the floor, where his head made a distinct cracking noise as it collided with the smooth concrete.

Kline grinned. Good fun.

He turned to Brian, whose expression of fury had become a burning, beautiful thing. His eyes blazed.

"I. Am. Going. To. *KILL*. You," Brian said. His arms and legs strained against the steel ties as he spoke.

Kline nodded. "That's exactly what I'm talking about, Brian. The frustration that you're feeling. The helplessness. You can see what's happening, even understand it. But you can't stop it. And that's me every damned *day*." He sighed. "You're right here, but you can't do anything. Look." He pointed at Jerald, who's body was now sprawled out on the concrete floor. Blood was pooling up near the crack at the side of his head. He wasn't moving anymore. "If you weren't tied up," Kline said slowly, "you could have done something. Or if you were strong enough to break through those steel straps, you could wrestle this nail gun away from me and call the hospital. Or maybe if you hadn't agreed to take that tranquilizer an hour ago, then the two of you could have stopped all of this before it had even started." He nodded thoughtfully. "It's all about the choices we make, and that's the real irony. Just like the choice I made two years ago. When I hired you two to build my TMS Isolator prototype."

"I'm going to rip out your fucking *heart*," said Brian.

"No, you're not," Kline said mildly. "Not after I'm through with you." He picked up the gardening shears. The new blades twinkled in the overhead lights. "Do you know what it's like to feel as though your arms and legs are missing?" He paused, then wagged a finger at the engineer, as if he could hear what was going through the man's head. "No, not paralyzed – that's not the same thing – I mean *missing*, as if your limbs aren't even there anymore." Kline moved in closer. "Here, I'll show you."

The shears' cutting mechanism was based on a ratcheted lever pressure design, and Kline was able to remove Brian's right arm with no more difficulty than if he had been pruning a tree branch. The blades had been designed for slicing through thick sections of wood; they made easy work of tendons and bone.

Brian passed out from pain halfway through the removal of his left arm, which Kline found disappointing. But he did revive briefly, thanks to an aerosolized stimulant from Kline's own personal stash. In the few seconds he was conscious, Brian Patton saw all four of his limbs laid out neatly before him.

Kline smiled for the second time that afternoon. The brief look of horror on Brian's face made everything worthwhile.

It was dark by the time Kline finished his work in the prototyping center, so he decided to stay the night. He found a cot in one of the small warehouse offices.

The morning light woke him, and now he was out on the highway, looking for a ride. Because it was all well and good to use threats – he was trying to induce paranoia, after all – but he still intended to pay Carlisle a visit. He wanted his old partner scared, but he also wanted him dead. And he had a very special disposal method in mind. Something oh-so-appropriate.

There were plenty of cars on the interstate this morning. Kline wasn't worried about picking up a ride. The large North Face backpack he still wore made his disheveled hair and dirty clothes look like the result of outdoor living, rather than sloppiness or penury.

I look like an Appalachian Trail hiker, he thought.

And who would be afraid of a friendly hiker? No one, Kline hoped.

The sun was still low over the horizon when a car with Massachusetts plates stopped to pick him up. It was a big old Cadillac, looking as if it could use some maintenance. The driver leaned over as he rolled down the window.

"Heading North?" he said.

Kline crouched down to speak into the car. He saw that the man inside was old and weathered, but strong. His arms were thick with muscle, and he had angry eyes.

"Going anywhere near Dartmouth?" Kline asked.

The man nodded. "Miracles will happen. Throw your bag in the back."

Kline stepped into the car. He was coming into a Scarecrow phase, and sitting down was a relief. The driver glanced at him.

"Outdoorsman?"

Kline smiled. "Yup. Got a little winded, though."

"Happens to everyone. Going to catch a rest in Hanover?"

"That, and visiting an old friend. You?"

The driver took a breath, as if reminding himself not to shout. "Just going up to say hello to my daughter," he said. "She's a freshman."

"Bet she'll appreciate a visit."

The man grinned. "Well, maybe. Lots of excitement up there recently. I figured I could use the 'comforting-father' excuse."

Kline was confused. "Excitement?"

"Well, the murder."

Kline froze.

Wait a minute. "I didn't hear," he said slowly.

The man shrugged. "I guess you wouldn't. Not too many chances to watch the news when you're hiking." He pointed at the radio. "It was on the morning report. Some professor from the medical center. Killed last night, they said."

No. It's not possible.

Kline fought to control himself.

“Did they give a name?”

The driver paused. “I don’t… wait, yeah. Fred, I think. But different, like it was European.”

“Frederick?”

“That’s the one.”

Damn.

The driver gave Kline a quick glance. “You know him?”

Kline shook his head quickly. “Used to have a friend named Frederick, that’s all.” *And I was hoping to slice him open like a trout. For starters, anyway.* He tried to change the subject. “I’m Nathan.”

The man nodded. “Good to meet you, Nathan. I’m Martin.”

The big Cadillac pulled away from the shoulder, gravel shooting from beneath the tires. They were on their way.

3

Morning classes at Dartmouth were starting. Students filed into the Psychology 10A lecture hall, chatting in low voices. Professor Carlisle had not yet arrived. Jeff Gooding, the young teacher Carlisle had provoked in the first class, was there at the front. He shuffled papers around the desk, humming to himself. He didn't seem worried by Carlisle's lateness. "Okay, let's get started," Gooding said.

The students ignored him.

He tried again. "Excuse me, class is now in session."

No one was listening. There was a buzz going around the lecture hall. "Something's going on," whispered a boy near the front. "Carlisle's never late. *Never*."

"I heard a rumor," said a girl behind him.

The boy twisted in his seat. "About Carlisle?"

"Yeah. He's *not* late."

"Then where is he?"

The girl's eyes sparkled with the excitement of inside information. "He's gone," she said breathlessly. "Gone, as in dead."

Far in the back, crouching in the last row of seats, Melissa and Lea and Jason and Garrett waited silently. They listened. And they watched.

Melissa didn't like what she was hearing. It couldn't be true – there were no murders on college campuses. Not outside of television. Still, the professor's lateness was worrisome. He was supposed to be back today. She wanted to speak with him. Badly.

The other three were thinking the same thing.

There was more whispering in the lecture hall. Something about a girl in the class who had gone to Carlisle's office that morning for extra help. And talk of a body. Specifically: Carlisle's dead, mutilated body.

When ten minutes had gone by and the professor had still not appeared, people began leaving the lecture hall *en masse*. The four at the back glanced at each other, then got up quickly and headed for the rear exit.

Most of the students went trotting off happily to the dining halls for some late breakfast. Some returned to the dorms to catch up on sleep. But not the four in the back. They went walking *away* from the main campus. Toward the medical center. On the way, Jason shot a curious glance at Garrett. None of them had seen Garrett since that afternoon in Carlisle's office two days ago. "So," Jason said. "What's your problem?"

Garrett looked at him quickly. "What?"

Lea could see the defensiveness on Garrett's face, and she spoke up. "It's okay. We're all going through really weird stuff because of Carlisle's experiment."

Garrett shook his head. "No, Carlisle fixed me. He cured my headaches, put me back to normal. I've got no problems." He glanced at them suspiciously. "Why? What's happening with you guys?"

They looked at each other for a minute. Then Melissa shrugged. "I've got the nose of a bloodhound, Lea can tell what people are thinking just by looking at them, and Jason remembers everything he's ever heard or seen."

Garrett laughed. "Right."

Melissa fixed Garrett with a tired, withering stare. "Hanging out with some swim team girls, are we?"

"What?"

"Please." She lowered her head and took a step closer to him. "Women swimmers have a distinctive odor, Garrett. The chlorine, for one thing. It takes days to wash out of their hair."

Garrett was momentarily speechless. He looked at Melissa as if she might be trying to trick him.

"What are you… I don't know anything about – "

"Yes, you do," Lea said quietly. "You just don't want to know. I can see it."

"You can see *what*?"

"You," said Lea. "I see your attitude. The specifics of what you say aren't important. It's how you say it."

Garrett smiled. The absurdity of the conversation was making him feel better, giving him back his confidence. "So you can read my mind? You're a magician now?"

"Not your mind. Your face. And your tone."

Garrett rolled his eyes. "Whatever. Sounds like something I saw on *Copperfield* once. And I don't believe in magic anymore."

"Then why are you scared?"

That made Garrett pull up short. "I'm not – "

"Save it," said Jason, shaking his head. "Lying to Lea is like trying to fool a CT-Scan. It's a waste of time. She sees right through you."

Garrett turned to him. "You're buying into this crap?"

"It's happening," Jason said with a shrug. "Why argue?"

"Because you people are talking nonsense. I'm supposed to believe that you're suddenly Mr. Super Memory? If that were true, why would you be complaining? Why would *any* of you complain?"

Jason scowled. "Have you ever gotten a really bad song stuck in your head, Garrett? One that sticks there for hours and hours?" He put a finger to his ear and made a circling motion. "Imagine having *every* song stuck in here. Every movie, every conversation, every phone call. They're all on a permanent loop, and I can't turn it off." He blew out a long breath. "I'm starting to go a little crazy."

Lea nodded in agreement. "I can't interact normally with people anymore. Everyone looks like a bad actor in a terrible theatre production. Practically everyone is lying all the time. It's exhausting."

"I throw up every five minutes from the smells," Melissa added. "You wouldn't believe how many things are nauseating when you can smell them well enough."

Garrett tried to laugh, but it didn't come out sounding right. "You're all a bunch of nut jobs. But that's beside the point. I'm not going through anything like that."

Lea stared at him. There was a little smile on her face.

"What?" Garret said.

"You're not a very good actor, that's all."

He frowned at her. "I'm not acting."

Melissa broke it up. "Suit yourself, Garrett. Either way, we all need to get our hands on that antenna device again. And we're going to need Carlisle's help to use it."

The medical center was just over the next hill. They picked up the pace.

The Dartmouth Hitchcock Medical Center was a mob scene when they arrived. There were police everywhere, and blue barriers had been put in place to keep curiosity seekers at bay. Reporters crowded the area, jockeying for position around the building as if they were waiting for a Hollywood starlet to emerge. Photographers passed the time by snapping off pictures of the crowd itself.

Jason put his hands on his ears, as if the noise from all the onlookers was too much for him. "What is all this?"

"He's dead," Lea said suddenly.

Garrett turned to her. "What? You can't know that. Maybe someone just got hurt."

"Their faces." Lea pointed at the policemen. "This is no accident scene. It's a murder."

Melissa nodded "Listen to her. I doubt all this press would be here for an accident. *Someone* is dead, that's for sure. But there's no guarantee it's Carlisle."

Jason looked determined. "I'll go find out."

He walked over to a policeman standing near one of the blue crowd-barriers, then smiled and pointed at the medical building. But the cop shook his head and put his hands up. Jason persisted. The cop frowned and looked angry. Then he shouted something and gestured away from the barriers.

Jason retreated. He came back to them looking disappointed. "Mind your own business," he said, imitating the cop's voice. "Police activity here, can't you see the barriers? Now back away or I'll have you thrown in the drunk tank."

Garrett stared at him. "Jesus. You sound like a tape recorder."

"Yeah, well. That's my thing now. Want me to recite some poetry? I took a class in seventh grade once." He turned to the others. "Anyway, that cop was having none of it. Wouldn't tell me a thing."

Lea had stopped listening. She was lost in thought, staring at the lines of policemen at the barricades. "Try him," she said, pointing.

They looked at the man Lea had chosen.

Garrett laughed. "The old guy? He's *definitely* a hard-ass. Just look at that scowl."

"I *am* looking," Lea said. "That cop likes to talk. He's friendly."

"What? There's no way you could – "

"Garrett," Melissa said gently.

"Yeah?"

"Have you been listening? You just said yourself that Jason seems like a tape recorder. And that's because he *is* a tape recorder." She nodded at Lea. "This girl can see things. If she says that cop is friendly, then he's friendly."

Garrett shrugged as if it were just more nonsense, but Melissa stared him down, her strong eyes digging into him. Garrett tried to stare back, and he almost succeeded. Lea watched them carefully, enjoying the private wrestling match. *It's like watching lions in a courtship ritual*, she thought.

"All right," Garrett said finally. "So Lea is the character expert around here. I'll go talk to Mr. Good-Times Cop, then."

"No, I'll do it," Jason said, and started to walk away.

Garrett grabbed him. "Easy, big man. This is my job."

"And why is that?"

"Because he left something out," Lea said. "He's good at this, somehow."

Garrett glanced at her. Then he smiled. "Okay, Miss Watchful. Yes. Carlisle's antenna thing did… *something*. I think I'm sort of persuasive."

Jason looked skeptical. "How?"

"What is this, science class? Do you know how you're a tape recorder?"

Melissa said something then. Very quietly. All three of them turned to her, but she seemed strangely embarrassed.

"What?" Lea whispered. "Once more, Melissa?'

"He smells good," she said, louder this time. Her eyes were closed. "He smells *incredible*."

Jason shook his head. "I don't smell anything."

Melissa opened her eyes and gave him an exasperated look. "So what?" Suddenly she sounded almost frantic. "It doesn't matter what *you* can smell, your nose is nothing but a – "

She stopped. Took a breath, collected herself. When she spoke again, her voice was subdued. Apologetic. "You use Colgate toothpaste, Jason. And even though you brushed your teeth before coming to class, I can tell that you had a burger for dinner last night and cheerios for breakfast. Okay?"

Jason put his hands up in surrender.

"More importantly," Melissa went on, "I can tell that Garrett smells better than the rest of us. I'm not even sure what the smell is, but it makes me want to rub my face against him. He smells like sex. He smells like *good* sex."

They stared at her without speaking. Lea noticed that she was breathing fast. The quiet stretched out, awkwardly.

"Sorry," Melissa said finally. "Didn't mean to freak everyone out."

Garrett smiled. "Not at all. Nice to be appreciated."

"Oh, shut up."

Jason still looked uncomfortable. He glanced at Garrett. "I guess you're elected."

"On my way."

Garrett was successful, as both Lea and Melissa had known he would be. The old, grumpy-looking cop lit up when Garrett started talking to him, and soon the two of them were walking past the blue barriers, all the way up to the building itself. The policeman even escorted Garrett inside.

"Wow," Jason said. "I wouldn't have believed that it if I hadn't seen it."

"Doesn't surprise me," said Melissa.

"So the old cop is gay?"

Lea shook her head. "He's not."

"But you said Garrett smelled like sex."

Melissa shrugged. "It's not just sex. He smells like authority. Like power. Safety, even."

Now it was Jason's turn to be cynical. "Come on. How can someone smell like *safety*?"

Melissa considered. "Smell is probably the wrong word. It's more than that. It's like an emotion, but coming through your nose." She squinted at him. "You buying this?"

"I don't know, but I wish *I* smelled like that."

"You do," Melissa said, glancing at Lea. "Just not as much. You're a guy, so you have it. But Garrett has it a *lot* right now. It's his thing. Like your memory."

"Yeah, I guess." Jason didn't sound convinced.

Garrett emerged from the building five minutes later. The friendly policeman was still with him, looking very pleased.

"He wants to keep talking," Lea said. "The cop, I mean."

Melissa watched, and she could see that Lea was right. Garrett was nodding, thanking the man, but he couldn't get away. Finally he began gesturing to the blue barricade.

"He's telling him he should probably be standing guard," Lea said.

After another minute of cajoling, Garret managed to get free. He came back looking dejected.

"You were right," he said, nodding at Lea. "Carlisle's deader than a post." He sighed heavily.

Lea frowned as she read his expression. "Oh, *shit*," she said.

Melissa looked at them. "What?" she said. "What, *what*?"

Garrett closed his eyes. He could feel another headache coming on. A bad one. "I looked everywhere," he said. "I even had that cop show me an inventory of any items that were confiscated for fingerprinting. But it wasn't there."

Jason cursed under his breath.

Melissa shook her head. "No," she said. "I can't handle this for much longer."

"You're going to have to," Garrett said sadly. "Because that antenna thing is gone. Whoever killed Carlisle must have taken it."

4

There was a sudden murmur in the crowd, and the four students stopped their conversation to watch. Several policemen were moving barriers aside. A group of EMT personnel came out of the building with a stretcher between them.

There was a body bag on the stretcher.

The EMT men hustled into a waiting ambulance while reporters' cameras flashed around them like a fireworks display. "What's the point of the ambulance?" Garrett said. "Isn't he dead already?"

"He's been dead for hours," Melissa said. Her voice was strange, and they turned to look at her.

"Melissa!" Lea ran to put her arm around her friend's waist, but Melissa's knees had already buckled.

"I'll be okay in a second," she said weakly. She leaned heavily on Lea's arm and glanced toward the EMT men. "He's in the truck now," she said. "Those doors are shut tight. It's not as bad anymore."

Jason stared at her. "You smelled him from all the way over here?"

"As if I were lying next to him in the bag."

"How do you know he's been dead for so long?"

"The same way you'd know if meat in your refrigerator had gone bad a week ago. He was rotten." She took a deep breath, and this seemed to steady her. "I can't live like this. It's too disgusting. Jason, do you remember if Carlisle said anything about this stuff wearing off? Just a little bit?"

Jason shook his head. "He was very specific. 'Previous trials have shown ongoing effectiveness. In all cases, secondary treatment is necessary for symptom reversal.' " He shrugged. "It sounds like we're stuck like this until we get our hands on that T.V. antenna again."

Garrett looked sullen. "How come he gave *you* all the info?" he said.

"Beats me."

"Because he knew," Melissa said.

"What?"

"Carlisle knew that Jason would have a perfect memory. That's why he told him everything."

Lea nodded. "We probably wouldn't even have remembered Carlisle's name without Jason here to remind us."

"Terrific," Garrett said. "Did he tell you what to do in case he got killed in the meantime?"

Jason didn't look amused. "It didn't come up."

"I really need that antenna thing," Garrett said again.

"We *all* do," said Melissa.

Garrett winced suddenly. He put one hand on his head. "Fuck." He closed his eyes. "My headaches are coming back. I need that thing *now*."

"So do I," Lea said, sounding piqued. "So does Jason. So does Melissa."

"So let's go *find* it," Melissa said.

"And how are we going to do that?" Garrett asked. He was almost shouting now.

Melissa smiled. She was the only one who didn't look rattled. "You aren't using your imagination," she said.

As soon as the ambulance pulled out of the parking lot, the crowd began to evaporate. Photographers unloaded their rolls of film, collapsed their tripods, and packed their cameras away. A few reporters tried again to get comments from officers on the scene, but their efforts were firmly rebuffed. Most of them headed for their cars, heads bent over notepads, scribbling madly. The four students from Carlisle's psych 10A class made no move to leave. They were still waiting for Melissa to explain herself.

"You think *we* can find the antenna?" Garrett said. "We're not the cops. How do we even know where to start?"

Melissa seemed not to hear the question. She turned to Lea. "Hey. Check out all the plainclothes cops. Who's in charge?"

Lea scanned the crowd of officers. She saw that several of them were dressed casually, rather than in the starchy blue uniforms of the beat police. They wore permanent frowns, and walked around in an endless rush, as if they were annoyed at something. Without uniforms or stripes to look at, it was impossible to tell who the highest ranking officer might be.

But not for Lea. She inclined her head at a lady standing near the edge of the crowd. The lady was wearing a dark gray blazer, neatly tailored. She wasn't frowning like the others; she seemed perfectly calm.

"Try that one," Lea said.

Jason looked at the woman and rolled his eyes. "I don't think she's even a cop."

Garrett nodded in agreement. "I doubt she's in charge of *anything*. Isn't she's a professor or something?"

Lea sighed. "Watch her a little bit."

They did. For a few seconds, nothing happened. The woman barely seemed interested in the scene before her. She looked as if she were waiting to be let back into the building.

Garrett huffed. "How long do you want us to – "

"Shut up and *watch*."

As if on cue, one of the plainclothes cops walked over to the woman and spoke for a minute with her. She produced a pad from the inside pocket of her jacket and made some notes. Then she said something and pointed, as if giving instructions. The cop nodded and walked off.

Melissa smiled. "What do you think, guys? Still think she's a professor?"

Garrett and Jason looked at the ground.

Melissa grinned at Lea, who looked ready to burst with pride. "Okay, then," Melissa said. "Garrett, you're our point man. Soften her up and bring her over."

"Excuse me?" Garrett shook his head. "We're not talking about some flatfoot this time. That lady could probably lock me up for tying my shoes wrong."

"You can't handle it?"

"I didn't say that."

Melissa waved at him. "So get going."

Garrett took a deep breath, as if he were about to jump into a pool of very cold water. "Here we go," he said quietly.

"Now," Melissa said, "as soon as he brings her back, I'm going to – "

"What if he can't?" Jason asked.

Melissa stopped and looked at him. Her eyes softened. "Try not to get distracted."

"What?" Jason said, sounding defensive. "I know he's a sex God and everything…"

"Jason, please – " Lea began.

"It's just that he didn't seem that sure of himself this time. That's all."

Lea sighed. "Don't be jealous about this."

"I am *not* jealous."

Melissa shook her head. "All right, enough." She looked at the ground, then seemed to make a decision. She turned to Lea. "What did you think about Garrett at first? As a *guy*, I mean."

Lea was startled by the question. She bit her lip, remembering. "He was… good looking." She glanced nervously at Jason. "But not… anything so special."

"Right," Melissa said. "And now?"

Lea reddened.

"It's okay," Melissa said. "It's only lust. You can admit it."

"*Melissa*!" Lea's eyes went wide with embarrassment. She dropped her voice to a whisper. "I don't see how this helps with the jealousy."

Melissa shrugged. "It's a *smell*. I'm feeling it too. Just answer the question." She stared at Lea gravely, as if this were an interview. "So, once again: what do you think of Garrett?"

Lea threw her arms up in resignation. "He's attractive, okay? Is that enough?" She was careful not to make eye-contact with Jason. "It's not his face, or his body, or… anything. It's just…" She shook her head, looking defeated. "Actually, I don't even know *what* it is."

Melissa nodded, as if this were exactly the response she had been looking for. "And do you *like* him?" She made her voice sound like an eight-year-old's. "As in, more-than-a-friend?"

Lea scowled at her. "No!"

"And who *do* you like?"

Lea said something very quietly. Too quietly to be heard.

"What?"

"You *know*," Lea whispered, tilting her head almost imperceptibly in Jason's direction.

Melissa kept pressing. "Really? Even though Garrett's all hot-to-trot and everything?"

"Yes."

"Thank you." Melissa glanced at Jason. "You feel better now?"

Jason ran a hand through his hair. He tried to collect himself; to seem serious. But it was hard for him to hide his smile. "Yeah, okay," he said finally.

"No more juvenile comments about Garrett being a sex god?"

"No."

"And you?" Melissa looked at Lea. "You're going to survive the indignity of all this?"

Lea nodded silently.

"Good." Melissa blew air through pursed lips like a weary parent. "As I was saying: when Garrett brings that lady back, I'll try to get some information out of her. Lea, you're on truth patrol."

Lea grinned. "Got it."

"And Jason – look at *me*, please, not Lea – I need you to remember everything this lady cop says. And I mean everything."

Jason nodded. "It's not like I have a choice. I remember everything *anyone* says." He tipped his head back, as if the weight of so many memories was throwing him off balance. "I don't discriminate."

Melissa seemed satisfied. She glanced in the direction of Hitchcock Medical Center. "Our charmer still has his stuff. Here he comes."

Garrett was walking toward them. The lady in the gray sports coat was following close behind. She looked delighted.

"I see you've met our friend," Melissa said.

The woman smiled, but did not take her eyes off Garrett. "Mmmm," she said, as if Garrett were a chunk of creamy chocolate in her mouth. "Yes, I have."

"Good. Then we can – "

But suddenly Melissa discovered that she could barely concentrate. Garrett's odor had intensified noticeably in the last three minutes. Melissa stepped back a pace and took a little breath through her mouth. Her head cleared a bit, and this allowed her to refocus. She returned her attention to the detective. "Could I ask you a few questions about the murder?"

The woman frowned. She looked offended by the question, as if such a request might actually be illegal. But then Garrett spoke up. "We don't want to be a nuisance," he said. "Detective Perth, I'm sure you need to attend to matters on the scene..." He began inching away from her.

"No, no," the woman said quickly. She took a step toward him, closing the gap between herself and the pheromone factory standing next to her. "Ask your questions," she said.

Melissa bit her lip to keep from smiling. Detective Perth had her own set of distinct smells – good perfume, wool fibers – and she smelled *smart*. But apparently brains didn't matter when you were up against Garrett Lemke.

"First of all," said Melissa. "What time was Carlisle killed?"

The detective responded without hesitation. "We won't know for sure until we get the report back from the medical examiner," she said, her eyes still locked on Garrett. "But the best guess right now is around three this morning."

"And how was he killed?"

"Blunt trauma to the head."

Lea made a coughing sound. Melissa glanced behind her, and Lea shook her head slowly.

"I don't think so," Melissa said, turning back to the woman.

There was a flash of annoyance in the detective's eyes, but Garrett swooped in like a well-trained butler preventing a spill. "We're doing a study," he said smoothly. "For a class. I *promise* this isn't going to show up in the papers. I would never do that, Detective Perth. Not to *you*." He smiled warmly.

"His face was ripped off," the detective purred, as if she were delivering a come-on line. Garrett managed to hold his smile steady.

"Who are your suspects so far?" Melissa asked.

"Everyone. Disgruntled students, competing professors. He wasn't a popular man."

"And what – "

Lea made her coughing sound again. Melissa turned around, and Lea mouthed a word silently: *more*.

Melissa turned back. "Are there any *specific* suspects you're planning to investigate?"

The woman paused. She looked up at Garrett, then back at Melissa. She seemed torn. The question had touched something sensitive, and Detective Perth had reached some sort of balance point.

Jason gave Garrett a nudge. *Time to pour it on, champ.*

Garrett dropped his head briefly. He looked like someone going into meditation. Then he raised his eyes and stared at the woman in front of him. He stared at her with longing. With *heat*. As if she were the last woman on earth.

Melissa took a quick step backward, looking slightly unsteady on her feet. "God," she said. "Jason, could you – " She gave him a pointed look, and he moved quickly to the space where she had been standing.

"You were saying about the suspects?" Jason prompted the detective.

"Yes," she said softly, her hesitation gone. She was now gazing at Garrett as if he were Adonis himself. "Here's the list so far: Chris Hershel, a sophomore who failed Carlisle's psych class last year. Martha Lynch, a junior who's rumored to have had a brief relationship with Carlisle. And Jeff Gooding, whose tenure has apparently been derailed several times by Carlisle's influence in the psych department."

Jason nodded. "Got it." He glanced behind him. Melissa seemed okay, but she was still keeping her distance. "Anything else?" he asked.

"Clues," Melissa said.

Jason returned his attention to the woman. "Is there evidence on the scene? Any fingerprints, stuff like that?"

The detective shook her head dreamily. "Not a thing. Looks like the room was tossed, but we have no way of knowing whether that's just a smokescreen. Any fingerprints we find will probably belong to people who would have been in Carlisle's office anyway."

Jason frowned and looked back at Lea for confirmation.

No evidence?

Lea shrugged.

Jason cleared his throat. "But if you *did* find a new set of prints, someone new…"

"It would kick off all kinds of alarms," the woman said. "But trust me, that's not likely to happen. People watch too many crime shows on television. Fingerprints don't just turn up like little Easter eggs. They get smudged, stepped on, messed up. Carlisle's office is a wreck. We'll be lucky to get three clean prints out of that place, and all of them will probably be the janitor's."

Jason looked behind him, and Melissa made a flicking motion with her hand.

That's enough. Let the lady go.

Jason gave Garrett another poke. "Thanks so much for your help, Detective Perth. Good luck with the rest of your investigation."

The woman smiled and nodded without even glancing at him. Garrett began walking away, leading her back to the blue crowd-barriers. Several uniformed and plain-clothes cops were waiting there, giving Garrett strange looks.

With Garrett now farther away, Melissa took a deep breath of relief. Her stomach finally began settling down. Almost without being aware of it, she found herself staring after Garrett.

I don't care if it's the smell, she thought. *He's nice to look at.*

It took a few minutes for Garrett to extricate himself from the group of policemen. A number of them – mostly the women – seemed eager to chat. The head detective, in particular, looked very disappointed that he was leaving. By the time he came back, Melissa discovered he was bearable once again.

Garrett shook his head in disappointment. "It sounds like they don't have much to work with."

"That's not exactly true," said Jason. "Time of death, three viable suspects and plausible motives, including retribution for academic injustice, professional competition – "

"Okay, Big-brain," Garrett said quickly, cutting him off. "Enough with the memory demonstration."

Jason grinned. He looked very pleased with himself.

"I don't think it's so hopeless," said Melissa.

"They couldn't arrest anyone even if they wanted to," said Garrett. "There's no murder weapon. No prints."

"We don't need those things," Melissa said.

"We?" Garrett laughed. "*We* can't arrest anyone at all, evidence or not. I think I left my badge in my other pair of jeans. Anyway, that detective didn't seem too optimistic about their chances."

Melissa shrugged. "Who cares about arrests? I'm not interested in taking over the legal system. We just need to find that antenna, remember? And based on this first test-run, I'd say we have the potential to be pretty effective in our own investigation." She turned to Jason. "You got it all, right? You won't forget?"

Jason shook his head and grinned. "Not likely."

"And we know the detective didn't mislead us, or leave anything out." She glanced at Lea.

"Correct."

"I think we're ready. You can keep up the charm, right Mr. Love?"

Garrett sighed and rubbed his temple. "Sure. If my head doesn't crack open first."

Melissa looked at him with concern. "The headaches are getting bad?"

"Nothing compared to a few days ago. But I'll be useless before too long." He made a face, and Lea saw it all in his expression. "If I lose my focus," he added, "I'm going to lose it all the way. I made a fool of myself a few days ago. Little run-in with the swim team. Not pretty."

Melissa nodded. "So let's get going." She turned to Jason. "Who's first on the list?"

The hockey player's eyes moved briefly, as if he were reading. "Hershel, Chris. Failed Carlisle's psych class last year."

Melissa smiled. "Oh, yes. The 'bitter student' angle. Let's go have a talk with Mr. Hershel." The four of them headed back toward the main campus, with Melissa leading the way.

Grim Research

1

The reporter covering the story had all his facts together, and he was ready to write. The only problem was the overflow factor: too much blood, too many severed limbs. And the nail gun, which was such a tangible, almost obscene detail, and what about –

He couldn't decide where to begin.

The *Boston Globe* seldom covered events in Concord, NH, but this one was a no-brainer. His editor had signed on after a five-second pitch.

"Go," the editor said, pointing at the door. "Get it. Move."

The reporter moved. The last story he had covered in New Hampshire had been a gopher assignment – just a blurb about an orderly who got roughed up by a mental patient – but that had been over a year ago. He hadn't really known what he was doing.

Now he knew. He knew to ask about the little things. The details.

Two victims, names withheld. Brothers. Both in their mid-thirties, neither one married. Nothing much on the social scene, but he wouldn't be looking into that. Their jobs were more interesting than their nighttime habits, anyway. They were prototypers.

And what was a prototyper?

Someone who builds prototypes, naturally. Because when some nutty farmer or a college professor got an idea for a new machine, you needed someone to build the first model. He had looked up some of the stuff the victims had built, just in case his editor wanted extra background. A lot of it was pretty technical: they put together special electrical equipment, customized motors, and a few devices using large electromagnets. Their claim to fame was the *Segway*, that upright, overpriced scooter toy that had been big news for a while. Apparently they had built the original testing model. It was weird science stuff, mostly. Toys for nerds.

Anyway, the cops told him that one man – or woman – had probably killed them both. It looked like the murderer had just walked in during business hours and started cutting. No one had heard anything, because these guys worked in an old warehouse just off I-89. Land wasn't worth a dime. Plenty of room to work.

Plenty of room to have your arms and legs sawed off.

The reporter had searched for personal tidbits, but both victims were pretty boring. They kept to themselves, watched TV, paid their taxes, and stayed clear of the law. Not even a DUI, which was remarkable. Getting pulled over for drunk driving in New Hampshire was almost a rite of passage in the state, but these brothers were clean. Boring clean.

Their family was no better. You had the grieving father and the tearful younger sister, but nothing to make you really care. No one with cancer. No wives or children left behind, sobbing inconsolably. The human-interest angle was a dud.

The real story was the murder itself. The way they had died was terrific.

And horrible, the reporter thought quickly, chastising himself. *Horrible and bad. Tragic.*

But no. For the purposes of the story, it *was* terrific. He couldn't wait to see his by-line on this one.

The first guy had been found sprawled out on the warehouse floor, blood pooled around his head. There were thirty nails embedded in his skull. Fifteen per ear. The reporter shook his head in disbelief every time he thought of it. *Thirty* nails, not twenty-nine. Such precision.

Apparently the nails weren't the cause of death, however. His source at the precinct had told him that. It didn't make any sense, and the reporter said so.

"It was the knock on the head," said the source. "That's what killed him."

But how could that be right?

The 2-inch-long roofing nails had been driven deep – *all* the way in – so that the flat heads were flush with the victim's skull. Close-up photographs showed a neat cluster of dark gray circles completely obscuring both of the man's ears, as if he had been trying to put on a pair of steel earmuffs.

Or trying to prevent himself from hearing anything ever again.

"Yeah, but the doctor said they barely caused any bleeding," the precinct source explained over the phone. "Plugged him right up."

"You're trying to tell me they didn't hurt him?"

"Well, doc says they would have destroyed the guy's balance, but that's it."

Balance? Who gives a fuck? "I've been drunk before…" the reporter began.

"No," said the source. "Not like that, not just wobbly. We're talking *no* balance. Doc said this guy couldn't have told you which way was up. His vestibular something-or-other was completely destroyed."

"Okay, but the nails eventually – "

"Yeah, they *would* have killed him. Thirty roofers in your skull won't help a man. But they didn't do the job. The fall took care of that. He fell *hard.* Someone must have pushed him, the doc said. Cracked his head wide open on that concrete floor. Bled to death. Like I told you, the knock on the head."

Thirty roofers won't help a man, the reporter thought, jotting down the phrase. He wondered if he could work that into the story somehow.

The second victim had not been shot with nails, and the cause of death in his case was much easier to determine: his limbs had been cut off. All four of them. They had been cut off *high*, tight with the body. The police found what looked like a giant pair of tree-pruning sheers next to his corpse, and there were fingerprints all over the handles.

Good fingerprints.

The reporter managed to contact one of the medical examiners, who told him that the man's arms were probably the first to go, based on the higher "blood exit volume," whatever that meant. The murderer had taken them off at the shoulder, leaving only the ragged ends of cartilage and tendons. "Like he was ripping out a lobster's claw for dinner," said the examiner, who sounded a little bit loopy over the phone. "With a big set of those nut-cracker-looking things, you know? Same principal."

The victim's legs had been removed the same way, just below the pelvis. With this done, the man had been reduced to nothing but a torso. A torso that had done a lot of screaming, the reporter guessed. The man's limbs were found lined up in front of him, just a few inches away from his immobilized head.

"What for?" the reporter asked. "Any ideas?"

"Who knows?" said the precinct source, who was beginning to sound annoyed. "Murderer might have been putting them on display for the guy. To taunt him or something. Doc over here said the victim might have been conscious. He'd have died pretty quick, but not before he saw his own stuff laid out in front of him. Like he was shopping for some new parts, you know? At the arm-and-leg trade show."

"Nice. Can I quote you?"

"Suit yourself. Just don't use my name."

"Got it."

He hung up the phone and smiled. It was such a great story. Now, if he could just figure out where to start writing.

Something about the roofer nails. Or maybe the arm-and-leg trade show. He liked the sound of that.

2

Officer Jim Watts was a new Dartmouth employee. He had moved to New Hampshire just last year, all the way up from New York City. It was a sort of retirement for him, though not in the working sense. He needed to get out of Manhattan, was all. He couldn't afford it.

Living up here in Hanover was a good thing, but getting information was difficult. He didn't have access codes to any of the police databases, nor could he request information from precincts. He did, however, have public access to the Dartmouth computer center in Kiewit Hall. There he could get the basic college administration files, and, of course, he could get on the internet.

The internet was much, much better than nothing.

The best thing about the web, in Officer Watts' opinion, was the association game. You typed a name into Google, and the links that came back gave you the beginnings of a network. A network, in this case, of people who were associated with the name you had entered.

For instance: the name Frederick Carlisle.

When Officer Watts put in that name, Google came back with dozens of hits on scholarly papers published under the professor's by-line. That much Watts had expected. More interesting, however, was the second name. The one right next to Carlisle's at the top of almost every paper.

The name was Dr. Nathan Kline.

So here was the missing partner the nurse had told him about. But where was Dr. Kline now?

Another Google search gave him the answer.

Kline's name came back with links to plenty of research papers of his own, but most of those were near the bottom. They were less "relevant" matches, at least in the opinion of the Google search algorithms. Translation: fewer people were looking at those links. The popular matches were at the top, and the very top link with Dr. Kline's name was part of a court case. Same with the number-two link. And number three, four, five, six... all for the same legal proceeding.

It was a hot case, evidently. And Kline had been the defendant.

"Convicted of manslaughter" was the summary description Watts found when he clicked on the document. Skimming over the details, it looked as though the case had concluded with an alternate sentencing protocol.

Kline hadn't gone to prison.

Instead, he had gone to the loony bin. And the center where they sent him was right here in New Hampshire. Watts licked his lips.

He looked up the number for the institution, and then stepped out of Kiewit with his cell phone. In less than a minute, he had the state ward's main operator on the line.

"New Hampshire Corrections."

"Yes," Watts said, unsure of how to begin. "I'm trying to locate a patient. Nathan Kline."

"Transfers, please hold."

"No," Watts said quickly. "I just want to know if – "

But she was already gone. Hold music began playing through the phone. In another minute, a new voice came on. Another woman's voice.

"Yes?"

"I think I may have been put through in error..." Watts began.

"Patient name?" the woman said briskly.

"Nathan Kline."

There was a brief silence. Then: "Kline, Nathan. Transferred fourteen months ago. Clancy Hall, Massachusetts."

"Wonderful. Is there a number for Clancy Hall?"

Another pause. "No."

"Do you think that you could – "

Watts heard a click. That was all the help he was getting from the people in Concord.

It took him only two more minutes on the computer to locate a number for Clancy Hall. He went back outside and made the call.

"Clancy, hello."

"I'm trying to locate a patient," Watts said for the third time in ten minutes.

"Name?"

"Nathan Kline."

There was a long, long silence on the line.

"Are you a family member, sir?"

"No, but I need to know whether – "

"We have spoken with every press organization already," said the man on the other end, sounding testy. "And Dr. Levoir has no more time for any of you people. In fact, he's away on vacation right now. The answer is *no comment.*"

Watts took a moment to collect his thoughts.

Press organizations?

"I'm not a reporter," he began.

"Sure," said the man, sounding utterly unconvinced. "And I suppose this has *nothing* to do with the events in Concord last week."

Not a minute ago, no, Watts thought. *But it does now.* "Yes, the events in Concord," he said slowly, "but I just need to know if – "

Another click. Watts stared at the receiver. That was the second time he had been hung up on in ten minutes. He went back inside and sat down at his computer. Something was happening – or had already happened – in Concord. Something with Carlisle's old partner, Dr. Nathan Kline. He ran another search, using the words 'Concord,' 'New Hampshire,' and 'Kline.' Then he thought for a moment. Something in the voice of the man at Clancy Hall… Watts started typing again. Next to the first three search terms, he added another word.

Murder.

He hit the 'enter' key. The Google results came back, and Watts' mouth hung open.

"*The arm and leg trade show…?*"

He stayed in Kiewit, pouring over the article in the *Boston Globe*, for a very long time.

3

"I appreciate the lift," Dr. Kline said, as the Cadillac began picking up speed on the highway. "I'll pay for your gas, how's that?"

"Sounds just right." Martin signaled and moved into the passing lane, leaving a lone truck in their wake. Before long they were cruising along at 80 MPH, and the big car wasn't having any difficulty maintaining its speed. Both men stared out the front windshield, thinking of the people they needed to see. Of the things they needed to do. They drove for a while in silence, and Kline found himself thinking of Alexandra again. It was a pleasant exercise. His daughter usually came to him only when he was dreaming, but sleep had not been easy lately. He wondered where she might be at that moment. Nowhere near New Hampshire, that much he knew. Joanne had moved away, taking Alexandra with her.

Far away, if he knew his wife at all.

"I miss her," he said suddenly, out loud.

The man behind the wheel glanced at him. "You say something?"

"I was thinking about my daughter."

"She die or something?" Martin didn't sound very sympathetic.

"No, nothing like that. She just moved away."

Martin was quiet for a moment. "You have any sons?"

Kline shook his head.

"I did. Passed on early, though. In the crib. Now *that's* a real letdown, you know?"

Kline looked at him. Paused before answering. "What do you – "

"Losing a girl is one thing," Martin went on, "but they're not good for much, are they?" He tightened his fingers around the wheel, and his knuckles showed white through the skin. "Goddamned daughters, you know?"

Kline did not answer. He decided to keep looking straight ahead.

Martin continued talking. He kept his voice low, but he didn't seem to care if Kline heard him or not. "No sense of duty," he whispered. "Take everything you got, try to tell you to get out of your own damned *house…*"

Dr. Kline stayed quiet. Over the last several days, he had methodically tortured and murdered three people with a car battery, a nail gun, and a pair of garden shears; only minutes ago, he had been fuming over the possibility that someone might have beaten him to the task of killing his former lab partner. And yet suddenly he felt uncomfortable. Unsafe. He began inching his body toward the right edge of the seat. When he had moved over as far as he could go, he concentrated on keeping his mouth shut and his body very still.

This guy might be crazy, Dr. Kline thought to himself.

Meltdown

1

"Wait a minute," Melissa said. "Where are we going? How are we supposed to find this guy?"

The other three stopped and looked at her. Then at one another. "I thought you…" Jason began.

Melissa shook her head. "What am I, the school directory? I expected Garrett to know who he was."

"Why me?"

"You're a senior. You're supposed to know everybody."

Garrett smiled. "Maybe if we were searching for a *girl*. But I don't know any Chris Hershel. We should look him up on the school's intranet. Find his dorm."

"Hold on," said Jason. His eyes were moving quickly again. "Not the dorms," he murmured, like someone talking to himself. "Phi-Delt. That's our best chance."

Lea frowned. "Phi-Delt?"

"Phi-*Delta*," Garrett said, and he turned to Jason. "How do you know the guy lives there?"

"Saw his picture on the wall inside."

"When?"

Jason shrugged. "Last year. Friday, April twenty-second. Party co-sponsored with Chi-Gam. They hired the Tin Chickens to handle the music. In the room off the entryway, there's a photo-montage of all the members. Hershel's picture is fourth from the right on the third row. The kid next to him is Dave Evans. The one on the other side is – "

"Okay, enough." Garrett put both hands up. "I believe you. Let's go."

"Where?" Lea asked.

"Frat row."

Jason watched Melissa as they walked. "What happened to you back there?"

Melissa looked up. "When I got queasy?"

"Right, with the detective. Was it because of Garrett?"

She nodded.

"His sex thing?"

"Yup. It was strong for a minute. I thought I was going to throw up again. Or maybe strip my clothes off in front of everyone."

Behind them, Garrett made a face. He seemed torn between pride and embarrassment. "Hello? I'm right here. Can everyone stop talking about me like I'm a human dildo, please?"

Jason frowned. "I still don't understand… Lea, you felt it, right? The Garrett-thing, I mean."

Lea looked uncomfortable, but she held her ground. "Definitely. It got more intense. Don't read anything into it – "

"No, I'm just curious. I thought it was supposed to work on men, too."

"It does," Melissa said. "Don't you remember the friendly cop? Garrett charmed him into letting him into the building."

"That's right," Garrett said, flashing them with a sarcastic grin. "I'm hot with everybody now. Girls, guys, keepers of the peace, mail carriers…"

"Fair enough," said Jason. "But why don't I feel it? I don't think Garrett could talk me into buying life insurance right now, let alone convince me to do special favors for him."

Garrett twisted his face into an expression of mock-hurt. "Oh, come on, honey," he cooed. "Don't you find me… desirable?" He batted his eyelashes a few times.

Jason ignored him and turned to Melissa. He shook his head. "Nothing."

Melissa sighed. "Jason, I told you before. It's okay. Feeling attracted to Garrett doesn't mean you're homosexual – "

"No, I'm serious. I don't feel a *thing*."

Melissa studied him. Then she glanced at Lea. "Well?"

"What?" Lea looked confused.

"Is he telling the truth or not?"

"Oh, sorry." She gave Jason a once-over, then nodded. "He's on the level."

Melissa frowned. "You're sure?"

Now it was Lea's turn to sigh. "Melissa, I know you've got the power-sniffer around here, but trust me on the true-false stuff. Jason's not hiding anything. If he were, I'd spot it immediately. He's reacting to Garrett pretty much the same way you'd react to a tree stump."

Jason pointed triumphantly at Lea. "There, see? Thank you."

Lea smiled and dropped her eyes.

Melissa shrugged. "Okay, so you're immune. You're an über-hetero. Who knows why? I can only tell you what Garrett smells like to me."

"Right," Jason said quickly. "But that's exactly the problem. There's something else going on here."

"What? You're not making any sense."

Jason took a couple of quick, sniffing breaths through his nose. Then he shook his head. "I can't smell anything anymore. Maybe Carlisle's funhouse antenna did more than we realize."

Garrett suddenly seemed interested. “More how?”

“I’m not sure…” Jason was speaking slowly now. Carefully, as if afraid of saying too much. “My vision is a little hazy, for one thing.”

Garrett looked disappointed. “That’s it? I’ve been wearing contact lenses since the fourth grade. Welcome to my world.”

Jason shook his head. “Not me. I’ve always had perfect eyesight. Until an hour ago, anyway. And that’s not the only thing. My ears feel a little clogged. Not to mention my skin, which is getting sort of numb all over. Like I’ve been given some sort of low-grade anesthetic.”

They stared at him silently.

“It’s pretty obvious what’s going on,” Jason said. “It’s not just my eyes. *All* of my senses are shutting down.”

2

No one spoke, and Jason seemed to be holding his breath. He was waiting for them to respond. To say anything at all.

Finally, Lea started nodding. "I knew something was bothering you," she said. "But I didn't want to ask."

Garrett frowned at Jason. "You're going *blind*?"

"That's not what I said. Things are fuzzy at a distance, that's all. But it's getting worse. Same goes for my hearing. It used to be perfect, but now it's as if I'm in a tunnel. And what about the numbness everywhere? *And* the difficulty smelling? I don't think it's a coincidence."

Melissa was already shaking her head. "Nothing is a coincidence."

"Is it only me?" Jason sounded very worried now. "Are you guys… " His voice trailed off.

Lea removed her glasses and began wiping them nervously. "I'm having some… difficulties," she said quietly. "But not the same kind. I can, um… I can *see* okay." She put her glasses back on and glanced furtively at Melissa and Garrett. "I can tell you guys are in… trouble too, but I guess we all need to make our own – " She paused and looked at the sky. She seemed to be searching for her words." – our own decisions about what… about what we're ready to talk about."

Melissa studied the ground at her feet. Garrett made a huffing sound, as if he were becoming impatient with the whole conversation.

"I'm *dandy*," Garrett said. "Can't we just find the antenna and fix all this stuff?"

"Right," Melissa agreed quickly. She seemed very uncomfortable. "We can't waste any more time. Where's that fraternity?"

The Phi-Delta house was not difficult to find. Frat row, smack in the center. The building had "ΦΔ" painted above the door in black, foot-high letters. There was a frayed brown couch out on the porch, and a pair of fake columns on either side of the entrance. The whole building looked as if it could use a fresh coat of paint. Ten yards from the door, Melissa paused. "Great place to live," she said, wrinkling her nose. She could already catch the stench of old beer and urine coming from inside. "The cigarette butts on the lawn are an especially nice touch."

"Depends on what you're hoping for in a residence," Garrett said with a smile.

Melissa cupped a hand over her face, and she began backing away. When she had retreated to a safe distance, she sat down on the grass. "I'm not going to be able to go in there."

Lea nodded. "I can smell it too," she said sympathetically. "And I don't even have a super… um, a super nose. Why don't you just wait… just wait out here for us?"

"I've got a better idea," Garrett said. "Melissa and I will go talk to Muffy, and you two can handle this kid in Phi-Delt." He glanced at Melissa. "The sorority will smell a lot better, I promise. And then we can all meet back here in fifteen minutes. Compare notes. How's that sound?"

Melissa's eyebrow shot up. "I'm sorry, did you just refer to our next suspect as 'Muffy'?"

Garrett reddened. "I meant to say Martha."

"Of course you did." Melissa was smiling now. "I don't suppose you happen to know where Muffy lives?"

"KDE."

"Yes, KDE. Wonderful." She smiled brightly at Garrett, as if he were a naughty child. "Been there a few times, have you?"

"Christ. Let's just get going."

"Right behind you, Muffin."

"Shut up."

Melissa got to her feet slowly. She moved haltingly, as if she couldn't quite get her balance. Lea opened her mouth to say something, but then seemed to think better of it.

Garrett turned around to watch Melissa catch up. "You okay?"

"I'm fine," Melissa said. "I'm just starting to have some – " She stopped. "We shouldn't waste any time, that's all."

Lea's face was twisted with anxiety. "Wait, can't we all… can't we wait a second?"

They looked at her, but she seemed unsure of what to say next. "Can't you guys just… I mean, who are we… who are we trying to fool, here?" She looked at them, pleading with her eyes. But Garrett and Melissa both stared at the ground. There would be no discussion about these things. Not yet.

Melissa caught up to Garrett, and they headed down frat row together. Jason watched them go. When they were far enough away, he turned to Lea. "They don't seem to like each other very much. You think they'll avoid getting in a fight before they get back?"

Despite her own worries, Lea smiled. She would keep this particular secret to herself. "I think they'll be fine."

Jason shrugged. "Then let's go interrogate this kid."

They walked into Phi-Delta.

3

Once inside, it took them a moment to adjust to the dark. Tapestries hung over the windows in the common room, creating a permanent twilight. A huge television dominated the far wall, surrounded by three weather-beaten couches that resembled the one on the porch outside. ESPN's *SportsCenter* blared on the television, and there were several students stretched on the couches. Jason squinted as he tried to make out their faces. "It's too dark in here," he said, "but I think that's him." He pointed.

Lea nodded. "How do you want… do you want to… to handle this?"

Jason looked back at her. He seemed surprised. Without Melissa there, the two of them were briefly lost.

"I'll start," Jason whispered finally. "You keep him honest."

She nodded.

"What are you… going to ask?" Lea said.

Jason looked at her. There was a little gleam of mischief in his eyes. "The most obvious things."

"Are you Chris Hershel?"

The boy on the couch looked up with a tired stare. He barely moved. "Sure."

"Did you kill Professor Carlisle?"

"*Jason*!" Lea hissed.

Jason turned to her. "What? Just watch him and tell me. That's your trick, right? Did he do it or not?"

For a moment Lea looked as though she might start yelling at him, but then her face cleared. "No, you're… you're right." She glanced at Hershel, who was still stretched out on the couch. Then she nodded.

"He's clean."

"Okay then," Jason said dismissively. "That was easy. Let's get out of here."

Hershel sat up. He shook himself, as if coming out of a stupor. "Huh? What do you guys want?"

"Nothing," Jason said. "We already got it."

"Did you just accuse me of killing Carlisle?"

"No," Lea said quickly. "My friend was… was only asking if – "

"Because I *would* have, you know." Hershel spat on the floor. "Total dick of a prof. Failed me for turning in a paper a few days late."

Lea stared at him for a beat, and then she smiled. "A few days?"

Hershel scowled. "Whatever. So maybe it was a few weeks. He was a dick, that's the point. I wish I *had* killed him."

Lea marveled at the boy's false bravado. Was this cool somehow, to talk as if you should be a suspect in a murder case?

"He's really dead?" Chris asked.

Jason nodded. "Yes, he's *really* dead." They turned to go. "Thanks for your help."

4

The Kappa-Delta-Epsilon yard was neater than the one in front of Phi-Delta. There were no stray bottles or cigarette butts. The entrance was better maintained, too. It looked as though the building had been renovated within the last couple of years.

"Much better," Melissa said. "This I can handle." She turned to Garrett. "So, Martha. No, wait, I'm sorry – *Muffy*. What's she look like?"

Garrett sighed and rubbed his temple absently. His head had started to throb again. "Exactly what you think she looks like."

Melissa put a confused expression on her face. "What *ever* do you mean?"

"Thin and blond and perky and all that stuff. Give me a break, will you?"

"No. I don't think I will."

The common room inside the sorority was aggressively feminine. Every couch had been upholstered in Laura Ashley patterns, and the seats were arranged into a rough circle. The windows were open wide, letting the sheer curtains billow and puff in the autumn afternoon air. Melissa appreciated the breeze. There was no beer or urine smell to contend with here, and the girls in this sorority seemed to know what a shower was for.

They even use soap, she thought with relief. She could almost convince herself that she didn't feel dizzy anymore.

A small group of girls sat chatting on the couches, their legs folded in studied poses of leisure. Several of them were wearing identical, white-and-flower-print pajamas. None of them looked as though they had gone to class that day – or even outside – though it was now four in the afternoon. One of them turned around as the two visitors walked through the front door. "Hey, there's no boys allowed now," she said.

"Please, Heidi," said another. "Van's still upstairs, and you snuck Kevin in here two nights ago."

The girl opened her mouth to retort, then closed it again.

"Anyway," said the second girl, "that's just Garrett. He's always here."

Melissa smiled ruefully, and Garrett made several coughing noises into his fist. "My head hurts," he grumbled.

At the sound of Garrett's voice, a third girl turned around. She was smaller than the others, and her hair was a shade blonder. A shade less natural, perhaps. "Garrett? Hey, sweetie!" Her voice was light and full of energy.

Garrett smiled uncertainly. "Hey, Muffy."

The girl sprang up and vaulted over the couch like a gymnast. Melissa stepped back.

"You look great, Gar," said Muffy. She took a deep breath, then stepped closer to Garrett. "I mean, *great*." The top of her head reached only to the middle of his chest, and she gazed up at him with heavily made-up eyes.

Still in her pajamas, thought Melissa. *And yet that eye-shadow smells fresh from this morning. Does she put it on before she gets dressed?*

"Thanks," Garrett said slowly. He tried to put some space between them, but Muffy was too quick. She stayed with him.

"Hey, *Gar*?" Melissa whispered, barely keeping the sarcasm out of her voice. "You want me to handle this?"

"No, I got it." Garrett took a breath and tried to give Muffy a no-nonsense look. "I need to ask you…" he began, then winced and pressed a knuckle to his forehead.

"Yeah?" said Muffy softly. She put a hand on his arm.

"Um…"

"…if you were sleeping with Professor Carlisle," Melissa finished loudly.

Muffy kept her eyes on Garrett. She didn't seem concerned by the girl standing next to him. "Definitely," she said, leaning her head onto Garrett's chest. "We hit it off for a while. But that was last year, second semester." She closed her eyes and smiled, as if she had never been so happy. "What an asshole he was."

"Did you… kill him?" Garrett managed to ask, gritting his teeth through successive waves of pain.

"No, baby," Muffy whispered. "Would have been happy to, though."

Melissa shrugged, feeling satisfied. Lea wasn't there to pick out people's lies for them, but this girl was no criminal mastermind.

"Why?" Muffy said, glancing up suddenly. The subject of murder seemed to have broken the Garrett spell for a moment. "Is he dead?"

Garrett took the opportunity to back up a few paces. He shook his head gingerly, and blinked his eyes like someone walking into a too-bright room. His current headache was sending him to brand new levels of distraction. "Yeah," he said. "Someone killed him last night."

A loud voice boomed from the top of the stairs. "Someone killed *who*?" They all turned to look, and an athletic, buzz-haired boy came walking down. Muffy sprang back from Garrett as if his skin were hot to the touch, and almost fell over the flowered couch behind her.

"Hey, Van!" she chirped, trying to maintain her balance. The boy walked over and planted a kiss on Muffy's cheek. "What's up, sex-pot?" He seemed oblivious to her near-infidelity, and he grinned at Garrett and Melissa. "Hey, it's the late-comers."

They looked back at him blankly.

"You guys were late to psych class two days ago, right?" Van nodded his head, answering his own question. "Man, Carlisle was all *over* you. He got you to participate in some experiment or something, right? How'd it go?"

Garrett and Melissa exchanged glances. "We'll let you know,"

Melissa said.

Van shrugged. "Who'd you say got whacked?"

"Professor Carlisle."

Van's eyes went wide with shock. And maybe a little bit of glee. "Wow, seriously? No class for a few days, I guess. They know who did it?"

"That's what we're trying to find out."

"It was probably Gooding." Van nodded wisely, as if this declaration were the result of hours of careful thought.

"Jeff Gooding?" Melissa looked at Garrett, whose eyes were now shut tight against the pressure building inside his skull. "He's on the suspect list," she said, turning back to Van. "What makes you think he did it?"

Van seemed pleased that his suggestion was being taken seriously. "Are you joking? Gooding hated that dude. I was in Cog-Sci with him last year, and half the time he just ranted about what a jerk Carlisle was. About how all his research was so *der*-something."

"Derivative?" Melissa suggested.

Van pointed at her, impressed. "Right, what you said. Gooding's line was that Carlisle couldn't come up with a new idea to save his life."

Muffy was holding onto Van's arm as he spoke. At the same time, she was staring hungrily at Garrett. As if he were a favorite food that she had been craving.

"We should go," Melissa said uneasily, glancing at Garrett with concern. Both of his hands were on his head now, and Melissa could tell that he was lost inside his pain. "Good to meet you, Muffy."

Muffy ignored the pleasantry. "See you, Gar." There was a distinct note of longing in her voice.

Melissa led Garrett out of the sorority by one hand. His eyes were still closed, and he was starting to talk to himself. "Just need another… one more quick shot of the buzz, loosen everything up make it STOP why can't you just help me?"

He was getting worse, and fast. Melissa walked him off the path, between two of the frat houses, to a patch of grass that was out of the way. They were hidden on both sides from wind and people. She thought the quiet might help keep him calm until his headache subsided. Her mother had never suffered migraines – only a debilitating sadness – and she was unsure of what to do.

Maybe he'll feel better lying down.

Her own head was starting to spin in a loopy, rolling way that made the ground seem to go slanting off at irregular angles; she felt like lying down herself. With a few awkward lurches, she helped him ease back onto the grass.

This seemed to fix him for a moment. He paused in his ranting. But then his head began moving from side to side, as though he were in the middle of a nightmare.

"Just help me just help me just HELP ME," he said, over and over again.

Melissa was genuinely alarmed now, and she leaned over him. "I'm trying," she said. "Open your eyes and look at me. Focus. Think about something else."

At first she thought he couldn't hear her. But then his head stopped its thrashing, and he did open his eyes. They were frantic, bloodshot eyes. Full of pain. Then, all at once, they cleared. And Garrett took a long, shuddery breath. "Oh you're so beautiful," he said.

Melissa felt a warmth go moving through her. Down and around and in her. She was aware, somewhere in the back of her mind, that Garrett's smell was mostly responsible for this reaction. But she realized she didn't care. The smell, after all, wasn't the *only* reason. It was quick work to slip out of her jeans, and then she felt herself melting. She leaned forward and put her face in the hollow of his neck, and let her hips move as they wanted to.

She thought she could have stayed there, that way, forever.

Garrett sat up, looking dazed. Melissa was already beside him, clothing back in place, hair slightly mussed.

"I feel much better," Garrett said.

I don't, she didn't say. *My head's scrambled, the ground is still spinning, and none of my limbs seem to be working properly. And you still smell fantastic, which isn't helping.*

Instead what she said was: "Good. So get up. And then help *me* up. They'll be waiting for us."

5

Melissa needn't have worried. When she and Garrett returned to Phi-Delta, Jason and Lea didn't look impatient at all. In fact, they seemed mildly put out by the interruption. Jason's cheeks were shining, as if he'd just gone for a run. Lea did her best to act normal. To pretend she didn't want to stand here talking to this boy *forever*.

Except, of course, that talking for Lea – just *talking* – seemed to be getting harder every minute. She turned to them. "Did you two… find out any…" Her voice faded away as she read the information hidden in Melissa's eyes. Melissa tried to look elsewhere, but it didn't make any difference.

"Oh," said Lea quietly.

Garrett picked up the slack. "We need to visit that teacher," he said hastily. "Jeff Gooding."

"That's right," Melissa added quickly. "Unless you two turned up anything, he's our best bet. Let's go see him immediately. I'm actually getting sort of desperate."

"We're *all* going… downhill," Lea said. She took a deep breath. "I can see it in… see it in each of you."

"Gooding is the one," said Melissa, trying to sound confident. "He'll know where the antenna is. Everyone just hold on for a little longer…" As she spoke, she began leaning slightly to the right. It looked to the rest of them as if she were being buffeted by wind. Lea was the first to see what was happening, and she moved quickly.

"Damn," Jason said, reacting when he saw Lea lunge. He got his arms under Melissa and helped her sit down slowly. "What happened?"

"It's nothing," Melissa said. "I'm just a little dizzy."

Garrett maintained his distance. "Is it me again?" He looked distressed. "My smell, or whatever? I wasn't even thinking about women that time."

"No, its nothing."

Lea looked torn. She seemed to be making a decision. "I can't – " She stopped. "I can't remember words," she blurted out.

They all stared at her. Jason looked thunderstruck.

"What?"

Lea put a hand to her head. "The… *big* words, I mean." She was clearly struggling. "I have to… have to think harder than before. To talk. To say… things." She sighed heavily, as if the admission had tired her out. "Also, I'm not getting… not getting some of the things you guys say. It's as if you're… going in and out of a… of another language."

They watched her silently, absorbing this new information. Melissa was still on the ground. She looked up at Lea with gratitude.

That was brave. Thanks for taking the attention off me.

Lea glanced at her and smiled. *No problem.*

Melissa spoke up. "My balance is starting to go, if you guys couldn't tell already." She sounded embarrassed. "I thought it was just because of all the nausea at first, but things are really starting to spin."

"Can you walk?" Garrett asked.

Melissa nodded slowly. She looked run-down. "I think so. My arms and legs feel as if they're going to sleep, but whatever. I'll need to put my hand on someone, that's all. Just in case."

"I'm… I'm up for it," Lea said.

"Speaking of that," said Jason, "I could use a guide too. My eyesight is getting really bad. I'm going to start running into things if I'm not careful."

Garrett sighed. "We're turning into quite a crew. Anyone need to be carried? I could go look for a hand-truck."

"Cut it out," Jason said. "Get over here and help. Lea shouldn't have to lead this train all by herself."

"Take it easy, Helen Keller." Garrett walked over to Jason and studied him critically. "You can still see me?"

"Yeah, barely. But it's – "

"Good. You're fine. Just stay on my left shoulder." He glanced at Lea and Melissa. "You guys set?"

Melissa nodded. "Good for now."

"Everyone try to use… to use small words," Lea added.

Garrett nodded. "Jeff Gooding, here we come."

"He'd better have some answers," Melissa said.

"He will." Garrett sounded calm. His head had stopped bothering him for the time being, and he flashed Melissa a smile. If Jason had been able to see better, he might have found the gesture puzzling. "We'll *take* our answers from him if we need to," Garrett added.

"You're right," said Melissa. She breathed in his confidence. "We will."

Fathers

1

With a different riding companion, Dr. Kline decided he might have enjoyed the trip to Dartmouth. The drive up Interstate 89 to Hanover, New Hampshire, was a scenic one: evergreens and oak trees crowded at the edges of the road for most of the way, with the leaves and pine needles battling for space. The shoulder of the road was narrow in places, overgrown and wild, as if to show travelers that nature could not be held back forever. Farther north, great valleys appeared without warning from around the corners, and the space stretched out, silent and immense. The horizon lost itself in miles of hills and haze.

Martin Hartman did not notice the natural beauty unfolding around him. His foot was heavy on the gas, and he was still muttering to himself about the endless problems that daughters were likely to cause their fathers. "They're all rude," he grumbled. "Rude, strong-willed, smart-aleck pests."

He didn't wait for a response from Kline. In fact, none of his comments seemed to invite conversation at all. With each muttered curse, his foot came down harder on the accelerator. The big Cadillac, still comfortably within its operating range, was soon hurtling across the New Hampshire countryside at better than 90 MPH. They charged past an old blue pickup truck as if it were standing still.

Dr. Kline kept silent and motionless in the passenger seat. His ability to understand language had deserted him forty-five minutes ago, and he was glad that Martin was not looking for conversation. Not that he would have started chatting anyway. He could still tell, after all, that the sounds coming out of Martin's mouth were decidedly unhappy sounds, and the charged atmosphere in the car was making him increasingly nervous. Almost as nervous as how damned fast they were going. It wasn't a matter of fear, necessarily; Dr. Kline was not afraid to die. He suspected that he would be meeting his end in a matter of days, if not sooner. However, he did not want to die right *now*. Not here. Not in a lumbering, sky-blue 1992 Cadillac, tearing along an empty stretch of New Hampshire Interstate 89. He still had errands to run. For example, there was the matter of finding out who was responsible for Carlisle's death. And then having a talk with that person.

A very serious talk.

Nearly an hour after the aphasic period had begun, Kline detected a sense of returning clarity. Words, like clouds at first, crept into his mind. The temporal lobe deficit was passing. Thirty seconds later, as the phrase "driving too fast" occurred to him in all of its sharp, bright-edged detail, he heard the sound of… what were those things called?

Sirens.

The word triggered a flood of relief, and Kline felt as though he had been rescued. They would have to slow down now. In fact, they would be pulling over shortly. And then they would actually come to a complete stop. Wonderful. His relief was short-lived, however. It only took him a few more seconds to remember that the police would probably be far more interested in *him* than in Martin. Speeding tickets were one thing, but murder was quite another.

He had been very busy, after all.

Martin cursed under his breath. He brought the Cadillac to a gradual stop at the shoulder and hung his head over the steering wheel. "Mother *fucker*." A quick glance at Kline, and then a rueful smile. "Typical, right?"

Kline nodded silently. He could see the police car sitting behind them, its lights flashing. The officer was taking his time, sitting in the car and writing something on his little pad.

Probably checking the license plate, Kline thought.

After a minute, the cop climbed out of the cruiser and made his way slowly toward the Cadillac. Kline eyed his NorthFace pack in the backseat. He considered making a lunge for the automatic nailer inside, but then decided against it. The cop would surely be carrying a real gun, and he probably wouldn't appreciate having a carpenter's appliance pointed at him.

Kline thought quickly.

Could I hold Martin hostage? Maybe if he threatened to kill Martin with the Hilti, the cop would back off.

No. A quick look at Martin's bulging arms convinced him that this plan would fail horribly. He could imagine Martin elbowing him swiftly in the chin, then shoving him to the side and beating him senseless, all while shouting at him about what a bitch his daughter was.

There was no good plan here. The cop had already arrived at the driver's-side door, and it was too late for heroics.

This could be messy, Kline thought.

The cop took his time coming up to the Cadillac's driver-side door. He was very large.

But he's also sort of pleasant-looking, Kline thought. *As if he's just here to let us know that one of the tires on the Caddie is running a little low.*

When the cop leaned over to peer inside the window, his face did seem kind. "Afternoon," he said. "License and registration, please."

Martin pointed to the glove compartment, and Kline fished the documents out.

The cop looked the papers over carefully. Then he gave both Martin and Kline a good stare-down. Kline felt his skin start to crawl. "Had you fellows at ninety-four," said the officer. His tone was still easy. Conversational. "Ninety-four in a sixty-five. *Way* too fast. Going to be a very expensive ticket, I'm afraid."

Martin said nothing. He stared straight ahead, as if he couldn't hear the policeman talking.

The cop waited for a moment, perhaps expecting an argument or excuse. When none came, he resumed his little speech. "No call for that kind of speed around here," he said. "None at all. You boys sit tight, and I'll be back in a few."

He walked away.

Dr. Kline sat and debated. With the edges of his aphasia still lingering, some of the cop's words had sounded foreign. The flipside, of course, was that he had been able to read the truth in the man's face. And the lies, as well.

It was easy. It was like reading a newspaper.

That was the thing with aphasia: when the actual meaning of words faded, you couldn't be deceived by them anymore. Only the non-verbal cues remained. Tone, body language, and facial expression took on brand new significance. They were dead giveaways.

The cop had recognized him from somewhere, that much was clear. Probably a wanted poster or an APB description. Kline supposed that being able to spot a super-tall, super-skinny man was no big trick.

He took a long breath. The decision had been made for him, really. It was time to act. "Cop's lying," he announced suddenly.

Martin turned toward him. "What?"

"He isn't writing up a ticket back there. He's calling for backup."

"No he is *not*."

"Wait and find out." Kline leaned back in his seat. "Makes no difference to me. I'm just a hiker. But it looks like you're in some kind of trouble."

Martin scowled. It was an expression his daughter would have recognized. "There's no way," he muttered. "They could never have put it all together that fast."

Kline had to struggle to contain his smile. Paranoia was such an easy emotion to evoke. He had no idea what Martin might have done, but he could see the guilt on his face. In fact, he had seen it hours ago, as he was first climbing into the car. Maybe the man had knocked off a convenience store, or maybe he had too many parking tickets. It didn't matter. An unclean conscience was a powerful thing. "Just watch him for a while," Kline said, adding fuel to the fire. "He's not even bothering with the ticket. He's going straight for the radio."

Martin turned to look, and Kline knew he had won. Because the cop *was* talking on the radio. It made the whole story seem more plausible. The only inconsistency being, of course, that the man was surely not calling for backup on account of Martin.

It was all for the sake of Dr. Nathan Kline.

"Fuck," Martin growled. "I don't need this right now. I really don't."

"What are you going to do?" Kline tried to make himself sound scared. It was important, he knew, to make Martin feel as though he was the one taking the initiative. The technique, a sort of passive guidance, was something he had learned as a college professor years ago.

"I'm taking care of it," Martin said curtly. "Just sit still and don't say anything."

"You're the boss," Kline said meekly.

Martin stuck his head out the car window. "Officer!" he yelled. "Officer, we've got a problem over here!"

The cop looked in their direction. He seemed annoyed at the interruption. "I'll have your ticket in a few minutes," he yelled back to them. He made no move to get out of the cruiser.

"No," Martin shouted. "This is a *serious* problem. I can come and show you, if you want…"

That did it. "Stay right there," the officer said. He climbed out of his car and came walking toward the Cadillac.

The cop came up alongside Martin's window. "What is it?"

"My friend and I were talking," Martin said, "and we're lost. Can you help us out?"

The cop's expression switched from caution to relief. "That's it? Let me finish with these tickets first – "

"We've got the map right here," Martin said, reaching into the pocket on the driver's side door. "Let me show you."

The policeman saw the danger, and he tried to go for his gun. But Martin had timed his move very carefully. He watched for that split second of relaxation after his insipid "we're lost" announcement, and the cop's defenses didn't return to normal quite fast enough.

Just like that, Martin was holding a gun under the cop's chin.

Kline raised his eyebrows.

This guy might be crazy, he thought. *But he's also very fast.*

Martin climbed slowly out of the Cadillac, being careful to keep the muzzle of his Magnum pressed firmly into the soft flesh underneath the cop's jaw. He unsnapped the holster on the officer's hip and threw the service revolver onto the pavement.

"Hop in," Martin said. "Make a move and I'll blow you away."

Kline smiled. He couldn't have said it better himself.

"Now, then," Martin said, when they were all back in the car. "Let's talk about this." He flicked the gun barrel at the cop, who was sitting with his hands on his head.

"What?"

"Don't 'what' me!" Martin barked. "Tell me how much you know."

"About…?" The cop sounded genuinely perplexed. "I'll need some help. How much do I know about what?"

"About me, you idiot. Who tipped you guys off? The insurance agent? Or was it that real estate bitch? She called an arson inspector, I suppose. That house was a piece of shit, anyway. It's not as if anyone was going to buy it. I did everyone a favor by burning it down." Martin shook his head. "How many units are after me?"

The cop gave Martin an exasperated look. "Nobody's after you," he said, sounding more frustrated than scared. He nodded at Dr. Kline.

"It's *him*."

2

They were back on their way. Martin wasn't driving anymore, busy as he was with pointing a gun at the cop. He kept asking for more speed, but Dr. Kline was determined to hold them under eighty. As before, he simply wasn't ready to die. There were too many loose ends that needed his attention.

"He doesn't even *care* about me!" Martin shouted, glaring at the policeman.

Kline nodded silently. He could understand Martin's frustration. In the backseat, the cop seemed to be holding back a grin. Martin scowled. "For a man with a gun pointed at him, you're in an awfully good fucking mood."

"Sorry," the cop answered softly. "I must be in shock. Hostage syndrome, or something."

"Yeah, my left nut. Come on, Kline. Faster."

"This is probably far enough."

"*I'll* decide what's far enough. Shit. I'm done listening to you."

Kline ducked his head like a turtle.

"Okay," Martin said finally. "Take that fire road."

Kline pulled the big car off the highway and through a gap in the trees. They bumped along the dusty, partially mowed path until they came to a clearing, where Kline brought the car to a stop. Martin helped the officer out of the backseat. He took the handcuffs off the man's belt and pointed to a tree. "Go hug it."

The policeman, ever pleasant, did as he was told. Martin kept the gun pressed against his head as they walked, and he gave the handcuffs to Kline.

"One on each wrist," Martin instructed. "I want him married to that thing."

When Kline was done, they both stepped back to inspect the arrangement. Martin nodded with satisfaction. The officer's arms were hooked to one another behind the trunk. "He's going nowhere," said Kline.

"I know." Martin raised the gun to shoulder-level.

The officer spoke up quickly. "Whoa. Hey, now. Don't go doing that."

Kline marveled at the man's calm. *He sounds like a father warning his child not to touch a poison ivy plant.*

Martin paused, lowering his weapon a few inches. "And why shouldn't I?"

"Because you haven't done anything worse than a college fraternity prank so far." The cop's voice was still easy, almost amused. "The frat brothers up at Dartmouth do this kind of thing to sophomore pledges all the time. The kids get a bunch of mosquito bites along the way, but that's about it." He pointed his chin at Kline. "It's your friend there who's in trouble. *He's* the murderer. You don't want to do anything to change that distinction."

Surprise registered on Martin's face, and he glanced at Kline. *Murderer?*

Kline shrugged. *Yeah, so?*

"If you pull that trigger," the cop went on, "you'll be right there with him. They'll hunt you down. *Both* of you."

Martin lowered his gun a little farther, and the cop pressed his advantage. "Just take off. Leave me here. Like your friend said, I'm going nowhere. Eventually my guys will find me, but that won't be for at least a day. Maybe two. And I won't tell them who did this. That'll be my little gift to you." He smiled. "For sparing my life."

Martin's eyes narrowed. "You already called in the arrest," he said. "When you were sitting in the car."

The officer nodded slowly. "Right. Which is why they *will* find me, eventually. But I was calling about *him*, not you. They don't know your license plate, make, or model. And they sure don't know your name. I was too busy requesting backup." The officer paused. Something seemed to occur to him.

"Wait a second," he said. "Was this gentleman *hitchhiking*?"

Martin frowned. "What if he was?"

The cop started to laugh, and they stared at him in disbelief. The man was handcuffed to a tree, miles from anything, with a cocked gun pointed at his head. And he was laughing.

"You don't even know who this *is*," the cop said.

Martin raised the gun again, as if to encourage a more honest conversation. "Educate me."

"That's Dr. Nathan Kline." He spoke the name with reverence, as if it were a dignitary's. Kline felt a little welling of pride in his chest. "He's wanted for – " The cop searched for an appropriate description. " – for a whole lot of killing."

A mild way of putting it, Kline thought.

Martin didn't seem impressed. "Who cares?" He looked again at Kline. "You're a bad guy, huh?"

Kline decided to keep quiet. He had a dog phase coming on, and he could already smell the fear in the air. *You're doing a very good job of hiding your emotions, officer.*

He could smell Martin, too, and he didn't like what he smelled there. Not one bit.

"Let's go," Martin said suddenly, lowering the gun for the last time. He turned and headed for the Cadillac. "You coming?"

Kline nodded. He spared a last glance for the cop. *Try not to wet your pants until we're gone.*

To his credit, Officer Barnhart maintained his placid demeanor until the Cadillac was out of sight. Then he lowered his large head and leaned forward. Very quietly, he began to cry. His massive shoulders shook, and his arms rubbed up against the bark of the tree. The tension leaked out of him in huge, shuddering waves.

After a few minutes of sobbing, he felt much better.

Members of the 2nd precinct squad found him a day and a half later. He was very thirsty, and, as he had predicted, thoroughly bug-bitten. But otherwise he was in good spirits. He kept his word to Martin Hartman, refusing to divulge any details of the incident that had brought him there. His superiors pressed him, but he had always been a stubborn man. Stubborn, and unerringly pleasant.

Not that his integrity made much of a difference in the end. By the time he was rescued the next afternoon, Martin and Kline had both found what they were looking for, and it was all over.

3

The big Cadillac was back on the highway. Martin had calmed since their adventure with the patrolman, and he wasn't driving quite as fast. Also, he had stopped talking about daughters. About how much he hated wives, sisters, and women of all kinds. Kline was glad for the break.

After a few minutes of silence, Martin gave his passenger a sideways glance. "You going explain it to me?" he said suddenly. "Why they're chasing you, I mean?"

Kline didn't turn his head. "Got into some trouble," he said quietly. "Like the officer told you. Never messed with anyone who didn't deserve it, though."

Martin grunted. He seemed to like this answer. "You got *that* right. Sometimes they're just asking for it." He gripped the steering wheel, and his fingers went white again. The calm atmosphere in the car evaporated, and Martin's foot came down on the accelerator. The big car leapt forward.

Kline said nothing. He was right in the middle of the dog phase, and it was all he could do to cope with Martin's scent.

The man smelled like *rage*.

The Other Teacher

1

When he was done reading through the information on Dr. Nathan Kline, Officer Watts sat back and tried to collect his thoughts. This was a very dangerous man, this doctor. And apparently he was on the loose.

Who in God's name decided to let him out? Someone at Clancy Hall?

He shook his head. Blame wasn't important now. Kline was murdering people; that was the issue. Watts needed to know if Kline was responsible for *this* killing – the murder of Professor Carlisle. Not that he expected to actually apprehend Kline himself. That would be a job for the Hanover PD.

But I can do some more looking on my own, Watts thought. *I can help. No law against that.*

Dutifully, he began researching some of Carlisle's closer associates. Surely he could find someone who would have liked to see Carlisle dead.

People hated that man, the friendly nurse at the medical center had said to him.

It was simple enough to find a list of names on the psychology department website. Watts began playing the Google game again, working his way through the teaching staff. Progress was slow. After several hours of tedious searching, he was almost ready to call it a day. The computer screen was starting to blur in front of his eyes, and he was nearing the end of the psych faculty list. There was no one left now except tenure-track associates and teacher's assistants.

But then, just as his eyelids were becoming almost too heavy to hold up anymore, Watts found some information.

Some very odd information.

He had typed in the name of a second-year hire, some guy named Jeffrey Gooding. The search returned most of the usual junk links: a few journal papers, a biography from the college website, a stray resume. Near the bottom of the page, however, the Google engine returned a link that looked different.

Watts clicked on it, then sat back with his mouth open.

He had heard of this kind of thing, of course. He had just never actually seen it in person. And certainly never in connection with a teacher. This was a special web page. And the longer Watts stared at the screen, the more confused he became.

I'm not sure if this is even relevant, he thought.

Still, it was worth investigating. Watts felt his energy returning. He glanced at the clock on the wall; it wasn't six yet, and he could probably catch Gooding in his office if he hurried. He got up quickly, not bothering to log off the machine. He wanted to settle this before the day was out.

Mr. Gooding had some explaining to do.

2

The four students didn't talk much on the way to Jeff Gooding's office. Jason could remember seeing the teacher's name on a list under the Silman Hall directory, so they knew which building to visit. "Is that it?" Jason asked.

"Not yet, Blind Man," Garrett said. "Third one on the left."

Melissa kept one hand on Lea's shoulder, for balance. She looked confused by Jason's directions. "I don't understand this. Why isn't his office in the Medical Center, like Carlisle's?"

Garrett shrugged. "Who cares? Let's just try to get there."

Lea nodded in agreement, even though she could now understand only bits and pieces of what the others were saying.

Garrett didn't knock on Gooding's door. He and the other three students walked into the office without pausing, as if they had an appointment. Gooding was sitting behind a large desk. He looked up in surprise at the group of teenagers before him.

Jesus, he thought. *What's wrong with these kids?* The students seemed – he struggled for the right term – *debilitated.* As if they had just made a break from the infirmary to visit his office. He recognized the hockey player, Jason Bell, from Carlisle's psych class a couple of days ago. Bell was standing next to the senior who had wandered in late that day.

No, not just standing next to him. *Holding* him. As if the hockey player needed a seeing eye dog. And the two girls: Gooding recognized them as well. The thin, pretty one with the glasses. And the gorgeous one. The one with hard, strong eyes.

She looks like she's about to topple over.

"What can I do for you?" Gooding said.

The senior stepped forward. He spoke through clenched teeth, as if enduring some unseen, unimaginable pain. "Did you kill Professor Carlisle?"

Gooding's mouth dropped open, but no sound came out.

The students stared back at him, faces blank. *We're not here to be polite*, those faces said. *We are busy people with things to do.*

Gooding finally found his voice. "You can't come in here and – "

"Just answer the question," Garrett said with a sigh. "Did you kill him or not?"

Lea watched carefully for the reaction. Very carefully.

The teacher shook his head. "I am *not* going to sit here and be subjected to an inquisition. Please leave immediately."

Unfazed by Gooding's indignation, they turned to Lea.

So? Is he our guy?

But Lea looked confused. "He doesn't… talk like…"

"Did he *do* it?" Garrett said, as if Lea might have forgotten why they had come to Gooding's office. "Did he kill him? And what about the antenna thing? Did he take it?"

"Shut up," Melissa said sharply. "Let her think."

Lea bit her lip. "Something… strange," she said, struggling to find each word. "I can't… with him… don't know." She dropped her head, as if she had let them all down. "Sorry," she whispered.

Melissa's hand was still on Lea's shoulder, and she gave her a small squeeze of encouragement. "What's wrong?" she said softly. "Is it wearing off?"

"No," Lea said, her head coming back up. "I … still see… *you.* All of you." She looked fearfully at Gooding, as if he were a ghost. "Not… *him.*"

Melissa nodded. "Don't worry. We have other tricks." She turned to Garrett. "Can you get him to open up?"

Garrett rubbed his temple. "I can try."

Jeff Gooding watched all of this with a rising anger. He was being treated as if he were invisible, and he didn't like it. "Did none of you hear me? I said get out!"

"Absolutely, Professor," said Garrett, changing his voice to a mellow drawl. "And we will, in just a minute. But wouldn't you like to chat a bit?" His tone was warm and friendly.

Gooding's eyebrows shot up, as if Garrett had just asked him to come dancing with him. "Are you joking? Get out of here! All of you!" He gave Garrett a little sneer. "You too, Barry White! Why are you talking like that? What *is* this nonsense?"

Garrett was speechless, shocked by the hostile reaction. He glanced behind him. Melissa was already starting to look woozy, and Lea had stars in her eyes.

It's working, Garrett thought. *My juice is on. Why doesn't he feel it?*

He took a deep breath and forced a smile. "But Professor," Garrett said, "why don't you and I – "

"*OUT*!" yelled Gooding. "Out before I have you all sent to the disciplinary committee!" He stood up and jabbed his finger at the door. "This is unbelievable!" he barked. "Who are you people to come in here and – "

"Okay, come on," Melissa said suddenly. She seemed eager to escape the cramped quarters of the office. Lea helped her out, and Garrett and Jason followed. They didn't bother closing the door. Gooding was still shouting as they walked down the stairs.

3

It took less than five minutes for Officer Watts to make his way from the computer center to Silman Hall. He passed a small group of haggard-looking students just outside the building, and he thought he heard Jeff Gooding's name mentioned.

"…couldn't get a thing out of that guy…"

Watts assumed the students were trying to negotiate better grades for a class project. He hoped they had met with some success.

They don't look happy, he thought, as he ran up the stairs.

Gooding's office door was open, which Watts found strange. Regular office hours didn't usually go this late into the day for teachers. "Afternoon, Mr. Gooding," Watts began. "I wonder if I could – "

"*Now* what?"

Watts paused, started again. "This won't take long. I just have a few questions."

Gooding head was resting in his hands. He looked up slowly. "Can it wait? I don't know if you've heard, but my mentor was found dead this morning."

Watts nodded. "That's what I'm here for."

"Really?" Gooding's expression turned superior. "Didn't realize murder investigations fell under campus security's jurisdiction."

Watts sighed.

Jerk.

"We handle lots of things," Watts said calmly. "But my questions are more about you than your mentor."

"All the more reason to postpone. I have a lot of paperwork that needs – "

"It's about your prior."

Gooding froze, and his face went pale. Watts thought he looked like a man who had just been kicked in the shins.

"Would you mind closing the door?" Gooding said, so quietly that Watts could barely hear him.

"Not at all." The security officer swung the heavy door shut without turning around.

"Now then," Gooding said, his voice shaking. "I must have misunderstood you."

"Your prior conviction, sir. I believe it was something – "

"No!" Gooding sputtered, leaping up from his chair. "I have no idea what you're talking about!"

Watts almost laughed. He wouldn't be needing any special interrogation techniques here. "I think you do know," he said evenly. "And in case you're wondering, these situations fall squarely under campus security's jurisdiction."

Gooding waited a beat before answering. Then he collapsed back into his chair. "How did you – ?"

"Changing your name doesn't work anymore," Watts said. "Not these days."

Gooding swore under his breath. "Useless…" he muttered. Then he looked up quickly. "This has nothing to do with Carlisle," he said. "I would never – "

"Wouldn't you?" Watts' eyes narrowed. "*I* found your record. What would stop a smart man like Professor Carlisle from digging it up? And if he had leverage over you…" Watts shook his head. "I don't know what I would do in your shoes, if someone threatened to leak that kind of information about me."

Gooding's face turned purple. "Carlisle did *not* find out!" he yelled. "No one found out!"

Watts shook his head. "Why should I believe that? Carlisle made the discovery about you, and you had to keep it quiet to hold on to your job. It's a simple explanation, and it makes you a perfect candidate for the murder."

"Christ," Gooding whispered to himself. "I should have just – " He took a breath, but it didn't seem to help him. "I knew someone would get wind of this bullshit, and then they'd start making assumptions." He glared at Watts. "Just like you're doing right now."

Watts shrugged. "Set me straight. Show me the flaw in my argument."

"Fine. We'll start simple: did you find the terms of my conviction? Or just the rap sheet?"

"Just the sheet."

Gooding looked disgusted. "Of course. You want to hear the rest of the story?"

Watts nodded, and Gooding gestured to the chair opposite the desk.

"Have a seat."

4

Outside Silman Hall, Garrett took a moment to walk around in the fresh air. He waited until he could see Melissa's face beginning to clear, and then he made his way back to the group. He was shaking his head in frustration. "What just happened? I couldn't get – " He grimaced as an especially strong wave of headache pain hit him. He had felt good for five minutes after his encounter with Melissa, but that relief was leaving him fast. " – couldn't get a thing out of that guy."

Melissa put one hand up, motioning for Garrett to stay away. She continued holding onto Lea for support. "I don't know," she said. "But keep your distance for another minute, please. You're a walking hormone factory, and I'm dizzy enough as it is."

"Somebody's losing his magic, I guess," Jason said with a grin.

Lea shook her head. "No," she said. "Garrett's still… attractive. He – "

"I know, I know" Jason said, sounding defeated. "Garrett's still the sexiest man alive."

"It's not *Garrett*," Melissa said sharply. "It's *Gooding*. Didn't you hear Lea when we were inside? There's something weird about that guy."

She paused and put a knuckle to her lips, as if to reassure herself with the scent of her own skin. "I couldn't zero in on him either. He smelled like… nothing. And he didn't – "

"No," Garrett interrupted. "He was wearing cologne, wasn't he? Even I smelled it."

"That's not what I mean. That's just surface stuff." Melissa frowned, remembering the teacher's scents. "I'm talking about the elemental things. What was underneath. His *sweat*. It was strange. Really strange. He didn't smell like a man."

Jason gave her a puzzled look. "What's that supposed to mean?"

Melissa sighed. "I don't know. He's too clean, somehow. It's like smelling…" She stopped and squinted into the distance, as if the answer might come walking around a corner. Then, suddenly, she opened her eyes wide. She had the expression of someone who has finally remembered the name of an old friend. "He smelled like a *boy*," she said at last.

Garrett looked puzzled. "I thought you just said he didn't smell like a guy."

"Didn't smell like a *man*," Melissa corrected.

"Man. Boy." Garrett shrugged. "What – " He winced again, and seemed almost to choke on the pain. " – difference does it make?"

She winked at him, and for just a moment Garrett completely forgot the terrible pressure building up behind his eyes. She really was a beautiful girl.

"It makes all the difference in the world," Melissa said with a grin.

5

Officer Watts made himself comfortable in the large chair opposite Gooding's desk. "So," he said, "I've been trying to figure this out ever since I found that file of yours. How does a convicted child molester get a job at an Ivy League College?"

Gooding bristled. "I'm not – " He bit his lip and closed his eyes. "I don't molest children," he said. "It was ruled 'statutory rape,' and I think you'd agree if you saw the girl. She looked older. Much older."

"Fine. How does a convicted rapist get a job at an Ivy League College, then?"

"Will you stop calling me – " Gooding forced his mouth shut. With another visible effort at control, he began again. "Do you want to hear this or not?"

Watts held his hands out like an indulgent father.

The floor is yours.

"It was a mistake," Gooding said slowly. "That's all. I was young, but yes, she was younger." He laced his fingers together on the desk. "The judge, thank God, was reasonable. Anyone would have been. Even the district attorney was sympathetic. So they let me plead out."

"Keep going."

"I was sentenced to take Depo-Provera injections indefinitely. In return, the state agreed to seal the record once I had served my sentence."

Watts sat forward "Depo-who?"

"Provera. It's a drug. Hormone therapy."

"What's it do?"

"Usually it's for preventing unwanted pregnancies. But that's when it's taken by a woman, as a birth control device."

"And when taken by a man?"

"It induces chemical castration."

Watts' eyes opened a little wider.

"Your body stops producing testosterone," Gooding went on. He smiled humorlessly. "I haven't had sex in over five years. I still *could* – all the equipment works, I think – but I never feel like it anymore."

Deep lines of suspicion appeared on Watts' forehead. "Sounds a little convenient. A drug can turn you into a sexless robot? Just like that?"

"It's not that simple. Depo-Provera causes exhaustion and depression in men. All the energy – all the life – gets sucked right out of you. The first few months are terrible, and you never really get used to it. It's not natural."

Watts was silent for a moment. "I don't see how this changes anything," he said. "If Carlisle was the first one to discover your little secret, then you still might have decided to get rid of him."

Gooding put a hand to his forehead. "You're not listening. I'm not a sexual predator, and I've taken extraordinary steps to guarantee that fact. If Carlisle *had* found out, I would have told him exactly what I just told you. He was a bastard, but he would have understood. Just like the judge on the case did. And like the district attorney did." He looked earnestly at Watts. "Just like *you're* starting to understand. Right now."

Watts kept silent. He didn't look convinced.

Gooding, on the other hand, now seemed more relaxed. He almost acted pleased with himself. "I'll bet I know what you're thinking," he said suddenly.

"Oh?"

"You're disappointed that I seem so sincere. Because you're starting to believe me. And it's ruining all your theories."

Watts shifted in his chair. "That's not true."

"Of course it is. But I can help you. Because I've been thinking about Carlisle's death since this morning. Since *before* this morning, actually."

Watts sat up.

Carlisle's body wasn't discovered *until this morning.*

"Now you're interested," Gooding said. "And you should be. Because I know who killed him."

Watts tried to smile. "Don't be absurd. You would have said something earlier."

"No. Because I did have something to hide. Something other than the conviction. And I was hoping to keep it to myself."

Watts shook his head. "This approach isn't helping your credibility."

"You'll change your mind," Gooding said, rising from his chair.

"Where are you going?"

"I'll tell you on the way."

"On the way *where*?"

Gooding smiled. "The scene of the crime, of course. Dartmouth-Hitchcock Medical Center."

6

Lea was nodding. Despite her increasing difficulty with language, she had figured out what Melissa was suggesting, and she agreed with the idea. It all made sense.

"Imagine trying to seduce a 5-year old boy," Melissa said to Garrett. "That's why your charm didn't work on Gooding. That's why he smelled so clean to me."

"And no… match," Lea managed to sputter.

"Exactly," said Melissa. "I don't know how Lea's face-reading trick works, but I'll bet Gooding's manners and expressions don't match up at all. He's all off-kilter. He may *seem* like a normal guy, but he isn't.

"But how do you turn yourself into a five-year-old?" Garrett said through gritted teeth. His eyes were squeezed shut against the pain pulsing through his head. Sweat ran down his cheeks. "And *why*? He doesn't look any different to me. I don't see how this – "

Garrett's eyes suddenly flew open. Melissa thought he had come to some incredible realization, but Lea could see what was really happening. She moved quickly, running to Garrett's side. Melissa found herself dropped rudely on the grass.

Lea caught Garrett just as his eyes began to roll back into his head. She staggered under his weight, lurched hard to the left in a way that made Melissa afraid she was about to fall, and then eased Garrett down to the ground.

"Will someone please tell me what the hell is *happening*?" Jason shouted. He was the only one in the group still standing. "I can barely hear anything, and I can't see you guys anymore."

"Garrett's having some kind of seizure," Melissa said.

Jason's face clouded over, and he crouched low to the ground, staring at the spot where Melissa's voice seemed to be coming from. "Is he all right?"

"I don't know."

"What?"

"*I don't know!*"

Lea held Garrett's head in her hands, positioning it so that the trembling whites of his eyes faced skyward. She could remember seeing people do something like this in a safety video.

Or is his head supposed to be turned to the side?

She couldn't remember. Behind her, Melissa and Jason were shouting. She didn't understand the words, but she assumed they were discussing Garrett.

I hope they're not trying to give me instructions. That would be a waste of time.

Garrett's body was moving in a way that scared her. Every muscle was locked. A vein stood out in the middle of his forehead, making him look angry. It was as if he were being electrocuted.

Wake up, Garrett, she thought desperately. *Please stop this and wake up.*

And then, suddenly, he did. His pupils swam back into view, and he blinked. Lea let out a long, shuddery gasp of air, and she realized she had been holding her breath. She waited for the rush of relief, but none came. Looking at him, she saw that something was still very wrong.

What happened to his face? This isn't Garrett. This is something else –

The thing that looked like Garrett sat up quickly and glanced around like a startled animal. His eyes fell on Melissa. She couldn't see him the way Lea could, and she tried to comfort him. "You're okay," Melissa said. "You were just – "

"Of course I'm *okay*," he spat. Melissa recoiled. Garrett's tone was harsh and unfriendly. "But where is this?" he said. "What the fuck happened to Carlisle?"

"That's what we're trying to figure out," said Melissa.

"I need that antenna thing again," he said angrily. "I need it *now*."

"I know, we all do, and – "

"Shut up, *SHUT UP!*" the Garrett-thing yelled. He jumped to his feet, and his eyes went dark. His hands were clenched into fists. His stance made him look almost as though he were readying himself for a charge.

Melissa Hartman felt something come over her. A sudden calm. She was back home, in the living room. She could smell the tired, hopeless odor of her suicidal mother, oozing out of the rug like a poison. Her father loomed above, glaring at her. He was asking her about all this *crap* on the floor.

What is all this crap? You call this art?

It took enormous concentration for Melissa to stand up without stumbling, but somehow she managed it. She knew that if she tried to move from this spot, she would fall.

No matter.

"Don't shout at me," she said softly. "You smell like a sickness. It's in your sweat."

Garrett's eyes flickered. He hesitated. "Tell me what – "

"I *did* tell you. We're looking for the antenna. Do you know who I am?"

More uncertainty. "I know… you're the one who…"

"I'm the one who helped you to bed when you were passed out on the sofa."

Garrett looked offended at this. "No."

"Yes, Garrett. And outside that sorority an hour ago, you told me I was beautiful."

A long, long pause. Then Melissa thought she saw him nod. "We were together," he said. "And – "

His voice caught in his throat.

Lea made a frightened, anguished noise, and she darted to Garrett's side as his eyes rolled back again. She caught him awkwardly this time, and could not support his weight for more than a moment. His head hit the turf with a thud.

Melissa felt her own legs go limp as the adrenaline left her, and she crumpled quickly to the ground.

"What's happening?" Jason shouted. "Is everybody okay?"

"No," Melissa said, too softly for Jason to hear. "Everybody is not okay." She let out a small hysterical giggle, sounding very unlike herself. "In fact, everybody is pretty much fucked."

7

Jeff Gooding was almost running as he headed down the stairs of Silman hall. Officer Watts had to hustle to keep up.

A flash of clarity.

"*You* discovered the body," Watts said suddenly. "Hours before that freshman girl ever did."

Gooding nodded.

"Why didn't you report it?"

The teacher smiled. "How far did your research take you, Officer? Do you know what Professor Carlisle was working on?"

"Something with the brain. I'm not a neuroscientist. I didn't understand the details."

Gooding scoffed. "There *weren't* any details. No real ones, anyway. Carlisle never published them. Anything you found was probably just pseudo-scientific doubletalk."

"The work was secret?"

"Not the work. The *method*."

They exited Silman Hall and set out toward Hitchcock Medical Center. Daylight was fading, and neither one of them noticed the small group of students crouched in a patch of grass by the side of the building. If they had, they might have wondered why the four students were all on the ground. Why one of them was lying so rigidly on his back, as though frozen there. Why the others were looking at him with expressions of such deep concern.

"Everybody knew that Carlisle was trying to validate Charcot's Genius Postulate," said Gooding. "But he was very secretive about his approach."

Watts waited silently for an explanation.

"Jean-Martin Charcot," said Gooding impatiently. "The father of clinical neurology?"

Watts shrugged. "I'm a campus security guard, remember? Besides,

I thought Sigmund Freud was – ”

“Freud was one of Charcot’s students,” Gooding said. Without Charcot, there *is* no Freud.”

“Fine,” said Watts, sounding impatient. “And what’s the Genius Possibility?”

“*Postulate*,” Gooding said, correcting him. “Like a theory, but more fundamental. And more important. The way the story goes, Charcot had discovered the key to intellectual greatness. Basically, he had found a way for anyone to become a genius. Unfortunately, this idea was too revolutionary for people to swallow. He was a well-respected doctor by this time, but he couldn’t get anyone to take him seriously; all his peers decided he had gone senile, and they called him a crackpot. It was a major embarrassment, and Charcot never published his findings. In fact, he tried to disclaim the entire notion, and no historian has ever been able to directly link Charcot to the Postulate.”

“So it’s just a rumor?”

Gooding shrugged. “You could call it that. You’re not going to find it in any psychiatry textbooks, if that’s what you mean. I don’t even think it shows up on the internet.”

“Then why would Carlisle be wasting his time – ?”

“Because the Genius Postulate was always intriguing to anyone who heard about it. And it never really went away. It turned into a sort of urban legend for neurologists. Every once in a while, someone would claim they had discovered a method for showing that the Postulate was true, but no one ever came forward with any solid experimental data.”

Watts raised his eyebrows. “You think Carlisle discovered a way?”

“I know he did. The device was still there when I found his body, along with his notes.” He looked pointedly at Watts. “*All* of his notes.”

“So you took them,” Watts said, understanding. “And then you didn’t tell anyone about what you had found. You were probably hoping – ”

Gooding nodded. “That I could tackle the Genius Postulate on my own, yes. I’d have to wait for the dust to settle on Carlisle’s murder, of course. A few years, at least. Enough time to make it plausible that I had come up with the solution independently."

"But that plan is out the window now," Watts said "*I* know you didn't come up with the solution."

"Really?" There was a spark in Gooding's eyes. "You know I didn't kill him, and that's all that matters. What's the point of letting this cat out of the bag? I'll solve the Postulate, and you can have ten percent of the profits when my invention goes public."

Watts didn't even consider it. "You can forget that idea," he said. "You're still a suspect as far as I'm concerned."

They were almost at the medical center, and Gooding quickened his pace again. He grinned at Watts. "Please. You're just trying to negotiate. Besides, I can prove I'm not a suspect. Carlisle's notes had more than just the technical data for his machine – he also kept records of his most recent experiments."

"So what?"

"So – "

Gooding suddenly darted to the side, grabbing Watts' arm as he did. There was a police guard stationed outside the entrance to the medical center, but Gooding had spotted him before they got too close. He ushered Watts around to the side of the building.

"So those records make it clear," Gooding whispered, producing a key from his pocket. He unlocked the side door and led Watts into the semi-dark hallway.

"Make *what* clear?" Watts hissed. "Where are we?"

"East wing. Near the holding rooms for violent patients."

"But why would we – ?"

"Quiet. We're on our way to the lab where Carlisle did his experiments." In the low light of the hallway, Gooding's features were difficult to make out. Watts thought he saw something strange in his expression. It might have been anticipation. "There's something I want you to see," Gooding said quietly.

8

Garrett's second episode was shorter than the first. When he awoke, the first thing he saw was Lea Redford's face hovering above him. There was concern in her eyes. Then he saw her expression turn to relief.

It's Garrett, she thought. *It's really him this time.*

She helped him sit up, and she was immediately rewarded by a warm gush of fluid on her arm. Garrett was vomiting.

"Sorry," he said weakly. Then, as an afterthought: "Wow this hurts."

"Garrett?"

"Jesus, Melissa, not so loud, okay?"

Much softer: "How do you feel?"

"Is that a joke? Like my head got stuck in a wood-shredder. What am I doing on the ground?"

Melissa glanced at Lea, who read her friend's confused expression in an instant.

Lea shrugged. *I don't know what happened. But he's back now.*

"You had a seizure or something," Melissa whispered.

"You mean I dozed off?"

"No. You were – "

Garrett made another effort at getting to his feet. He had more success this time, though it looked as if the process caused him a lot of discomfort.

"You were definitely not dozing," Melissa finished. "We need a doctor."

Garrett frowned. "No way. We should get back in there and take another crack at Gooding."

"Garrett, look at us. Look at this group." Melissa nodded at Jason and Lea. "I can't stand up on my own anymore, and these two are fading fast. Jason is blind and deaf, and Lea doesn't know how to talk. And you…" She stopped and shook her head. "Well, we *all* need medical attention. Carlisle's mad-house antenna will have to wait."

"No doctors," Garrett said, sounding defensive. "What I need is a triple-strength dose of Excedrin, a plate of eggs and bacon, and a ten-minute session with that antenna strapped to the back of my head."

Melissa looked purposefully at Lea, who understood immediately.

Lea walked over to Jason, who was still waiting patiently for someone to guide him to their next destination. He was completely helpless.

"Hey," Jason said happily, as Lea took his hand. She led him over to Melissa, who used the former hockey player's body like a ladder, hoisting herself up off the ground. The three of them stood there, facing Garrett. Jason's sightless eyes looked off into the distance. "Did we find it?" he asked hopefully. "Are we going somewhere?"

"We're going to the medical center to get some help," Melissa said. She looked at Garrett tenderly, almost begging him with her eyes. "Please come with us."

Garrett glanced behind him at Silman Hall, as if wondering whether he could make a run at Gooding's office on his own. Then he shrugged. "Fine," he said dejectedly. "I'll tag along."

The four of them set out toward Hitchcock, with Garrett shuffling and dragging his feet like an unhappy fifth grader forced to leave a carnival. "Not *my* fault you're all falling apart," he said. "There's nothing wrong with *me*."

9

"This is the lab," Gooding said, still in a whisper.

Watts scanned the room doubtfully. He couldn't see anything that looked like scientific equipment. There were four chairs in the middle of the room and a series of cabinets along the wall, but nothing more. "Not much to it," he said.

"Look again." Gooding pointed to the thick, double-looped canvas restraints. "Do those chairs look like they were made to hold anyone willingly?"

Watts rolled his eyes. "It's a mental ward. Those restraints don't necessarily mean – "

Gooding wasn't listening. He walked quickly to one of the cabinets on the wall, opened the door, and pulled out a small, gleaming object. It's size and shape reminded Watts of an old television antenna.

"This is what I wanted to show you." Gooding opened another cabinet and retrieved a stack of papers. "And these."

Watts stared at him in disbelief. "You…?" He pointed at the unlocked cabinet. "You hid the stuff in *there*?"

Gooding shrugged. "Most of the staff have access to the room, but none of them would have recognized this for what it is. They'd probably try to get free HBO with it." He motioned for Watts to follow him. "There's more to see in his office."

"Isn't it blocked off?"

"From the outside, yes. But I have a key to this door, and that cop's a good fifty yards away from the front entrance. He won't notice anything if we keep our voices down."

"But what if we – "

"Stop stalling. You want to know what happened, right?"

Watts nodded. He followed Gooding into the office.

This was the wrong decision.

10

It was dark outside when the big Cadillac finally pulled into Hanover. Martin slowed the car to a town-safe speed of twenty-five miles per hour, but he didn't seem to be looking for landmarks or street signs. He drove like a man who knew that fate would guide him. His face was like stone.

Kline thought he heard him say something. "Did you – "

"Fucking *mistake*," Martin whispered, still looking straight out the front windshield. "A mistake to be *corrected*."

Kline pretended not to hear. He had his own agenda to worry about. "The medical center is coming up on our right," he said. "You can drop me off anywhere here."

"It's *easy* to correct," Martin whispered. "I can start over. Like before."

As the Cadillac pulled to a stop beside Hitchcock Medical Center, Kline reached behind him to retrieve the backpack. The Hilti nailer was still safely inside, and it reassured him to feel its heft through the bag. He would probably need it at least once more.

Next to him, Martin was still whispering.

"I'll *correct* her."

Kline wondered if the man even realized he was speaking out loud.

11

Inside Carlisle's darkened office, Gooding pointed to a crack in the doorframe. Then at a dent in the metal table. "See these?" he whispered. "Professor Carlisle wasn't just murdered."

He paused and looked grimly at Watts.

"The man was *abused.* Beaten like a dog. Pummeled."

Watts examined the places Gooding had indicated. He didn't have much experience in reading this type of evidence – he *was* only a security guard, after all, and he could barely see in here without any lights turned on – but Gooding's explanation sounded reasonable. The broken spot in the door frame, and the dent in the desk… they looked as though they only could have been caused by extreme physical violence.

"Whoever came in here that night," Gooding went on, "was *furious* with Carlisle. And psychopathic. The killer didn't care about keeping quiet, or covering his tracks. And he wasn't here to get his hands on Carlisle's research."

"You took care of that," said Watts quickly.

Gooding didn't respond. He held up the pile of notes he had taken from the cabinet. "If you read these – and I have, carefully – you'll see that there is only one person who could be angry enough, sick enough –"

There was a swift, whickering noise from somewhere behind the security guard. Something was being swung quickly through the almost-dark.

Something heavy.

The last thing Officer Watts experienced in this life was a feeling of intense, overwhelming pressure at the back of his skull. The bones there tried gamely to distribute the impact around and away from his brain, but they were unsuccessful. Jeff Gooding heard a cracking sound that made him think of a hard-boiled egg being dropped onto a cement sidewalk, and then he saw the security guard go down hard. Watts' knees seemed to turn to rubber, and he toppled forward like a felled oak.

He did not put his hands out to break his fall, and his face smacked into the office floor with resolute finality.

Behind him, holding the broken wooden leg of a table from the asylum common room, stood the little man with the pointy nose. The one Lea Redford had thought looked so angry during Professor Carlisle's tour of the neurological ward. Had she been there, Lea might have said that Mr. Pointy now looked even angrier than when they had last met.

"Shit," said Gooding, backing up quickly.

"No, I think I'll make you into paste," said the little man. He eyed the device Gooding was holding, and he shook his head. "You people," he said, sounding disgusted. "Isn't it enough that I'm already crazy? You have to come and try to fuck me up a little more?"

"I didn't invent it," Gooding said lamely. His heel struck the wall behind him, and he found that he couldn't back up any farther.

"I didn't invent blunt force trauma," said the pointy-nosed man. He grinned and stepped forward with his homemade club. "But it turns out I'm good at it just the same."

He moved in with the table leg.

12

The Hanover beat cop who had been assigned to monitor the Carlisle murder scene that night was feeling drowsy, so it took him a moment to understand the sounds he was hearing behind him. At first he thought a tree branch had snapped and fallen to the ground. There was a muffled cracking noise, and then a thud as something heavy came down to earth. He even felt a brief, delayed tremor pass through his feet from the impact.

Heavy branch, the cop's mind whispered to him.

But then he heard shouting. And just after that, pleading.

By the time he had woken up enough to realize that these sounds were coming not simply from behind him, but from *inside* the very room he had been instructed to guard, the pleading had been joined by other noises.

Cracking, crunching noises.

Though out of shape and still feeling drowsy, Officer Green ran toward those sounds as fast as he could.

He would not be nearly fast enough.

The little man with the pointy nose needed less than thirty seconds to turn Jeff Gooding's head into an almost unrecognizable mass of blood and broken bones. When he was through, he sacrificed a single moment to stare down at the teacher. One of Gooding's eyes was still partially free of blood, and that one eye stared up at the pointy-nosed man with sightless intensity.

"See how *that* feels," the little man said, and smiled. He didn't sound angry anymore.

Tucking the broken table leg under one arm, he turned and jogged back the way he had come: through the door to Carlisle's office, through the access door to that hateful, sanitized treatment room, and finally down the long hall to the ward's common area. There he found several orderlies bent over a large, heavy game table. The table had been flipped over on its back, and one of its legs had been removed. Broken off, in fact. The orderlies were peering at the damaged piece of furniture with puzzled looks on their faces.

"It's right here," the little man announced happily. He held up the table leg, its edges now caked with blood and hair and skull fragments.

The orderlies turned. They hesitated at first, because none of them had ever seen this particular patient – this extremely *dangerous* patient – out of his room before. To a man, each assumed his eyes were playing tricks. Something with the overhead lighting. *That* patient would never be walking around on his own. But then a big, panting Hanover policeman came bursting into the room through another door, and the silence was punctured.

"Two bodies in the office," the cop gasped. This simple declarative fragment was all Officer Green could manage with the breath left in his lungs, but he used his remaining energy to gesture emphatically at the pointy-nosed man, who was now holding up the bloody table leg like some grisly Statue-of-Liberty prop.

Me, the little man's dancing eyes seemed to say. *That panting idiot is trying to tell you that it was me.*

The orderlies broke out of their frozen state. They lunged for the patient. The little man dropped his table leg and darted for the nearest hallway. He moved with surprising speed, and he avoided them easily.

The light this way was not as good. He probably realized that no exits could be found in the direction he was running, but he didn't seem to care. The point wasn't to escape, apparently, but to keep this little field trip going for as long as possible. As he ran, a little smile crept across his face. He looked like someone who was having the time of his life.

Together

1

From *Getting to Know Patient Nathan*:

The police reports from the day of Nathan's death are incomplete. Or at least, that's how they seem to me. It's as if entire sections have been deleted, leaving only those events that an average reader would expect.

Leaving only what is plausible.

I have often wondered if these deletions were due to politics within the Hanover Police Department. Was pressure applied by the college? Or did the police themselves, fearing sanctions over a particularly bloody chapter in their town's history, initiate the changes on their own?

I am being too cynical, you will say. It may have been something as simple as a misunderstanding. Or disbelief. After all, even I had difficulty adjusting to Nathan when I first encountered him. And I have been trained to deal with mentally disturbed patients.

We do still have the newspaper articles from that day. These provide a more telling – if slightly exaggerated – account of the doctor's last hours. For anyone who is so inclined, it is possible to piece together an accurate chronology by combining and comparing the stories from different papers. This does take some time; many of the reported facts seem to be contradictory.

Personally, I didn't mind. I had the time. And the curiosity. One thing all the papers seemed to agree on is that Nathan arrived in Hanover that day with a traveling companion. Further, this man was apparently quite dangerous in his own right. I have heard it said that this man came to Dartmouth with the intention of killing his own daughter.

I cannot imagine what kind of monster would try to do such a thing.

Beyond the information provided in the newspaper reports, I find myself speculating. What if Nathan had been picked up by some other driver? Someone who was calm, and stable? It seems reasonable to assume that he might have survived, had this been the case. Couldn't we have helped him, then? Surely there was more that we could have done. More *I* could have done.

There are so many things I still want to ask him.

2

Dr. Kline opened the Cadillac's door before the vehicle had come to a complete stop. Despite the darkness, he felt no disorientation as he stepped out into the cool Hanover air. He was home. The Hitchcock medical center was there, just to his right. Carlisle's office – or what had been his office – was in that small outcropping at the side. Everything looked exactly as he remembered it, and he could feel his focus returning. He forgot about Martin, shook off those last few awful hours in the car, and even stopped thinking about the dog phase that was now letting him smell every organic compound within a 500-yard radius.

He was here. He was ready.

There was only one, simple goal left: find and eliminate all traces of the experiment. It felt good to be clear-headed again. Purposeful. He would start with an investigation of Carlisle's office, and then –

"There's someone. Ask that guy." A voice coming up behind him. A young, worried voice. "Sir, do you work at Hitchcock? We need help."

Dr. Kline turned quickly, ready to lie. Ready to tell whoever this was that he knew nothing about the medical center. Anything to be left alone so that he could go about his business. His focus was so complete, he almost missed the strange sound of that voice. It was familiar, somehow. As if he were listening to a younger version of himself.

When he turned around and saw the students, he almost fell back.

The after-effects of Frederick Carlisle's latest experiments were unmistakable. Looking at the four young adults coming toward him, Kline made a series of instantaneous diagnoses. It was a reflex. He saw Melissa first: her unsteady gait, and the way she leaned on Lea's shoulder like an invalid.

Proprioceptive and vestibular deficits. Not yet complete, but getting worse.

Jason's problem was even easier to see. The former hockey player was clutching at Lea's other shoulder with the dependence of someone who had gone recently blind.

Degenerative neuro-paralysis. Temporal lobe. Also progressive.

Lea's handicap was different, and particularly touching. He could see the desperate, searching expression in her eyes; their nervous motion, like a lost child's. That feeling was one he knew too well: being able to see so much, but understand so little.

Aphasic. She wouldn't understand a word I said to her. But she'd probably be able to catch me lying in any language.

Then there was the last one. Despite an entire year of planning, Kline's primary objective was briefly forgotten as he studied the fourth student coming along the path toward him. And for the first time in months, he found himself thinking about the Genius Postulate.

Does it matter anymore? Did it ever *matter? Is anything worth this much?*

Because there, still shuffling a few yards behind the others on the path, was Garrett Lemke.

Oh, Jesus, thought Dr. Kline. *Look at this.*

3

Lea brought the group to a careful stop in front of the tall, gaunt man with the backpack. He had looked different from afar. Calm, and somehow distinguished. That was why Melissa had thought he might be a Hitchcock employee. Now, up-close and lit by the dim, strange-shadow light of a street lamp, she thought he seemed more like a homeless person.

A *miserable* homeless person.

He was looking at the four of them as if he had just heard the most depressing news. That Christmas had been canceled, or that someone's dog had died. That love, as an idea, was at its end.

No, it's something worse, Melissa thought.

"I see you've met Dr. Carlisle," the tall man said sadly.

Lea reacted first. She saw his face, listened to him speak. And then she jumped. Actually *jumped* into the air, as if she had been stung. Jason and Melissa, both dependent on Lea's shoulders for physical support, were put off-balance. They clutched at her like nursing-home patients reaching for their walkers.

Lea began pointing wildly at the man, and from her mouth came a series of urgent bleating noises. Melissa watched her with distress. It was impossible to decipher any of the sounds she was making. "I can't – " Melissa waved at her, signaling for her to calm down. "I can't understand what you're saying."

Lea stopped her bleating, but she continued to point.

"Okay," Melissa said, still trying to calm her. "Okay." She looked up at the tall man. "How do you know Carlisle?"

He took a long, slow breath. "So many questions," he said, almost to himself. He looked thoughtfully at Melissa. "Let's skip ahead, shall we? I helped to design the machine that did this to you."

Lea was following the conversation in her own way, and she saw from Melissa's shocked expression that the necessary information was being communicated. She smiled and stopped pointing. Surely Melissa would know what to do now.

Melissa, however, seemed to need a moment to digest.

"You…" she began. Then she stopped. Started over. "The antenna thing?"

The man nodded.

Melissa took a breath. Considered. And then she demonstrated once again why she had become the *de facto* leader of this strange little group. She did not waste time with irrelevant questions.

"Can you help us?"

Kline studied the tall, beautiful girl before him, and he felt something click over in his head. She reminded him of someone. There was a barely controlled anger in her eyes, and the way she held herself showed a deep foundation of confidence. Even as she leaned on the aphasic girl for support, the strength inside her was obvious. He realized suddenly that he *wanted* to help her. The emotion surprised him.

"I might be able to do something," Kline said slowly. "But I don't know if –"

"Fucking *WOMEN*," came a shout from behind them. Then the slam of a long, heavy car door.

The Cadillac never pulled away, Kline realized suddenly. *It's been there this whole time.*

"They're always asking for help," Martin continued, stepping onto the path. His fury had made him larger, like an animal preparing for a fight, and he walked as though his shoes were made of lead. His gun hung loosely in one hand. "They take everything they can," he growled. "Take your wife, take your dignity, take your damned *house*."

A change came over Melissa. She straightened up, and her eyes went dark. It made the two of them, father and daughter, look strangely similar. "Hi, Dad." Her voice was soft, almost a whisper. "Did you come to visit me? You smell like the man on the street corner again. And angry, too. Like one of the stray dogs behind the trash bins."

Dr. Kline took a short sniff through his own, currently hyper-sensitive nose, and found that he agreed. Martin smelled worse than ever. Hot, perspiring, and breathless.

Almost rabid.

Lea Redford was still watching them all very carefully. She saw, with her increasingly accurate emotional sense, that the man with the gun was Melissa's father. And she also saw what Melissa and Dr. Kline could not. That Martin was not simply angry.

That his plans here were specific.

4

"I burned down your precious house," Martin said. There was a look of triumph in his eyes. "And I made sure they'd know it was arson. No insurance money for you. Not one fucking dime."

Melissa nodded thoughtfully, as if her father had told her she'd have to wait another year before he could buy her that new bike she'd been wanting so badly. "Okay, Dad. Sorry to hear that."

The light in Martin's eyes faded. "You're such an idiot," he hissed. "Just like your mother."

"Like Mom?" Melissa's voice went up a notch. She smiled. "You've never really talked to me about her. How did you two meet?"

"We –" Martin bit his lip, and his face twitched. "I'll tell you about your mother," he said slowly. "She was weak. And ugly. And absolutely fucking useless, just like every other woman who ever – "

Melissa's laughter, high and bright, cut him off.

5

Dr. Kline had found himself riveted by the exchange, and now he watched in wonder as the tall, beautiful girl transformed herself yet again. Melissa's dark eyes flashed with delight, and she became gorgeous as she laughed. She laughed at this man who was calling her mother useless, laughed the way one laughs at a burbling, fussing infant.

Aren't you cute, with your loud noises and your red face?

She was not intimidated, Dr. Kline saw. Not even a little bit. And now he realized why the girl had seemed so familiar.

She was Alexandra, of course.

She had come back to him somehow. Her hair was different – a shade lighter, perhaps – and there was a hardness to her face that hadn't been there before. But the laughter gave her away. The laughter, and the love he could hear in her voice.

6

Martin stood with his mouth open, shock and anger making his skin turn purple. He couldn't speak.

"I never saw it," Melissa said, still laughing between her words. "Not before. But Mom probably did. It's just *fear*, isn't it? You smell so scared now, Dad. What are you afraid of?"

Martin Hartman felt something lurch in his stomach.

She's reading my mind.

It was suddenly difficult to breathe. The girl in front of him... he had *thought* she was Melissa, but that had been a mistake. This girl was an apparition, something other-worldly. Her face threw out light that pulsed with the street lamp above. She seemed to glow.

And now she had turned into some kind of psychic.

Yes, you scare me, Martin thought. *And you always have. But you won't anymore. Not for long.*

7

Lea had been watching the man with the gun. Watching his eyes. She saw the decision he had made, saw it on his face before he even began to raise his arm. She stepped quickly in front of Melissa. It was a light, almost unconscious movement. The two girls might have been sisters in a shared bathroom, alternately vying for space in front of a narrow mirror.

I need to check my hair. Hang on a second.

8

Martin could no longer look directly at the laughing, black-eyed devil in front of him. She did *resemble* Melissa, but he knew this was only a trick.

He closed his eyes as he pulled the trigger.

9

Garrett had been focused on his headache, ignoring everything else.

I can make it to the emergency room, he thought. *I'll be okay.*

But then there was a strange, high-pitched noise, and he looked up. Garrett had seen enough James Bond movies to recognize the sound of a gun with a silencer attachment, and this sound probably meant that things were not okay. As he took in his surroundings, he saw that there were two strangers here now. One was tall, with a sad, haunted expression on his face. The other was stocky, and angry looking. And unless Garrett was seeing things, that angry-looking man had just shot Lea in the chest.

10

Jason Bell never heard the gun go off; his ears had become useless. But he was still holding Lea's shoulder, and he felt her body go jolting backward suddenly, as if she had been hit by a large rock. It was clear from her movements that she was going to fall.

Though now completely blind as well, Jason caught Lea easily, dropping down on one knee like a man about to propose. He supported her head with one hand, and slid a single strong thigh gently under her back. His sightless eyes searched the darkness, straining for a glimpse of her.

He tried hard to find her face.

"Oh," said Lea weakly. Her voice sounded wet, as though she were trying to speak while drinking a glass of water. She was dimly aware that she had been shot, and that her lungs were no longer working properly. More important, though, was that Jason had taken hold of her. His face, tense and desperate, told her stories. She saw how scared he was. How much he wanted to help her, protect her.

Save her.

She tried to say something else, but no more words came. The air stopped moving down her throat. If she had been able to speak, or even breathe, Lea would have tried to comfort him. To tell him that everything would be okay. It felt good to be held like this, even as blackness began to fill her field of vision. Jason's face hung over her, and she tried to smile.

Lea Redford felt happy then, and loved. She had found her perfect boy. But this did not keep her alive.

Jason felt the change, and he understood what he could neither see nor hear. He slumped over Lea, and sheltered her body from the world. To see them there, together under the streetlamp, you might have thought that they were kissing.

11

Melissa, too, had felt the jolt as the bullet went rocketing through Lea's chest. It passed in and out of her friend's quickly beating heart, through the delicate tissue of the left lung, and finally lodged itself in one of the ribs in Lea's back.

The bullet never found its way to Melissa.

Lea was caught by Jason as she fell, but the sudden movement sent Melissa tumbling backward, onto the ground. *She* had no savior to catch her, and Garrett was too busy staring at Martin to be of any help. Melissa realized then, too late, that her father was not simply scared. Was not just a misogynistic brute with a grudge. That he had, in fact, gone insane.

Some things are hard to sniff out, she thought.

Her sense of calm nearly deserted her, and she felt a sudden urge to get away. Anywhere away. She briefly imagined herself wriggling along the ground like an army cadet avoiding enemy fire, as if she might be able to crawl to safety. But instead she took a breath, and the moment passed. There would be no crawling. Not from the likes of Martin Hartman.

Martin, meanwhile, was peering down at Lea Redford's now lifeless body with a curious, bemused look on his face. "What the fuck was the point of *that*?" he said, and grinned crazily. The fear that had gripped him a minute ago was gone, replaced by exhilaration. He had let the gun drop for a moment, but now he raised it again. "Skinny bitch thought this thing came with just one bullet?" He turned his attention back to his daughter, who had fallen to the ground as if something were wrong with her balance. Strangely, she did not seem to be trying to get up or run away. Instead, she looked up at Martin with the same, peaceful expression she had always had for him, even as a baby.

Why doesn't she run?

Martin decided that he didn't care. He widened his stance for extra stability and adjusted the gun sight to line up with Melissa's chest.

He never saw Kline coming.

12

The Hilti nailer had jammed somehow, so Dr. Kline used his long arms – his "gangly" frame, as Nurse Bailer had always described it – to send the heavy carpenter's appliance whistling toward Martin's head in a wide, sweeping arc.

Garrett was still watching the scene unfold before him. He watched passively, as if he were simply at a movie. The grace in the tall man's movements surprised him.

Angry-Man's about to get bonked, Garrett thought.

Martin's sharp ears picked up something behind him, and he moved at the last second. The Hilti missed. Instead of colliding with his head, as Kline had meant it to, the tool smashed into the back of Martin's neck. He stumbled forward, and turned with the gun.

Kline held fast to his one available weapon, and he advanced quickly, before Martin could get a shot off. As he moved, he kept the heavy nail-gun swinging, throwing it backward and high over his head like a softball pitcher going into the windup. He stepped forward to add momentum, and the 20-pound appliance accelerated like a stone on a string.

Just before impact, Kline saw the shock on Martin's face. "What the fuck are you – "

Kline delivered his uppercut with grim, silent precision, and this time he found the mark. Martin's head snapped back with the sickening crunch of shattered bone and mashed cartilage, and he went flopping to the ground. The gun flew from his hand.

Kline was still moving, cursing himself under his breath. He had let Martin shoot the one girl, which was bad enough. Alexandra was still all right, but that wouldn't last if this lunatic was allowed to go on living. He straddled Martin's body, pinning the man's arms to the ground with his knees.

He examined the Hilti briefly. The tool looked in one piece; it had not even been dented by its encounter with Martin's face. It also looked as if the safety might be on. Which meant that it wasn't jammed after all.

Easily solved, Kline thought, as he moved his thumb over the trigger guard.

13

Melissa barely had time to register how close she had come to being shot. Her first instinct was simply to deny what had happened.

Lea's okay, she thought desperately. *She's fine. Jason will help her.*

But a quick glance in Lea's direction told her otherwise. Her friend was not moving, and Jason was hunched over her in a mourner's crouch.

She's gone.

Melissa did not have a chance to cry. Before she could give into her sadness, or even exhale, her father had been cracked in the nose by the tall man, and now Martin was lying stunned beside her on his back. A moment later, the man was straddling her father like a professional wrestler. She almost expected him to start bellowing in Martin's blood-spattered face.

"*Who's the champion now?*" the tall, hungry-looking man would shout.

Instead, he took what looked like an extra-large power drill and began jabbing Martin with it. Jabbing him in the face, in the forehead. In the neck. The last shot to the neck, in particular, produced a sudden, gushing stream of blood.

It's not a drill, Melissa realized dully. *He's shooting him with something. Shooting my father.*

The Hilti began making a dry, breathy sound, and the tall man tossed it away. He leaned forward and studied Martin critically, as though searching for signs of life. Finding none, he stood up. "It's okay," he said, glancing at Melissa. "The one in his carotid did the trick. He'll be dead in a minute." He spoke with a curt detachment, as though describing a roof-shingle repair he had just completed.

Melissa nodded slowly. She glanced at her father, who had stopped moving. Most of his upper body was now dotted with broad, silver nail-heads, like a badly upholstered easy-chair. Under his neck there was a quickly-expanding pool of blood.

"Okay, Dad," Melissa said quietly, and turned away. She was surprised to find that she was finally crying.

"Bye, dad."

14

There followed, then, a moment of calm. Jason was still down on one knee, cradling Lea's body and making low, guttural noises of grief. He wouldn't lift his head. Garrett, on the other hand, had finally broken out of his trance. He stepped forward to help Melissa off the ground. She let herself be helped, and avoided looking at her father as Garrett propped her up.

"Careful," said Garrett softly. He winced as a fresh wave of pain tore through him.

When the two of them were stable on one another, they turned their attention to the tall man. He was staring at them. The look in his eyes had reverted to one of sadness. And resignation.

Melissa brought herself under control. "Who – " she began.

"Dr. Nathan Kline," he said. "But it doesn't matter." Kline could see his mistake now. This girl wasn't his daughter. She wasn't Alexandra. Because Alexandra had left him. With her mother. Long ago. But the resemblance really *was* remarkable. And Kline supposed he had done the right thing in any case.

What was I going to do? A few minutes ago?

The focus Kline had felt when he stepped out of the Cadillac – it was gone. He couldn't remember why he had been feeling so aggressive. There was a remnant somewhere in his mind, a vestige of purpose, about destroying all the evidence of the experiment. But that seemed absurd now. He had been ready to kill people – even *more* people – but why?

"Tell me about the murder," he said quietly.

Melissa paused, reorienting herself. "You mean Professor Carlisle? He was killed sometime last night."

"By another teacher, we think," Garrett added. "A man named Gooding. We tried to shake him down, but there was something weird about that teacher. We couldn't – "

Kline held up a thin, bony hand, cutting Garrett off.

"It wasn't the teacher," Kline said softly. He looked at Garrett. "I'm pretty sure it was you."

15

Melissa and Garrett stared blankly at Kline for a moment. Then Garrett shook his head.

"You're pretty sure *what*?"

Kline nodded slowly. *You heard me*, he thought.

Now even Melissa looked confused. "That's the most ridiculous – " She stopped and threw up her hands. "Garrett needed Professor Carlisle. To fix his headaches. And just like the rest of us, he needed him *alive*."

Garrett nodded along.

"He wouldn't have had any motive," Melissa continued, but Kline was already shaking his head.

He smiled bitterly. "Motive?" Kline glanced down at Martin Hartman's nail-studded and quickly stiffening body. The blood had finally stopped flowing from the wound in his neck. "This man," Kline said, "whom I take to be your father, just finished murdering your courageous friend there. Next he tried to murder you, his own flesh and blood." Kline raised an eyebrow. "What were his *motives* for these acts, may I ask?"

Melissa didn't miss a beat. "He didn't mean to kill Lea. His target was always me. Plus, my father was crazy, and probably had been for years. Garrett, on the other hand – "

"Garrett, on the other hand," Kline interrupted, "has a massive, temporal lobe carcinoma. Otherwise known as a brain tumor. It's causing blackouts, seizures, and migraine headaches." He looked steadily at Garrett. "Right?"

Garrett frowned. "I don't know about any temporal lobe thing, but who cares if I'm getting headaches? Everybody gets them now and then." He spoke through a clenched jaw, doing his best not to let the pain show. "I'm fine."

Kline turned to Melissa. "His personality has been unstable, yes? Like a moody child?"

Melissa didn't answer, but a look of doubt began creeping over her face. She seemed less sure of herself.

Garrett rolled his eyes. "We just met," he said, a little too loudly. He jerked a thumb at Melissa as if she were a stranger who had approached him on a subway platform. "This girl doesn't know a thing about my personality. Anyway, I'm no idiot. You'd need all sorts of expensive equipment and tests before you could tell if I had something really wrong with my head."

"Normally, yes. But remember your brave friend there?" Kline tiled his head at Lea. "She could spot things no one else could, correct? I have similar abilities."

"Oh, I see," Garrett said sarcastically. "You know all the same tricks?"

Kline shook his head. "Not the same. That girl's vision was limited – language and facial interpretation only – whereas I see *everything*. And your symptoms are obvious."

"Sounds like a bunch of – " Garrett squeezed his eyes shut briefly, and a drop of sweat trickled down his temple " – a bunch of bullshit."

Kline nodded as if he had expected as much. "Fine. Then let's try something else." He crossed his arms. "Would you like to know why you're so good with the ladies all of a sudden?"

Garrett opened his mouth to respond, then closed it again.

How the fuck could he – ?

Dr. Kline sighed. "Yes, I can see that, too. Honestly, I'm amazed Carlisle went through with it. My partner was never an ethical man, but this represents a new low for him. He probably suspected what was wrong with you; even a cursory physical exam and a few simple questions would have uncovered all sorts of warning signs. The moral course of action would have been to fly you immediately to the Dana Farber Cancer Center in Boston. They'd have given you the necessary tests, and then they'd have started an emergency regimen of chemotherapy and radiation treatment."

Dr. Kline looked disgusted. "But instead, Carlisle strapped you into his machine – *our* machine, actually – and used you as one of his guinea pigs."

"You don't know what you're – "

"Yes, I do. And so did Professor Carlisle. He knew – he *knew* – that amplifying cerebral activity could have disastrous effects. He knew because of what had happened to me. But he went ahead with it anyway."

Melissa's eyes flickered, as if she had suddenly come to an understanding of something. "Amplifying cerebral… what are you saying? That Carlisle turned up our brains? Like stereo equipment?"

"Not you." Kline held up a finger. "With you and the other two – " He nodded at Jason and Lea. "– Carlisle seems to have employed a more conservative method. He turned your volume *down*. And for that you should be glad. It's a safer procedure."

Melissa's eyebrows arched. "Safer? I don't know if you've noticed, but I can barely stand on my own feet anymore. And Jason's gone blind and deaf."

Kline shrugged. "Carlisle obviously hadn't yet worked out the precise levels of the new treatment, and he went too far. But your condition will be easy to fix." He turned to Garrett. "You, my friend, are a different story altogether."

"I'm through listening to this crap," Garrett said. "You're a psycho."

Kline kept talking as if he hadn't heard. "Carlisle used the old technique with you, unfortunately. He turned your systems way up – particularly your pituitary gland. That's the region of your brain that controls gonadotropin-releasing hormones. Want to take a guess what those do?"

Garrett didn't say anything.

"They make you attractive," Kline went on. "And persuasive. As if you've just doused yourself in the most expensive, most potent, most hypnotic cologne ever made. And, of course – " Kline leered at Garrett, as if he were describing a pornographic picture. " – all this makes you very, very sexual." He turned to Melissa, his face serious again. "Isn't that so?"

There was a silence. Then, very slowly, Melissa began to nod.

"Oh, cut this shit out," cried Garrett. He put both hands to his head, as if to keep it from falling off the top of his neck. Then he glared at Kline through eyes that were only partly open. "Even if any of this were true, being *Don Juan* doesn't make me a murderer. It just makes me lucky."

Kline nodded his head sadly. "That might be so, if it weren't for the tumor. But turning up your pituitary gland only made the seizures worse, and the hormones flooding your system right now are making you aggressive. That's not good for an epileptic. Plus, there's a funny thing about patients like you, with your deep temporal lobe tumors. Especially those with heightened metabolic rates." He waited a beat, then glanced at Melissa, whose expression had turned to one of dread. "Go ahead," Kline said to her. "Spill it. You're not protecting him from anything but the truth." But Melissa wouldn't open her mouth, so Kline turned back to Garrett. "Patients in your condition have been known to experience prolonged periods of waking forgetfulness."

Garrett scoffed. "Uh-huh. The fuck is *that* supposed to mean?"

Melissa spoke up suddenly. "It means you don't know what you're doing. You're a different person for a few minutes, and you don't remember it afterward."

Garrett glared at her. "Horseshit. That hasn't happened – you would have said something."

"It *did* happen," Melissa snapped back. "And I *did* say something." She looked miserable. "I said that you needed to see a doctor. But you couldn't hear me."

"You felt great at first," Kline prodded. "Didn't you? About twelve hours after Carlisle's treatment."

Garrett kept his eyes pressed shut. He nodded.

"But that was because the extra hormones being released into your system were acting as analgesics," Kline went on. "Which means they were hiding the pain caused by your tumor. So, naturally, after a while they couldn't keep up. And the headaches started coming back. At that point, like any patient given a taste of morphine, you realized there was only one thing that could make you feel better: another taste."

Garrett frowned. His forehead wrinkled in concentration. "I was with that swim team girl… and then, yeah, I started to get another headache. I remember thinking Carlisle's machine could help me out." He looked up, staring at the black sky above. His eyes were glassy. "And I remember setting out for his office. But then…"

"But then *you don't remember*," Dr. Kline finished for him.

Garrett's shoulders fell, as if he were finally surrendering to a deep, deep exhaustion. He looked at Kline. Then at Melissa. "Fuck this," he said.

Then he ran.

16

Melissa had been leaning on Garrett for support, and suddenly he was gone. For the third time that night, she found herself tumbling to the ground. Dr. Kline knelt down and scooped her off the grass in a single, swooping motion.

Melissa was surprised at his strength.

"We need to get you fixed," Kline said. "You and this boy." He nodded at Jason. "Right now."

"What about Garrett?"

Kline shrugged. "This is triage. Like in an emergency room. You help the patients who *can* be helped."

"But we can't just abandon him."

"Do you know where he went?"

"No."

"Neither do I, and I'm not going to go running around campus looking for a patient who's going to be dead within the hour no matter *what* I do."

"But he's – "

"Would you like to be normal again?"

That stopped her. "Yes. Very much."

Kline nodded again at Jason. "I'm sure your friend here would like that too. Let's see if we can convince him to leave this unfortunate girl behind."

Melissa relented. "Okay. You're right."

At first Jason refused to budge. He had his face pressed to Lea's forehead, his arms wrapped around her body in an immovable grip. Melissa tried talking to him, but his hearing was now utterly gone. "He's going nowhere," she said.

Kline frowned. "I'm going to leave you on your own for a moment," he said to Melissa. He helped her sit down, then turned his attention to Jason.

Melissa was afraid at first that Kline was going to try overpowering the hockey player, but in this she was mistaken. Instead, Kline began pulling gently on Jason's shoulders in a steady, rocking motion that mimicked the boy's own movements. Kline rocked with him as though comforting a son.

Seeming finally to understand, Jason let himself be pulled away.

Before helping Melissa back on her feet, Kline took a moment to pick up Martin's dropped gun. Just in case of… anything. They walked the last few yards to Carlisle's office as quickly as they could, looking like refugees from a war documentary: a tall, gangly man supporting two incapacitated hangers-on, one blind and deaf, one constantly struggling to keep her balance.

There was no one guarding the door to the office. The officer assigned to the post – officer Green – was still chasing after the little man with the pointy nose, who had killed Jeff Gooding and Security Officer Watts just ten minutes ago. Those two bodies were still there, cooling in the darkness of Carlisle's office, their sightless eyes looking up at the ceiling.

They waited, dead and patient, for Kline and his two new friends to arrive.

17

Garrett didn't stop running, even when he was sure they weren't trying to catch him. The noise and feel of the cold nighttime air rushing past his ears and cheeks was soothing, and he was able to imagine for a second that he hadn't just been accused of murder.

That he hadn't just been told he was going to die.

He hoped wildly that he would run into Allyson Morrone. Or anyone from the swim team. Because that would set things straight. Allyson wouldn't be spouting any bullshit about brain tumors or amnesia or gonad-hormones or whatever. She'd want to have sex. And more sex. Like before. And then he could forget about that tall, spooky-looking fucker with the hollow face. Jesus, that guy had been creepy. And the scariest thing was that he had almost started to make sense toward the end there.

But that's what really *insane people sound like*, Garrett reassured himself. *They sound like perfectly normal folks, but with a tendency for telling strange stories.*

Very strange stories. Very *convincing* stories.

As he ran toward the center of town, his breathing grew labored. Garrett heard the thump-thump-thump of his own heart beating loud in his ears. As if he had been running for hours instead of minutes. Approaching the intersection at Main street, he saw that the light was changing. On the other side of the street, he spotted a girl who might have been Allyson Morrone.

Oh, please.

Suddenly it seemed to him that making this light could turn out to be more important than anything.

I can make it, he thought. *And then I'll be okay. With Allyson.*

His cardiovascular system was already operating at it's peak, but Garrett Lemke nevertheless requested a burst of speed from his legs.

They responded dutifully, and his heart contributed its own surge of support. The blood pressure in his head, already dangerously high due to the growing blockage in his temporal lobe, spiked suddenly. For the last time.

18

At 10:16 PM on Saturday the 28th of September, Hanover dispatch received a 911 call from a payphone. The unidentified caller reported a man sprawled out in the intersection of Main and College avenues. No, the caller said, the man had not been hit by a vehicle. But he was not moving. Traffic was backing up in all directions.

"What? No, I have not begun CPR. No one has. The guy looks like *toast* to me, frankly."

"Sir, please stay on with me for a moment. Can you tell me if – "

But the connection had already been severed, and the line went dead.

19

Dr. Kline had not considered what he would do if the locks to his old office had been changed. But the situation did not present itself. Officer Green had unwittingly solved this problem when he dashed through Carlisle's door – unlocking it in the process – as he tried unsuccessfully to save poor Jeff Gooding from being beaten to death. Officer Green didn't think to turn the lock back as he left; catching the little man with the pointy nose had seemed more important at the time.

And so the door opened easily. As if it had been left waiting for them.

Kline stepped inside first, reached automatically for the light switch, and regretted it. He felt Melissa's hand go tense on his shoulder. Gooding and Watts lay on opposite sides of the room, sprawled out as if from exhaustion. They might have been simply resting there, except that their injuries were both grotesque and starkly visible. Watts was lying face-down, a deep, blood-caked indentation disfiguring the back of his skull. Gooding's back was to the far wall, and his face was now barely recognizable. His nose and mouth had been crushed inward, and his forehead still held the concave impression left by some sort of blunt instrument.

A thick, wooden chair leg, perhaps.

Jason, alone in his world of darkened silence, witnessed none of this. He had no way of knowing that he was walking through a room that held two dead bodies. Kline and Melissa, meanwhile, both reacted with their own version of carefully studied control. Dr. Kline assumed he was suffering a paranoid episode, and he discounted the dead bodies as either figments of his imagination or, more likely, as simply irrelevant. Melissa, who had detected the stink of death while still 30 meters away from the office, held her breath and looked away.

They were out of the room soon enough. Kline saw the TMS device lying at Gooding's feet, and he snatched it up without breaking stride. He steered Melissa and Jason carefully around the security officer's body, then through the door that led to the examination room.

Melissa said, “Could you close that door tightly behind us, please?”

Kline looked at her, saw how her nostrils were flaring. She looked ready to burst.

Of course, he thought, feeling selfish. *The smell.*

He took his hand from Jason’s shoulder and leaned heavily on the lab door, sealing off Carlisle’s office. Melissa exhaled with relief, then took a deep, shoulder-rolling breath. “Thank you.”

“Don’t mention it. Let’s get you set up.”

Dr. Kline worked quickly, moving with the efficiency of experience. The TMS device was wired, powered up, and fitted securely behind Melissa’s head in less than five minutes. She didn’t ask him if he knew what he was doing. Or whether it was safe. Her nose seemed to be getting more sensitive every minute, and she could smell his competence. It was in the way he breathed, in the cool smell of his skin. He reminded her then of Ms. Cooper, and the resemblance calmed her.

She did ask one question: “Will it hurt?”

Dr. Kline smiled. “It’s already on.”

“Oh.” She almost giggled with relief. “And how long will it take?”

Kline checked an oscilloscope readout. “Another minute ought to cover it.”

“Nothing feels any different yet.”

“It’s not going to. Not for about ten minutes after you’re done.”

“Why?”

Kline shrugged. “We’re ‘waking up’ the rest of your brain. I’m doing the first part with this machine, but you’re essentially coming out of a partial coma. It’s a gradual process.”

“And then? When everything’s up and working? Back to normal?”

“Yes, normal,” Kline said, and paused. “But it won’t seem that way.”

“What do you mean?”

“Just wait.”

In another minute he had the device off her and onto Jason. The former hockey player allowed himself to be led to one of the examination chairs. Then Kline and Melissa stood and watched. They waited.

Melissa turned to Kline suddenly, a curious look on her face. "What will you do after this?"

The question seemed to catch him off-guard. "After? I'm not sure." He grinned, and the expression briefly made him look less intense. More human. "I'm good at appearing sane now. I suppose I could – "

But Melissa never got to hear what Kline supposed he might do. Because at that moment the door to Carlisle's office swung open. Melissa was momentarily floored by the death-stench that came flooding into the room – her nose had not yet lost any of its power – and Kline stared at the man in the doorway as if he were having another hallucination.

The man had a tweed coat. And glasses.

"It can't…" Kline began. "You *can't* be here."

Melissa could see that the man was real enough, but she didn't much like the smell of him. Even with the reek of dead bodies still flowing through the doorway, she could pick out the undercurrents coming off this person in waves. He stank of treachery. Of manipulation.

"I *am* here, Nathan," said the man. And he smiled warmly.

Melissa shuddered.

20

Dr. Levoir took a step into the examination room, and Dr. Kline took a step back.

"How…" Kline began, fear in his voice.

"I just thought I'd drop by and check on you," Levoir said smoothly. "To make sure everything was moving along." He smiled like a proud father. "And you've been doing well, Nathan. So well. I couldn't be happier."

Melissa glanced at Dr. Kline. He didn't seem to be sharing in the good cheer. In fact, he was looking more bewildered every minute. "But you shouldn't *be* here," Kline said. "I never told you… it doesn't make any sense."

Levoir waved dismissively. "You were always such a worrier, Nathan. You could have gotten yourself released much earlier from Clancy Hall if you had only learned to relax. You worried about your unpredictable phases, and about others' perception of you, and of course about your daughter. You *never* stopped obsessing over Alexandra, even after I had explained that your ex-wife would never allow her to see you. Not after what you had done."

This last declaration seemed to hit Kline in the stomach. His head dropped, and his eyes clouded over. "Alexandra," he said softly, almost to himself. "But I never talked to you about her…"

"Don't be ridiculous," Levoir said cheerily. "You're becoming hysterical, Nathan. Try to remain calm."

Meanwhile, Melissa was aware of something unsettling going on inside her head. It felt as if a cool wind had suddenly gone blowing into one of her ears. And then, all at once, the world began to seem… *bland.* She felt as though someone were stuffing cotton up her nose. She couldn't smell the air anymore, or the floor of the room, or the leather of the examination chairs. And the people around her had gone gray. They seemed lifeless, colorless. She could barely smell any –

It's happening, she realized. *I'm losing the smell.*

As her nose grew steadily less powerful, Melissa found herself wondering whether she had made the right decision.

This is normal? It's like going blind, but worse. How do people live like this?

The man speaking to Dr. Kline, meanwhile, seemed to have transformed right in front of her. His threatening demeanor had vanished, and Melissa struggled to remember how she could have perceived him as manipulative. He was smiling so warmly. He was kind. Supportive.

He's obviously just here to help. I was only imagining things.

"You've done everything right," Levoir was saying to Kline now. "Exactly as we discussed. Wonderful."

Dr. Kline stared back at him, flabbergasted. "As we *discussed*?" He looked wildly around the room, as if to reassure himself that he had not somehow sleepwalked all the way back to Clancy Hall. "But I didn't… we didn't…"

Dr. Levoir nodded slowly. He seemed satisfied. "You're worrying again, Nathan. Try not to do that. Everything will be fine." He stared seriously at Kline for a moment, holding his gaze. And then his voice changed, dropping a notch.

"*I believe in you, Nathan.*"

Hearing these words, Dr. Kline straightened up like a cadet coming to attention. He seemed to take in his surroundings for the first time, and his air of uncertainty sloughed off of him like an old skin. Without looking away from Levoir, he removed Martin's gun from his waistband. Then he turned, aimed, and fired three quick shots into Jason Bell. Two in the heart, one in the head.

Jason never saw anything coming, and he didn't flinch. He was dead in seconds.

Melissa did not scream, but this was only because her breath had deserted her. She stood, frozen to the spot, and looked at Kline with eyes that were wide with shock. With an immense effort, she convinced herself to stay still. Running now would be useless. All she could do now, she told herself, was wait. And hope.

Dr. Kline turned to face Melissa, and he studied her as one might study an oil painting. He cocked his head to one side, watching. She was calm, this girl. Calm and beautiful. With strong, strong eyes.

Like Alexandra's.

Kline made his decision, and he brought Martin's gun back up quickly. He kept his eyes open, and this was something that Melissa would always remember afterward.

That man shot himself in the head, she would think to herself, *and he never even closed his eyes.*

The sound of the shot was muffled by the silencer, and the only noise in the room after Kline crumpled to the ground was Melissa's rapid breathing. Dr. Levoir assessed her critically, looking her over with an expression of murderous calm. Then he seemed to dismiss her, and he glanced down at Dr. Kline, lying motionless on the floor.

"I tried to stop him," Levoir said, very clearly, as if reciting a pre-written speech. "What a tragedy." He shook his head sadly.

Begin Again

Dr. Levoir took his time returning to Clancy Hall. He remained in Hanover longer than the police needed him, answering every question until they were bored with his jokes, tired of his easy, perfectly consistent story.

A violent patient. An overly optimistic release. A tragic relapse into psychosis.

"I'd like to stay as long as possible," Dr. Levoir said, playing the eager detective wannabe. "To help out in any way I can."

The police smiled solicitously at him. Tried to avoid patting him on the head. And then sent him away. They simply had no use for the friendly doctor; it was an open-and-shut case. Gory, yes. And bizarre. But once you sifted through the details, the same old characters turned up. A homicidal maniac with a penchant for appliance-style killings. A pissed-off, wife-beater dad with a gun.

Yawn.

On his way back to Massachusetts, Levoir kept a small bag next to him, in the passenger seat of the little Ford *Escort*. When he stopped once for gas and a soda, he took the bag with him out of the car. There was a device in there, one that looked like a little silver-and-copper television antenna. He had been trying to get his hands on it for almost a year now, ever since Dr. Kline had told him about it in their interview sessions.

Not that Nathan had ever *known* he was revealing such things; during most of those interviews, Levoir had kept him under the influence of sodium amytal.

And Nathan, bless him, had never suspected a thing.

Dr. Levoir had always been a methodical man, and he was not going to rush now. He had proceeded carefully with Nathan – convincing him, over the course of nine interminable months, that all traces of the original experiment should be erased, no matter what the cost – and he would proceed carefully this time, too.

Nathan and Professor Carlisle had *not* been careful enough, and they had failed massively. Gruesomely. But they had been hasty with their experiments. Hasty and greedy. They had been consumed by the potential of the thing.

Dr. Levoir would not let himself be hasty. He would study his notes from his sessions with Nathan, study them until he knew the theory behind the Kline-Carlisle procedure better than he knew his own name. *He* would not make any mistakes.

He would figure everything out.

First he would tackle the machine's basic mechanism. He knew that it was little more than a carefully arranged series of capacitors and electromagnetic coils, but that special arrangement obviously made all the difference.

Eventually he would understand it. All of it.

And then, after a series of closely monitored tests – using patients at Clancy Hall, naturally – he would make his announcement to the world. That the solution to Charcot's Postulate had finally been found.

Found by him, Dr. John Levoir.

The greatest, most legendary figure in the history of psychiatry.

A genius.

Melissa

From *Growing Up Fast*, by Melissa Hartman. Reprinted with permission.

My last three years at Dartmouth were easier than the first. More normal, some would say. No, I never had the sort of all-American, frats-and-football-games experience that Ms. Cooper had envisioned for me, but I did make progress. I learned how to open myself up to people, for one thing. To make friends more easily.

Lea was the one who helped me with that, I think.

I still miss my friends from that first month at school. Jason for his easy kindness, and of course Lea, for her infinite understanding. And yes, Garrett. Because even if he was a player, he was a sincere player. He was up-front with his objectives; he wanted what he wanted. And for a while there – brain tumor or not – he wanted *me*. He made me feel, for the first time in my life, that I was someone to be *desired.*

You say I didn't really need such an experience. You think that tall, long-haired girls have enough going for them already. But every girl deserves her own version of Garrett Lemke. We all need someone to be *crazy* about us, even if it's just for a little while. Garrett filled that role with distinction.

And so, with a whole lot of serious therapy, and with my new sense of self-worth held tightly to my chest, it was easier to jump into the college social scene. I took risks. I started friendships that seemed destined to fail. And sometimes they *did* fail. But sometimes I was surprised.

Not everything was so easy. I never did get used to having an "ordinary" nose, for one thing. Even to this day, I feel that some essential part of me has been ripped out, as if through rough surgery. People still tell me that I have a freakish sense of smell, but they don't know. They can't imagine what it's like to absorb someone's entire personality with a single breath. To be able to identify every smudge on a person's hands from a hundred yards away. To smell a man's fear in his sweat.

Always the sweat.

Thankfully, however, that particular skill – spotting a dangerous man by the stink coming from his pores – has become unnecessary. Because in my junior year I met a boy. A nice one. He reminded me of Charlie Lane back home.

And he still does.

Kline

The attending emergency room doctor had seen only two gunshot wounds to the head in his tenure at Hitchcock Medical Center, and both were DOA. But when the tall, thin man was brought in that night, he clearly wasn't dead. At least not yet. Blood was still leaking out the back of his skull, and his skin was warm to the touch.

"Time?" said the doctor.

"Less than a minute."

Dr. Hall looked quickly at the EMTs who had carried the man in, and then he noticed that they were *not* EMTs. Their uniforms were the standard-issue orderly gear from the psychiatric ward next door. "What – ?"

"He was in Carlisle's lab," one of them explained.

Dr. Hall raised an eyebrow. *Too much excitement in that lab*, he thought.

There was no debridement to speak of; the bullet had removed a small section of the man's skull at the back, but it was an amazingly clean wound, as if whoever had done the shooting had been holding the gun at just the perfect angle for the job. Surgery would still be necessary to cover the area, of course. Survival would depend on the extent of any brain trauma.

Out of the corner of one eye, Dr. Hall saw several officers standing at the door. They looked particularly interested in his patient.

"Come back in twelve hours," the doctor said, without looking up from his work. "I wouldn't hold your breath," he added. "There's a good chance this guy's never walking out of here."

The patient opened his eyes shortly after surgery, but this alone indicated nothing. Dr. Hall began administering the standard tests for the Glasgow Coma Scale. He checked for verbal responses, an ability to follow commands, and visual tracking.

The results were not good.

The officers were back the next day, still looking very interested. They pointed at the man, whose head was now wrapped in a gigantic white turban of post-operative bandages.

Dr. Hall frowned. "No," he said sternly. "Even if I were to let you talk to him, it wouldn't do you any good. You're free to come back in another twelve hours, but I doubt anything will change. He's essentially vegetative."

The officers nodded slowly, and turned to go. A few hours later, one of them spoke to that friendly, harmless doctor from Massachusetts, Dr. Levoir. The officer told Levoir, incorrectly, that the patient had died. A "vegetative" patient was no better than a dead patient if you were trying to conduct an investigation. From the officer's point of view, the two conditions were different only in name.

Vegetative. Dead. Whatever.

But Dr. Kline was not dead. He was not vegetative, either. Not remotely. He was thinking. And, as always, he had planned ahead.

He had given the Glasgow Coma Scale test himself many times, of course. Long ago, before all of this. And so he had known that it would be easy to fake the responses for a low GCS score. Fooling a general practitioner – an E.R. doctor, for example – would be simple.

He had known, also, that a bullet aimed just so – grazing the back of his skull – would bleed impressively without doing any real damage. Like most head injuries, it bled in great, scary pools of dark redness, spilling out onto the smooth floor of Carlisle's pristine lab and giving the impression of imminent death. But Kline knew help would arrive in time. He was already in a hospital, after all.

The one serious risk had been hitting the occipital lobes. He was not an expert with a gun. But this was an acceptable risk. Worst case, he would wreck his vision, and he had decided that he could live with vision problems. He could live with them *easily.* Compared to what he had been through over the past year, the prospect of bad eyesight was nothing.

Anyway, he hadn't hit the occipital lobes.

In fact, he hadn't hit anything but skull. And now that part of him was neatly patched up. He would probably need at least one more surgery, but there was no reason to have that surgery here.

When Dr. Hall sent the officers away for the second time, Kline saw his opening.

He rose once in the middle of the night, to remove some of the extra layers on his head bandage. Then, the next morning at 6 AM, during the shift change, he simply stepped out of his room, walked down the hall, and headed out the front door.

There were no balance problems. No sudden scarecrow phases. No paranoia or amnesia or aphasia. Just a tough headache at the back of his skull from the steel plate the doctors had screwed in place.

Nothing like the shockwave from a gunshot to set your mind right, Kline thought. *Who would have thought it could be so easy?*

He almost laughed out loud.

One of the incoming nurses, still groggy and grumpy at that early hour, wondered why the tall man who passed her in the parking lot was wearing such a large wool cap, or how anyone could possibly look so cheery coming out of a hospital. But she didn't dwell on these thoughts. She was tired, and her first cup of coffee had not yet taken hold. The idea that a patient might want to escape never crossed her mind.

And so Dr. Nathan Kline, one-time murderer, current gunshot wound victim and recently presumed vegetative patient, strolled calmly out of the building, into the bright New Hampshire morning, and out of the public eye forever.

He was on a bus within an hour, headed for somewhere, anywhere, else.

He had always enjoyed bus rides. They made him feel purposeful.

And he still had so much to do.

Made in the USA
Middletown, DE
19 October 2020

22315197R10205